Alfred Hitchcock's Tales of the Supernatural and the Fantastic

Alfred Hitchcock's Tales of the Supernatural and the Fantastic

EDITED BY

Cathleen Jordan

SMITHMARK

This edition published in 1993 by SMITHMARK Publishers Inc., 16 East 32nd
Street, New York, NY 10016

SMITHMARK books are available for bulk purchase for sales promotion and
premium use. For details write or call the manager of special sales,
SMITHMARK Publishers Inc., 16 East 32nd Street, New York, NY 10016;
(212) 532-6600.

Library of Congress Cataloging-in-Publication Data

Alfred Hitchcock's tales of the supernatural and the fantastic /
    edited by Cathleen Jordan.
        p.   cm.
    "A compilation of 33 mysterious and suspenseful tales of the
supernatural, culled from Alfred Hitchcock mystery magazine"—CIP
galley.
    ISBN 0-8317-0437-3
    1. Fantastic fiction, American.   2. Fantastic fiction, English.
3. Supernatural—Fiction.   I. Jordan, Cathleen.   II. Alfred
Hitchcock mystery magazine.
PS648.F3A465   1993
813'.0876608—dc20   93-20152
                                                                    CIP

Printed in the United States of America

10   9   8   7   6   5   4   3   2   1

Contents

Introduction

Alfred Hitchcock Mystery Magazine, in its more than thirty-five years of existence, has primarily focused on mystery and suspense short stories involving warm-blooded citizens with their feet flat on the ground. Occasionally, during its first quarter century, the magazine took a flyer into the Unseen (or Mostly Unseen) World. In the last ten years or so, the magazine's editorial staff have ventured even more frequently into those realms in which the crimes encountered rarely turn up in the job descriptions of the average policeman or private eye. The results, we hope, fit our mission of providing the reader with entertaining mystery fiction.

Of course, thanks must go to our amazingly resourceful authors. For not only are they skilled in the actual business of storytelling, they are able to conjure up worlds we've never even dreamed of: Charles Ardai's "Balancing Man," for instance, who teeters about above the ground in an old, red wood barn; Terry Black's inside-out realities in "It Ain't Necessarily So"; Marion M. Markham's trees full of creatures, whatever they are, in "There Are Fantasies in the Park"; the house wherein resides "The Ronnie," that touching little being revealed by K. D. Wentworth; and J. A. Paul's twilight world of "The Time Between."

A flock of regulation ghosts have put in appearances, too. One of them, in William T. Lowe's "Second Nature," is a butler. F. M. Maupin takes us to a haunted Welsh chapel in "An American Visit." A (very) chilling woman appears (or not) in Rob Kantner's "The Last Day." W. Sherwood Hartman introduces us to a friendly poltergeist.

There is a talking palmetto bug. An unknown-but-certainly-awful something from outer space. A vampire. A genie. A witch. That old, familiar fellow, Death. . . .

. . . And there's more: a new struggle for residence in the land of Oz, a case of spontaneous human combustion, dream tips, and a few stories that defy brief descriptions.

Among the authors presented in these pages, you will find a handful who preceded both Mr. Hitchcock and his magazine. Their stories possess timeless elements of the supernatural. Classic or contemporary, all of the writers herein have provided especially spectral tales—tales that have all appeared in *Alfred Hitchcock Mystery Magazine*.

We offer to you, then, our most spirited collection.

—CATHLEEN JORDAN

Alfred Hitchcock's Tales of the Supernatural and the Fantastic

The Time Between

by J. A. Paul

There's that time between day and night when it's neither. In some parts of the world the time between is so short you can't see it. Still, it must be there. It can't be day and night at the same time, any more than there can be life and death at the same time. In between the two is a flutter of both or neither. I'm not sure which.

Lord, I miss Eleanor. I didn't know a man could love a woman he'd been married to for twenty years as if it was their honeymoon. Even now, three years gone, it hurts just to think about her.

I tapped out my pipe. The entry was dated August, 1952, three years after my grandmother had been murdered by a drunken derelict. The old diary had been a surprise. It was hard to imagine grizzled old Grandpa writing down such thoughts. He wasn't a man to say much.

I was tired. I had been up since four A.M., when the hospital had called to tell me Grandpa had collapsed at the local tavern. It had taken them hours to find my number. I had driven most of the morning, hoping to see Grandpa before he died, and although I made it, it hadn't mattered much. He was no longer fully conscious. He didn't know me. I stayed at the hospital till mid-afternoon when exhaustion sent me to rest at his old farmhouse.

It was a small town and word traveled fast. I was Grandpa's only relative, a fact most of the townspeople knew, yet the kitchen table was laden with food. I got up to sample some of the baked beans, took a saucerful, and went back to the diary. It was by no means kept daily. Some entries were six months apart. It was an old fashioned blue cardboard covered looseleaf, quite full, to which pages could be added. There were fresh blank sheets at the back. I leafed through it, having nothing better to do with the remainder of the day. I hoped he would recognize me in the morning, that the phone would remain silent through the night.

Walter tried to fix me up on a date today. As if Eleanor could be replaced! He knows better. He loved her, too. I keep thinking I'll see her again, I mean besides that God-awful last time out in the front yard that comes every night at dusk. I hear you can sell your soul to the devil and get anything you want in return. I want Eleanor walking beside me again, but old Lucifer ain't made an offer.

A chill went up my spine. The entry was dated 1969. Grandma Eleanor had been murdered in the front yard in 1949. According to the entry, Grandpa had "seen" her moment of death every night for twenty years. Forty, if his hallucination continued. It was nightmarish. "Poor Grandpa," I told the empty room.

"You talk to yourself, too? Must run in the family."

I elevated three inches from the chair, heart pounding and hair on end.

"Didn't mean to spook you," said an old man from the other side of the screen door. "My name's Walter Bethroe. You must be the grandson."

Besides his appearance in the diary, my grandfather had mentioned Walter over the years. They had known each other forever. Although embarrassed at being caught redhanded talking to myself, I remembered my manners and let him in.

"I'm Howard Stintson," I said.

He nodded and held out yet another foil-covered pot. "This here is pork and sauerkraut," he said.

A man after my own palate.

"Join me?" I asked.

He did so, and except for my polite compliments on his meal, we ate pretty much in silence. From the looks of him, he and Grandpa were very much two of a kind. Walter was sturdy and weatherbeaten and, like Grandpa, alert for a man closing in on eighty. Over coffee he came out of his reverie.

"I'm gonna miss Thomas. I surely am."

I nodded but remained silent. What could I say? Grandpa's heart had been weak for years. He was dying and we both knew it. Walter had reached an age where few friends, if any, remained. His loss would run deep.

"It'll be dusk soon, almost time," Walter said.

"For what?" I asked. There were no animals to feed, I had checked.

"We ought to clear the table before all this food goes bad," was all he said.

We put pots and bowls in the refrigerator, dirty dishes in the sink. Walter neatly ran soapy water and left them to soak.

"You best sit down, boy," he said.

Did he want a card game? It was okay with me. He pulled up the window shade and looked outside.

"What do you know about your grandmother's death?" he asked.

The question surprised me. I would have thought he would tell anecdotes about Grandpa, if he wanted to talk at all. I thought back to what my father had told me. Familiarity with the story somewhat lessened its gruesome quality. "In 1949, Grandma was axed to death by an Indian. No one knew who he was. He was assumed to be a drifter who had too much to drink, saw a pretty woman, and for some reason went berserk. Grandpa had come in from the fields just after the killing and at the sight of Grandma went wild. He beat the Indian to death."

Walter nodded. "That's the way I told it," he said.

I didn't recall his presence being mentioned.

"You were there?" I asked.

"Only at the end," he answered. He folded his arms on the table and cleared his throat. "I don't know how to tell all this, boy. You'll likely think Thomas is crazy. He isn't, no matter how it sounds. I saw him at the hospital early this morning and I promised him I'd tell you the truth. There's something he's going to do tonight. If he does it, you might think you'd lost your mind. It would only last a few minutes, but he wants to spare you that. If he can't manage it, he still wants you to know the whole story."

"Manage, what?" Frankly I was a bit jealous that he had been there while Grandpa was still lucid.

"You'll see for yourself," said Walter pointing to the front yard. "It's Eleanor's death. It happens all over again. I saw it myself, years ago. Afterwards, I never came visiting at twilight again. Mornings or after dark, yes. Never again at dusk."

This was too much. Though it matched with what was in the diary, I was more inclined to understand Grandpa's mental aberrations than Walter's. It was Grandpa's wife who had died a horrible death. The trick his mind played for years afterward was strange, but probably an understandable result of psychological trauma. I didn't feel the same about Walter's claiming to have seen the crime again. I re-evaluated my former assessment of his mental capacities. There seemed to be only one remark in all he had said to which I might logically respond.

"I don't think Grandpa will be able to accomplish anything, Walter. He was in pretty bad shape when I left."

He said nothing.

I looked outside. Whatever they hoped I might see wasn't readily apparent. My car was parked under the thick old oak. There was a fence needing paint and a few cracks in the asphalt. There was nothing peculiar about any of it.

Walter rubbed his hands across the worn checkered oilcloth.

"I'll tell you how it was in the beginning," he said finally. "Tom, Eleanor, and me, we all grew up together. Eleanor was beautiful and sweet, and Thomas and I both loved her. We had a fight over her nearly every week from the time we were fourteen. People used to bet on which of us she'd marry. For sure it would be one of us. We were both from landed people, had ambitions to enlarge our property and better ourselves. We were churchgoers and decently educated. We were handsome, too, if I do say so. It was odd, what with the competition for Eleanor, but we were also the best of friends. If the truth be told, I thought Eleanor was favoring me. And then he came."

For a moment the old man was silent. I suppose he was lost in his memories. I was grateful the conversation had taken a normal turn.

"Who came?" I prompted.

"The Indian. Fleet. Half Indian, anyway. His ma had named him Fleet-footed something or other, but when they came here everybody shortened it to Fleet. They were from somewhere up by Lubec. We understood that his father was a Norwegian sailing man. He had his ma's coloring, though. His skin was dark, and his eyes and hair were black. He was full of fire and the girls in town near fainted when he was around. At the annual fair he knocked the rest of us boys off our pins in everything from horse racing to pistol matches. Eleanor wouldn't run after him like the other girls. She was too proud for shenanigans like that, and as it turned out, she didn't have to. Soon as Fleet saw Eleanor, it was like all the rest became invisible. Crazy about her, he was. Worse even than Thomas or me. What came as the surprise, though, was that she returned his feelings. You'd think it would've ended happy for them, but you got to remember it was still the twenties. No self-respecting family would allow their daughter out the door with a poor, half-breed Indian. Suddenly Eleanor didn't go anywhere without her ma. I guess they figured she'd get over him. Thomas and I sure figured it that way. Well, to make it short, Thomas and Eleanor's family both belonged to the same church, which gave Thomas the inside track over me. Eleanor was a good girl, the kind who listened to her family. The marriage was arranged and Thomas was in heaven. Can't say I blame him. I would have been, too." The old man stopped for a few moments to shake his head sadly.

"Trouble was," he continued. "Eleanor never was the same after that. She hardly ever smiled. The marriage took place and Fleet went back north somewhere. A year or two later your pa was born and she got a bit better, but still not the same." He stopped again and looked at me guiltily. "Son, I never thought to say it, and I hope you forgive me. About your pa, and your ma, too, though I never met her. I sure am sorry."

Both my parents had been killed in an auto crash about three years before. It was kind of him to mention it. "Thank you," I said.

The sun outside was definitely fading.

"I'd best hurry," said Walter. "Fleet started to come back. It wasn't often. He just turned up every couple of years or so, stayed out in the woods somewhere for a few days, then disappeared again.

I guess it was to see how Eleanor was doing. Lord knows, no one but us three ever saw him. He didn't socialize none. As it turned out, he must've been waiting till Eleanor was ready. I guess Eleanor was waiting till your pa went off to college. Don't fault her, though. She was only seventeen when she was forced to marry a man she didn't love. Thomas knew it was just a matter of time till she went off with Fleet. Years, maybe. But coming just as sure as old age. It was bad for Thomas, but son, I think we all knew it was worse for Fleet. He just kept coming back and going away, like the tide. It didn't look like he ever took a wife of his own. The woman he wanted belonged to another man. He was a sorry sight to see in them years. Pitiful."

I was shocked. It was pitiful, all right. However, my pity was reserved for the man who had spent twenty years married to a woman who didn't love him, my grandfather.

"It was late spring of 1949," Walter went on. "Thomas had a mare in foal. Like most farmers, he had a sixth sense about when the foal was coming. In those days, we used to have continuous barns, which means that out from the house was a lot of connected out-buildings. Nearest the house was the woodshed. In Thomas's yard that connected to an old carriage house, which went on to connect to the corn shed, cow shed, dairy, and barn. In other words, you could be out in the barn and pretty far away, and enclosed, too. Eleanor didn't know that Thomas had come in early that day to see to his mare. He'd have no reason to make any noise, and every reason to be quiet and soothing. He told me later that he heard a couple of cars, but hadn't thought anything of it. It was dusk when he got finished. He walked back through the buildings and came out the side of the woodshed which opened to the yard. The first thing he saw was Eleanor's things in the back of an old black Ford. I've often wondered why she waited till that hour before leaving. Thomas always came in from the fields about that same time. The only thing I can figure is that it took them longer to get her belongings than they thought it would. Anyway, Thomas saw the car first, then Eleanor and Fleet, and all three kind of froze. Now if he had come upon them someplace else, the story might have ended different. Thomas wasn't naturally a violent man. But he was in the woodshed, and the axe was right to hand. Sure, he says he knew for years that

Eleanor was going, but it wasn't right that he had to see it happening right in front of him like that. It was too much for any man to bear. He picked up the axe and charged out at Fleet like a bull gone mad."

I sat like stone, certain of the outcome of the story. Walter passed a hand through his sparse hair.

"My house," he continued, "is but a quarter mile down, the other side of the road. In those days we didn't turn on the TV the minute we walked in the door. It was quieter then. I heard a roar. It made my blood run cold. I'd never heard the like of it before. I rushed outside. It seemed to have come from Thomas's direction. I didn't even think to use my car. I just ran.

"Back here, Thomas was running at Fleet and Eleanor was trying to get in front of him to protect him. When Thomas saw Eleanor in the way, he tried to change the direction the axe was heading, but in that same fraction of a second, Fleet tried to protect her, too. He shoved her aside, right into the downswing. I won't describe that further. I was running down the road when I heard the next scream. I think that was Fleet. Thomas was bent over Eleanor trying to pull out the . . ." The old man gulped and took a breath. "Anyway, Fleet went mad. He pulled Thomas off with a rage that would scare the devil himself. Trouble was, for all his strength he swung wild, like he didn't know what direction to hit. I guess the thing that counted most was that Thomas was beyond feeling physical pain. Nothing short of a bullet would have stopped Thomas that night. I know. I tried. By the time I came running down that there driveway, Thomas was banging Fleet's head against the oak. It took me forever to pull him off. It took me even longer to convince him Eleanor was dead. He kept trying to get to her. Landed a few good ones on me before I got through to him. I got him into the house. At the time I naturally wasn't sure just which one had killed Eleanor, but I had no problem about which one I wanted to blame. I grabbed a bottle of whisky and went back out and poured it on Fleet. I brought Eleanor's clothes inside and threw them in the bedroom closet. Thomas was numb, sitting like one of them statues, except his face was bloody and swollen. I left it alone for the sheriff to see. Then I called him and told everybody the story you know. Nobody but the four of us knew how those two had waited twenty years. Nobody remembered Fleet. Nobody questioned my version. Thomas might have said something at the beginning, but it was weeks before he could say anything at all. Nor did he ever say anything about what I did. About six months later, though, he asked me to come here at dusk. I guess he wanted me to know that he never meant to hurt Eleanor. I thought he'd gone crazy when he told me what I'd see. Afterwards, I thought I had."

Well, I hadn't. I looked out again at the benign front yard. The two men had fed each other's imagination for forty years. Especially if Walter's current version was true, which I believed. Only a shared sense of guilt could prompt identical hallucinations. It was too late to help Grandpa. Maybe I could still help Walter.

"My grandmother's death was an accident," I said. "The Indian's probably qualified as self defense. Grandpa's lifting the axe, in all probability, would have been attributed to temporary insanity. You should put your mind at rest, Walter."

"It is, son. I have no regrets about what I did."

"Then what is this all about? Even if I did see the whole thing, what difference would it make?"

"None," he replied. "But Thomas says we won't see it the way it was the first time. It's going to come out different."

"How?"

"He's going to change it. Anyway, that's what he thinks. He tried before, but he said he couldn't get through from the living side. Then he figured it out, he said. But first, you got to understand Thomas. He was guilty about robbing them of the life they were supposed to have together. He said he had Eleanor for twenty years when he shouldn't have had her at all, and he was given a fine son in the bargain. He thought it only right for her and Fleet to have their time together like they always wanted."

"They have eternity together," I said coldly.

Walter smiled and shook his head. "Thomas didn't see it that way."

"Listen," I said using my most reasonable tone of voice. "No matter what my grandfather wanted to do, you mustn't expect miracles. History is unchangeable."

"Thomas said that between life and death is a time we don't

understand, when each side could get through to the other. If they met at the right time and place, they could change what happened the first time. He used to want to kill himself just to get it done and over with, but he couldn't figure a way that wasn't too fast. It had to come natural; then he had to hang on till dusk so he could meet them when they came again. Tonight's probably the night. We'll see."

What could I say to this old man? Even if he relived the killings, I certainly wouldn't. Changing history was even more preposterous. When the time came, should I humor him? Lie? I followed his gaze to the diminishing light of the front yard. Suddenly I hoped his imagination would allow him to see whatever he wished.

My first impression was puzzlement, my second disbelief. My Chrysler was gone. I experienced that disoriented feeling which comes from witnessing something either tragic or impossible. My car was there a minute ago. Now it wasn't. The paved driveway was gone. Now a dirt drive led out to a gravelly road. The oak stood slimmer. Under it was parked an ancient dusty black Ford. The car doors were open. Boxes and articles of women's clothing were visible. Near the car, two people materialized. One was a tall man whose face was more bone than flesh. The hollows of that face caught and held the shadows that fell around him. His eyes, dark as a moonless midnight, were captured by the woman facing him. He was about to help her into the car. I tried to look at Walter, I suppose to assure myself that I wasn't dreaming, or maybe to prove that I was, but found I was unable to do anything but stare at the unfolding scene. Outside, the two people hesitated, then turned together toward something beyond my vision. Only when the woman turned would I admit who she really was. It was my grandmother, Eleanor. I was amazed by her youth. She had seemed so much older in the family album. Here, she was no more than four or five years older than I. Her golden brown hair was in a loose bun at the nape of her neck. She wore an ankle-length dark brown skirt, and though she stood very erect, she barely reached the shoulder of her companion. Her eyes, when I finally saw them, were haunted and sad.

I didn't hear the roar Walter had heard, but I felt it. It isn't possible to describe this, but I "heard" it with a different, foreign, sense. I couldn't bear to watch the scene he had drawn so painfully clearly, and again I tried to look away. I couldn't. I was transfixed.

Another man appeared. He was not as tall as the first, but he was broader. His eyes were shocking in their intensity, his mouth a grim, bloodless line. He held an axe. Eleanor's face now streamed with tears. She stepped in front of the gaunt man, and I saw her mouth forming pleas. From behind, the Indian grasped her shoulders and moved her out of harm's way. My grandfather, for of course it was he, flew at his enemy like a majestic, crazed eagle. Massive and enraged, he raised the axe. Again Eleanor threw herself in front of the man she so obviously loved. Grandpa, eyes on fire, was now but a few feet away from the man who was thief of all he held dear. The axe stopped in mid-air. The scene froze.

If I should live a century beyond a normal life span, it won't feel as long as the moments that followed. My chest was constricted. I was sure my heart had stopped. My fingers gripped the table edge. I watched Grandpa's face soften, and his shoulders sag. I saw the axe fall harmlessly to the ground, and watched as he used the handle to lean upon. I never knew such pity existed as I felt when I witnessed resignation consume him. The Indian didn't hesitate. He swung Eleanor into the car as another man appeared, racing down the road. The third man stopped at the foot of the drive as the car turned right and drove out of sight. Of course it was a younger version of Walter, the man sitting next to me. He went to my grandfather, who was still standing in the yard, and they stood quietly together as night fell around them.

A highway light appeared and, with it, the outline of my car. I was grateful that a small part of reality had made an appearance.

"He did it," Walter whispered.

The phone rang. My world was back. I practically knocked it off the hook. "Stintson residence," I answered in a foreign voice. It was the hospital, of course. Grandpa was dead. I stumbled to his desk and my hands shook as I turned the pages of his diary. It looked the same. Why shouldn't it? Not once had he said that Eleanor was dead. I turned to the blank pages at the back and grabbed a pen.

"That's right, boy," said Walter. "Write it down quick before we forget."

Forget? Not likely. My problem is the memories crowding out all else. I remember Fleet who taught me to cast and fish in the turbulent Atlantic waters from a small island off the coast of Maine. I remember the small, happy bungalow on that island where I spent many youthful summers in the company of Grandma Eleanor and the rugged, rangy man who adored her. I remember attending his funeral, following so shortly the death of my parents. I had loved him more than the quiet, isolated man I had called Grandpa Tom, whom I now loved and understood more than I ever thought I might. Most of all, I remember, and must continue to remember, that these memories had not existed one half hour before. Two lifetimes had not existed.

I wonder about the impact of these events, and decide that except for the disappearance of some dusty old newspaper copy, there will probably be none.

Walter has memories of his own to contend with. He's at the sink methodically washing and rinsing the dishes. "Don't want Eleanor coming back to a mess," he says.

I remember that Grandpa sent Eleanor a letter, telling her the house is hers, that she must come home as soon as he's gone. I know now the reason for this. He wants Walter to look after her.

"Write it down, boy," Walter keeps repeating as my fingers try to fly over the pages. "You and me are the only ones who'll know what Thomas did. We mustn't forget." He's now washing cabinet doors and counter tops. A thought occurs to me as I look up at him.

"Walter, did you ever marry?"

"Me? No. Keep writing, boy."

"Don't worry," I say. "I'll write till it's finished."

Work for Idol Hands

by Charles Peterson

When a party has been out of stir for less than a year, you wouldn't think it so hard for this party to convince another party that he has no interest in a return visit, not even for the class reunion. I am finding it very difficult to get this point across to T. F. O'Toole, however.

"I would not have expected such a turndown," says T. F., shaking his head, "from such an ornament to the profession as Kit the Cat Burglar."

"You may erase the name 'Kit the Cat Burglar' from your memory banks," I reply. "He is no more. In his place you find Augie Augenblick, gainfully employed as caretaker for the estate of Professor Elbert Hufflemeyer. I gave much thought to the future of Kit the Cat Burglar while stamping out license plates, and decided he didn't have any. I am now a civilian."

T. F. looks unhappy, like a toad who has just snarfed an underripe bug—which is one reason he is widely known in the trade, behind his back, as "Toad-Face." I am about to remark on the resemblance when I recall what happens to the last guy who does so within O'Toole's hearing—a guy who winds up with so many stitches he looks like one of those things you hang on the wall that says "Bless Our Happy Home." So I stifle the comment as T. F. sighs, "Too bad! I understand the wall safe is packed with stuff your professor doesn't trust banks with—and is it really true about that doll with the diamond in her forehead?"

"It's not a doll; it's an idol from Africa. And it's not a diamond; it's an emerald the size of an egg. And it's not in the thing's forehead; it's the idol's right eye."

"Thank you," says Toad-Face, jotting all this down in a small notebook. "I like to have all the details clear." He tucks the notebook into a pocket and grins. "As I see it, that thing is worth a fortune and it's there for the picking. And you're just the guy to help me pick it."

Here we go again! I take a deep breath to explain once more why I won't touch this caper with a ten-foot pole. In fact, I won't even touch the pole not to touch it with.

But T. F. casts his eyes heavenward and continues in a thoughtful tone: "In my rambles to and fro about this establishment, I have noticed from time to time a certain very appealing dish with brown hair and blue eyes and a figure that won't quit."

This would be Angela Hufflemeyer, the professor's daughter, and I am more than somewhat taken aback at her sudden appearance in this conversation. "Yeah? What about her?"

Toad-Face delicately gnaws a hangnail and goes "Ptoo!" as he spits it on the sidewalk. "I also note that your hair seems to stand on end when you glance her way, and deduce that there is a certain jenny says quoi in your relationship—am I right?"

"Get to the point, O'Toole!"

"This point is, I am hopeful of your cooperation, because otherwise said dish might get a phone call telling her that she has an ex-con mooning about the premises. In addition to which, your parole board is apt to get the idea, from anonymous sources, that you have been associating with known criminals, in violation of your parole."

"I haven't either!"

"You're associating with me," retorts T. F. grandly, "and if I ain't a known criminal," he adds with pride, "the work of years is for naught. Think it over, Kit."

"Augie," I reply automatically, but my heart isn't in it. It is off somewhere looking for mittens and a muffler to overcome that cold feeling it gets as Toad-Face O'Toole strolls off, being careful not to step on the cracks in the sidewalk because he is superstitious about things like that.

*   *   *

There are several reasons why I like my job taking care of Professor Hufflemeyer's place, and cutting five acres of grass with the riding mower is the least of them. For instance, I like his house. It is one of those Victorian jobs in rough stone that looks incomplete without a moat and drawbridge and a few serfs. It has a lofty tower from which to keep an eye peeled for invaders such as traveling salesmen, and lots of high-ceilinged rooms full of Hufflemeyer's anthropological collections. These are mostly rather creepy: carved masks with glowering expressions, lots of knives and spears and bones, voodoo dolls and tom-toms and other odd-looking musical instruments you toot, twang, or bang.

I like the professor, who is small and wiry, with a white goatee, a peppery disposition, and a tendency to go into a lecture on primitive witchcraft at the drop of a hat.

But mostly I like Angela Hufflemeyer. She is, as T. F. O'Toole rightly observed, a dish, although I am not too sure that there is much of anything in the lid, the Hufflemeyer brain supply having evidently been ladled out to excess in the professor. She goes around asking if I don't think the petunias are really tiny ballerinas who pirouette in the moonbeams, and giving it as her opinion that the garden is populated by elves who swing on the spider webs, but what the hell? When she smiles, clouds disappear and birds sing, and if she says the stars are heaven's dewdrops twinkling in the blue, I'll go along with her. Besides, in the kitchen she's a genius.

There is something about being stuck on the horns of a dilemma that shows in a guy's face, I guess, because a few days later the professor is asking what's eating me, and I am denying that it is anything in particular, although it suddenly occurs to me that maybe I can talk him into putting in some burglar alarms that will discourage O'Toole and get me off the aforementioned horns. "I am somewhat worried about this collection of yours," I say. "I mean, it's worth a pile, obviously, yet you have no security system whatever. Anybody could bust in and walk away with a sackful."

"Augie," he says, "you are needlessly concerned. Have you ever heard me speak of M'Bonga-M'Bunga?"

"If so, it went in one ear and out the next."

"A good friend of mine, from my days in Africa. One of the more highly regarded witch doctors there. I had occasion to rescue him from a rhinoceros to which he was about to become a sort of hood ornament, and the dear chap was most grateful. Gave me a special incantation of his to safeguard one's goods and chattels and keep gnus out of one's boma. Used it himself with great success."

"I don't know about M'Bonga-M'Bunga's boma," I reply, "but what about this thingummy here with the emerald eye and curdled milk look?"

"Bama-Lolo?"

"If you say so. It'd take only about two seconds for somebody to pop that emerald out of there and make off with it."

Professor Hufflemeyer's eyes twinkle, like Angela's heavenly dewdrops. "As a matter of fact, this idol is part of M'Bonga's spell. Bama-Lolo," he goes on, addressing the idol and patting it on the head, "keeps that eye on everything. Don't you, Bam'?"

Well, I ask you, what are you going to do with a household like this, where one member sees petunias dancing in the moonlight and the other gabs with a hunk of kindling? I make one final attempt to persuade the professor to get the joint wired, but he turns testy on me.

"One of my bearers once tried to steal Bama-Lolo," he snaps. "Never saw him again. Come to think of it, every time I look at the idol I am reminded of him. No, Bama-Lolo can take care of himself—and when you finish the yard, Augie, I wish you'd take a look at the garage door. It sticks."

Like the garage door, I, too, am stuck. Angela, I find, won't dream of pressuring Daddy against his wishes and, being immersed in a new recipe for chocolate cookies, is not inclined to bend either of her shapely ears to my warnings. In a sombre mood, I trudge out to finish mowing and am not awfully surprised to find a snake in the grass—namely, T. F. O'Toole.

"Ah, there, Kit—er—Augie," says Toad-Face, genially. "Fancy running into you like this. Now, about this business venture of ours: Today is Tuesday, a day my horoscope says is ideal for making big plans and settling details. And by a happy coincidence, Friday finds the moon moving into the house of Scorpio, making it an excellent time for me to move into the house of Hufflemeyer. With your assistance, of course."

"Look, T. F.," I say, desperately, "your horoscope may be saying yes-yes-yes, but I'm telling you that house is a no-no. Hufflemeyer was just explaining to me, it's protected up, down, and sideways by African witch doctor spells. You could shrivel up and blow away or something."

"Pooh!" says T. F. "Of what avail are the mumblings of an ignorant savage, compared with the illuminations of those who read the stars? Modern science is on my side, and besides," he adds, digging into a pants pocket and pulling out a fuzzy object, "I not only have my rabbit's foot but shall be wearing my good luck derby—the one I was wearing the night I lifted the Vandercook pearls. Now here's the plan. . . ."

It could not have been simpler. All I have to do is forget to check the latches on the french windows leading from the south portico into the trophy room. Toad-Face waits until I am back in my room in the servants' wing, of which I am the sole occupant anyway, and when he sees my lights go on therein, he nips into the trophy room, cracks the wall safe, trousers the idol's emerald eye, and nips out again with anything else that happens to stick to his fingers en route.

"And for that small lapse of memory," T. F. continues, "you collect a quick grand. Who knows? You may be inspired to come out of retirement, my boy. Think! The world needs talented performers like you."

"I don't want to collect anything!" I mutter through clenched teeth. "All I want is out of this!"

O'Toole shakes his head. "I was afraid you might take this attitude," he says. "I wonder; do you happen to have Miss Hufflemeyer's phone number handy? Never mind," he adds, in a kindly tone, at my yip of dismay. "I'm sure she's in the book. I already have the number of your parole board."

The rest of Tuesday is bad; Wednesday is worse. I am helping the professor rig up an intercom system with speakers so he can call me in any part of the house, and make one last effort to get him to listen to reason about his collection, but he is trying to fish wires through the walls and not doing very well at it, and is in no mood to talk about anything else. Afterwards I put it up to Angela again.

"I'm sure Daddy knows best, Augie," she says, looking so adorable in a flour-covered apron that it is all I can do to keep from sweeping her into my arms and kissing the chocolate frosting off her nose.

Then she disconcerts me with a sudden sharp look that goes through me like one of Daddy's Watusi spears. "Why are you so persistent, Augie? Do you think something's going to happen? Are you keeping something from me?"

Muttering something about my duties as caretaker having to do with taking care of things, I escape and spend the rest of the day pondering various ways to out-maneuver Toad-Face. The trouble is, you see, heavy planning is not really my bag—which is one reason I retired from cat burgling. Somebody with a brain, like O'Toole, who is so crooked he can hide behind a corkscrew, can think up a dozen plans a minute, but I always went in for direct action. Up the wall, across the roof, into the upstairs bedroom, snatch the sparklers or coins or whatever, and exit to a round of applause, was my shtick; and that it lacked something was brought home to me the last time when the round of applause came from a squad of cops watching me shinny down a drainpipe.

The problem is, if I tell the professor, he'll want to know the whole story. He and Angela will discover I'm an ex-con. He will fire me and she'll tell me never to darken her door again. And T. F. O'Toole will try to turn me into a wall sampler. If I don't tell the professor, he stands to lose a pile of money plus who-knows-what from his priceless collection. I will feel so guilty I'll have to quit and never darken Angela's door again. Either way, Angela's door is not going to be darkened by August J. Augenblick in the future, and I find this more than somewhat disheartening.

Nevertheless, by Thursday night I have made up my mind that I can't let O'Toole give a poke in the eye to two people who have always done right by A. J. Augenblick. An anonymous tip to the local gendarmes might do the trick, I think, so after dark I sneak out of the house and head for the public phone a couple of blocks away, since I don't want to chance anyone overhearing me on the house extension.

I have dropped the coins and am about to dial when I feel a sudden chill. This is caused by a knife blade at my throat, and it prompts me to hang up and turn around. Slowly, so as not to scrape anything—such as a jugular vein.

"O'Toole!" I exclaim. "What are you doing here? This is only Thursday!"

Toad-Face tips his lucky derby. "Today's wishing well in the newspaper told me to beware of double crossers named Augenblick, so I moved things up a day. I also had a stroke of luck in finding a former acquaintance at liberty and talked him into taking your place. You know Nobby the Knife?"

"How do?" says Nobby, though his eyes indicate he doesn't care at all whether I do or not. He removes the knife from my neck, it having been replaced by O'Toole's .38 in the small of my back, and we leisurely walk back to the house.

"Then you don't need me any longer?" I say, hopefully.

"Not so," says O'Toole. "I have merely recast the script. You may have noticed certain resemblances between you and Nobby? You are about six one; Nobby is about six one. You are on the lean side—" he says, a bit enviously, being a stylish stout himself "—and Nobby is on the lean side. You are wearing jeans and a plaid jacket; Nobby is wearing jeans and a plaid jacket. I think it likely that when we capture the professor and his daughter (a part of the plan I neglected to mention, dear boy), I may several times inadvertently refer to Nobby as 'Augie.' And since he will be wearing a ski mask at the time, an unfortunate impression may be left that you are masterminding this operation."

"I get it. You had it planned this way from the beginning—to make me the fall guy."

He shrugs modestly. "One does one's best."

"You can't get away with this, Toad-Face."

He stiffens at the appellation. "Why do you say that?"

I don't know really, but I have to say something. "Because a black cat just crossed your path, that's why."

O'Toole whips out his rabbit's foot and waves it in the air in a cabalistic pattern. "That takes care of that," he says, cheerfully. "Anything else?"

I am not sure of all the subsequent events, being unconscious a good bit of the time, but I assume things go about as T. F. expects. When I come to, I am in the trophy room trying to orient myself in the darkness. T. F. is at the wall safe. Nobby has O'Toole's .38 trained on me.

"Awake, are you?" says Nobby.

"What have you done with Angie and her father?" I demand.

"They won't bother us," says Nobby. "They're stashed in the tower, safe as houses."

"Shut up!" snaps O'Toole, straining to hear tumblers clicking.

There is dead silence, and all at once I am aware that the thumping sound I hear is not just my heartbeat. It sounds like a big drum being struck rhythmically, far away. This is a funny time for the professor to start practicing percussion, I think. And presently we hear a voice over the drumming.

"Toad-Face!" it says. "Toad-Face O'Toole!"

"Call me that one more time, Augenblick, and your next call will be for a hearse," snarls O'Toole.

"Boss, he didn't say nothin'," says Nobby, in a puzzled tone.

"Toad-Face!" says the voice again, and the drumbeats grow louder.

"Find out where that's coming from," O'Toole orders. "I can't hear myself think with that racket. Leave him," he says, when Nobby protests that he's guarding me. "He's tied up; he's not going anywhere—yet."

Nobby vanishes in the darkness. I find I am indeed tied up, but not very well, and in spite of a throbbing head my fingers still have a certain skill at picking knots. I work feverishly until I feel something give. Meanwhile, the voice continues calling Toad-Face, who is getting more incensed by the minute. When Nobby reports that he can't locate the source of the drumming, T. F. growls, "Never mind. Augenblick must have spilled the beans to the professor and that babe upstairs. Now they know who I am—and you know what that means! Take care of 'em—now!"

There is a sound that sounds like Nobby running into a door with an "Oof!" just as I find my wrists free. Then he is gone, and I am untying my ankles. Between the drumming and the voice, O'Toole doesn't hear me as I crawl into the hallway and, once there, I sprint up the stairs in Nobby's wake. He is nowhere to be seen and I am hoping I am not too late when, on nearing the door to the tower, I sense rather than see him making his way back toward me. I debate the feasibility of jumping him, but it is against my principles to tangle with a guy packing a .38, even in the dark.

"The key," he mutters as he pads by. "Forgot: O'Toole's got the key."

Since the key he refers to is undoubtedly one of the master set that should be hanging on my belt but isn't, I have almost as big a problem as Nobby in getting into the tower. But there is a window nearby and sliding it open I see the tower looming against the starlight, just beyond it. To an ex-cat burglar, the rough-cut stones are nearly as good as a ladder, and the window into the tower room, not anticipating any visits from ex-cat burglars, is beautifully unlocked. A moment later I am inside and falling over a body, which emits muffled sounds of protest. My delicate sense of touch indicates that it is not the professor. I fumble elsewhere and locate a gag to loosen.

"You're awfully fresh, whoever you are!" says Angela, and when I identify myself, she adds bitterly that she hopes I am satisfied with this evening's work, and how can I bite the hand that feeds me, and so on.

"Shut up," I tell her tenderly. "Where's your father? Never mind; I've got him."

Professor Hufflemeyer is also abrim with indignation as I untie him, but I cut him off. "Later, professor. In about thirty seconds a guy is coming through that door with a .38 to blow both of you away. Do you suppose you and Angela can manage to get over by the door and trip him up while I smack him with—with whatever this thing is?" Fumbling around in the blackness, my hand has found something hard and heavy—maybe a table lamp, maybe one of the professor's war clubs.

The key is rattling in the door as I speak. The professor and Angela scamper into position. The door opens, and a second later Nobby is on the floor, reduced to a neutral power. Simultaneously, the deafening drumbeats from downstairs hit a crescendo, then stop, and there is a horrible yell that echoes up the stairwell. Then nothing. In silence, I switch on the lights.

"Oh," says Angela, ogling the figure on the floor with the ski mask over its head. "That's not you, is it? Oh, Augie, I'm so glad!"

There is a whizzing sound and she is in my arms. There are smacking noises and she is kissing me. It is nice.

We make our way downstairs cautiously. The wall safe is open, but its contents seem undisburbed. All of Professor Hufflemeyer's artifacts are present and accounted for, including the emerald eye of Bama-Lolo, which glitters in the light as though it knows something. The only sign of O'Toole is his good luck derby on the floor.

"I think you scared him off with those sound effects—that voice and those drums over the intercom," I say at last.

The professor gives me a funny look. "Sound effects? Intercom? Augie, you know we didn't finish wiring the intercom this afternoon. And how could we have managed any sound effects, tied up in the tower?"

I scratch my head, but this produces no explanation, and the professor goes on, "You did nobly tonight, Augie. I shall certainly see that your parole board gets the whole story of your heroism."

"M—m—My pup—pup—pup?" I stammer. "Then you know?"

"Why, of course," says Angela. "One of Daddy's friends on the board recommended you."

"And you don't mind that I'm an ex-cat burglar?"

"We thought it might come in handy for cleaning the rain gutters and getting tennis balls off the roof," she says, smiling.

I turn to the professor, still stunned. "Well, sir, I hope this little episode has at least convinced you to install some burglar alarms?"

He grins and strokes his goatee. "N—no, Augie," he says. "I think I'll stick with Bama-Lolo."

He pats the idol with the emerald eye and I give the thing a double-take. It is a trick of the light, of course, plus the strain of events affecting my eyesight. . . .

But the damned thing looks a lot like Toad-Face O'Toole, all of a sudden!

Second Nature

by William T. Lowe

Old habits are hard to break, even when a person has been dead for fifty years. When I was in service at Mimosa Hall, one of my duties was to answer the door. Sometimes I forget that I am not to do that now; it does frighten people to see the big door swing open by itself. Now Miss Polly herself or Martha from the kitchen will answer the door while I just look on.

But today I was in the front hall when the knock came, and I simply forgot what I am. I opened the door. The man who stood there, gaping at the empty hallway, was Mr. Clayburn come again to call on Miss Polly. I remembered not to take his hat; that had been another old habit.

Miss Polly came hurrying into the hall from the parlor. "Why, Mr. Clayburn, how nice to see you!" She was all smiles and dressed for company. She took his hat and put it on.a small table and led her guest into the parlor. Of course he couldn't know I followed them.

Miss Polly had set out the best china for tea. I would have used the everyday service; I didn't care for Mr. Emmett Clayburn. He was too much a dandy, with his plastered hair and fancy suit and hightop shoes. He was the latest suitor to come calling on Miss Polly. Now he sat by the fire, smirking and drinking tea.

"You poor thing," he was saying. "Caring for a big estate like this must be dreadfully tiresome for you."

Miss Polly smiled and dimpled. "A person must do what is required," she said. Slender, with her mother's blonde hair and blue eyes and firm chin, Miss Polly was well past thirty but she still looked like a schoolgirl. And acted like a schoolgirl, in my opinion. Mr. Emmett Clayburn was as transparent as well water.

Of course he knew about Mimosa Hall and our five hundred acres of farmland and timber. Anybody in town could have told him that the Pollards were one of the richest families in this part of Virginia, and that Miss Polly lived here alone, since her brother had been killed overseas.

"I always say that men have a natural aptitude for agricultural management," he was saying. "Don't you agree, Miss Polly?" He took a sharp look at her rings and the big brooch she always wore.

"More tea, Mr. Clayburn? Another of these little cakes?"

He managed to touch her arm as she poured him more tea and gave her what he thought was a warm smile. He looks like a fox circling a henhouse, I thought.

"I do believe Martha has some chocolates in the pantry," Miss Polly said. "I'll just go and fetch them."

When she left the room, he got to his feet. First to the mantel where he inspected the signature on the Sargent hanging there. Then he lifted all the silver pieces to look for the sterling hallmarks. Then he went around the room looking at the other paintings, fingering the rugs on the floor, appraising everything in sight. Of course he thought he was alone.

Miss Polly and I have an understanding. She knows what I am and that I belong here. She knows that cats and dogs and other animals are afraid of me. She has made it plain that I am not to annoy anyone, except of course when there might be a burglar or a prowler, and I am not to interfere with the way she runs the house. She doesn't understand that I feel responsible for her just as I did for her mother. Sometimes, not often, I take some liberties with my position.

I did now. Miss Polly might enjoy the company of Mr. Emmett Clayburn, but to me he was nothing but a fortune hunter. This would have to be his last visit.

I began by making the room darker. He glanced about nervously and retreated to his chair by the fire. The air around him became quite chilly. He leaned toward the fire and held out his hands.

The fire went out. Slowly at first, then it died down quickly until there were only a few embers glowing on the hearth. He reached for his cup; it glided away from his hand. I knew from his expression that he was recalling the gossip that Mimosa Hall was haunted.

An ominous creaking from across the room made him jump. He looked over his shoulder to see the door to the front hall opening slowly. Then the set of fireplace tools rattled, and he jerked around to see the poker rise into the air and hover over his head. He cowered in his chair, his face white, the hair on his neck rising.

A few more minutes of the dark and the cold and the dancing poker would send him pelting out the door, and that would be the last we would see of Mr. Emmett Clayburn.

But I heard Miss Polly's step in the hall from the pantry. I brightened the room and sent the poker back to its bracket. When she came in with a plate of candies, the fire was crackling again. She stared at her visitor's pasty face.

"Why, Mr. Clayburn, is something the matter?"

He gulped twice before he could speak. "Why, no, Miss Polly," he stammered. "I've just remembered an urgent appointment." He launched himself out of the chair and made for the door. "You will excuse me."

"Of course, Mr. Clayburn." Miss Polly frowned at the mantel above the fireplace. But like her mother, she was a good hostess.

"I have enjoyed your visit," she began, but he was already at the front door. I couldn't let him forget his hat; it rose from the table and settled gently on his head. He squeaked and was through the door and gone.

I was afraid Miss Polly would be angry, and she was. She stamped her foot and glared around the hall.

"Jonathan," she said in her most severe tone, "in the parlor. Right now."

She marched back inside and stood before the mantel. She frowned at the two silver candlesticks on the mantelpiece. "All right, Jonathan. You did it again. I know you're in here. Answer me."

The candlestick on the right tilted once, then settled back. That meant I said "yes." Tilting the left candlestick meant "no." Tilting both of them meant "maybe" or "I don't know." Communication had always been a problem, and the candlesticks were all we had. Her mother had told Miss Polly about them when Miss Polly was grown up enough to accept my being there. She also explained that in my day servants were not expected to read and write.

"I know you scared off Mr. Clayburn, Jonathan," Miss Polly said sternly. "I didn't see you do it, but I know you were up to your tricks again, weren't you?"

I couldn't deny it. The right candlestick moved gently, meekly. "Yes."

"That's the third gentleman caller you've run off this year!" She glared at the mantel and stamped her foot. "Explain yourself, Jonathan." She stamped her foot again. "Oh, I know you can't tell me that. You just decided you didn't like him. Is that it?"

Both candlesticks tilted toward each other. I thought a "maybe" was better than a "no."

"You don't think he was good enough for me?"

Right candlestick. "Yes."

"You think he just wanted to get his hands on my money?"

The right candlestick bounced into the air. "Yes."

"Well, maybe you're right. I didn't like him much myself."

The right candlestick spun in the air and dropped back into place.

"But, Jonathan, do you think I want to be an old maid all my life?"

"No."

Just like her mother, Miss Polly never stayed angry very long. Usually she began to giggle at the notion of standing by the fire in an empty room talking to the mantel. As always, I had to be sure Martha didn't come in from the kitchen and hear her, or see the candlesticks moving. She would have been frightened out of her wits, and good help is still hard to get.

"Oh, Jonathan," Miss Polly said, "I know you mean well." She stared into the fire. "But will I ever meet someone we both like?"

I can't foretell the future any better than a living person, but of this I was sure. The right candlestick sprang off the mantel and flew around the room, turning cartwheels, diving under tables, brushing the ceiling over her head.

Miss Polly laughed. "All right, Jonathan. That's a promise." She started out to the kitchen, but at the door she turned back. "But next time, let me make up my own mind. You hear me?" All the Pollard women have to have the last word.

Miss Polly was my favorite. It was she who had years ago found out what my name was. With the candlesticks we were on speaking terms, although she still turned pale sometimes when she caught me dusting the furniture. One day she took the family Bible off the table where it was always kept and opened it. "Who exactly are you?" she demanded.

I turned to the correct page and made a teaspoon hover over one line.

"Anson Pollard," she read. "Died May 14, 1872." She looked around the room. "Are you my Great-uncle Anson?"

The teaspoon waggled and pointed to a smaller line below that one.

"He and his faithful servant Jonathan killed by lightning during a storm." She looked up from the page. "Jonathan? You are Jonathan?"

"Yes," said the teaspoon.

"If you're here, where is Uncle Anson?"

The teaspoon pointed at the floor.

"Down there? Oh, dear." She was quiet for a moment. "Well, Jonathan," she said stoutly, "I'm sure you served the family very well." I am proud to say that I did, and I've been serving the family ever since.

Maybe this time I tried too hard to be helpful because a few days later I almost got Miss Polly arrested for horse stealing.

That would have been the talk of the county and a family disgrace. There are the new automobiles now, but horse stealing is still a very serious offense. When the sheriff came, I let Miss Polly answer the door herself. I remembered the sheriff as one of the Culpepper children who used to raid the Pollard orchard many years ago; now he was an embarrassed old man, twisting his hat in his hands.

He refused Miss Polly's invitation to step inside. "I'm afraid I'm here on business, Miss Polly," he said.

"Yes, Sheriff Culpepper?"

"It's about that new neighbor of yours down the road. Mr. James Howell, who bought the old Simpson place?"

"I've heard about him. We've never met."

"Well, he's raising thoroughbred horses, those Morgan horses, and it seems one of his mares is missing. A right prize animal, he says."

"I'm sorry to hear that, but what has it to do with me?"

The sheriff's face was as red as a brick. "Well, Miss Polly, it seems that one of Mr. Howell's hands done seen that mare in the corral outside your stable."

"Outside my stable? Well, surely the horse must have just wandered in there."

The sheriff twisted his hat completely out of shape. "No, ma'am. It seems that the gate is latched on the outside. With Mr. Howell's mare on the inside."

Miss Polly stared at him. "You mean . . . you mean . . . ." She drew herself up and stamped her foot. Just like her mother, I thought. "Sheriff, if you think for one minute that I stole that horse! Well, I never!"

"No, not at all, Miss Polly. There's got to be some mistake. I mean, what would you folks at Mimosa Hall want with another horse?"

Miss Polly had heard enough. "Yes, there most certainly is a mistake. If Mr. Howell thinks I am harboring an animal of his, then let Mr. Howell come here and tell me so himself. Good afternoon, Sheriff Culpepper!"

He left quickly. Miss Polly closed the front door firmly and marched into the parlor. "Jonathan," she said, "are you here?"

The right candlestick said, "Yes."

"Is there a strange horse in our pen?"

The left candlestick said, "No."

"This whole thing is a mistake?"

"Yes."

"All right. I'm sure the sheriff can straighten it out. Tell Martha we'll have roast pork for dinner. Oh, never mind. I'll tell her."

In my second existence I have learned what I think is known as discretion. The candlesticks answer questions. They don't always tell the truth.

That evening I waited in the front hall, hoping we would have another visitor. Since Martha always leaves before sundown, Miss Polly would have to answer the door herself. When the knock came at the door, she came down the hall from the kitchen, wearing an apron with a frown on her face and a smudge on her cheek.

She opened the door and stared at the man standing there, a tall, handsome man wearing casual work clothes. He smiled politely and took off his hat.

"Miss Pollard? Good evening. My name is James Howell."

"Yes?" Then Miss Polly recognized the name. "Oh, Mr. Howell. You bought the Simpson place. You're the man who is raising horses."

"Yes, Miss Pollard. May I come in?"

Miss Polly was flustered, and I knew why. She hadn't expected a caller, the fire hadn't been lit in the parlor, neither tea nor coffee was ready, and, even worse, she was wearing an apron. And this was the man who thought she had taken one of his horses.

But she was the lady of the house and she knew her manners. "Do come in, Mr. Howell," she said graciously. Her mother would have been proud of her.

From there on things went smoothly. Miss Polly led him into the parlor, saying, "I'm afraid we weren't expecting company." But when she opened the door she saw that lamps had been lit in corners of the room and a cheery fire was blazing in the fireplace. She shot a look at the mantel, but said nothing. She motioned her guest to one of the chairs by the fire. "Please have a seat."

James Howell walked over to the fireplace, and when his back was turned Miss Polly's apron whisked itself away and vanished under a seat cushion. There was a light touch on her face as the smudge disappeared from her cheek. She put her hand on her face and looked again at the mantel.

From the pantry came the whistle of a teakettle on the boil. Mr. Howell looked at the table on which the good tea service stood waiting. "Do I hear a teapot calling?" he asked pleasantly.

"Why, yes," Miss Polly stammered. "Would you care for a cup?"

"Thank you, if it's not too much trouble."

In the pantry Miss Polly found a plate of sliced fruit cake ready and waiting. "Jonathan, what in the world are you doing?" she whispered. Of course there was no answer. She poured hot water into the teapot and carried it and the plate of cake back to the parlor.

When they were settled by the fire and Mr. Howell had sampled his tea, he glanced around the room. "What a charming home, Miss Pollard. I wish I had come calling sooner. But there's been so much to do since I moved here. I live alone, you know, and I have to supervise all the work."

Miss Polly came directly to the point. "But now I assume you've come to inquire about your horse?" she asked sweetly.

"Now that you mention it. May I call you Miss Polly?"

In spite of herself, she smiled and the dimples appeared in her cheeks. "Please do, Mr. Howell."

"James, please."

He stretched out his legs and leaned back. "I don't have to inquire about Rose, Miss Polly. I know she's in good hands. I saw her out back before I knocked at your front door."

"So she is here." Miss Polly glared at the mantel where the candlesticks stood silent and still. To Mr. Howell she said, "And how did you know where to find her, Mr. Howell?"

"James, please. Actually, I followed the same trail Rose did when she came here. It led me right to your stable door."

"I don't understand." The firelight made golden highlights in her hair; James Howell looked at it with appreciation. "I thought the horse just wandered in here," Miss Polly said. "You followed a trail?"

"Yes. A trail of grain. There was a trail of grain from my pasture up the road and down your lane and into your stable yard. Rose loves grain, naturally, and when she found my own gate open, she just followed it."

"A trail of grain? But how in the world . . ."

It was then I made a mistake, a very bad mistake. Just when everything was going so well. Here was this handsome new neighbor, a man who lived alone, a man who had resources enough to raise horses and employ workers, sitting by a cosy fire in our parlor. Here he was with Miss Polly and they were smiling at each other. And their teacups were empty.

Old habits are hard to break, especially when a person spends a lifetime in household service and takes pride in his work. It was still second nature to me to answer the door, to tend the fires, to dust, to wait on the table, to fill water and wine glasses. And teacups.

The teapot lifted itself off the table and floated through the air toward our guest. It deftly poured more tea into his cup and then sailed across the hearth and filled Miss Polly's cup and went back to the table.

It was a terrible mistake because both of them saw it happen. Miss Polly gasped. "Jonathan!" she hissed at the fireplace. "Be careful!" Her eyes were wide with alarm as she turned to our guest.

"Now don't be alarmed, James," she said. "I know you must have been startled, but you mustn't be frightened. It's nothing to be afraid of. . . ."

He held up his hand and smiled at her. I was pleased to see that it was a genuine, unafraid smile. "Don't upset yourself, Miss Polly." He looked around the room and in spite of myself I ducked behind a loveseat.

"Jonathan, is it?" he said. "Do you know, Miss Polly, I have someone who looks after me, too." He grinned at the incredulous look on her face. "Yes, I do. Old Miss Fanny Simpson still, ah, still resides on the farm I bought." He saw relief dawning on Miss Polly's face.

"Yes, she does. Miss Fanny passed away at the turn of the century, but she's still there. She looks after me when she thinks I need it."

After a moment Miss Polly began to smile and then they were both laughing. He held out his hand and Miss Polly took it. I suppose sharing a secret will bring two people together.

A bit later Miss Polly murmured, "I guess we'll never know who put out that trail of grain, will we?"

The candlestick on the right hopped into the air, but neither of them noticed. Slowly it sank back to its place on the mantel. It didn't matter if they ever knew or not.

I knew.

The Balancing Man

by Charles Ardai

I was eleven when my brother Friendly took me to see the balancing man.

The day we went was a hot spring Wednesday, the kind when it can be three o'clock but the sweat in you thinks it's high noon. Friendly and I were slacking off behind the heaven elm in the school courtyard, lazing in its shade and putting off going back inside as long as we could. School was no place to be on a day like this. Anyone with half a brain could see that, Friendly said.

It wasn't long before it became too late for us to go to class with an excuse about forgetting what time it was—exactly when we passed the point of no return I can't say but at one point we both knew that we had. The only thing keeping us where we were then was the shade of that towering elm . . . but it was hardly the only tree around. So we got to our feet and stepped out into the sun, crimping our eyes shut and wiping our necks and foreheads as trickles of sweat started bubbling up.

We dashed up over Morton's Hill and into the wilds at the edge of school grounds, plunging through the forest and changing course to meet any big tree we saw, among whose roots we could spend a few minutes lying around and breathing in the scent of the damp earth. Friendly climbed some trees, too, because that's the sort of thing he liked to do; as for me, I like the ground and was more than happy to stay on it.

For a while our path kept us in sight of the schoolyard—we

ducked into the undergrowth and held our breaths whenever we thought someone in the yard was looking our way—but pretty soon we'd wandered far enough to be completely lost. Luckily, Friendly had a good sense of direction and he was able to tell where we had gotten to just by looking at the moss on the trees or something like that. I trusted him and he trusted himself; so we kept on walking and whistling and sitting under trees until we came to a path and I realized that we hadn't just been wandering, we had been heading somewhere.

Now, I wasn't angry really, because I had no call to be, but I was a little peeved that Friendly had known all along where we were going. The whole point of wandering is not having to get somewhere, and knowing that we'd had a goal all along took away some of the fun.

"Ted," Friendly said when I told him this, "you don't know anything. Where we're going's better than just wandering. You'll see." And that took care of that, because when Friendly said something like that, he meant it.

We went down the path till it crossed Tocolow Road, then took a shortcut through someone's property and over an old wood bridge. Eventually we found ourselves on another dirt path, this one even narrower than the first. It looked like a driveway someone had started and then abandoned when he decided not to bother building a house after all. Sure enough, where the path ended there was no house, just a cleared area and a tall red wood barn.

No house, but a barn? Friendly was right. This was interesting.

"Now, listen," he told me. He bent over with his hands on his knees even though I was almost as tall as he was. I bent over, too, so he could whisper in my ear. "You've got to do exactly as I say. Okay?"

I nodded.

"When we go inside," he said, "you can't talk. You can't make any noise at all. You understand?"

I nodded.

"And when I pull on your arm like this—" he tugged on one of my sleeves "—you just follow me out. Got that?"

I nodded. Friendly straightened up and started off down the

path, but I ran after him and caught one of his belt loops. He spun around.

"Friendly, what's inside?" I said.

He clamped his hand over my mouth and darted glances left and right. "Shhh!"

I tried to talk through his hand but couldn't make a sound, so I licked his palm. He jerked it away and wiped it on his jeans. This time I whispered.

"Friendly, what's in there?"

"You'll see," he said. "Come on."

He took one of my hands in one of his and pulled me toward the barn. As we got closer, he slouched down a little and took his steps more slowly, careful not to make a sound. I did the same.

We ran out of path about five yards short of the barn, and from there I could see that the doors were already open a little. I wondered if Friendly had known they would be, and if so how, but I had promised not to talk, so I didn't. Friendly crept up to the doors and stuck his head in, then waved his hand for me to join him. I went as quietly as I could, though when I reached Friendly's side he frowned in a way that told me I had made too much noise. He put his finger to his lips again, stepped through the door, and pulled me inside by my shirt collar.

I must have looked completely confused—I remember that my eyes opened so wide they hurt—because Friendly broke his own rule. He stuck his mouth right up against my ear and hissed, *"It's the balancing man."*

It certainly was.

The inside of the barn was hollowed out: no stables, no loft, no troughs, nothing you'd expect to find in a barn. But it wasn't empty. It was the furthest thing from empty. It was full. Only it wasn't full of anything that made sense.

It was full of trestles and sawhorses, pewter cooking pots and lacquered settees, long dangling hanks of rope and window shutters and automobile doors. It was full of garden hoses, long canvas mail sacks, and a jackhammer. It was full of television antennas and serving platters.

Right in front of us, perched on a pair of cinder blocks, there was a refrigerator, turned over on its side. On top of the refrigerator there was a hat stand, and wedged on top of the hat stand was an extension ladder stretched out horizontally to its full length of ten feet or so. At either end, the ladder was strung with lengths of copper wire; the wire went straight up for maybe twenty feet, where it was looped on one side around a pair of umbrellas and on the other around a metal statue of a baseball player. I can't tell you what the umbrellas and the statue were connected to since that would just bring up the same question again and it would all take too long in the telling; but I'll tell you, looking around the barn I saw more *things*, connected up in more ways, than I'd ever seen before.

There was a grandfather clock with its pendulum missing dangling high overhead. There was a set of golf clubs roped together to prop up an upended washbasin. There was a well bucket tied to the end of a long, colorful scarf. There was a tambourine. There was a box of crackers. Anything you'd care to name was in there somewhere.

All this stuff was piled up like a mighty ziggurat, only instead of coming to a point at the top, it came to maybe a dozen points, each sticking out like a turret from a castle. The turrets were tied to each other with thick cables of wire, like tightropes in the circus. On one of these cables I could see a lemon crate, and sticking out of the lemon crate there was a sword, and balanced on the pommel of the sword there was a bicycle seat. Squatting on the bicycle seat, forty feet up, was an old man.

He sat, and he looked straight ahead, and he seemed not to notice the extremely perilous position he was in. For although the structure had outcroppings in every possible direction and at every possible location, he had chosen the one spot I could see where a slip would be certain to pitch him the whole forty feet to the ground.

It was something like watching an act in the circus, except that nothing happened. The man sat, and he sat, and he didn't budge, and though I couldn't tell from so far below, I wouldn't have been surprised to learn that he wasn't even blinking. I remember thinking that if *I* were perched on a bicycle seat, on a sword, on a lemon crate, on a highwire, I wouldn't budge either.

I looked away from the man, away from the huge tower of odds and ends, at the only spot of sense my eyes could find: my own shoes. But no sooner had my head stopped spinning a little than Friendly was tugging on my sleeve. My first thought was that we were leaving, but when I looked up I saw that Friendly was pointing. The man now had his hands pressed down on the bicycle seat with his long legs extended out to either side of him. As I watched, he turned himself over entirely, resting the top of his head on the bicycle seat and curling his arms around his chest and his legs around each other.

Then he didn't budge again for the longest time.

I didn't want to stay. I was frightened for the old man; he was sure to fall and I didn't want to see it happen. So I tugged on Friendly's sleeve and pleaded with him silently.

He ignored me and started walking around the base of the ziggurat, poking a finger in here, staring through a gap there. I wished that he would stop, but there didn't seem to be anything I could do to make him. I followed him around the wall of the barn, once or twice glancing up and then glancing down again quickly.

When we reached the side of the barn opposite where we had come in, I saw three other kids already there, huddled in the shadows, watching the balancing man. I looked at the three boys closely, but I didn't recognize them. They looked about my brother's age or maybe a little bit older.

They made room for us on the floor. Friendly sat down, so I had to, too. They all looked up with big smiles on their faces, as though there were a giant television screen under the roof and it was showing their favorite program.

The balancing man was still standing on his head, and it was then that I realized just how old he was. His beard hung down at least two feet in front of his face, long and off-white, the color that curtains get if you don't wash them very often. He was wearing a black turtleneck shirt and a black vest with black trousers, but because of his position I could see bits of his arms and legs, which were very thin: he looked like a doll made out of straw.

But he must have been strong! Stronger than anyone in the world, to be able to balance the way he did! And more than strong; he must have been . . . I couldn't think of the word I wanted. Today, I think of the word "agile," but that falls so far short of describing this extraordinary man that I think I was better off when I couldn't think of a word at all. I was amazed, and more than amazed: I was shocked. I was impressed. I was frightened. And I was embarrassed for watching, for Friendly and the other boys' gawking. Because I knew now, from the way Friendly had spoken, that this wasn't the first time he had come here.

At least the balancing man didn't seem to know we were there; I was glad about that. But I was also terrified. What if one of us should bump into something, or stick his finger where it didn't belong? It would be a tragedy.

I closed my eyes and pressed my chin to my chest and didn't look up again even when Friendly tapped on my shoulder and tried to lift my chin. I didn't open my eyes until Friendly hissed in my ear, "Okay, come on!"

The other three boys were already halfway to the door and Friendly was edging in that direction. I went with him. Still, I couldn't resist the urge to look up once more, and when I didn't see the balancing man on the crate my heart leapt up into my throat. Then I caught sight of him only a few feet away, walking easily along another of the cables. His stride was long and brave, and so perfectly composed—he even had his hands in his pockets!—that I felt sure for a moment that walking on a wire must be the most natural thing on earth for him. He had such an air of unconcern about him that I felt as though my amazement at his performance was somehow unwarranted. How much of a fool would I have thought someone who had praised my ability to lie in bed without falling out, or to comb my hair without putting out an eye?

My head swam with confusion and I was so relieved when we reached the door that I ran through it and down the driveway without waiting for Friendly.

I didn't run far, though, and Friendly caught up with me quickly. We sat down together in the woods. He looked at me with a sort of sly pride in his face, as though he had just initiated me into some delicious, illicit pleasure.

"So? What'd you think?"

I shook my head. It didn't help. "Who is he?" I asked.

"Who cares?" Friendly said. "He's some guy. He's a nut. He's an alien from outer space. What difference does it make? He's just someone. What do you think?"

"I don't get it."

Friendly laughed and lay back against the root of a tree. "Nope, I bet you don't."

"Do *you*?" If anyone understood this, I was sure it would be Friendly.

"Sure," he said. "The man's a loony-tune."

"But how does he do it?" I asked.

"How? He probably collects up junk from around here. Maybe he steals things."

"No, I mean how does he . . . balance?"

Friendly shrugged. Then he said very quietly, "I hear that crazy people are twelve times stronger than normal people."

"Really?"

Friendly nodded. Then he sat up and put his hands on my shoulders. "You can't tell anyone about this," he said. "Especially Mom and Dad. You understand?"

I nodded.

"Good." He ruffled my hair and stood up, brushing soil off his jeans. "Now let's go home."

It wasn't easy, but as Friendly led me home, I forced myself to remember the path we took.

The second time I went by myself. It was a Saturday, and I told everyone that I was going to meet Jesse at his house. I told Jesse, too, and he said he'd cover for me.

This time the barn doors were closed, but they still weren't locked. I opened them gently, just far enough for me to squeeze in. To make sure that I was alone I walked all the way around the barn. I was.

Then I looked for the balancing man, but I couldn't see him—it was still too early in the day for much light to come in through the barn's windows. I stood where I was and I waited, and in a while my eyes adjusted until I could make out the old man's shape up on the highest point of the tower.

Both of his feet were crowded onto the top of what was either a basketball or a volleyball. The ball itself was perched at one end of a steep wooden plank and I couldn't see why it didn't roll down and take him with it.

In one hand he had what looked like a metal coffeepot and he was using it to water some plants that were growing out of a porcelain bathtub. When he was done, he set the pot down on the edge of the bathtub and turned completely around with a single, sudden twist of his torso. The ball started to carry him down the incline, slowly at first, then at a tremendous rate. At the end of the plank there was a circular hole through which the ball dropped into a net—but the balancing man sailed off the end of the platform, aimed right at the wall of the barn.

As he flew, he stretched one of his arms out behind him and snagged an upright flagpole, which whipped him around in a half circle and deposited him on a small wooden platform a few feet below. My heart very generously started beating again.

I had to fight a strong urge to run away. I wasn't even sure why I had come. Crazy people were twelve times stronger than regular people, after all—of which strength I had just seen a fine demonstration—so I was scared.

But there are some things in life which you can't just see once and pass over without questioning. There are some bits of food which are too big to swallow unchewed. Even at eleven I wasn't like Friendly, who could see the balancing man and think only of his own entertainment. What I didn't realize until much later is that people like Friendly are, perhaps, to be envied.

I waited until the balancing man was balanced steadily on his bicycle seat and then I said, "Good morning." I didn't want to startle him—I certainly didn't want him to fall—but somehow I was confident that I wouldn't and he wouldn't. I spoke loudly, but not suddenly.

He looked down and I could almost see him straining to make me out. "Good morning," he said.

His voice was small and distant, which was not a surprise. But it was also clear and deep, with none of the taints that age so often brings. He did not seem disturbed by my presence.

"My name is Ted," I said, a little louder.

"Mine isn't," he said.

"What is your name?" I asked. He didn't answer. This he didn't seem to have heard.

I cupped my hands around my mouth and shouted: "What are you doing up there?"

"I'm balancing," he said.

"But why?" I asked.

"Because if I didn't balance," he said, "I'd fall."

He slid off his perch and sat down on the cable, his skinny legs dangling over the edge.

"Why don't you come down?" I shouted.

"Why don't you come up?" he said.

I didn't know what to say. "Because I don't know how! I wouldn't be safe! I'd fall!"

"Exactly," the balancing man said. As though this was his reason, too.

"Don't you *ever* come down?" I said.

"No. It's dangerous."

I waved my arm at the structure beneath him. "Where did this come from?"

"Where did that come from?" The balancing man pointed out one of the windows. "Where did you come from?"

"I came from home," I said. "I wanted to know if you needed any help."

For a long time he didn't speak. I began to think he wasn't going to. Then he said, "No, you didn't. You don't understand me. You are afraid of me. That's why you came."

It was, more or less, the truth.

"The feeling," he said, and here his voice trembled a little, "is mutual."

"What does that mean?" I asked.

"It means, young man, that I am afraid of you."

"Of me?"

"No," the balancing man said. "Of *you*."

"I don't understand—"

"Please," the old man said suddenly. "Leave me alone."

I was surprised at this and a little bit hurt. Neither of us moved for a good five minutes, and then I lowered my head and walked out. I did not go back.

Friendly did go back. I couldn't stop him. In all honesty, I didn't try; but it wouldn't have mattered if I had. It was a hangout for those kids we had seen there and a couple of others. (Friendly told me names, but I've forgotten them, if I ever remembered.) They were his friends now, and you could have made him give up his own family before you'd have gotten him to stop going to that barn.

Once he asked me to go with him again; when I refused, he made fun of me. Another time he tried to take me there without telling me where we were going, like the first time, but I got wise when we hit Tocolow Road and I screamed at him like I had the devil in me. I said I'd tell Mom and Dad. He told me to go to hell then, that he'd stab me in my sleep if I did any such thing. Friendly and I didn't talk much after that day.

But I knew he kept going back because it showed in his face, the way it would show when he had his hands behind his back in the wintertime and you could just *tell* that he had a snowball he was about to throw. He had a secret, and he wanted it to stay that way, but part of him wanted to shout it out to the world: *I'm Friendly Cooper and have I got something to tell you!* That was the part that showed in his face.

And sometimes it wasn't even a matter of reading his face. Sometimes he'd just come right out and tell me, almost like he was daring me to do something about it. He told me when they snuck eight people in there at once—*and the guy didn't notice a thing! What do you think of that, Ted?* He told me when Martin, or Mark, or someone, burped real loud and someone else laughed, *but that guy must be blind, or deaf maybe, 'cause you could see he didn't hear a thing!* He told me the day one of them climbed up on top of the refrigerator and sat on it—*and then he got down real quick, but nothing happened, the guy didn't notice.* So of course they all had to do it. And then, of course, someone climbed a little higher.

And then one afternoon Friendly came home glowering, his eyes set in furious determination, his breathing deliberate like a bull's when he's led into the ring. Martin had climbed up past the refrigerator, Friendly said, over the ladder, through the barrel, and up over the automobile tires when that old monster came up behind him and kicked him off. He just *kicked* him off. He put his foot on Martin's back and pushed, and the whole stack of tires fell and Martin fell with them, maybe fifteen feet. The others picked him up because he couldn't walk, and they beat it the hell out of there. When they got to Martin's house, they told his mother he'd fallen out of a tree. She took him to a doctor in Port and the doctor said his leg was broke clean through.

Friendly's face was white with terror and red with shame and black with anger as he told me this. Until you see a face like that you can't imagine what it looks like. I hope you never do.

I never have since, except that I've seen it quite a lot in my dreams. Usually it's superimposed over a headline from the Gavin County *Dispatch*. The paper's dated a week later and the headline says

FIRE DESTROYS TWO ACRES

and the story tells how the volunteer fire department managed to contain a potentially devastating fire on one small plot of land. The story is basically an upbeat one, and why not? No one lived on that land; it was just being used as a dumping ground by people in the area, judging by the burned-up junk the firemen found at the center of the blaze. And the firemen got there in time to put it out before it spread. A happy day all around.

If I'm lucky, the dream stops there—I wake up sweating into my sheets like I'm under a heat lamp and my heart's beating so hard my ribs ache, but at least I'm awake. Then there are the other nights, the ones when the dream goes on the same as it did the first time, when I was eleven years old and sleeping right down the hall from my parents.

Sometimes Friendly's in it, sometimes he's not. Sometimes I'm in it. Sometimes I pour the gasoline and light the match. But the part that's always the same is what comes next, after the boys all run away.

Flames bite into the walls of the barn, climb gently, slowly up toward the roof, lighting the red wood a fine, smoldering orange. And as the flames climb, a spark catches here, on the wooden stave of a barrel, a spark catches there, on the fringes of a scarf held up with clothespins.

The old man squats on his bicycle seat, on the sword, on the lemon crate, on the highwire, forty feet up, and he doesn't notice right away. Then he smells something; then he glimpses the first flames; then he sees the barrel collapse onto itself, all flame and ashes, the scarf curl up and blacken in an instant.

He jumps off the seat onto the cable, and the crate, the sword, and the seat fall the forty feet and smash on the floor. He sees more flames: in front of him, so he turns around, but they're behind him, too. He shimmies up a wire, climbs over some boxes, and then the flame's under him, slapping hungry tongues against his feet. Soft metals melt, wood burns, cloth vanishes; and all the connections come apart one by one. A turret tips and falls. The cable snarls under his feet and he leaps to another cable, a higher plank, until he's all the way up by the bathtub with his plants.

At this point, the dream can go one of two ways, depending on whether the plank he's standing on burns up quickly enough or the roof collapses, crushing him first.

If I'm lucky here, I wake up in tears. If I'm unlucky, I dream it all over again.

And you wonder, why? I said it myself, I couldn't have talked Friendly out of going; and even if I could have, the others would still have been there. Nothing would have been different. Maybe at eleven I'm entitled to a measure of irrational guilt, but at forty?

But you've got it wrong. It isn't guilt and it never has been. It's grief.

I'll be honest with you. I hadn't had this dream in a long time. Years. I hadn't thought about any of it in ages. The only reason it came back now is because of another headline I read, just last week:

WEEKEND RAMPAGE

It seems that some teenagers went into Central Park late last

Saturday night, found a dozen homeless people sleeping in card-board boxes, and set them on fire. Then they went home.

And I can't help but think about the old man on his highwire saying he was afraid not of me, but of *us*.

He had every reason to be.

Enter the Stranger

by Donald Olson

When the young man with the dream-scarred eyes finally found his way to Windfall, De Vore Goring's secluded estate, he stood trembling in the rain under the lighted windows, and not even the thunder rumbling over the wooded foothills behind him sounded louder in his ears than the frantic drumming of his own heart, a disturbance caused less by awe than by joyful anticipation, and when he passed through the gate and sounded the bell he did so without a tremor of shyness.

The aged housekeeper looked at him the way most people looked at him, with that eye-squint of uncertainty he'd learned to counteract, as he did now, with a disarmingly boyish smile. He asked for Goring and when the housekeeper wanted to know his name he said merely that he was a friend of Penelope's.

The woman looked at him oddly for a moment but then responded with a comprehending chirp of approval. "Friend of Penelope's, are you? Oh, ha-ha, yes, I see. Well, come in, then, come in. I'll see if he's still up."

He glanced behind him before following her inside and in a flash of silvery lightning noticed once more how totally isolated the house was.

She returned in a few moments and conducted him to a room at the head of the stairs, leaving him outside the open door.

With the greedy eyes of a traveler overjoyed to be home again, he tried to take in everything at once: the shelves of books, the huge mahogany desk, the marble fireplace, the picture of the young girl over the mantel, so that it was all a shimmery blur made worse by the tears filming his eyes, those dreamy slate-colored eyes that betrayed the presence of some wound or flaw or sorrow lurking just below the surface of his personality.

There was Goring himself, dear old Uncle Dev, with the familiar white hair and mustache, bushy brows and tame-lion eyes.

Goring waited for his tongue-tied caller to speak. When he did not, he lifted a frail hand from his blanketed lap and beckoned the young man closer.

"I'm Goring. Mr. . . . ?"

The visitor stepped eagerly forward to clasp the outstretched hand, somewhat startling Goring, making him feel uncomfortably like St. Peter in the Vatican, fearing for a moment that the fellow might be going to kneel and kiss his toe.

Instead, he moved back as if to give the older man a better look at him and said, with his too-generous smile: "Don't you recognize me?"

Goring stared, murmured an apology.

"I'm Jack!"

"Jack? Hmm . . . I'm still afraid . . ."

"*Jack.* You know—the Mysterious Stranger!"

Goring's hand rose to his eyes. "I'm afraid you still have me at a disadvantage, young fellow. An old man's memory . . ."

The caller looked more impatient than annoyed. "Gee, I recognized you right away. You're just like I knew Uncle Dev would be."

Goring became alert now in a more than socially attentive way. "Wait a minute. You don't mean you're—not *our* Jack."

As he said this he waved toward a certain shelf of books directly behind the desk. The visitor pounced on them, ran trembling fingers across their brightly jacketed spines.

"Yes! Jack, the Mysterious Stranger. I'm him!"

"Are you in*deed?* Well, fancy that." Although truly flabbergasted, a well-trained imagination helped Goring maintain his aplomb.

A blunt-tipped finger plucked one of the volumes from the shelf. "*Penelope and the Coral Reef.* Wow! That was super. But I don't see how Penelope could have thought I was one of the *bad* fishermen. I kept trying to warn her about Chang. But she kept running away."

He raced on in this vein, darting from one book to another, from *Penelope and the Deadly Amulet* to *Penelope and the Enchanted Valley*, from *Penelope and the Travisham Ghost* to *Penelope and the Smuggler's Revenge*, recalling delightedly how in each adventure he had come to Penelope's rescue.

Goring listened to all this with an emotion so singular he could not have defined it; it was as if one of his characters had magically come to life and burst through the study door to confront him at the very spot where Goring had created him. The emotion was certainly disturbing but not ungratifying. Recognition he'd had, to a degree, but this was in its way the supreme compliment.

The *Penelope* books, some two dozen of which had been published over the past couple of decades, had grown out of a simple story he'd written to amuse his young niece, based on one of his archaeological expeditions. He would never have tampered with the stories' formula—his teenage readers would not have tolerated it—and in each book Penelope would accompany Uncle Dev to some distant spot and be plunged into an exotic, danger-filled adventure. A conventional figure in each of the plots was a shadowy young man named Jack, a Mysterious Stranger who invariably popped up when Penelope was about to be fatally bitten by a cobra, suffocated in a mine cave-in, drowned in a scuttled yacht, or shot in a bandit's hideout. Any young reader of average intelligence could have told Penelope—Goring had scores of letters to prove it—that ever since *The Opal Talisman* adventure Jack had been wildly in love with her, yet she remained, book after book, annoyingly oblivious to his affection.

Only now did the visitor become aware that Goring was in a wheelchair.

"Did that bullet wound in *The Mandarin's Hatchet* really injure you, sir?"

Goring sighed and was on the point of explaining that nothing more dramatic than degenerative arthritis accounted for his condition when the caprice seized him to humor the lad's delusion.

Or was the impulse quite that innocent?

It was second nature to Goring to invent fictional plots and already certain elements of a curious scenario may have been shaping themselves in his mind, a mind grown bitter with jealousy and illness.

So he said, "Not really, no. It was that fall in *The Temple of the Sun Dragon*, remember? When I fell down the thousand and one steps?"

The man who thought he was "Jack" looked sympathetic to the point of tears. Feeling guilty, Goring insisted his visitor tell him more about himself. "I could offer you some refreshments, but I told Mrs. Harkins she could go to bed. And I'm quite helpless, as you see."

The visitor's face grew surprisingly hostile. "Is *that* why Penelope's going to marry Howard Rashbrooke?"

Goring's mind, until now only toying with that dangerous scenario, not really believing he could connect those various elements, seized upon the young man's hostility with furtive delight, as if the key to that shadowy plot had suddenly dropped into his hand.

"Er—no. No, of course not."

"Because she mustn't, you know. Rashbrooke's nothing but a fortune hunter. Can't you *see* that?"

The sorrows which had been Goring's only company ever since Sheila had begun the affair with Harry Lawton, the affair she thought Goring knew nothing about, were momentarily forgotten, the pain no pills could conquer half-forgotten.

"Rashbrooke claims to be in love with Penelope," he said slyly.

"Penelope *can't* love *him*. She loves *me*. She always has, ever since I kissed her in *The Opal Talisman*. She slapped my face, sure. Any decent girl would have done the same thing if a mysterious stranger kissed her. But she never forgot the kiss. No! She can't marry Rashbrooke. She can't!"

The young man had jumped to his feet and assumed a pose, legs apart, fists jammed against hips, which Goring recognized as characteristic of Jack. For a moment he felt a bit like Frankenstein and, like Frankenstein, he had passed beyond the point where he might still have abandoned his perilous experiment. It was as if fate had sent him this instrument, this human tool.

Goring implored the visitor to sit down. "You were going to tell me about yourself. How did it begin? I mean, when did you first know?"

"That I was Jack? Gosh, ages ago. When I was still in the orphanage. The other kids, they liked *Tom Swift* and *Nancy Drew*, but the minute I read *Penelope and the Jade Tiger* . . . well, Jack was *me*. He looked like me and he was an orphan and he never belonged anywhere. I must have read that book twenty times. And the others . . . all the others."

Goring was silent, watching the emotions glide swiftly over his visitor's young-old face, while outside the window the artillery rumble of thunder drew closer, and rain, like cold-fingered refugees fleeing before the guns, tapped urgently upon the pane. In spite of what he knew he was going to do, Goring was still deeply touched by the young man's tale, never dreaming that his unambitious labors could have wrought so lastingly vivid an effect upon a childish mind. How dismaying to realize that he had provided another human being with so total an escape into fantasy.

The caller's voice droned on, ". . . and when I read *The Missing Cipher* last month and Penelope actually got *engaged* to Howard Rashbrooke I knew I had to do something. I couldn't let it happen. I knew I had to come here and find her and tell her I love her . . . Where is she, Uncle Dev? Where's Penelope?"

Goring's mind was busy with the various aspects of his scenario that must be made coherent and viable.

"Tell me, Uncle Dev. Where is she?"

Where indeed? *No motion has she now, no force, she neither hears nor sees* . . . Only her name in real life was Polly, that adored little niece who had died in Goring's arms, and with her had died the only thing in the world he'd ever truly loved. He had been unable to keep Polly alive, but he could be sure that Penelope, the shadow child of his imagination whose adventures had so enthralled his little niece, would never die.

This reminded him of Sheila and a wave of hatred darkened his face.

"Uncle Dev? *Where is Penelope?*"

Goring knew it was his last chance to tell the truth, his last chance to scrap the grisly scenario in his mind. And what if he did? What if he were to tell "Jack" that all this time he had been idolizing a dead girl? What effect might such a revelation have on his already clouded mind?

The thunder, closer now, as if the furious armies in the sky were battling above the very roof, seemed to echo the words: "*Where is she, Uncle Dev?*"

"She's not home this evening, Jack. She had to go out."

"With *him?*"

"No. Not with him. She went to visit a sick friend."

Sheila, damn her, had insulted his intelligence with the same brazen excuse. A sick friend! Did she think he was senile, that he would swallow as phony an excuse as that? But then, it gave her pleasure to insult his intelligence just as it gave her pleasure to see him sitting in that wheelchair, helpless and vulnerable and so totally at her mercy.

"That's just like Penelope," the young man murmured. "Where is she, Uncle Dev? Tell me how to get there."

"If you found her, what would you do?"

"Why, tell her, of course."

"That you love her?"

"Yes."

"And want to marry her?"

"Yes!"

"What if she refused?"

"She wouldn't. She loves me."

"But what if she did?"

"I'd kill myself!" All his utterances were as melodramatic as a child's, and as artlessly sincere.

"Ah, my boy, it's no good. She has to marry Rashbrooke whether she wants to or not."

The young man was actually trembling with excitement. "You're wrong, Uncle Dev! I'll help her escape. Like I always do."

"You don't understand, lad. You don't know what Rashbrooke is."

In Goring's mind the scenario assumed its final shape.

"He's nothing but a lousy fortune hunter, Uncle Dev."

"He's more than that. Much more." Goring pointed to the manuscript on the desk. "It's not finished. But read the title."

A sudden shattering clap of thunder seemed to make the house tremble on its foundation as the young man picked up the manuscript and looked at it, his lips shaping and reshaping the words before speaking them aloud. "*Penelope and the Final Escape* . . . I don't get it, Uncle Dev. *Final* escape? That doesn't mean—"

"Marriage will bring Penelope's adventures to a logical conclusion."

Not his idea, never his idea; if he'd had anything to say about it Penelope's adventures would never end, not so long as he had breath in his body. Only he didn't have anything to say about it; he was powerless to cope with Sheila, the woman who had entered his house for the first time as a hired secretary when arthritis had afflicted him shortly after the fourth *Penelope* book and who, as his wife two years later, was writing the books herself. No one knew, of course, not even his publisher; she had become an expert at aping Goring's style. As the royalties had rolled in in greater and greater abundance she had grown indifferent to Goring and his suffering and had begun the affair with Lawton almost under his nose, until finally a day had come when she declared that she was sick of Penelope and she had embarked upon *The Final Escape*, intending to bring the series to a close.

Now Goring wheeled himself to the young man's side and calmly took the manuscript from his hand. "You remember Anaxos in *The Greek Uprising?*"

"Sure. He was one of Chang's men."

"Well, so is Rashbrooke."

The effect of this upon his visitor was enough to make Goring lower his eyes in shame even while his heart pounded with excitement.

"But, Uncle Dev, you can't let her do it!"

Goring spread his hands. "I'm helpless, as you can see. There's nothing I can do."

Gradually a sly, deliberate smile swept the anxiety from the young man's face. "I'm not helpless, Uncle Dev. I can help her get away from Rashbrooke just like I helped her escape from Anaxos."

Now that he could no longer dismiss it, Goring tried to tell himself that the idea for this monstrous scenario wasn't really his at all, but something evil and hideous spawned by the Devil of Pain that had made its home in his crippled body.

"You'd be risking your life, Jack. If you were caught they'd never believe you. You know what they'd say, don't you? That Penelope and Rashbrooke are only figments of the imagination, characters in a book."

The caller's smile grew noticeably slyer. "That's what Mrs. Brooks said when I went back to visit her once at the orphanage and told her all about my adventures. She said I was all mixed up. She said they were only characters in a book. And you know what I said, Uncle Dev? I said, if they're not real, then I'm not real either. She couldn't argue with *that*. That stumped her, let me tell you. Because I was right there talking to her and she couldn't say *I* wasn't real."

The hideousness of what he was doing brought a cold sweat to Goring's hands. "Go away, boy. While there's still time. Forget about Penelope."

"Where is he, Uncle Dev? Tell me where to find Rashbrooke. I'll take care of him just like I took care of Anaxos."

Once more his hand darted toward the desk, this time grabbing up a silver letter knife. "I don't have that Persian dagger I used on Anaxos, but this will do just fine." He smiled at Goring. "How do I find him, Uncle Dev?"

Goring looked very old and very tired. "You'd never find him. Not unless I called him and told him to come here."

Tiny flames burned behind the dream-scarred eyes. "Then call him, Uncle Dev. Right now."

With a curious, passive sense of having delivered himself into the power of an emotion he could neither understand nor resist, Goring picked up the telephone, then paused. "Listen, Jack, while I'm calling him you go downstairs and unlock the front door. Don't make any noise. We don't want to wake Mrs. Harkins."

As soon as the young man was out of the room Goring dialed the number with an aching, stiff-jointed finger. They would be together, of course, Sheila and Lawton. Suppose Sheila were to answer. But of course she didn't.

"Lawton? It's me, Goring, I've got to see you . . . Yes, yes. I know what time it is, but it's important . . . There's something I've got to tell you. About Sheila. Something she mustn't know. You've got to come right now. Sheila's visiting a friend and I've got to see you before she gets home . . . Yes . . . The door will be unlocked. Come straight up to my study." He hung up and pressed his fingers to his eyes. That would give the precious pair something to think about and he'd come. He'd come running to find out what it was all about. Sheila would make sure of that.

When the young man returned, his face was deeply flushed and the paper knife still gleamed in his clenched fist. "Did you reach him, Uncle Dev?"

"Yes. He's on his way." Goring wheeled himself to the door. "Switch off that light, Jack. Just leave the desk lamp burning."

In its greenish glow Goring's face looked as dead-white as a cadaver's. "I'll wait in the next room. Be quick about it, and be silent."

The young man nodded, then spoke just as Goring opened the door. "Uncle Dev?"

Goring looked back at him.

"I just want you to know something. Whatever happens to me, this has been the happiest day in my life."

Goring quickly withdrew. In his darkened bedroom he opened a drawer in the bedside stand, removed the revolver which he kept there, and slid it under the blanket on his lap.

He waited. The sound of thunder was now no more than a distant cannonade.

He didn't hear the car when it drove up and the first sound that reached his ear was a soft but impatient tap on the study door.

For perhaps a second or two he remained immobile, unbreathing, but the wild impulse of remorse which sent him hurtling toward the door came an instant too late. The man he had said was "Rashbrooke" gave a muffled cry as the paper knife drove fiercely into his heart.

Goring froze, then reacted with the calm, fatalistic precision of a sleepwalker, gently pushing the door open wider, raising the gun and firing.

He was almost sure that the young man who thought he was "Jack" never knew what happened, never knew that it was Uncle Dev who killed him.

The sensation it caused was, of course, considerable, but not so great as it would have been had Goring permitted reporters to step foot upon the grounds. His story was simple. A young man had come to the house, Mrs. Harkins confirmed that she had let him in ("he had real funny-looking eyes") and taken him upstairs to Goring's study. Goring stated that the caller had babbled incoherently, seemed to have confused some of the *Penelope* stories with real life, and when Harry Lawton had arrived unexpectedly the young man had gone berserk, seized up a paper knife from the desk, and stabbed Lawton in the heart. Before he could turn on Goring, the older man had been able to reach his revolver and shoot the intruder.

Goring would remember with utmost satisfaction the look on his wife's face when she arrived home just as they were removing her lover's body from the study. He wondered, with no particular alarm, if she would tell the police that Lawton had received a call from Goring. If she did Goring was prepared to deny it, but he didn't really expect her to, since it would mean confessing that she had been with Lawton.

He was right. She said nothing about that call, not to the police and not to him.

Instead of aggravating his condition as it might have been expected to do, the events of that night had quite a different effect upon Goring, for days afterward his aches and pains seeming to enter upon a period of remission, raising his spirits to the point where he actually expressed a desire to return to work.

His wife stared at him in amazement. "Work? *You?*"

"Why not?"

"You haven't worked in years."

"Well, now I feel like working. I've got two or three ideas churning around up here," and he gaily tapped his forehead.

"You're out of your mind," she said coldly. "Dr. Simpson would never approve. And you'd never stand the discomfort. That's why you hired me in the first place, don't forget. Every time you struck a typewriter key you winced with pain, and you know you were never any good at dictating your novels."

"Oh, I don't know. Maybe I didn't have the right *kind* of secretary."

He wheeled himself to the desk, picked up the unfinished manuscript of *The Final Escape* and with a look of infinite satisfaction calmly forced his crippled fingers to rip it into shreds.

"I've got a much better idea. How's this for a title? *Penelope and the Evil Bridegroom.* We'll take the little darling right up to the altar with that scoundrel and then, when things look absolutely hopeless, when there seems to be no conceivable way out of the situation— *enter the stranger.*"

The Griffin and the Minor Canon

by Frank Stockton

Over the great door of an old, old church which stood in a quiet town of a faraway land there was carved in stone the figure of a large griffin. The old-time sculptor had done his work with great care, but the image he had made was not a pleasant one to look at. It had a large head, with enormous open mouth and savage teeth; from its back arose great wings, armed with sharp hooks and prongs; it had stout legs in front, with projecting claws; but there were no legs behind—the body running out into a long and powerful tail, finished off at the end with a barbed point. This tail was coiled up under him, the end sticking up just back of his wings.

The sculptor, or the people who had ordered this stone figure, had evidently been very much pleased with it, for little copies of it, also on stone, had been placed here and there along the sides of the church, not very far from the ground, so that people could easily look at them, and ponder on their curious forms. There were a great many other sculptures on the outside of this church—saints, martyrs, grotesque heads of men, beasts, and birds, as well as those of other creatures which cannot be named, because nobody knows exactly what they were; but none was so curious and interesting as the great griffin over the door, and the little griffins on the sides of the church.

A long, long distance from the town, in the midst of dreadful wilds scarcely known to man, there dwelt the Griffin whose image had been put up over the church door. In some way or other, the old-time sculptor had seen him and afterward, to the best of his memory, had copied his figure in stone.

The Griffin had never known this, until, hundreds of years afterward, he heard from a bird, from a wild animal, or in some manner which it is not now easy to find out, that there was a likeness of him on the old church in the distant town.

Now, this Griffin had no idea how he looked. He had never seen a mirror, and the streams where he lived were so turbulent and violent that a quiet piece of water, which would reflect the image of anything looking into it, could not be found. Being, as far as could be ascertained, the very last of his race, he had never seen another griffin. Therefore it was that, when he heard of this stone image of himself, he became very anxious to know what he looked like, and at last he determined to go to the old church, and see for himself what manner of being he was.

So he started off from the dreadful wilds, and flew on and on until he came to the countries inhabited by men, where his appearance in the air created great consternation; but he alighted nowhere, keeping up a steady flight until he reached the suburbs of the town which had his image on its church. Here, late in the afternoon, he lighted in a green meadow by the side of a brook, and stretched himself on the grass to rest. His great wings were tired, for he had not made such a long flight in a century, or more.

The news of his coming spread quickly over the town, and the people, frightened nearly out of their wits by the arrival of so strange a visitor, fled into their houses, and shut themselves up. The Griffin called loudly for someone to come to him but the more he called, the more afraid the people were to show themselves. At length he saw two laborers hurrying to their homes through the fields, and in a terrible voice he commanded them to stop. Not daring to disobey, the men stood trembling.

"What is the matter with you all?" cried the Griffin. "Is there not a man in your town who is brave enough to speak to me?"

"I think," said one of the laborers, his voice shaking so that his

words could hardly be understood, "that—perhaps—the Minor
Canon—would come."

"Go, call him, then!" said the Griffin; "I want to see him."

The Minor Canon, who was an assistant in the old church, had
just finished the afternoon services, and was coming out of a side
door, with three aged women who had formed the weekday congregation. He was a young man of a kind disposition, and very anxious
to do good to the people of the town. Apart from his duties in the
church, where he conducted services every weekday, he visited the
sick and the poor, counseled and assisted persons who were in
trouble, and taught a school composed entirely of the bad children
in the town with whom nobody else would have anything to do.
Whenever the people wanted something difficult done for them,
they always went to the Minor Canon. Thus it was that the laborer
thought of the young priest when he found that someone must come
and speak to the Griffin.

The Minor Canon had not heard of the strange event, which was
known to the whole town except himself and the three old women,
and when he was informed of it, and was told that the Griffin had
asked to see him, he was greatly amazed and frightened.

"Me!" he exclaimed. "He has never heard of me! What should he
want with me?"

"Oh! you must go instantly!" cried the two men. "He is very angry
now because he has been kept waiting so long; and nobody knows
what may happen if you don't hurry to him."

The poor Minor Canon would rather have had his hand cut off
than go out to meet an angry Griffin; but he felt it was his duty to go,
for it would be a woeful thing if injury should come to the people of
the town because he was not brave enough to obey the summons of
the Griffin. So, pale and frightened, he started off.

"Well," said the Griffin, as soon as the young man came near, "I
am glad to see that there is someone who has the courage to come to
me."

The Minor Canon did not feel very brave, but he bowed his head.

"Is this the town," said the Griffin, "where there is a church with
a likeness of myself over one of the doors?"

The Minor Canon looked at the frightful creature before him and saw that it was, without doubt, exactly like the stone image on the church. "Yes," he said, "you are right."

"Well, then," said the Griffin, "will you take me to it? I wish very much to see it."

The Minor Canon instantly thought that if the Griffin entered the town without the people's knowing what he came for, some of them would probably be frightened to death, and so he sought to gain time to prepare their minds.

"It is growing dark now," he said, very much afraid, as he spoke, that his words might enrage the Griffin, "and objects on the front of the church cannot be seen clearly. It will be better to wait until morning, if you wish to get a good view of the stone image of yourself."

"That will suit me very well," said the Griffin. "I see you are a man of good sense. I am tired, and I will take a nap here on this soft grass, while I cool my tail in the little stream that runs near me. The end of my tail gets red-hot when I am angry or excited, and it is quite warm now. So you may go; but be sure and come early tomorrow morning, and show me the way to the church."

The Minor Canon was glad enough to take his leave, and hurried into the town. In front of the church he found a great many people assembled to hear his report of his interview with the Griffin. When they found that he had not come to spread ruin, but simply to see his stony likeness on the church, they showed neither relief nor gratification, but began to upbraid the Minor Canon for consenting to conduct the creature into the town.

"What could I do?" cried the young man. "If I should not bring him he would come himself, and, perhaps, end by setting fire to the town with his red-hot tail."

Still the people were not satisfied, and a great many plans were proposed to prevent the Griffin from coming into the town. Some elderly persons urged that the young men should go out and kill him; but the young men scoffed at such a ridiculous idea.

Then someone said that it would be a good thing to destroy the stone image, so that the Griffin would have no excuse for entering the town; and this plan was received with such favor that many of the people ran for hammers, chisels, and crowbars, with which to tear down and break up the stone griffin. But the Minor Canon resisted this plan with all the strength of his mind and body. He assured the people that this action would enrage the Griffin beyond measure, for it would be impossible to conceal from him that his image had been destroyed during the night. But the people were so determined to break up the stone griffin that the Minor Canon saw that there was nothing for him to do but to stay there and protect it. All night he walked up and down in front of the church door, keeping away the men who brought ladders, by which they might mount to the great stone griffin, and knock it to pieces with their hammers and crowbars. After many hours the people were obliged to give up their attempts, and went home to sleep; but the Minor Canon remained at his post till early morning, and then he hurried away to the field where he had left the Griffin.

The monster had just awakened, and rising to his forelegs and shaking himself he said that he was ready to go into the town. The Minor Canon, therefore, walked back, the Griffin flying slowly through the air, at a short distance above the head of his guide. Not a person was to be seen in the streets, and they went directly to the front of the church, where the Minor Canon pointed out the stone griffin.

The real Griffin settled down in the little square before the church and gazed earnestly at his sculptured likeness. For a long time he looked at it. First he put his head on one side, and then he put it on the other; then he shut his right eye and gazed with his left, after which he shut his left eye and gazed with his right. Then he moved a little to one side and looked at the image, then he moved the other way. After a while he said to the Minor Canon, who had been standing by all this time:

"It is, it must be, an excellent likeness! That breadth between the eyes, that expansive forehead, those massive jaws! I feel that it must resemble me. If there is any fault to find with it, it is that the neck seems a little stiff. But that is nothing. It is an admirable likeness—admirable!"

The Griffin sat looking at his image all the morning and all the afternoon. The Minor Canon had been afraid to go away and leave him, and had hoped all through the day that he would soon be satisfied with his inspection and fly away home. But by evening the poor young man was very tired, and felt that he must eat and sleep. He frankly said this to the Griffin, and asked him if he would not like something to eat. He said this because he felt obliged in politeness to do so; but as soon as he had spoken the words, he was seized with dread lest the monster should demand half a dozen babies, or some tempting repast of that kind.

"Oh, no," said the Griffin; "I never eat between equinoxes. At the vernal and at the autumnal equinox I take a good meal, and that lasts me for half a year. I am extremely regular in my habits, and do not think it healthful to eat at odd times. But if you need food, go and get it, and I will return to the soft grass where I slept last night and take another nap."

The next day the Griffin came again to the little square before the church, and remained there until evening, steadfastly regarding the stone griffin over the door. The Minor Canon came out once or twice to look at him, and the Griffin seemed very glad to see him; but the young clergyman could not stay as he had done before, for he had many duties to perform. Nobody went to the church, but the people came to the Minor Canon's house, and anxiously asked him how long the Griffin was going to stay.

"I do not know," he answered, "but I think he will soon be satisfied with regarding his stone likeness, and then he will go away."

But the Griffin did not go away. Morning after morning he came to the church; but after a time he did not stay there all day. He seemed to have taken a great fancy to the Minor Canon, and followed him about as he worked. He would wait for him at the side door of the church, for the Minor Canon held services every day, morning and evening, though nobody came now. "If anyone should come," he said to himself, "I must be found at my post." When the young man came out, the Griffin would accompany him in his visits to the sick and the poor, and would often look into the windows of the schoolhouse where the Minor Canon was teaching his unruly scholars. All the other schools were closed, but the parents of the Minor Canon's scholars forced them to go to school, because they were so bad they could not endure them all day at home—Griffin or no Griffin. But it must be said they generally behaved very well when that great monster sat up on his tail and looked in at the schoolroom window.

When it was found that the Griffin showed no sign of going away, all the people who were able to do so left the town. The canons and the higher officers of the church had fled away during the first day of the Griffin's visit, leaving behind only the Minor Canon and some of the men who opened the doors and swept the church. All the citizens who could afford it shut up their houses and traveled to distant parts, and only the working people and the poor were left behind. After some days these ventured to go about and attend to their business, for if they did not work they would starve. They were getting a little used to seeing the Griffin; and having been told that he did not eat between equinoxes, they did not feel so much afraid of him as before.

Day by day the Griffin became more and more attached to the Minor Canon. He kept near him a great part of the time, and often spent the night in front of the little house where the young clergyman lived alone. This strange companionship was often burdensome to the Minor Canon; but, on the other hand, he could not deny that he derived a great deal of benefit and instruction from it. The Griffin had lived for hundreds of years, and had seen much, and he told the Minor Canon many wonderful things.

"It is like reading an old book," said the young clergyman to himself; "but how many books I would have had to read before I would have found out what the Griffin has told me about the earth, the air, the water, about minerals, and metals, and growing things, and all the wonders of the world!"

Thus the summer went on, and drew toward its close. And now the people of the town began to be very much troubled again.

"It will not be long," they said, "before the autumnal equinox is here, and then that monster will want to eat. He will be dreadfully hungry, for he has taken so much exercise since his last meal. He will devour our children. Without doubt, he will eat them all. What is to be done?"

To this question no one could give an answer, but all agreed that the Griffin must not be allowed to remain until the approaching equinox. After talking over the matter a great deal, a crowd of the people went to the Minor Canon at a time when the Griffin was not with him.

"It is all your fault," they said, "that that monster is among us. You brought him here, and you ought to see that he goes away. It is only on your account that he stays here at all; for, although he visits his image every day, he is with you the greater part of the time. If you were not here, he would not stay. It is your duty to go away, and then he will follow you, and we shall be free from the dreadful danger which hangs over us."

"Go away!" cried the Minor Canon, greatly grieved at being spoken to in such a way. "Where shall I go? If I go to some other town, shall I not take this trouble there? Have I a right to do that?"

"No," said the people, "you must not go to any other town. There is no town far enough away. You must go to the dreadful wilds where the Griffin lives; and then he will follow you and stay there."

They did not say whether or not they expected the Minor Canon to stay there also, and he did not ask them anything about it. He bowed his head, and went into his house to think. The more he thought, the more clear it became to his mind that it was his duty to go away, and thus free the town from the presence of the Griffin.

That evening he packed a leathern bag full of bread and meat, and early the next morning he set out on his journey to the dreadful wilds. It was a long, weary, and doleful journey, especially after he had gone beyond the habitations of men; but the Minor Canon kept on bravely, and never faltered.

The way was longer than he had expected, and his provisions soon grew so scanty that he was obliged to eat but a little every day; but he kept up his courage, and pressed on, and after many days of toilsome travel, he reached the dreadful wilds.

When the Griffin found that the Minor Canon had left the town he seemed sorry, but showed no desire to go and look for him. After a few days had passed he became much annoyed, and asked some of the people where the Minor Canon had gone. But, although the citizens had been so anxious that the young clergyman should go to the dreadful wilds, thinking that the Griffin would immediately follow him, they were now afraid to mention the Minor Canon's destination, for the monster seemed angry already, and if he should suspect their trick he would, doubtless, become very much enraged. So everyone said he did not know, and the Griffin wandered about disconsolate. One morning he looked into the Minor Canon's schoolhouse, which was always empty now, and thought that it was a shame that everything should suffer on account of the young man's absence.

"It does not matter so much about the church," he said, "for nobody went there; but it is a pity about the school. I think I will teach it myself until he returns."

It was the hour for opening the school, and the Griffin went inside and pulled the rope which rang the school bell. Some of the children who heard the bell ran in to see what was the matter, supposing it to be a joke of one of their companions; but when they saw the Griffin they stood astonished and scared.

"Go tell the other scholars," said the monster, "that school is about to open, and that if they are not all here in ten minutes I shall come after them."

In seven minutes every scholar was in place.

Never was seen such an orderly school. Not a boy or girl moved or uttered a whisper. The Griffin climbed into the master's seat, his wide wings spread on each side of him, because he could not lean back in his chair while they stuck out behind, and his great tail coiled around, in front of the desk, the barbed end sticking up, ready to tap any boy or girl who might misbehave.

The Griffin now addressed the scholars, telling them that he intended to teach them while their master was away. In speaking he tried to imitate, as far as possible, the mild and gentle tones of the Minor Canon; but it must be admitted that in this he was not very successful. He had paid a good deal of attention to the studies of the school, and he determined not to try to teach them anything new, but to review them in what they had been studying; so he called up the various classes, and questioned them upon their previous lessons. The children racked their brains to remember what they had learned. They were so afraid of the Griffin's displeasure that they recited as they had never recited before. One of the boys, far down in his class, answered so well that the Griffin was astonished.

"I should think you would be at the head," said he. "I am sure you have never been in the habit of reciting so well. Why is this?"

"Because I did not choose to take the trouble," said the boy, trembling in his boots. He felt obliged to speak the truth, for all the children thought that the great eyes of the Griffin could see right through them, and that he would know when they told a falsehood.

"You ought to be ashamed of yourself," said the Griffin. "Go down to the very tail of the class; and if you are not at the head in two days, I shall know the reason why."

The next afternoon this boy was Number One.

It was astonishing how much these children now learned of what they had been studying. It was as if they had been educated over again. The Griffin used no severity toward them, but there was a look about him which made them unwilling to go to bed until they were sure they knew their lessons for the next day.

The Griffin now thought that he ought to visit the sick and the poor; and he began to go about the town for this purpose. The effect upon the sick was miraculous. All, except those who were very ill indeed, jumped from their beds when they heard he was coming, and declared themselves quite well. To those who could not get up he gave herbs and roots, which none of them had ever before thought of as medicines, but which the Griffin had seen used in various parts of the world; and most of them recovered. But, for all that, they afterward said that, no matter what happened to them, they hoped that they should never again have such a doctor coming to their bedsides, feeling their pulses and looking at their tongues.

As for the poor, they seemed to have utterly disappeared. All those who had depended upon charity for their daily bread were now at work in some way or other; many of them offering to do odd jobs for their neighbors just for the sake of their meals—a thing which before had been seldom heard of in the town. The Griffin could find no one who needed his assistance.

The summer had now passed, and the autumnal equinox was rapidly approaching. The citizens were in a state of great alarm and anxiety. The Griffin showed no signs of going away, but seemed to have settled himself permanently among them. In a short time the day for his semiannual meal would arrive, and then what would happen? The monster would certainly be very hungry, and would devour all their children.

Now they greatly regretted and lamented that they had sent away the Minor Canon; he was the only one on whom they could have depended in this trouble, for he could talk freely with the Griffin, and so find out what could be done. But it would not do to be inactive. Some step must be taken immediately. A meeting of the citizens was called, and two old men were appointed to go and talk to the Griffin. They were instructed to offer to prepare a splendid dinner for him on equinox day—one which would entirely satisfy his hunger. They would offer him the fattest mutton, the most tender beef, fish, and game of various sorts, and anything of the kind that he might fancy. If none of these suited, they were to mention that there was an orphan asylum in the next town.

"Anything would be better," said the citizens, "than to have our dear children devoured."

The old men went to the Griffin; but their propositions were not received with favor.

"From what I have seen of the people of this town," said the monster, "I do not think I could relish anything which was prepared by them. They appear to be all cowards and, therefore, mean and selfish. As for eating one of them, old or young, I could not think of it for a moment. In fact, there was only one creature in the whole place for whom I could have had any appetite, and that is the Minor Canon, who has gone away. He was brave, and good, and honest, and I think I should have relished him."

"Ah!" said one of the old men very politely, "in that case I wish we had not sent him to the dreadful wilds!"

"What!" cried the Griffin. "What do you mean? Explain instantly what you are talking about!"

The old man, terribly frightened at what he had said, was obliged to tell how the Minor Canon had been sent away by the people, in the hope that the Griffin might be induced to follow him.

When the monster heard this he became furiously angry. He dashed away from the old men, and, spreading his wings, flew backward and forward over the town. He was so much excited that his tail became red-hot, and glowed like a meteor against the evening sky. When at last he settled down in the little field where he usually rested, and thrust his tail into the brook, the steam arose like a cloud, and the water of the stream ran hot through the town. The citizens were greatly frightened, and bitterly blamed the old man for telling about the Minor Canon.

"It is plain," they said, "that the Griffin intended at last to go and look for him, and we should have been saved. Now who can tell what misery you have brought upon us."

The Griffin did not remain long in the little field. As soon as his tail was cool he flew to the town hall and rang the bell. The citizens knew that they were expected to come there; and although they were afraid to go, they were still more afraid to stay away; and they crowded into the hall. The Griffin was on the platform at one end, flapping his wings and walking up and down, and the end of his tail was still so warm that it slightly scorched the boards as he dragged it after him.

When everybody who was able to come was there, the Griffin stood still and addressed the meeting.

"I have had a very low opinion of you," he said, "ever since I discovered what cowards you are, but I had no idea that you were so ungrateful, selfish, and cruel as I now find you to be. Here was your Minor Canon, who labored day and night for your good, and thought of nothing else but how he might benefit you and make you happy; and as soon as you imagine yourselves threatened with a danger—for well I know you are dreadfully afraid of me—you send him off, caring not whether he returns or perishes, hoping thereby to save yourselves. Now, I had conceived a great liking for that young man, and had intended, in a day or two, to go and look him up. But I have changed my mind about him. I shall go and find him, but I shall send him back here to live among you, and I intend that he shall enjoy the reward of his labor and his sacrifices.

"Go, some of you, to the officers of the church, who so cowardly ran away when I first came here, and tell them never to return to this town under penalty of death. And if, when your Minor Canon comes back to you, you do not bow yourselves before him, put him in the highest place among you, and serve and honor him all his life, beware of my terrible vengeance! There were only two good things in this town: the Minor Canon and the stone image of myself over your church door. One of these you have sent away, and the other I shall carry away myself."

With these words he dismissed the meeting, and it was time, for the end of his tail had become so hot that there was danger of its setting fire to the building.

The next morning the Griffin came to the church, and tearing the stone image of himself from its fastenings over the great door he grasped it with his powerful forelegs and flew up into the air. Then, after hovering over the town for a moment, he gave his tail an angry shake and took up his flight to the dreadful wilds. When he reached this desolate region, he set the stone griffin upon a ledge of a rock which rose in front of the dismal cave he called his home. There the image occupied a position somewhat similar to that it had had over the church door; and the Griffin, panting with the exertion of carrying such an enormous load to so great a distance, lay down upon the ground and regarded it with much satisfaction. When he felt somewhat rested he went to look for the Minor Canon. He found the young man weak and half starved, lying under the shadow of a rock. After picking him up and carrying him to his cave, the Griffin flew away to a distant marsh, where he procured some roots and herbs which he well knew were strengthening and beneficial to man, though he had never tasted them himself. After eating these the Minor Canon was greatly revived, and sat up and listened while the Griffin told him what had happened in the town.

"Do you know," said the monster, when he had finished, "that I have had, and still have, a great liking for you?"

"I am very glad to hear it," said the Minor Canon, with his usual politeness.

"I am not at all sure that you would be," said the Griffin, "if you thoroughly understood the state of the case; but we will not consider that now. If some things were different, other things would be otherwise. I have been so enraged by discovering the manner in which you have been treated that I have determined that you shall at last enjoy the rewards and honors to which you are entitled. Lie down and have a good sleep, and then I will take you back to the town."

As he heard these words, a look of trouble came over the young man's face.

"You need not give yourself any anxiety," said the Griffin, "about my return to the town. I shall not remain there. Now that I have that admirable likeness of myself in front of my cave, where I can sit at my leisure, and gaze upon its noble features and magnificent proportions, I have no wish to see that abode of cowardly and selfish people."

The Minor Canon, relieved from his fears, lay back, and dropped into a doze; and when he was sound asleep the Griffin took him up, and carried him back to the town. He arrived just before daybreak, and putting the young man gently on the grass in the little field where he himself used to rest, the monster, without having been seen by any of the people, flew back to his home.

When the Minor Canon made his appearance in the morning among the citizens, the enthusiasm and cordiality with which he was received were truly wonderful. He was taken to a house which had been occupied by one of the banished high officers of the place, and everyone was anxious to do all that could be done for his health and comfort. The people crowded into the church when he held services, so that the three old women who used to be his weekday congregation could not get to the best seats, which they had always been in the habit of taking; and the parents of the bad children determined to reform them at home in order that he might be spared the trouble of keeping up his former school. The Minor Canon was appointed to the highest office of the old church, and before he died, he became a bishop.

During the first years after his return from the dreadful wilds, the people of the town looked up to him as a man to whom they were bound to do honor and reverence; but they often, also, looked up to the sky to see if there were any signs of the Griffin coming back. However, in the course of time, they learned to honor and reverence their former Minor Canon without the fear of being punished if they did not do so.

But they need never have been afraid of the Griffin. The autumnal equinox day came round, and the monster ate nothing. If he could not have the Minor Canon, he did not care for anything. So, lying down, with his eyes fixed upon the great stone griffin, he gradually declined, and died. It was a good thing for some of the people of the town that they did not know this.

If you should ever visit the old town, you would still see the little griffins on the sides of the church; but the great stone griffin that was over the door is gone.

Roughing It

by Michael Beres

The motor home was a class A, at least a thirty footer with twin rear axles. It swayed majestically on its air shocks as it lumbered into the campground, steering its way along the narrow, one-way graveled path, missing trees on either side by mere inches. It drove slowly to the far reaches of the camp beneath the shade of closely grouped oaks. The yellowed leaves of the oaks gave the site a golden tint, the abundance of trees and the overcast sky summoning a premature dusk. The motor home parked in a narrow site between two small tents. In the distance, where most campers had set up closer to the restrooms, orange fire flickers winked.

"They've got a lot of nerve. All those empty spots and they've got to park that damn thing right between the only two tents out here."

"Don't get so upset, dear. They've got all the right in the world to take whichever site they prefer. Besides, there's no electricity on these sites so at least we won't have to listen to someone's air conditioner all night."

Fred and Renee sat in their lawn chairs near the fire, keeping off the autumn chill. Fred poked at the fire with an empty hot dog stick while he stared at the motor home.

"Fine thing, our first camping trip without the kids and that thing probably has a dozen brats inside who'll explode out of there any second."

"What's that round thing on top?" said Renee. "Look, it's turning."

"It's the damn directional TV antenna," said Fred.

"But if they don't have electricity—"

Then it happened. A gasoline generator hidden behind one of the panels on the motor home's lower flank coughed and sputtered into life.

"I don't believe it," said Fred.

"We could always move," said Renee.

"No," said Fred. "I want to watch this. I'd like to see what kind of clowns would park a motor home bigger than our damn house back here in this so-called primitive area."

"I didn't see them driving. Did you?"

"No. The windows are too heavily tinted."

"I suppose they have to come out eventually."

But no one came out of the motor home. Fred had several beers, Renee had one. They made baked potatoes in foil and hot dogs. They finished eating and alternated their trips to the restrooms so one could keep watch and still no one came out.

As he sat in the dark, Fred stared at the windows of the motor home. Lights were on but curtains were drawn at every window. Occasionally he saw a shadow pass in front of the windows; at the same time he noticed that the motor home swayed noticeably, not as much as it would when driven but it did sway.

"They must be real porkers in there," said Fred.

Renee was knitting at the picnic bench under the light of their lantern. "Why do you say that?"

"Because when they move around in there the whole thing tips. Maybe they can't fit out through the door. Maybe that's why they don't come out."

"Or," said Renee in a whisper, "maybe they're disabled. Did you ever think of that?"

"Hey. Wait. The door's opening."

And the door did open. It opened just enough to allow a small dog to come out. The dog was light colored, and in the dim light from the other campfire on the far side of the motor home, Fred could see it cross under the motor home and sniff around. Then the dog disappeared into the dark undergrowth at the rear of the site.

A few minutes later Renee let out a yelp because the small dog had crept up on her. "He scared the daylights out of me."

"Aw, he's just looking for a handout. Come here, boy."

Fred got a hot dog out of the cooler, gave half to the dog, who ate it quickly then headed back to the motor home. Fred whistled and made clicking sounds with his tongue. He offered the rest of the hot dog but the dog would not come back. Then the door of the motor home opened a few inches and the dog jumped inside.

That night in their tent, ensconced within their zip-together sleeping bags, Fred and Renee further speculated about the occupants of the motor home. They spoke of kidnappers with their victim locked up inside. They spoke of ghosts and wondered if, since houses could be haunted, why not motor homes.

Sometime in the middle of the night the generator turned off. A little while later Fred heard footsteps in the weeds. The footsteps encircled the car, then the tent. He imagined someone with an ax outside the tent circling in for the kill. He was afraid to make a sound or to move for fear he'd awaken Renee and she'd make the sound that would bring the ax blade down upon them. But the footsteps moved off, crunched on the gravel for some distance, then went back into the weeds in the direction of the motor home, perhaps beyond it.

He did not sleep for the remainder of the night because he kept hearing footsteps and a sound like something heavy being dragged along the ground in the direction of the motor home. Finally he thought he heard the click of a door. Then all was silent.

Fred woke Renee at dawn and they were gone before sunrise. They drove west, farther from the crowds at all the modern campgrounds. Fred consulted the camping directory while Renee drove.

After a stop for lunch a state patrol car pulled them over. The trooper said there had been an incident at the last campground they were at. The police had gotten the license numbers of everyone who had camped there. The trooper had Renee and Fred follow him to a nearby state police headquarters.

A thin, sleepy-eyed sergeant questioned them.

"Did you see anything unusual besides the motor home?"

"No."

"And all you heard were footsteps?"

"Yes. That's all. Now please tell us what this is about. Was someone murdered or something?"

"What makes you say that?"

"I don't know. I just figured it had to be serious for you to trace all those campers."

"No. No one was killed as far as we know. But it seems a pair of campers, a young man and woman, have disappeared. Their tent and equipment and car are still there, but the couple's gone. They were the ones parked on the other side of that motor home."

"Didn't you get the motor home's license number?"

"No. It seems they came in late and didn't register."

That night Fred and Renee stayed at a campground in a wilderness area farther off the main roads. The camping directory said the campground had no electricity or water hookups for motor homes. When they arrived they didn't even have to sign in. They just picked a site with a picnic table and made camp along with about three other tenters spread evenly in the camp so that no one was within fifty yards of anyone else.

"This is more like it," said Fred as he sat in front of the fire sipping a beer. "This is what camping is all about."

"I still think you should have told the police you heard someone dragging something."

"Yeah, and we would've still been there. They would've brought in pictures of different kinds of motor homes and made me reconstruct the damn thing. No, my vacation is too important to spend it at a police station. Besides, we never saw anything except their dog, and if they did do something to that couple, it's too late to do anything about it."

After stuffing themselves with two large steaks they had grilled over the fire, Fred and Renee sat in their lawn chairs and watched squirrels collecting acorns and storing them away for winter.

"That's how I feel," said Renee.

"What?"

"That squirrel on the tree over there by the outhouse is trying to stuff another acorn into a hole where it won't fit."

"Sure is peaceful here," said Fred.

"Sure is," said Renee as she reached over and patted Fred's gut.

After dusk a wind came up and acorns fell from the oaks in rushes that sounded like rain. The wind continued after Fred and Renee retired into their tent. Occasionally an acorn hit the tent and rolled down its slope. But later the wind died down and it was silent. Dead silent. It was silent until the sound of an engine and the sound of acorns popping under large tires came closer and closer.

Fred and Renee did not hear the engine or the acorns popping. They did not see the spotlight sweep across their tent. The heavy steak dinner and a bedtime brandy to celebrate their find of a peaceful campground unfettered by so-called modern conveniences had put them into a deep slumber. Later, after the sounds of the engine and popping acorns had ceased, they did not even hear the generator cough and sputter into life, and they did not hear the footsteps in the weeds.

On the other side of the campground, Chuck and Cindy, on their first camping trip in Chuck's jeep after their marriage two months earlier, were testing the integrity of their tent by kicking out sporadically at the side wall with their bare feet.

"Must you breathe so loud?" said Cindy between fairly deep breaths of her own.

"Don't worry," panted Chuck. "No one can hear us except the squirrels. And they're probably as busy as us."

But then Cindy heard something. "Wait. What was that?"

"What?"

"Wait, Chuck, will you? Listen."

It was a high-pitched sound. An animal sound. No, not an animal.

"It's somebody screaming, Chuck."

"Aw, come on, Cindy. It's probably just a coyote or something."

"Do they have coyotes around here?"

"I don't know. I just couldn't think of any other animal."

"Listen. There it is again, only it's a different voice this time. Hear it? Someone's screaming. It's someone muffled or gagged and they're screaming."

Cindy did not want Chuck to leave her alone in the tent, but he insisted on having a look. He put on his jeans and sweatshirt and she also dressed even though she stayed behind.

While Chuck was gone Cindy listened but heard no more screams. When she heard footsteps in the weeds she thought it was Chuck. But the footsteps were light and rapid and she knew it was some kind of animal. When she finally did hear heavy footsteps she aimed the flashlight at the tent flap and saw first a hand, then a sleeve, then Chuck's great big grin.

"I didn't see anything," said Chuck, a little out of breath. "Nothing except a mile-long motor home. They've got a generator going and everything. We probably heard the TV or radio or something."

"You didn't see anyone outside at all?"

"No. Just a little puppy running around that I almost stepped on. Over by the motor home it smelled like they were cooking. When I walked past there was steam coming out of the stove exhaust vent."

"I'm scared, Chuck."

"Why?"

"Those screams. Even if it was a TV, it still scared me."

"Great," said Chuck as he hugged her. "Hey, I know. Tomorrow we'll go to a more remote place. Then there'll be no screaming."

"More remote than this?"

"Yeah. Not even outhouses."

Cindy kissed him, pulled his hair. "Boy, you really like to rough it, don't you?"

Outside the tent a small, light colored dog crept along in the weeds. The dog walked slowly and silently. Something rectangular was in the dog's mouth. The dog crept beneath the jeep that was parked nearby and lifted its head. When the dog came out from under the jeep its mouth was empty, and as it got farther from the jeep and the tent, it broke into a run toward a sliver of light at the open side door of the motor home.

*   *   *

At dawn Chuck and Cindy broke camp and left in their jeep. A little while later, when the sun was up, the only occupied sites in the camp were Fred and Renee's and the motor home parked next to them. But soon the engine on the motor home started and it lumbered out onto the acorn-strewn pathway. It stopped there, its driver pausing while the curious antenna loop on its roof circled twice before stopping and aiming. Then the motor home rolled forward, its springs creaking under its massive weight, and acorns popping like gunshots under its huge tires. Through the windshield, though it was heavily tinted, the outlines of two large figures could be seen in the driver and passenger seats, figures so large that it would have seemed impossible that they could get through the door of the motor home. Closer to the windshield, in fact right up on the dashboard, a small dog barked excitedly and pointed the way.

Life After Life

by Lawrence Block

When the bullets struck, my first thought was that someone had raced up behind me to give me an abrupt shove. An instant later I registered the sound of the gunshots, and then there was fire in my side, burning pain, and the impact had lifted me off my feet and sent me sprawling at the edge of the lawn in front of my house.

I noticed the smell of the grass. Fresh, cut the night before, and with the dew still on it.

I can recall fragments of the ambulance ride as if it took place in some dim dream. I worried at the impropriety of running the siren so early in the morning. They'd wake half the town.

Another time, I heard one of the white-coated attendants say something about a red blanket, and I recalled the blanket that lay on my bed when I was a boy almost forty years ago. It was plaid, mostly red with some green in it. Was that what they were talking about?

These bits of awareness came one after another, like fast cuts in a film, with no sensation of time passing between them.

I was in a hospital room—the operating room, I suppose. I was spread out on a long white table while a masked and green-gowned doctor probed a wound in the left side of my chest. I must have been under anesthetic—there was a mask on my face with a tube connected to it—and I believe my eyes were closed. Nevertheless, I was aware of what was happening, and I could see.

There was a sensation I was able to identify as pain, although it didn't actually hurt me. Then I felt as though my side were a bottle and a cork was being drawn from it. It popped free. The doctor held up a misshapen bullet for examination. I watched it fall in slow motion from his forceps, landing with a plinking sound in an aluminum pan.

"The other's too close to the heart," I heard him say. "I can't get a grip on it. I don't dare touch it, the way it's positioned. It'll kill him if it moves."

Same place, an indefinite period of time later. A nurse saying, "Oh, God, he's going," and then all of them talking at once.

Then I was out of my body.

It just happened, just like that. One moment I was in my dying body on the table and a moment later I was floating somewhere beneath the ceiling. I could look down and see myself on the table and the doctors and nurses standing around me.

I'm dead, I thought.

I was very busy trying to decide how I felt about it. It didn't hurt. I had always thought it would hurt, that it would be awful, but it wasn't so terrible.

But it was odd seeing my body lying there. I thought, you were a good body. I'm all right, I don't need you, but you were a good body.

Then I was gone from the room. There was a rush of light that became brighter and brighter, and I was sucked through a long tunnel at a furious speed. Then I was in a world of light and in the presence of a Being of light.

This is hard to explain.

I couldn't tell if the Being was a man or a woman. It could have been both, or maybe it changed back and forth—I don't know. It was dressed all in white, and it emanated a light that surrounded it.

And in the distance I saw my father and my mother and my grandparents—people who had gone before me—and they were holding out their hands to me, and beaming at me with faces radiant with light and love.

I was drawn to the Being, which held out its arm and said, "Behold your life!"

And I looked, and I could see my entire life. I don't know how to describe what I saw. It was as if my whole life had happened at once and someone had taken a photograph of it. I could see in it everything that I remembered in my life and everything I had forgotten, and it was all happening at once and I was seeing it happen. I would see something bad that I'd done and think, I'm sorry about that, then I would see something good and be glad about it.

At the end I woke and had breakfast and left the house to walk to work and a car passed by and a gun came out the window. There were two shots and I fell and the ambulance came and all the rest of it.

And I thought, who killed me?

The Being said, "You must find out the answer."

I thought, I don't care, it doesn't matter.

He said, "You must go back and find out the answer."

I thought, no, I don't want to go back.

All of the brilliant light began to fade. I reached out toward it because I didn't want to go back, I didn't want to be alive again. But it continued to fade.

Then I was back in my body.

"We almost lost you," the nurse said. Her smile was professional, but the light in her eyes showed she meant it. "Your heart actually stopped on the operating table. You really had us scared there."

"I'm sorry," I said.

She thought that was funny. "The doctor was only able to remove one of the two bullets that hit you, so you've still got one in your chest. He sewed you up and put a drain in the wound, but obviously you won't be able to walk around like that. In fact, it's important for you to lie absolutely still or the bullet might shift in position. It's right alongside your heart."

It might shift even if I don't move, I thought. But she knew better than to tell me that.

"In four or five days we'll have you scheduled for another operation," she went on. "By then the bullet may move of its own accord to a more accessible position. If not, there are techniques that can be employed." She told me some of the extraordinary things surgeons could do. I didn't pay attention.

After she left the room, I rolled back and forth on the bed, shifting my body as jerkily as I could. But the bullet did not change position in my chest.

I stayed in the hospital that night. No one came to see me during visiting hours, and I thought that was strange. I asked the nurse and was told I was in intensive care and couldn't have visitors.

I lost control of myself. I shouted that she was crazy. How could I learn who did it if I couldn't see anyone?

"The police will see you as soon as it's allowed," she said. She was terribly earnest. "Believe me," she said, "it's for your own protection. They want to ask you a million questions, naturally, but it would be bad for your health to let you get all excited."

Silly bitch, I thought. And almost put the thought into words. Then I remembered the picture of my life, and the pleasant and unpleasant things I had done and how they had looked in the picture.

I smiled. "I'm sorry I lost control," I said. "But if they didn't want me to get excited, they shouldn't have given me such a beautiful nurse."

I didn't sleep. It didn't seem to be necessary. I lay in bed wondering who had killed me.

My wife? We'd married young, then grown apart. Of course, *she* hadn't shot at me because she'd been in bed asleep when I left the house that morning. But she might have a lover. Or she could have hired someone to pull the trigger for her.

My partner? Monty and I had turned a handful of borrowed capital into a million-dollar business, but I was better than Monty at holding onto money. He spent it, gambled it away, paid it out in divorce settlements. Profits were off lately. Had he been helping himself to funds and cooking the books? And did he then decide to cover his thefts the easy way?

My girl? Peg had a decent apartment, a closet full of clothes. Not a bad deal. But for a while I'd let her think I'd divorce Julia when the kids were grown, and now she and I both knew better. She'd seemed to adjust to the situation, but had the resentment festered inside her?

My children? The thought was painful. Mark had gone to work for me after college. The arrangement didn't last long. He'd been too headstrong, and I'd been unwilling to give him the responsibility he wanted. Now he was talking about going into business for himself. But he lacked the capital.

If I died, he'd have all he needed.

Debbie was married, and expecting a child. First she'd lived with another young man, one of whom I hadn't approved, and then she'd married Scott, who was hardworking and earnest and ambitious. Was the marriage bad for her, and did she blame me for costing her the other boy? Or did Scott's ambition prompt him to make Debbie an heiress?

Who else? Why?

Some days ago I'd cut off a motorist at a traffic circle. I remembered the sound of his horn, his face in my rear view mirror, red, ferocious. Had he copied down my license plate, determined my address, lain in ambush to gun me down?

It made no sense. But it didn't make sense for anyone to kill me.

Julia? Monty? Peg? Mark? Debbie? Scott? A stranger?

I lay there wondering but didn't truly care. Someone had killed me, and I was supposed to be dead. But I was not permitted to be dead until I knew the answer to the question.

Maybe the police would find it for me.

They didn't.

I saw two policemen the following day. I was still in intensive care, still denied visitors, but an exception was made for the police. They were very courteous and spoke in hushed voices. They had no leads in their investigation and just wanted to know if I could suggest a single possible suspect.

I told them I couldn't.

My nurse turned white as paper.

"You're not supposed to be out of bed! You're not even supposed to move! What do you think you're doing?"

I was up and dressed. There was no pain. As an experiment, I'd been palming the pain pills they issued me every four hours, hiding them in the bedclothes instead of swallowing them. As I'd anticipated, I didn't feel any pain.

The area of the wound was numb, as though that part of me had been excised altogether. I could feel the slug that was still in me and could tell it remained in position. It didn't hurt me, however.

She went on jabbering away at me. I remembered the picture of my life and avoided giving her a sharp answer.

"I'm going home," I said.

"Don't talk nonsense."

"You have no authority over me," I told her. "I'm legally entitled to take responsibility for my own life."

"For your own death, you mean."

"If it comes to that. You can't hold me here against my will. You can't operate on me without my consent."

"If you don't have that operation, you'll die."

"Everyone dies."

"I don't understand," she said, and her eyes were filled with sorrow. My heart went out to her.

"Don't worry about me," I said gently. "I know what I'm doing."

"They wouldn't let me see you," Julia was saying. "And now you're home."

"It was a fast recovery."

"Shouldn't you be in bed?"

"The exercise is supposed to be good for me," I said. I looked at her, and for a moment I saw her as she'd appeared in parts of the picture of my life—as a bride, as a young mother.

"You know, you're a beautiful woman," I said.

She colored.

"I suppose we got married too young," I said. "We each had a lot of growing to do. And the business took too much of my time over the years. I'm afraid I haven't been a very good husband."

"You weren't so bad."

"I'm glad we got married," I said. "And I'm glad we stayed together. And that you were here for me to come home to."

She started to cry. I held her until she stopped. Then, her face to my chest, she said, "At the hospital, waiting, I realized for the first time what it would mean for me to lose you. I thought we'd stopped loving each other a long time ago. I know you've had other women. For that matter, I've had lovers. I don't know if you knew that."

"It's not important."

"No," she said, "it's not. I'm glad we got married, darling. And I'm glad you're going to be all right."

Monty said, "You had everybody worried there, kid. But what do you think you're doing down here? You're supposed to be home in bed."

"I'm supposed to get exercise. Besides, if I don't come down here, how do I know you won't steal the firm into bankruptcy?"

My tone was light, but he flushed deeply. "You just hit a nerve," he said.

"What's the matter?"

"When they were busy cutting the bullet out of you, all I could think was you'd die thinking I was a thief."

"I don't know what you're talking about."

He lowered his eyes. "I was borrowing partnership funds," he said. "I was in a bind because of my own stupidity and I didn't want to admit it to you, so I dipped into the till. It was a temporary thing, a case of the shorts. I got everything straightened out before that clown took a shot at you. Do they know who it was yet?"

"Not yet."

"The night before you were shot, I stayed late and covered things. I wasn't going to say anything, and then I wondered if you'd been suspicious, and I decided I'd tell you about it first thing in the morning. Then it looked as though I wasn't going to get the chance. You didn't suspect anything?"

"I thought our cash position was light. But after all these years I certainly wasn't afraid of you stealing from me."

"All these years," he echoed, and I was seeing the picture of my life again. All the work Monty and I had put in side by side—the laughs we'd shared, the bad times we'd survived.

We looked at each other, and a great deal of feeling passed

between us. Then he drew a breath and clapped me on the shoulder. "Well, that's enough about old times," he said gruffly. "Somebody's got to do a little work around here."

"I'm glad you're here," Peg said. "I couldn't even go to the hospital. All I could do was call every hour and ask anonymously for a report on your condition. Critical condition, that's what they said. Over and over."

"It must have been rough."

"It did something to me and for me," she said. "It made me realize that I've cheated myself out of a life. And I was the one who did it. You didn't do it to me."

"I told you I'd leave Julia."

"Oh, that was just a game we both played. I never really expected you to leave her. No, it's been my fault. I settled into a nice secure life. But when you were on the critical list, I decided my life was on the critical list, too, and that it was time I took some responsibility for it."

"Meaning?"

"Meaning it's good you came over tonight and not this afternoon because you wouldn't have found me at home. I've got a job. It's not much, but it's enough to pay the rent. I've decided it's time I started paying my own rent. In the fall I'll start night classes at the university."

"I see."

"You're not angry?"

"Angry? I'm happy for you."

"I don't regret what we've been to each other. I was a lost little girl with a screwed-up life, and you made me feel loved and cared for. But I'm a big girl now. I'll still see you, if you want to see me, but from here on in I pay my own way."

"No more checks?"

"No more checks. I mean it."

I remembered some of our times together, seeing them as I had seen them in the picture of my life. I went and took her in my arms.

Later, while Julia slept, I lay awake in the darkness. I thought, this is crazy. I'm no detective. I'm a businessman. I died and You won't let me stay dead. Why can't I be dead?

I got out of bed, went downstairs, and laid out the cards for a game of solitaire. I toasted a slice of bread and made myself a cup of tea.

I won the game of solitaire. It was a hard variety, one I could normally win only once in fifty or a hundred times.

I thought, it's not Julia, it's not Monty, it's not Peg. All of them have love for me.

I felt good about that.

But who killed me? Who was left on my list?

I didn't feel good about that.

I was finishing my breakfast the following morning when Mark rang the bell. Julia went to the door and let him in. He came into the kitchen and got himself a cup of coffee from the pot on the stove.

"I was at the hospital," he said. "Night and day, but they wouldn't let any of us see you."

"Your mother told me."

"Then I had to leave town the day before yesterday, and I just got back this morning. I had to meet with some men." A smile flickered on his face. He looked just like his mother when he smiled.

"I've got the financing," he said. "I'm in business."

"That's wonderful."

"I know you wanted me to follow in your footsteps, Dad. But I couldn't be happy having my future handed to me that way. I wanted to make it on my own."

"You're my son. I was the same myself."

"When I asked you for a loan—"

"I've been thinking about that," I said, remembering the scene as I'd witnessed it in the picture of my life. "I resented your independence, and I envied your youth. I was wrong to turn you down."

"You were right to turn me down." That smile again, just like his mother. "I wanted to make it on my own, and then I turned around and asked you for help. I'm just glad you knew better than to give me what I was weak enough to ask for. I realized that almost immediately, but I was too proud to say anything. And then some madman shot you and—well, I'm glad everything turned out all right, Dad."

"Yes," I said. "So am I."

Not Mark, then.

Not Debbie either. I always knew that, and knew it with utter certainty when she cried out, "Oh, Daddy!" and rushed to me and threw herself into my arms. "I'm so glad!" she kept saying. "I was so worried."

"Calm down," I told her. "I don't want my grandchild born with a nervous condition."

"Don't worry about your grandchild. Your grandchild's going to be just fine."

"And how about my daughter?"

"Your daughter's fine. Do you want to know something? I've really learned a lot these past few days."

"So have I."

"How close I am to you, for one thing. Waiting at the hospital, there was a time when I thought, God, he's gone. I just had this feeling. And then I shook my head and said, no, it was nonsense, you were all right. And you know what they told us afterward? Your heart stopped during the operation, and it must have happened right when I got that feeling."

When I looked at my son, I saw his mother's smile. When I looked at Debbie, I saw myself.

"And another thing I learned was how much people need each other. People were so good to us! So many people called and asked about you. Even Philip called, can you imagine? He just wanted to let me know that I should call on him if there was anything he could do."

"What could Philip possibly do?"

"I have no idea. It was funny hearing from him, though. I hadn't heard his voice since we were together. But it was nice of him to call, wasn't it?"

I nodded. "It must have made you wonder what might have been."

"What it made me wonder was how I ever thought he and I were

meant for each other. Scott was with me every minute, except when
he went down to give blood for you—"

"He gave blood for me?"

"Didn't Mother tell you? You and Scott are the same blood type.
Maybe that's why I fell in love with him."

"Not a bad reason."

"He was with me all the time, and by the time you were out of
danger I began to realize how close we'd grown, how much I loved
him. And then when I heard Philip's voice I thought what kid stuff
that relationship of ours had been. I know you never approved."

"It wasn't my business to approve or disapprove."

"Maybe not. But I know you approve of Scott, and that's important to me."

I went home.

I thought, what do You want from me? It's not my son-in-law. You
don't try to kill a man and then donate blood for a transfusion.
Nobody would do a thing like that.

The person I cut off at the traffic circle? But that was insane. How
would I know him? I wouldn't know where to start looking for him.

Some other enemy? But I had no enemies.

Julia said, "The doctor called again. He doesn't see how you could check
yourself out of the hospital. He wants to schedule you for surgery."

"Not yet," I told her. "Not until I'm ready."

"When will you be ready?"

"When I feel right about it," I told her.

She called him back and relayed the message. "He's very nice,"
she reported. "He says any delay is hazardous, so you should let him
schedule the surgery as soon as you possibly can."

I was glad he was a caring man, and that she liked him. He might
be a comfort to her later when she needed someone to lean on.

Something clicked.

*　　*　　*

I called Debbie.

"Just the one telephone call," she said, puzzled. "He said he knew you never liked him but he always respected you and he knew what an influence you were in my life. And that I should call on him if I needed someone to turn to. It was kind of him, that's what I told myself at the time, but there was something creepy about the conversation."

What had she told him?

"That it was nice to hear from him, and that, you know, my husband and I would be fine. Sort of stressing that I was married but in a nice way. Why?"

The police were very dubious. It was ancient history, they said. The boy had lived with my daughter a while ago, parted amicably, never made any trouble. Had he ever threatened me? Had we ever fought?

"He's the one," I said. "Watch him," I told them. "Keep an eye on him."

So they assigned men to watch Philip, and on the fourth day the surveillance paid off. They caught him tucking a bomb beneath the hood of a car. The car belonged to my son-in-law, Scott.

"He thought you were standing between them. When she said she was happily married, he shifted his sights to the husband."

There had always been something about Philip that I hadn't liked. Something creepy as Debbie put it. Perhaps he'll get treatment now. In any event, he'll be unable to harm anyone.

Is that why I was permitted to return? So that I could prevent Philip from harming Scott? Perhaps. But the conversations with Julia, Monty, Peg, Mark, and Debbie, those were fringe benefits.

Or perhaps it was the other way around.

They've prepared me for surgery. And I've prepared myself. I'm ready now.

The Last Day

by Rob Kantner

Hell probably won't be much hotter than this, Kramer thought as he stared intently at the snapshots arrayed on his desk. The building management, apparently for energy reasons, turned off the air conditioning on weekends, and the heat had risen through the building to the point where here, on the eleventh floor, it was smothering. It mottled Kramer's broad, fleshy face with patches of red, caused sweat to run down his flanks under the open-necked dress shirt, made him feel like he was breathing scorched cotton.

The suite was Saturday-silent save for Kramer's labored breathing and the murmur of someone's neglected radio, playing easy-listening music in one of the other offices. He tried to focus on the snapshots. Newborn faces, crawling faces, toddler faces. He shuffled and rearranged them like puzzle pieces. He squinted down through weary eyes at the backgrounds, trying to find clues. This one had to be Debbie. No doubt about it. But was this one Davey or Tom?

The little reddish faces blurred and began to look alike. Ignoring the rest of the packing work he had to do, Kramer grabbed more snapshots out of the box on the floor next to him and spread them out, turning them right side up, scanning the faces. They defiantly blurred into a single unidentifiable one. Finally he made a sound between a growl and a moan and sat back from the desk, almost in a trance, panting heavily.

Suddenly she was there before him, seeming to fill his office. He looked up at her numbly; he'd heard or seen nothing of her approach. She was erect, staring emptily, wearing a blue two-piece suit and unseasonably heavy black dress shoes. In the silence she sat down on the well-worn, wood visitor's chair in one fluid movement. Then she jerkily clenched her hands together and shivered.

"God, I'm cold."

Amherstburg, *the past*

Tricia jerkily clenched her hands together and shivered. "God, I'm cold."

Kramer's car sat next to the bridge where Sibley Road crossed the river. The near bank began just at the right side of the car, and plunged steeply down drifts of snow to the ice-choked water. The far side of the river was invisible, obscured by the driving sleet that came down in parallel, solid ranks, occasionally twisted into implike gyrations by gusts of frigid wind. The car's residual heat was fading, but Kramer didn't notice, thanks to his usual lunch of Rusty Nails chased with beer. Tapping the steering wheel impatiently, he said curtly, "Should have worn your coat."

"I barely caught you as it was, you ran out of the office so fast. I thought you were going to leave me standing there in the parking lot." She laughed nervously. "Did Hopkins see you leave?"

"Who cares? I'm through as of tomorrow. What's he gonna do, fire me?" He thought, come on, let's get it over with.

The light was fading fast. An occasional car whooshed past on the slushy road. In the distance to their right, where the reddish sun made its pathetic last stand, the ugly towers and stacks of the Axle plant loomed. Gradually the windshield fogged, then iced over. Kramer stared straight ahead, seeing nothing, but aware that Tricia was looking down at her fingernails, lips pursed, figuring out how to approach it. She said quietly, "When do you leave for Cincinnati?"

"Sunday. Job starts Monday." He didn't bother to conceal the harshness in his voice.

"And Elaine's staying?"

He leaned his head back and laughed, squinting. Oh boy, was she ever, and who could blame her. If there were a Purple Heart for wives, Elaine would win it with oak leaf clusters. Not that he'd ever confessed about Tricia. He wasn't that dumb. He'd observed Lenny Bruce's dictum to "lie and keep on lying."

But at the end it had made no difference. Not after the drunken binges and all-night parties. The foreclosures and repossessions and disconnects. The screaming and throwing and poisonous arguments. The terrified, bewildered faces of the small children looking frantically back and forth from parent to parent.

Tricia took his arm; he barely felt her hand through his thick coat and numb skin. He jerked away. She said softly, "Then take me with you."

"No can do," he said with finality.

She pressed herself against him, using her body as a method of persuasion as she'd done so many times before, desperately trying to make eye contact. "But it's all perfect now. No more ties for either of us. I love you, I want to make it better for you—"

He struck like a panther, spinning and shoving her away from him. "Forget it, see? I'm loose and I'm staying that way."

The headlights of a passing car splashed whitely on her face, showing tear trails. "This isn't fair. I've played the game your way for months now. Sneaking around, secret meetings, waiting for hours, just to protect you and your job and your marriage." In the darkness there were no more tears in her voice, just anger. "Now you're free. And you owe me. And I'm collecting."

There had been so many voices shouting at him lately. On the phone, at home, at the office. All the shouting voices had merged into one by now. It was him versus It. He had borne it and borne it and would bear it no longer.

With a crash he flung himself across the seat against her. One hand smashed her head against the window, the other pawed for the door handle. The door flew away into the white-streaked darkness as a blast of wintry wind roared hungrily in. Tricia gave one terrified shout as she spun off-balance out of the car, and he got a glimpse of blue skirt and tan stockings and sturdy black shoes as she tumbled silently down the lumpy, ice-blanketed riverbank into the darkness beyond.

Cincinnati, the past

"Here's your office," Hedgepath, the marketing director, said casually. "Get settled. I'm holding a product manager's meeting at ten."

Kramer dumped his two worn cartons of belongings on the bare, chipped wood desk and laid his briefcase on the cold gray steel table behind it. The single uncurtained window gave a glum view of Government Square and the snowcapped Procter & Gamble headquarters. He turned and pulled his creaking chair back and sat down. Outside his office, fellow employees whose names he'd already forgotten buzzed back and forth on Monday morning New Year business, some of them making mechanical welcoming smiles as they caught his eye.

The walls, pocked with nail holes and naked picture hangers, seemed so close that he could reach out and touch the opposite ones with both hands. Shaking himself out of his reverie, Kramer reached out and opened the first carton. Right on top: a large brown manila envelope stuffed with snapshots of his children. Now what the hell is this doing here? he thought as he tossed it on the table behind him.

"God, I'm cold."

It came from outside his office. Kramer went dead still, then rose uncertainly. The voice spoke again, saying something indistinguishable. He strolled out of his office and went around the corner. The voice issued from behind an orange acoustic divider. Kramer hurried around to the entrance and peered in; a woman there smiled and waved mechanically. The voice came from behind him now, echoing into the distance. He stood, staring after it in the unfamiliar suite, then trudged back into his office and resumed unpacking.

Hedgepath introduced Kramer, and the faces of the five other product managers focused on his expectantly. The marketing director folded his hands on the conference room table and said, "He'll be responsible for the heat inverter. This is, as you know, an energy saving device for manufacturing plants designed to recirculate hot air from the ceilings down to the ground level where it's needed. You'll recall that we have two thousand completed units in inventory, ready to ship. I expect Mr. Kramer to develop a plan that will sell them." He slid a thick blue three-ring notebook across to Kramer. "Here's background on the product and the market. Good luck!" He made the briefest mechanical smile, then went on to other business.

As befitted the most junior product manager on the staff, Kramer had the seat farthest away from Hedgepath, next to the half-open conference room door. He smoked cigarette after cigarette as the marketing director droned on and on, and glanced periodically at his watch, counting the minutes till lunch.

"God, I'm cold."

Kramer jerked himself straight in his chair and involuntarily shot a glance at the open conference room door, then back at Hedgepath. The marketing director was in the middle of a closing soliloquy and Kramer fidgeted, staring at the ceiling, trying to keep from looking at the door. Finally the meeting was done and everyone rose, the mood breaking with conversation and laughter. Kramer hoisted his notebook and shot through the door. The lobby area was deserted except for the receptionist and a female figure in a navy blue suit walking away from him toward the fire stairs. As she disappeared behind the clicking door, Kramer said to the receptionist, "Who was here just now?"

Like most recently emerged adolescents in positions of quasi-authority, she was swelled with self-importance. "Nobody in particular, why?"

"She sounded—looked familiar, that's all," Kramer said uncomfortably.

"Just the new girl down on ten," the receptionist lectured. "Lots of new people around here today."

"Thanks," Kramer said without thinking, and headed toward the fire stairs. But Hedgepath's voice halted him.

"Better see me in about an hour once you've gone over those notes on the inverter," the marketing director called from the conference room door. The product managers clustered around Hedgepath eyed Kramer like he was a specimen.

Kramer reversed course smoothly. "Right, okay, boss," he said, making his best, most confident smile.

"You know, Kramer, you ought to clean up your act," Stedman said, eyeing him from across the booth through thickish glasses.

Ogden's Pub was jammed tight with lunch customers, its long windowless length noisy and stuffy and humid from the bodies and the warmish spring weather outside. Kramer tossed back the last of his Rusty Nail and said, "Whaddya mean? I'm doing great. You ought to see the dealer orders we're booking on the heat inverter."

Stedman was senior product manager, a steady, quiet, sober sort with the kind of confidence that made his work look effortless. He shook his head patiently and said, "No, I mean *that*," gesturing at the empty glass.

Kramer picked up his beer mug and took a pull. "You know the routine," he said ingratiatingly. "This is a tough line of work. You gotta keep loose."

Stedman frowned, looking up, then leaned forward and said, "You look like hell, Kramer." His mild voice belied the harshness of his statement. "You eat garbage, if anything at all. You got extra weight, you're bleary, I been watching you, you don't track so good sometimes." When Kramer didn't answer, Stedman said, "It's a pity, really. 'Cause I think there's a real sharp guy in there trying to get out."

Kramer drank some more beer and wiped his mouth clumsily, ignoring Stedman's quiet eyes on him. "My problem, pally," he whispered.

"God, I'm cold."

It was literally a voice in a crowd, a long way off but definitely from behind. Kramer set his mug down much harder than he'd meant to and turned and looked back over the back of his booth toward the rear of the pub. Finally he made his eyes focus in the dim light on the back of a woman's head, the distinctive tilt, the familiar sweep of dark hair. With her in the booth sat another woman who was completely unknown to him.

Stedman said, "What's up?"

Kramer turned uncomfortably back to him. "Familiar voice I thought I heard."

Stedman hitched himself up and squinted. "Couple of girls from ten. You know them?"

"No," Kramer said thickly, sure it was the truth. He rushed on, "But really, this inverter is moving pretty good. Not bad for four months on the job."

"Good for you," Stedman said casually. "That product's broken a lot of hearts." He glanced at his watch. "Got a meeting. You coming?"

Kramer stood and turned unsteadily toward the rear of the pub. "No, I got to take a squirt. See you back there."

He shuffled half unwillingly down the aisle, determined at last to set eyes on the face and listen to the voice and find out. But when he got there, the booth was empty.

Many Cincinnatians referred to summer as "monkey's armpit weather." The fire stairs were stiflingly hot as Kramer puffed up them from ten and emerged into the reception area of his floor. He strode into the offices, trying to get control of his breathing, trying to keep from shouting. Missed her again. As usual. He'd heard it all. "Away from her desk." "Off sick." "Out to lunch." "Had to run some errands." All he ever got was a glimpse of her back here, the sound of her voice there, always from around corners, in crowds, in the next room. Once—he was sure—he even passed her car going the other direction on Fort Washington Way. He'd doubled back and given chase but lost her on Mount Adams. . . .

He was almost to his office when Hedgepath passed him. "In my office," the marketing director said without explanation, and without stopping.

Kramer cruised up to Hedgepath's open office door, his heavy notebooks in hand, trying to get his mind on business and—with no success—to anticipate the subject of the meeting. Hedgepath pointed him to a chair, leaned forward with his chin on his fists, and said, "You seen the dealer return figures on the inverter?"

"Yeah, I haven't analyzed them yet, but—"

Hedgepath held up a hand. "Well, allow me to analyze them *for* you. It's a rout, my friend. Our sales figures are going to have to be revised downward about ninety percent."

"Guess the field people couldn't make them stick," Kramer said nervously.

"I guess," Hedgepath said evenly, "you didn't market them properly."

"Hey, you approved the plan, you saw the orders—"

"Hey, I delegated the whole thing to you. You got lots of dealer orders, but dealer orders aren't sales if the dealers send the product back. In other words, just to make it absolutely clear to you, loading the pipeline isn't the same thing as sales. Or did you know that?"

"I got some feedback from the field," Kramer said, trying to keep his tone constructive. "The inverter requires AC outlets in the ceilings. Most plants don't have them and can't justify the cost of installing them, despite the potential energy savings."

"Tell me something I don't know. You know how long we've been trying to sell that miserable stillborn heat inverter? You know how many different things we've tried? Including, may I add, hiring Mr. Hotshot Kramer, veteran product manager. You loaded the pipeline, and it's backing up into us. It's the joke of the industry, my friend."

Kramer wanted to explode, to accuse Hedgepath of sandbagging him with a worthless product and to protest the unfairness of judging Kramer's ability on this effort alone. But the best he could do was to sputter weakly, "I—I did the best I could."

Hedgepath smiled grimly and shook his head. "That's loser talk. The bottom line is all that matters. The guy who sleeps the workday away and sells the product is a hero. The guy who puts in eighteen hours a day—and fails—is, for lack of a better word, fired."

Kramer's arms and legs felt leaden. His pulse raced. He felt an unbelievable hot flash start at his neck and flow in waves over his face. He stared dully at Hedgepath, barely comprehending his next words.

"I want you off the premises right now. Tomorrow's Saturday; you can come back in and collect your stuff." He turned away, leaned on his credenza, and stared out the window. Kramer sat there a long time before he could get up and leave.

Cincinnati, the last day

Kramer didn't notice his children's faces staring up at him from the desk. His throat was so dry he could barely swallow. He squinted through sweat-moistened eyes at the woman. She stared at him from a great distance, rubbing her hands together as if they were frozen.

He said in a hoarse, cracked voice, "You can't imagine what it's been like. I had it all. I was on top of it. I'd made it. Finished with the marriage, better job, big exciting city. Instead this." He paused and licked his lips with a dry, furry tongue. He noticed that the color was going out of her face and hands. "It's all gone so incredibly sour. I got crippling money problems. Job that's rotten to the core. Nothing's fun any more." Her skin was now dry-bone white and seemed to be hardening. He said, "Nobody to talk to. And, God, I miss Elaine and the kids and I can't see them. And now I'm fired. I've got nowhere to go and no one to be with." He looked at her stark, staring, expressionless face. "I'm glad you came anyway. Despite what I did."

Her convulsion nearly made him jump. It was a savage, palsied shaking, as if the woman were penetrated to the core by incredible cold. Her breathing became rapid and shallow and rasping, and she swallowed uncontrollably over and over again. And she said: "Too late too late too late." Her eyes rolled up in their sockets and her clothes became damp and dirty, then went white with a coating of unclean ice. "Too late too late too late" came the voice, way back and almost gone.

Kramer pitched forward on his desk. It was as though someone had grabbed his shirt front and yanked him down. His chin bounced on the hard wood with a crack, his legs bounced and jerked, he gasped and choked, and then he lay still, eyes frozen open.

Cincinnati, the present

"Mr. Hedgepath?" asked the frizzy-haired older woman in her whining yet commanding voice.

"Yes, Greta?"

"There's no word on Patricia."

"Who?"

"Patricia. The new dark-haired girl on ten." Though Greta didn't mention it, she took some grim pleasure from the nickname the other girls had hung on Patricia: The Spook. "Her apartment is empty and she left no forwarding address."

"So she ankled. Big deal. Hire somebody else."

Greta held up a yellow piece of paper. Sometimes you had to explain *everything*. "Where shall I send her final check?"

"How about the circular file? She leaves without notice, she takes her chances."

Greta put a chubby hand up and leaned on the doorframe, the natural-born gossip in her aroused. "Don't you think it's odd? You wouldn't think a person would just up and leave the day before payday. At least not without getting her check."

"Any other decisions I can make for you, Greta? I'm busy."

Well, who wasn't? She brought her hand down. "Uh, yes, as a matter of fact. Mr. Kramer's office. I suggest we leave it empty for a while. Until the memory of, uh, the event, fades a little."

"It's an office, not a historical site. Have it ready by the tenth. That's when the new heat inverter product manager starts."

"Very well."

Greta trudged away from the office, absently fanning herself with the check. Her feet were tired and sore. Never any satisfaction from anybody. First this one complains, then that one wants something. Now she'd have to figure out whether to fix or replace the carpet in Kramer's office. That big wet spot refused to evaporate. That big, wet, bitterly cold spot.

Don't Make Waves

by George Ingersoll

Hardy was a sombre fellow, not to say downright morbid, but verbose. He didn't cut a prepossessing figure. In late middle age, his appearance would make a barber laugh and a dry cleaner cry, but he had one blessed attribute: Hardy had tenure. He kept this priceless fact stowed away, to be pulled out and examined now and then, like a wino surreptitiously peeling back the bag to assure himself that the jug was still half full. Hardy taught math at a respectable New England college, and with tenure, they couldn't bigod lay him off unless the entire institution went belly-up. With no wife or family to trouble him, his modest salary and the income from his equally modest investments were all he needed. To look at him, nobody would have picked Hardy out of a crowd as the one to trigger the most awesome cataclysm in historic times.

He was surely not regarded as Mr. Chips by his students, but his verbosity was prized. If one could just manage to get him going, he was likely to go on for a whole class about something or other, and maybe even forget assignments. This was infinitely preferable to being zapped with calculus. And so it turned out on the final day of spring semester. The atmosphere was charged; the students were as Indy 500 drivers, rounding the final turn, pace car left behind, awaiting the green flag, release from constraints. It was all but over; exams complete, scores known, freedom thirty minutes away. Teaching and learning were equally impossible, and a sophomore unleashed Hardy's verbosity with a carefully crafted, seemingly innocent question.

He stood with his back to the windows, hands on hips, and glared around the room.

"Here I am. I try to teach. There you are. A few of you try to learn. A lot of you seem to think mainly of sex and cars. A few of you, I believe, don't think at all. And yet, out there beyond those lovely old elms, away from this sequestered campus, there are five or six billion people, all milling around, doing all of the inspiring and unspeakable things they've always done, and do you know what?"

He glared around again. "They're doing all those things like so many mindless bacteria on a shingle!

"You, who consider yourselves dedicated environmentalists . . . think upon how poorly this planet is assembled. A skin, thinner in proportion than the shell of an egg, separating us from the white hot magma below, and even this eggshell is flawed. All cracked into a lot of plates, floating around on that magma like so many shingles in a bathtub, nudging each other, and every shingle crawling with us microbes. And the lousy shingles are porous. Just let one of those pores ooze a bit of pus from below and the microbes have Krakatoa . . . Vesuvius . . . Mt. St. Helens.

"You children play at your nuclear protest movements, and well you might. If my colleagues in the physics department were to put together a big enough fusion device and detonate it at the right juncture of a few of those shingles, the microbes could quit worrying about fallout. Penetrate to that magma and let the oceans in, and it would be all over for this planet in less than two minutes. It would come apart like a fragmentation grenade, shingles, bacteria, and all."

Hardy paused, then went on, uncharacteristically quietly.

"Most of you passed. Don't thank me. You've only slogged through the Slough of Despond . . . differential calculus. From here the road gets steeper and more rocky. If any of you ever make it to the mathematical summit and elect to put your knowledge to work examining our shingle, you surely won't thank me. Who enjoys living under the Damoclean Sword?"

He checked his watch.

"Only fifteen minutes to go. Close enough. This class is over. Enjoy your summer." He spoke this last to a lot of rapidly receding backs.

Hardy went to the windows and stood watching as the trickle of departing students became a stream, then a torrent, pouring from every building on campus. "Someone must have sprayed behind the baseboards," he muttered sourly. The clamor and vroom-vroom of eighteen hundred vigorous kids eager to be gone is considerable, and masked the ever-so-faint tremble of the old floor beneath Hardy's feet. That's how it began.

The shingle called the Atlantic plate had shifted ever so slightly, like an old dog twitching in its sleep. The twitch didn't deserve the name earthquake, merely a minor redistribution of stresses. An observer on the shoreline might have noticed a brief period of un-usual wave activity, but none did. It went unnoticed except by a few readers of seismograph charts, who noted it routinely and forgot it. It stirred up a little mud from the ocean floor and dislodged from the ooze a curious greenish flask which had lain, covered, for millennia.

That was all.

When the zoo beneath the windows had subsided a bit, Hardy followed his students at a more leisurely pace. His car, gassed up and ready, awaited him in the faculty parking lot. While the kids were mainly speeding south, he would be heading east, to the coast. While they were fornicating in the sweaty nexus of Florida beaches, he would be enjoying the austere solitude he preferred. No wet T-shirt contests for Hardy. In two hours' time he would be crossing the bridge onto Cape Cod. Another hour, east then north, and he would arrive at the simple beach cottage which had been his inheri-tance, perched high on the lip of the great gaunt bluffs, looking out onto the Atlantic. As he drove he wondered what damage the winter storms had done this year, and how much of his little holding had yielded to the inevitable march of erosion.

Hardy was on schedule when he crossed the boundary of the National Seashore, approaching his cottage. "Only smart thing the bureaucrats ever did was to save this place from the developers," he grumbled. He followed the blacktop road, with its neat National Park Service traffic signs, to the familiar branch, swung left, and drove around the RESIDENTS ONLY BEYOND THIS POINT proclamation. He was on a part of the seashore legally accessible only to those who'd owned property there (or their heirs or assigns) at the time the area had become a national park. The bureaucrats at whom Hardy sneered did their best to assure the privacy of these folks.

Hardy talked to himself with increasing frequency these days. "If I had my way they'd take down that silly sign and replace it with a good high chain link fence with razor wire on the top." Among the hordes of summer visitors were always a few who, innocently or otherwise, violated the private lands. Hardy was usually the first to call the ranger station and scream. He was relieved to find his cottage intact, and that he'd only lost two feet of his back yard to the sea over the winter.

It was two mornings later that Hardy found the flask. He'd spent the day after his arrival taking down the plywood over the windows, turning on the water, and generally making the place livable. On this day he would get to do what he really wanted: walk the great beach in the early morning. Tourists seldom came this far up the beach from the public area, but if he got out early enough, he could usually avoid even the ones who did. In defiance of park regulations to stay off the faces of the high, steep bluffs, Hardy half-climbed, half-slid down over the convoluted clay and sand and landed on the beach amid his own little avalanche. He chose to walk north.

He very nearly missed seeing the flask; its dark greenish color blended with the patches of kelp that dotted the shore. He prodded it disdainfully with his toe. "More litter . . . damn kids . . . probably a beer bottle." But it wasn't. Curious, he picked it up. Too small for a beer bottle. Opaque. He wasn't even certain it was glass. Odd stopper, too . . . looked like lead, with some nearly-obliterated design stamped into the surface. Perfume? Too large for that. Some exotic liqueur, drifted ashore from a yacht? He shook it; it felt empty.

Hardy got out the absurdly large lock-back knife he carried in a belt sheath and attacked the stopper. It *was* lead, and solidly driven in. The stopper fought him, then suddenly yielded, as though pushed from within. He thought he heard a slight hiss and saw a tiny transient puff of vapor. Something had been released. He sniffed cautiously and smelled only a faint mustiness. He inverted the flask, but nothing ran out. He tossed the flask and stopper back onto the sand and trudged on.

Hardy was neither an antiquarian nor a scholar, only a mediocre math teacher. He had little imagination, and had never in his life read anything fanciful. He had no idea what he'd held, nor what he'd released. He may have remembered childhood legends of the Djinn, with their infernal powers, and how recalcitrant Djinn could be imprisoned in tiny flasks, and so rendered harmless, by the might of the seal placed upon the stopper. Invariably, the ancient wisdom holds, if the Djinn is released by the seal's removal, the liberator is rewarded by the granting of wishes. If Hardy did remember this, he certainly never connected it with the bit of flotsam he'd discarded. He was surely oblivious to the tiny breath of tenuous mist moving behind him.

His innate perversity had, that morning, taken the form of a mild crankiness at his inability to find anything to complain about. He gazed sourly at the flawless blue sky and virgin beach of late spring. Then he focused on the tiny, benign wavelets patting the sand gently. "Typical, for this time of year," he grunted. "Little six-inch waves that go on and on. I'd like to see one big wave, just to break the monotony, but just one. More, and we'd be swarmed over by screaming surfers." It was as close to being a frivolous thought as Hardy ever generated. It wasn't heard by anyone; he was alone, except for a wisp of mist.

As Hardy spoke, a curious phenomenon began. Far out at sea two waves met and merged their masses into one. This was unusual behavior in an area of opposing wind and current, where the norm was a confused chop. Then another added its mass . . . and another. The process had begun. All day it continued, unobserved by man, and by nightfall, the process was complete. The mass of bearded gray-white water had formed and begun to move on its course, accelerating. The course? Due west. At the speed of an airplane.

Considering the vastness of the sea it was minuscule. It was no larger than Vermont, and its plateau was only two hundred feet above the surface of the surrounding sea. A mere solitary scout, dispatched by the forces of the oceans to probe the alertness of the land's outposts.

At the following dawn Hardy strode to his accustomed vantage point on the lip of the eastern bluffs and stared below him. He grunted his surprise. The tide was far lower than ever in his experience. Rank after rank of sand bars marched outward from the beach for, he judged, half a mile. Clouds of gulls were feeding voraciously on fish trapped in the pools between the bars. Lunch, thought Hardy, and ran to the cottage for his spinning rod. He was bracing for his scramble down the bluffs when an inexplicable sense of unease impelled him to stop and survey the horizon. Unease escalated to premonition when he saw, far out to sea, a dark cloudbank rising, stretching in both directions to the limits of his vision. "Freak spring storm?" Spinning rod forgotten, he watched. The cloudbank seemed to be advancing rapidly, which Hardy thought odd; what breeze there was was offshore.

It came on with uncanny speed, silently, climbing until it obscured the dawn sun. He began to feel the edges of fear. This was unnatural. Then, at once, he was transfixed. Belief lags comprehension when one is confronted with the unbelievable. Unbelief dissolved into sheer animal terror. A white fleck in the face of the cloudbank had come into focus for what it was . . . the eighty-foot hull of an ocean-going trawler, tumbling like a bathtub toy. The cloudbank had revealed itself in an instant as a supernal wavefront, a sheer cliff of water higher than Niagara, advancing as inevitably as time itself. No man had ever seen such a tsunami, and Hardy faced it alone.

The wave would roll over Cape Cod, impeded no more than by a child's sand castle. A pilot on approach to Hyannis would see, and scream into his radio. A radio ham on the heights west of Hyannis would see, with one minute's margin. He would put out an immediate and hysterical Mayday. Both would be heard, and neither would be heeded. Nantucket would vanish, and the gingerbread houses of Martha's Vineyard would be drowned for all time. Slowed, now, by the rising of the sea bed, its speed would drop to seventy-five miles per hour when reaching landfall on the mainland at Onset. There would be no time for warning and escape.

The water would move inexorably inland, slowing as it went, as its incalculable energy would be sapped by the forces of the land which men called friction and gravity. It would finally stop, one hour and fifteen minutes after Hardy's demise, when the water was ankle-deep in the streets of Providence.

It would lie still briefly, exhausted, then begin its retreat. The ultimate, terrible, ever-accelerating outwash would begin, scouring a new face upon the land, and carrying with it all life and most of the recognizable works of man east of a line from Boston to Point Judith.

The loss in lives would, of course, never be accurately known. It would be estimated at five million. No rigorous attempt would ever be made to estimate the loss in treasure. The search for answers would begin even as the waters receded, but none would ever be found.

Hardy was never to know any of this. He lay on the lip of the bluffs, curled into foetal position, awaiting the wave. Poor fool, he never knew he had two more wishes due him.

An American Visit

by F. M. Maupin

Gwillam Eyer, aged eighteen and very angry with himself, gazed through the ruined door at his unwelcome houseguests spread out on his lawn. Because it *was* his lawn, he told himself resentfully: and his ruin, and his land, and, incidentally, his ghost. And his country!

He knew that most Americans were not like this, he knew they weren't, to go around barging into English houses. They were not typical, it was some nightmare: and there he stood, the spineless fool that he was, wholly unable to cope. But, in the same moment, his painful reserve returning, he knew that he could never tell them to leave.

He was never going to be able to manage anything. They were perfectly right: he was even afraid of a ghost.

"Will-ll-ll-ly!"

He shuddered, and not from the cold vault behind him. He hated nicknames.

"Pull yourself together, Eyer," he told himself miserably, "you just have to tell them to go. You didn't invite them, you don't want them, so why can't you tell them to shove off?"

Well, he heard his own conscience remind him, they'll say you got sore—that's the phrase—when we dared you to look in that church.

And did you?

Yes, I did.

"Now, no kidding," he heard Bob's ponderous voice saying, "is it true that you English believe in hoodoo—you know, ghosts and all that? I read a paper about it, scientific. How half of you English won't go in their own house on account of the spooks. Is that so?"

"Certainly not."

Gwillam cursed them once, well, in flawless Cantabrigian, and then for good measure in Welsh. But he felt no better.

"Now, see here," he told himself firmly, "you're going to go through this church once, thoroughly. There's nothing in here but yourself—nothing to be afraid of. You're not afraid, are you? And then you're going to go out there and tell them to pack up and go. Is that clear?"

It was clear. And he shivered.

"Oh, tell me," he found himself raging, "how did you get yourself into this mess in the first place?"

It was the ring he was wearing that started the whole affair.

He had been coming down here from Northampton, from his aunt's house—there were still details from his mother's death—and they had all piled on in Stratford. They not only took over the carriage, they had openly boasted among themselves that their tickets were second, not first.

In that odd American way, they had used the nominative of address with every breath, so it was impossible not to know their names: Bob and Pat, and the little one was Honey. They went to some strange university, and were a year or so older than he. Gwillam, who had no wish to be drawn into their chatter, had sunk into his corner, staring at the green fields outside where his own thin face floated in the air. Much good it had done him. Honey had leaned over, swooped up his hand in hers, and stroked the gold band on his finger.

"Oh, isn't that cute!" she exclaimed. "Is that a school ring?"

Gwillam looked at her blankly. School had been for him, till this year, the small class at the vicarage; and he pulled back his hand.

"I don't know what you mean."

The rounded English "o" sounded cold and unfriendly even to his ear, so he reluctantly added, "I can't take it off; it's too small for me. It's a family ring."

Bob had put down his ubiquitous newspaper and regarded him owlishly.

"You a duke or something?"

Gwillam, his color rising, said, "I'm not a duke."

The dark one, Pat, drew herself up with that impossible air she affected, and said distantly, "We wanted to meet some members of the British upper classes."

"Yeah," put in Bob, "live in a castle, and all that jazz."

Live in a castle? Gwillam found himself grinning. As much as he loved the far-flung line of fortresses that crowned the hills of Wales—and he did love them, passionately, with all the inherited love of his forebears—he would hardly have lived in a castle. A bit drafty, what?—when all that rain poured in? Perhaps they were thinking of Scotland?

He said, "Well, we live in a house that was built in the fifteen hundreds—I mean, I live there. Part of it, rather, the part Cromwell didn't get. But there're ruins there older than that, going back to King Edward. There's a piece of a priory, and a chapel. Really it's a church, but a little one. Nobody ever goes into that, though. There's a curse on it."

Honey had squealed so ecstatically that he had jumped.

"A curse? Not really? A real ghost?"

Bob had begun on the hoodoo then, and the English. His argument had been, not that the English believe in ghosts, but that they were "scared of" them. He thinks we're Jamaicans, Gwillam had thought; no, Haitians, with oo-angas and pins sticking in them.

"Certainly not."

"Ooh, you're just wonderful," Honey had cooed. "I think it's the most exciting thing I ever heard. Do go on. Tell us about the ghost."

So, of course, he had.

Now, in the brilliant summer afternoon, he stared through the vine-draped door of his own ruined church, to the sunlit lawn where his guests lingered over the crumbs of their picnic. His dislike was so strong that it startled him. Was he really angry at himself? Did he really hate them, or himself? How did he let them get him into this place at all? Well, they believed he was afraid.

And was he afraid?

Yes, he was.

He turned and, blinded by the sunlight, peered into the murk of the ruin.

It was a tiny place, really—it would have fitted in toto into a good-sized Mayfair drawing room—and was intact except for some missing stones at this door and the far one. Built in barrel style, the three vaults made three separate tunnels, parallel to each other, and each invisible to the others, except as you passed the spaces between the thick pillars. The sun never shone here, for the round, grudging windows had long since been sealed by the ivy, as the other door was sealed; and as this door had been before Bob had torn the stems aside, covering his hands with the viscous sap which the limbs spat out.

Gwillam said angrily, aloud, "I'm alone. There's nothing in here but myself. I'm alone. I'm alone."

"Oh-hhh-hhh," breathed the vault over his head, and kept quiet.

Alone?

Cato—no, Cicero—it was Cato: what is the worst that could possibly happen? If you know that, you're no longer afraid. Well, you could die. In an empty building? Killed—whatever next!—by a man six hundred and fifty years dead himself? How could you? Gwillam's father was dead, somewhere over the Channel: and Gwillam, well-taught by the vicar, by no means supposed that they would meet in this world.

". . . the time was, then the brains were out, the man would die, and there an end . . ."

How did it go on?

". . . but now they rise, with twenty trenched gashes on their heads to push us from our stools . . ."

So he had a good memory for verse, and why shouldn't he? Any lad in the village could sing all the hymns in the book, by memory. And there, as the play said, an end.

There an end?

He looked down at the torch in his hand. Honey had pressed it on him, limping out.

"I like to broke my neck," she said, "you've got holes in that church of yours. My foot went right through the floor—" and at his expression, she said, "I declare it did. Isn't that so, Pat? Oh, you-all had left. Well, I beat it right out of there, after that stone broke. Here, you take this, Willy. It's your turn now to go in there, unless—" she paused just for a second too long "—unless you don't want to."

Holes in the floor, a stone floor? She must have tripped on some up-ended paving, he would have to be careful.

So he really was going to look through the place, wasn't he?

"Like you said," Bob had grunted, "that ghost has it in for you in particular. He won't show up for us."

Gwillam felt cold fear, laid like a wet snake across his chest and stomach.

Talk to an American about his money; a Frenchman, his mistress; a German, his theories; an Englishman, his place in the country. It works every time. But how did they get invited? He had no more thought of inviting them than of asking his tenants to come in for tea.

And yet, here they were.

He had started to talk about the farm, of course; but they wanted more of the ghost. And so—because in truth he loved to speak of home—he had begun to tell the old story.

"It was really a question of family," he had told them. "It made a lot of difference which was the older son. My ancestor was the younger brother, and he wanted his elder brother dead so that his own sons could inherit. He locked his brother up in the tower—there're pieces of that around, too—and starved him."

"To death?"

"Oh, yes, to death."

"And nobody did anything to him?" asked Honey, shocked.

"Nothing except the curse, no."

Gwillam had gone on to explain about the curse. The dying man had sold his soul to the devil—so the story went—in exchange for his life.

"But you said he died."

"He did—but he was to come back to life. He was to stay dead until his grave was opened again, and the first man to see his dust was to change places with him, while he came back to life again."

"What do you mean, change places with him?"

Gwillam was rather enjoying this. He usually found it hard to talk to people he did not know, but this rapt attention was very flattering.

"Well, in his grave, I suppose. We always thought that the curse was meant to light on one of our family—you know, to wipe out our line, too, as his had been stopped. I think that was the idea. The children from the village, they sometimes play in there—but we've never gone in. The church he was buried in, I mean. It's not consecrated any more. It's just a ruin."

"You're saying," said Bob, incredulous, "that your family won't go in this church, for fear of running into that spook?"

"Well, in a way, yes."

"Your father never went in there?"

"No, he didn't."

"Because of a spook. Now, I call that chicken!"

The color flared in Gwillam's fair cheeks; he could feel it burn. He said carefully, "My father was killed in the war, before the Americans came in."

Bob stared at him, his mouth open like a fish.

But Honey put out her hand and said vaguely, "Oh, I'm sorry, how awful, oh, Bob, do let's go down and see this place."

She had quite left out Gwillam as she turned to the others and rattled on. "You never want to go anywhere with anybody we meet, it's half of traveling to get to know the people, how they live and all. Oh, you-all, do say yes, we can take a day off of Edinburgh."

Pat said remotely, "I want to see the castle of the Duke of Argyle. We're related, of course."

"Let's cut out Ee-lie," said Bob suddenly, "just another cathedral, Gee-sus! If I see another cathedral, I'll croak. Okay, couple of days, why not? Might get some sun in. Hate to go back white like this."

Honey hugged him deliriously. "You old dear. I know you'll love this, you'll just love it, ghosts and all."

She turned to the speechless Gwillam.

"Just a few days," she said. "We'd just love it. We'll love your ghost. I think you're sweet."

They hadn't, of course. They had looked at his velvet-green domain with those blank, flitting tourist glances, and dismissed it at once as second rate.

"You call that a river?" asked Honey, amazed. "Now, back home, it's just an itsy-bitsy little creek."

Nor the village either, though he had taken them into the pub, where the village boys, returning from the football match, had—for themselves, not the outsiders—put on a round of singing that would have graced a Continental stage. Gwillam, to whom song came as naturally as breath (it was one of the pains of his youth that he could not go down to play in the village), had listened, heart-wrung, to the liquid language that pressed into the old hymns all the griefs of mankind; and was outraged when Bob, off-key and strident, began to hum loudly, waving his hand to keep himself in time.

Had they been sympathetic he could even have conquered his shyness to tell them the old legends he loved. It was on that dark mountain opposite where the last of the bards of Wales had flung himself down on rocks, rather than kneel to an English king; and his own kinsmen had most unwillingly been bowed to Edward's heirs.

But none of this interested them. If it had, they might have understood better why the past was such a real thing to him.

"I don't know where my own grandfather came from," Bob had said. "Germany, somewhere. We don't think all that kind of stuff's important."

Well, I do, thought Gwillam mutinously, the past is still alive to me.

You don't say?

In what way?

And curses, too, are they real after almost seven hundred years?

". . . it will have blood, they say; blood will have blood; stones have been known to move . . ."

He had said, "Of course you can go in; but I won't. Of course I'm not scared of the church. Don't be daft. We just never go in it, that's all. We just never do."

But it didn't work out that way.

He turned the torch over in his hand; it was a big American one, a "flashlight." Darkest England: one should be prepared. He had never spoken this way to them, but he was going to. First once through the church, and then out, and he'd say it.

"Meant to mention it," he would say. "I've been called down to Cardiff; business, you know, the farm. Wish you could stay longer, I really do. It's been splendid." It sounded false even to him. They weren't going to believe him. But at least they couldn't say that he threw them out because he wouldn't go into his own church.

With an awful clearness, there in the darkness, Gwillam realized how much he had been taken in. They had imposed on him, they had imposed on him utterly. He had never been treated this way, he had no defense to put up. If he had left home earlier . . . if he had had sisters and brothers . . . if his birth had not set him off from the village children . . . oh, surely, in time he would learn how to handle such people! But now, as a final imposition, they had goaded him into this place, where his own shattered confidence was forcing him into a course which he himself saw to be wholly unnecessary.

Unnecessary?

No, not to him. In his desperate confusion and anger he would have done anything, anything, to restore what was left of his pride. He turned on the torch. It was dimming; and the reddish beam of light danced crazily along the curve of the vault.

Through no will of his own, he said softly, aloud, in the melodic Welsh which he almost never used, "Are you there?"

There was no answer but the humming of bees in the clover outside, and a rustle of ivy.

The stone to his touch was cold. He shoved his hand into his pocket, and moved slowly along the tunnel, the dirt thick on the floor at his feet. Ahead of him, the back door gleamed greenly, shut with leaves. Still fighting with each breath the desire to run, he stumbled along the short passage, till he came to the door and stood shaking, emptied of thought. The blood pounded at his throat, and his head swam with the numb sickness of a taker of drugs. He was past turning back. He whispered, his words as precise as before, in his ancestors' tongue, "Are you there?"

The ivy behind him sighed softly, faced out to the sun.

He swung into the tunnel at his right, and staggered down it like a sleepwalker. The dim light of the fading torch splashed in reddish pools on the ancient dirt. Ahead of him now, a shadow broke the floor, and, without words, he recognized it as the stone that had fallen in.

But he inched past it before he turned. Then he came slowly around. The pit gaped open before him, a shadow in the shadows. In that moment he knew—he must have known—but quietly, as hopelessly as a child, he took his hand out of his pocket and held it out, waiting, to the shadow at his feet.

"Come on," he said, "I'm here," and with the other hand shone the light down into the darkness.

Out in the sunlight, the three sat restless. Honey had taken out her mirror and scrutinized her face.

"Did you tell him?" Bob demanded.

"How can you?" said Pat, "I mean, you can't say I'm bored to death so I'm leaving."

Bob looked up from his paper. "It's perfectly simple," he said, exasperated, "just say we have to catch the five-oh-five."

"Honey's going to tell him."

"Well, she better hurry. It's four now. You all packed?"

They nodded. He had worked it all out: a half hour to the station, a half hour to get in and out of the house.

"I think he's glad we're leaving," Pat said. "He doesn't like us."

"Oh, yes, he does," said Honey, "it's just the accent."

"No, he doesn't," said Bob, "not two cents. I wouldn't be surprised if he lit out the back of that place and kept going, just so as not to have to talk to us. I should think the Americans'd be popular around here, us winning the war and all." There was a pause. Then he said, "My God, he's been in there twenty minutes. I bet he lit out back."

Honey stood up. "Oh, look!" she exclaimed, "what's that?"

Pat stood up, too. "Look, Bob," she said, "it's a monk. Didn't Willy say there were monks around here?"

"That was Win-chester."

"It's a judge," Honey said, "you know, in the movie about the French Revolution. The wigs and all."

Bob dragged himself up and looked over the fields. "I don't like that get-up," he said briefly, "looks too much like a dress. Looks funny on a man."

"Not if you've lived in Italy," Pat said coldly.

Honey glanced around. "I think we're being mean," she said. "I'm going in and look for Willy. You coming?"

She set out for the church alone, as the monk, or the judge, or whatever he was, walked on through the distant fields.

It was empty, of course, the church; but Bob had been right. The church had been left by the back, for the ivy was broken. Honey stooped and picked up her flashlight, still lit, from the broken floor. Its weak beam caught a flash of metal, and she leaned and fished up something small from the dirt in the hole. The others were already fixed to go, the picnic remains shoved to one side on the lawn. They decided to leave without saying goodbye. What could they do?—he had gone, he was rude, and not they.

Bob examined Honey's find as she smoothed back her hair. "You can give it to one of his coolies. He's got enough of them 'round, Lord knows."

Pat said suddenly, "I don't like to stay with people; it's murder. Isn't it, Bob?"

He grunted, but Honey was always polite. She took back the golden ring, with its crest, and turned it to gleam in the sun. She was not really listening at all, she was already half on the train. "Murder," she said agreeably, stroking the ring, "absolute murder."

The Man Who Could Work Miracles

by H. G. Wells

It is doubtful whether the gift was innate. For my own part, I think it came to him suddenly. Indeed, until he was thirty he was a skeptic, and did not believe in miraculous powers. And here, since it is the most convenient place, I must mention that he was a little man, and had eyes of a hot brown, very erect red hair, a mustache with ends that he twisted up, and freckles. His name was George McWhirter Fotheringay—not the sort of name by any means to lead to any expectation of miracles—and he was a clerk at Gomshott's. He was greatly addicted to assertive argument. It was while he was asserting the impossibility of miracles that he had his first intimation of his extraordinary powers. This particular argument was being held in the bar of the Long Dragon, and Toddy Beamish was conducting the opposition by a monotonous but effective "So *you* say" that drove Mr. Fotheringay to the very limit of his patience.

There were present, besides these two, a very dusty cyclist, landlord Cox, and Miss Maybridge, the perfectly respectable and rather portly barmaid of the Dragon. Miss Maybridge was standing with her back to Mr. Fotheringay, washing glasses; the others were watching him, more or less amused by the present ineffectiveness of the assertive method. Goaded by the Torres Vedras tactics of Mr. Beamish, Mr. Fotheringay determined to make an unusual rhetorical effort. "Looky here, Mr. Beamish," said Mr. Fotheringay. "Let us clearly understand what a miracle is. It's something contrariwise to the course of nature done by power of Will, something what couldn't happen without being specially willed."

"So *you* say," said Mr. Beamish, repulsing him.

Mr. Fotheringay appealed to the cyclist, who had hitherto been a silent auditor, and received his assent—given with a hesitating cough and a glance at Mr. Beamish. The landlord would express no opinion, and Mr. Fotheringay, returning to Mr. Beamish, received the unexpected concession of a qualified assent to his definition of a miracle.

"For instance," said Mr. Fotheringay, greatly encouraged. "Here would be a miracle. That lamp, in the natural course of nature, couldn't burn like that upsy-down, could it, Beamish?"

"*You* say it couldn't," said Beamish.

"And you?" said Fotheringay. "You don't mean to say—eh?"

"No," said Beamish reluctantly. "No, it couldn't."

"Very well," said Mr. Fotheringay. "Then here comes someone, as it might be me, along here, and stands as it might be here, and says to that lamp, as I might do, collecting all my will—'Turn upsy-down without breaking, and go on burning steady,' and—Hullo!"

It was enough to make anyone say "Hullo!" The impossible, the incredible, was visible to them all. The lamp hung inverted in the air, burning quietly with its flame pointing down. It was as solid, as indisputable as ever a lamp was, the prosaic common lamp of the Long Dragon bar.

Mr. Fotheringay stood with an extended forefinger and the knitted brows of one anticipating a catastrophic smash. The cyclist, who was sitting next the lamp, ducked and jumped across the bar. Everybody jumped, more or less. Miss Maybridge turned and screamed. For nearly three seconds the lamp remained still. A faint cry of mental distress came from Mr. Fotheringay. "I can't keep it up," he said, "any longer." He staggered back, and the inverted lamp suddenly flared, fell against the corner of the bar, bounced aside, smashed upon the floor, and went out.

It was lucky it had a metal receiver, or the whole place would have been in a blaze. Mr. Cox was the first to speak, and his remark, shorn of needless excrescences, was to the effect that Fotheringay was a fool. Fotheringay was beyond disputing even so fundamental a proposition as that! He was astonished beyond measure at the thing that had occurred. The subsequent conversation threw absolutely no light on the matter so far as Fotheringay was concerned; the general opinion not only followed Mr. Cox very closely but very vehemently. Everyone accused Fotheringay of a silly trick, and presented him to himself as a foolish destroyer of comfort and security. His mind was a tornado of perplexity, he was himself inclined to agree with them, and he made a remarkably ineffectual opposition to the proposal of his departure.

He went home flushed and heated, coat collar crumpled, eyes smarting, and ears red. He watched each of the ten street lamps nervously as he passed it. It was only when he found himself alone in his little bedroom in Church Row that he was able to grapple seriously with his memories of the occurrence, and ask, "What on earth happened?"

He had removed his coat and boots, and was sitting on the bed with his hands in his pockets repeating the text of his defence for the seventeenth time, "I didn't want the confounded thing to upset," when it occurred to him that at the precise moment he had said the commanding words he had inadvertently willed the thing he said, and that when he had seen the lamp in the air he had felt that it depended on him to maintain it there without being clear how this was to be done. He had not a particularly complex mind, or he might have stuck for a time at that "inadvertently willed," embracing, as it does, the abstrusest problems of voluntary action; but as it was, the idea came to him with a quite acceptable haziness. And from that, following, as I must admit, no clear logical path, he came to the test of experiment.

He pointed resolutely to his candle and collected his mind, though he felt he did a foolish thing. "Be raised up," he said. But in a second that feeling vanished. The candle was raised, hung in the air one giddy moment, and as Mr. Fotheringay gasped, fell with a smash on his toilet table, leaving him in darkness save for the expiring glow of its wick.

For a time Mr. Fotheringay sat in the darkness, perfectly still. "It

did happen, after all," he said. "And 'ow I'm to explain it I *don't*
know." He sighed heavily, and began feeling in his pockets for a
match. He could find none, and he rose and groped about the toilet
table. "I wish I had a match," he said. He resorted to his coat, and
there were none there, and then it dawned upon him that miracles
were possible even with matches. He extended a hand and scowled
at it in the dark. "Let there be a match in that hand," he said. He felt
some light object fall across his palm, and his fingers closed upon a
match.

After several ineffectual attempts to light this, he discovered it
was a safety match. He threw it down, and then it occurred to him
that he might have willed it lit. He did, and perceived it burning in
the midst of his toilet table mat. He caught it up hastily, and it went
out. His perception of possibilities enlarged, and he felt for and
replaced the candle in its candlestick. "Here! *you* be lit," said Mr.
Fotheringay, and forthwith the candle was flaring, and he saw a little
black hole in the toilet cover, with a wisp of smoke rising from it. For
a time he stared from this to the little flame and back, and then
looked up and met his own gaze in the looking glass. By this help he
communed with himself in silence for a time.

"How about miracles now?" said Mr. Fotheringay at last, addressing his reflection.

The subsequent meditations of Mr. Fotheringay were of a severe
but confused description. So far as he could see, it was a case of pure
willing with him. The nature of his first experiences disinclined him
for any further experiments except of the most cautious type. But he
lifted a sheet of paper, and turned a glass of water pink and then
green, and he created a snail, which he miraculously annihilated,
and got himself a miraculous new toothbrush. Somewhen in the
small hours he had reached the fact that his willpower must be of a
particularly rare and pungent quality, a fact of which he had certainly had inklings before, but no certain assurance. The scare and
perplexity of his first discovery were now qualified by pride in this
evidence of singularity and by vague intimations of advantage. He
became aware that the church clock was striking one, and as it did
not occur to him that his daily duties at Gomshott's might be miraculously dispensed with, he resumed undressing, in order to get to

bed without further delay. As he struggled to get his shirt over his head he was struck with a brilliant idea. "Let me be in bed," he said, and found himself so. "Undressed," he stipulated; and, finding the sheets cold, added hastily, "and in my nightshirt—no, in a nice soft woollen nightshirt. Ah!" he said with immense enjoyment. "And now let me be comfortably asleep. . . ."

He awoke at his usual hour and was pensive all through breakfast-time, wondering whether his overnight experience might not be a particularly vivid dream. At length his mind turned again to cautious experiments. For instance, he had three eggs for breakfast; two his landlady had supplied, good, but shoppy, and one was a delicious fresh goose egg, laid, cooked, and served by his extraordinary will. He hurried off to Gomshott's in a state of profound but carefully concealed excitement, and only remembered the shell of the third egg when his landlady spoke of it that night. All day he could do no work because of this astonishing new self-knowledge, but this caused him no inconvenience because he made up for it miraculously in his last ten minutes.

As the day wore on his state of mind passed from wonder to elation, albeit the circumstances of his dismissal from the Long Dragon were still disagreeable to recall, and a garbled account of the matter that had reached his colleagues led to some badinage. It was evident he must be careful how he lifted frangible articles, but in other ways his gift promised more and more as he turned it over in his mind. He intended among other things to increase his personal property by unostentatious acts of creation. He called into existence a pair of very splendid diamond studs, and hastily annihilated them again as young Gomshott came across the counting house to his desk. He was afraid young Gomshott might wonder how he came by them. He saw quite clearly the gift required caution and watchfulness in its exercise, but so far as he could judge the difficulties attending its mastery would be no greater than those he had already faced in the study of cycling. It was that analogy, perhaps, quite as much as the feeling that he would be unwelcome in the Long Dragon, that drove him out after supper into the lane beyond the gasworks, to rehearse a few miracles in private.

There was possibly a certain want of originality in his attempts,

for apart from his willpower Mr. Fotheringay was not a very exceptional man. The miracle of Moses' rod came to his mind, but the
night was dark and unfavorable to the proper control of large miraculous snakes. Then he recollected the story of "Tannhäuser" that he
had read on the back of the Philharmonic program. That seemed to
him singularly attractive and harmless. He stuck his walking stick—
a very nice Poona-Penang lawyer—into the turf that edged the foot
path, and commanded the dry wood to blossom. The air was immediately full of the scent of roses, and by means of a match he saw for
himself that this beautiful miracle was indeed accomplished. His
satisfaction was ended by advancing footsteps. Afraid of a premature
discovery of his powers, he addressed the blossoming stick hastily:
"Go back." What he meant was "Change back"; but of course he was
confused. The stick receded at a considerable velocity, and incontinently came a cry of anger and a bad word from the approaching
person. "Who are you throwing brambles at, you fool?" cried a
voice. "That got me on the shin."

"I'm sorry, old chap," said Mr. Fotheringay, and then, realizing
the awkward nature of the explanation, caught nervously at his
mustache. He saw Winch, one of the three Immering constables,
advancing.

"What d'yer mean by it?" asked the constable. "Hullo! It's you, is
it? The gent that broke the lamp at the Long Dragon!"

"I don't mean anything by it," said Mr. Fotheringay. "Nothing at
all."

"What d'yer do it for then?"

"Oh, bother!" said Mr. Fotheringay.

"Bother, indeed? D'yer know that stick hurt? What d'yer do it for,
eh?"

For the moment Mr. Fotheringay could not think what he
had done it for. His silence seemed to irritate Mr. Winch. "You've
been assaulting the police, young man, this time. That's what *you*
done!"

"Look here, Mr. Winch," said Mr. Fotheringay, annoyed and
confused, "I'm very sorry. The fact is—"

"Well!"

He could not think of no way but the truth. "I was working a miracle." He tried to speak in an offhand way, but try as he would he couldn't.

"Working a—! 'Ere, don't you talk rot. Working a miracle, indeed! Miracle! Well, that's downright funny! Why, you's the chap that don't believe in miracles. . . . Fact is, this is another of your silly conjuring tricks—that's what this is. Now, I tell you—"

But Mr. Fotheringay never heard what Mr. Winch was going to tell him. He realized he had given himself away, flung his valuable secret to all the winds of heaven. A violent gust of irritation swept him to action. He turned on the constable swiftly and fiercely. "Here," he said, "I've had enough of this, I have! I'll show you a silly conjuring trick, I will. Go to Hades! Go, now!"

He was alone!

Mr. Fotheringay performed no more miracles that night nor did he trouble to see what had become of his flowering stick. He returned to the town, scared and very quiet, and went to his bedroom. "Lord!" he said, "it's a powerful gift—an extremely powerful gift! I didn't hardly mean as much as that. Not really. . . . I wonder what Hades is like!"

He sat on the bed taking off his boots. Struck by a happy thought he transferred the constable to San Francisco, and without any more interference with normal causation went soberly to bed. In the night he dreamt of the anger of Winch.

The next day Mr. Fotheringay heard two interesting items of news. Someone had planted a most beautiful climbing rose against the elder Mr. Gomshott's private house in the Lullaborough Road, and the river as far as Rawling's Mill was to be dragged for Constable Winch.

Mr. Fotheringay was abstracted and thoughtful all that day, and performed no miracles except certain provisions for Winch, and the miracle of completing his day's work with punctual perfection in spite of all the bee swarm of thoughts that hummed through his mind. And the extraordinary abstraction and meekness of his manner was remarked by several people, and made a matter for jesting. For the most part he was thinking of Winch.

On Sunday evening he went to chapel, and oddly enough, Mr. Maydig, who took a certain interest in occult matters, preached about "things that are not lawful." Mr. Fotheringay was not a regular chapel goer, but the system of assertive skepticism, to which I have already alluded, was now very much shaken. The tenor of the sermon threw an entirely new light on these novel gifts, and he suddenly decided to consult Mr. Maydig immediately after the service. So soon as that was determined, he found himself wondering why he had not done so before.

Mr. Maydig, a lean, excitable man with quite remarkably long wrists and neck, was gratified at a request for a private conversation from a young man whose carelessness in religious matters was a subject for general remark in the town. After a few necessary delays, he conducted him to the study of the Manse, which was contiguous to the chapel, seated him comfortably, and, standing in front of a cheerful fire—his legs threw a Rhodian arch of shadow on the opposite wall—requested Mr. Fotheringay to state his business.

At first Mr. Fotheringay was a little abashed, and found some difficulty in opening the matter. "You will scarcely believe me, Mr. Maydig, I am afraid"—and so forth for some time. He tried a question at last, and asked Mr. Maydig his opinion of miracles.

Mr. Maydig was still saying "Well" in an extremely judicial tone, when Mr. Fotheringay interrupted again: "You don't believe, I suppose, that some common sort of person—like myself, for instance— as it might be sitting here now, might have some sort of twist inside him that made him able to do things by his will."

"It's possible," said Mr. Maydig. "Something of the sort, perhaps, is possible."

"If I might make free with something here, I think I might show you a sort of experiment," said Mr. Fotheringay. "Now, take that tobacco jar on the table, for instance. What I want to know is whether what I am going to do with it is a miracle or not. Just half a minute, Mr. Maydig, please."

He knitted his brows, pointed to the tobacco jar and said: "Be a bowl of vi'lets."

The tobacco jar did as it was ordered.

Mr. Maydig started violently at the change, and stood looking from the thaumaturgist to the bowl of flowers. He said nothing.

Presently he ventured to lean over the table and smell the violets; they were fresh-picked and very fine ones. Then he stared at Mr. Fotheringay again.

"How did you do that?" he asked.

Mr. Fotheringay pulled his mustache. "Just told it—and there you are. Is that a miracle, or is it black art, or what is it? And what do you think's the matter with me? That's what I want to ask."

"It's a most extraordinary occurrence."

"And this day last week I knew no more that I could do things like that than you did. It came quite sudden. It's something odd about my will, I suppose, and that's as far as I can see."

"Is *that*—the only thing? Could you do other things besides that?"

"Lord, yes!" said Mr. Fotheringay. "Just anything." He thought, and suddenly recalled a conjuring entertainment he had seen. "Here!" He pointed. "Change into a bowl of fish—no, not that—change into a glass bowl full of water with goldfish swimming in it. That's better! You see that, Mr. Maydig?"

"It's astonishing. It's incredible. You are either a most extraordinary . . . But no—"

"I could change it into anything," said Mr. Fotheringay. "Just anything. Here! be a pigeon, will you?"

In another moment a blue pigeon was fluttering round the room and making Mr. Maydig duck every time it came near him. "Stop there, will you," said Mr. Fotheringay; and the pigeon hung motionless in the air. "I could change it back to a bowl of flowers," he said, and after replacing the pigeon on the table worked that miracle. "I expect you will want your pipe in a bit," he said, and restored the tobacco jar.

Mr. Maydig had followed all these later changes in a sort of ejaculatory silence. He stared at Mr. Fotheringay and, in a very gingerly manner, picked up the tobacco jar, examined it, replaced it on the table. "*Well!*" was the only expression of his feelings.

"Now, after that it's easier to explain what I came about," said Mr. Fotheringay; and proceeded to a lengthy and involved narrative of his strange experiences, beginning with the affair of the lamp in the Long Dragon and complicated by persistent allusions to Winch. As he went on, the transient pride Mr. Maydig's consternation had caused passed away; he became the very ordinary Mr. Fotheringay of everyday intercourse again. Mr. Maydig listened intently, the tobacco jar in his hand, and his bearing changed also with the course of the narrative. Presently, while Mr. Fotheringay was dealing with the miracle of the third egg, the minister interrupted with a fluttering extended hand—

"It is possible," he said. "It is credible. It is amazing, of course, but it reconciles a number of difficulties. The power to work miracles is a gift—a peculiar quality like genius or second sight—hitherto it has come very rarely and to exceptional people. But in this case . . . I have always wondered at the miracles of Mahomet, and at Yogi's miracles, and the miracles of Madame Blavatsky. But, of course! Yes, it is simply a gift! It carries out so beautifully the arguments of that great thinker—" Mr. Maydig's voice sank "—his grace the Duke of Argyll. Here we plumb some profounder law—deeper than the ordinary laws of nature. Yes—yes. Go on. Go on!"

Mr. Fotheringay proceeded to tell of his misadventure with Winch, and Mr. Maydig, no longer overawed or scared, began to jerk his limbs about and interject astonishment. "It's this what troubled me most," proceeded Mr. Fotheringay; "it's this I'm most mijitly in want of advice for; of course he's at San Francisco—wherever San Francisco may be—but of course it's awkward for both of us, as you'll see, Mr. Maydig. I don't see how he can understand what has happened, and I dare say he's scared and exasperated something tremendous, and trying to get at me. I dare say he keeps on starting off to come here. I send him back, by a miracle every few hours, when I think of it. And of course, that's a thing he won't be able to understand, and it's bound to annoy him; and, of course, if he takes a ticket every time it will cost him a lot of money. I done the best I could for him, but of course it's difficult for him to put himself in my place. I thought afterwards that his clothes might have got scorched, you know—if Hades is all it's supposed to be—before I shifted him. In that case I suppose they'd have locked him up in San Francisco. Of course I willed him a new suit of clothes on him directly I thought of it. But, you see, I'm already in a deuce of a tangle—"

Mr. Maydig looked serious. "I see you are in a tangle. Yes, it's a difficult position. How you are to end it. . . ." He became diffuse and inconclusive.

"However, we'll leave Winch for a little and discuss the larger question. I don't think this is a case of the black art or anything of the sort. I don't think there is any taint of criminality about it at all, Mr. Fotheringay—none whatever, unless you are suppressing material facts. No, it's miracles—pure miracles—miracles, if I may say so, of the very highest class."

He began to pace the hearthrug and gesticulate, while Mr. Fotheringay sat with his arm on the table and his head on his arm, looking worried. "I don't see how I'm to manage about Winch," he said.

"A gift of working miracles—apparently a very powerful gift," said Mr. Maydig, "will find a way about Winch—never fear. My dear sir, you are a most important man—a man of the most astonishing possibilities. As evidence, for example! And in other ways, the things you may do. . . ."

"Yes, I've thought of a thing or two," said Mr. Fotheringay. "But—some of the things came a bit twisty. You saw that fish at first? Wrong sort of bowl and wrong sort of fish. And I thought I'd ask someone."

"A proper course," said Mr. Maydig, "a very proper course—altogether the proper course." He stopped and looked at Mr. Fotheringay. "It's practically an unlimited gift. Let us test your powers, for instance. If they really *are* . . . If they really are all they seem to be."

And so, incredible as it may seem, in the study of the little house behind the Congregational Chapel, on the evening of Sunday, November 10, 1896, Mr. Fotheringay, egged on and inspired by Mr. Maydig, began to work miracles. The reader's attention is specially and definitely called to that date. He will object, probably has already objected, that certain points in this story are improbable, that if any things of the sort already described had indeed occurred, they would have been in all the papers a year ago. The details immediately following he will find particularly hard to accept, because among other things they involve the conclusion that he or she, the reader in question, must have been killed in a violent and unprecedented manner more than a year ago. Now a miracle is nothing if not improbable, and, as a matter of fact, the reader *was* killed in a violent and unprecedented manner a year ago. In the subsequent course of this story it will become perfectly clear and credible, as every right-minded and reasonable reader will admit. But this is not the place for the end of the story, being but little beyond the hither side of the middle. And at first the miracles worked by Mr. Fotheringay were timid little miracles—little things with the cups and parlor fitments, as feeble as the miracles of Theosophists, and, feeble as they were, they were received with awe by his collaborator. He would have preferred to settle the Winch business out of hand, but Mr. Maydig would not let him. But after they had worked a dozen of these domestic trivialities, their sense of power grew, their imagination began to show signs of stimulation, and their ambition enlarged. Their first larger enterprise was due to hunger and the negligence of Mrs. Minchin, Mr. Maydig's housekeeper. The meal to which the minister conducted Mr. Fotheringay was certainly ill-laid and uninviting as refreshment for two industrious miracle-workers; but they were seated, and Mr. Maydig was descanting in sorrow rather than in anger upon his housekeeper's shortcomings, before it occurred to Mr. Fotheringay that an opportunity lay before him. "Don't you think, Mr. Maydig," he said, "if it isn't a liberty, I—"

"My dear Mr. Fotheringay! Of course! No—I didn't think."

Mr. Fotheringay waved his hand. "What shall we have?" he said, in a large, inclusive spirit, and, at Mr. Maydig's order, revised the supper very thoroughly. "As for me," he said, eyeing Mr. Maydig's selection, "I am always particularly fond of a tankard of stout and a nice Welsh rarebit, and I'll order that. I ain't much given to burgundy," and forthwith stout and Welsh rarebit promptly appeared at his command. They sat long at their supper, talking like equals, as Mr. Fotheringay presently perceived with a glow of surprise and gratification, of all the miracles they would presently do. "And, by the by, Mr. Maydig," said Mr. Fotheringay, "I might perhaps be able to help you—in a domestic way."

"Don't quite follow," said Mr. Maydig, pouring out a glass of miraculous old burgundy.

Mr. Fotheringay helped himself to a second Welsh rarebit out of vacancy, and took a mouthful. "I was thinking," he said, "I might be able (*chum, chum*) to work (*chum, chum*) a miracle with Mrs. Minchin (*chum, chum*)—make her a better woman."

Mr. Maydig put down the glass and looked doubtful. "She's—She strongly objects to interference, you know, Mr. Fotheringay. And— as a matter of fact—it's well past eleven and she's probably in bed and asleep. Do you think, on the whole—"

Mr. Fotheringay issued his orders, and a little less at their ease, perhaps, the two gentlemen proceeded with their repast. Mr. May- dig was enlarging on the changes he might expect in his house- keeper next day, with an optimism that seemed even to Mr. Fotheringay's supper senses a little forced and hectic, when a series of confused noises from upstairs began. Their eyes exchanged inter- rogations, and Mr. Maydig left the room hastily. Mr. Fotheringay heard him calling up to his housekeeper and then his footsteps going softly up to her.

In a minute or so the minister returned, his step light, his face radiant. "Wonderful!" he said, "and touching! Most touching!"

He began pacing the hearthrug. "A repentance—a most touching repentance—through the crack of the door. Poor woman! A most wonderful change! She had got up. She must have got up at once. She had got up out of her sleep to smash a private bottle of brandy in her box. And to confess it, too! . . . But this gives us—it opens—a most amazing vista of possibilities. If we can work this miraculous change in *her* . . ."

"The thing's unlimited seemingly," said Mr. Fotheringay. "And about Mr. Winch—"

"Altogether unlimited." And from the hearthrug Mr. Maydig, waving the Winch difficulty aside, unfolded a series of wonderful proposals—proposals he invented as he went along.

Now what those proposals were does not concern the essentials of this story. Suffice it that they were designed in a spirit of infinite benevolence, the sort of benevolence that used to be called post- prandial. Suffice it, too, that the problem of Winch remained un- solved. Nor is it necessary to describe how far that series got to its fulfillment. There were astonishing changes. The small hours found Mr. Maydig and Mr. Fotheringay careering across the chilly market square under the still moon, in a sort of ecstasy of thaumaturgy, Mr. Maydig all flap and gesture, Mr. Fotheringay short and bristling, and no longer abashed at his greatness. They had reformed every drunkard in the Parliamentary division, changed all the beer and alcohol to water (Mr. Maydig had overruled Mr. Fotheringay on this point), they had, further, greatly improved the railway communication of the place, drained Flinder's swamp, improved the soil of One Tree Hill, and cured the vicar's wart. And they were going to see what could be done with the injured pier at South Bridge. "The place," gasped Mr. Maydig, "won't be the same place tomorrow. How surprised and thankful everyone will be!" And just at that moment the church clock struck three.

"I say," said Mr. Fotheringay, "that's three o'clock! I must be getting back. I've got to be at business by eight. And besides, Mrs. Wimms—"

"We're only beginning," said Mr. Maydig, full of the sweetness of unlimited power. "We're only beginning. Think of all the good we're doing. When people wake—"

"But—" said Mr. Fotheringay.

Mr. Maydig gripped his arm suddenly. His eyes were bright and wild. "My dear chap," he said, "there's no hurry. Look—" he pointed to the moon at the zenith "—Joshua!"

"Joshua?" said Mr. Fotheringay.

"Joshua," said Mr. Maydig. "Why not? Stop it."

Mr. Fotheringay looked at the moon.

"That's a bit tall," he said after a pause.

"Why not?" said Mr. Maydig. "Of course it doesn't stop. You stop the rotation of the earth, you know. Time stops. It isn't as if we were doing harm."

"H'm!" said Mr. Fotheringay. "Well." He sighed. "I'll try. Here—"

He buttoned up his jacket and addressed himself to the habitable globe, with as good an assumption of confidence as lay in his power. "Jest stop rotating, will you?" said Mr. Fotheringay.

Incontinently he was flying head over heels through the air at the rate of dozens of miles a minute. In spite of the innumerable circles he was describing per second, he thought; for thought is wonderful—sometimes as sluggish as flowing pitch, sometimes as instantaneous as light. He thought in a second, and willed. "Let me come down safe and sound. Whatever else happens, let me down safe and sound."

He willed it only just in time, for his clothes, heated by his rapid flight through the air, were already beginning to singe. He came down with a forcible but by no means injurious bump in what appeared to be a mound of fresh-turned earth. A large mass of metal and masonry, extraordinarily like the clock tower in the middle of the market square, hit the earth near him, ricocheted over him, and flew into stonework, bricks, and masonry, like a bursting bomb. A hurtling cow hit one of the larger blocks and smashed like an egg. There was a crash that made all the most violent crashes of his past life seem like the sound of falling dust, and this was followed by a descending series of lesser crashes. A vast wind roared throughout earth and heaven, so that he could scarcely lift his head to look. For a while he was too breathless and astonished even to see where he was or what had happened. And his first movement was to feel his head and reassure himself that his streaming hair was still his own.

"Lord!" gasped Mr. Fotheringay, scarce able to speak for the gale. "I've had a squeak! What's gone wrong? Storms and thunder. And only a minute ago a fine night. It's Maydig set me on to this sort of thing. *What* a wind! If I go on fooling in this way I'm bound to have a thundering accident!

"Where's Maydig?

"What a confounded mess everything's in!"

He looked about him so far as his flapping jacket would permit. The appearance of things was really extremely strange. "The sky's all right anyhow," said Mr. Fotheringay. "And that's about all that is right. And even there it looks like a terrific gale coming up. But there's the moon overhead. Just as it was just now. Bright as midday. But as for the rest—Where's the village? Where's—where's anything? And what on earth set this wind a-blowing? *I* didn't order no wind."

Mr. Fotheringay struggled to get to his feet in vain, and after one failure, remained on all fours, holding on. He surveyed the moonlit world to leeward, with the tails of his jacket streamlining over his head. "There's something seriously wrong," said Mr. Fotheringay. "And what it is—goodness knows."

Far and wide nothing was visible in the white glare through the haze of dust that drove before a screaming gale but tumbled masses of earth and heaps of inchoate ruins, no trees, no houses, no familiar shapes, only a wilderness of disorder vanishing at last into the darkness beneath the whirling columns and streamers, the lightnings and thunderings of a swiftly rising storm. Near him in the livid glare was something that might once have been an elm tree, a smashed mass of splinters, shivered from boughs to base, and further a twisted mass of iron girders—only too evidently the viaduct—rose out of the piled confusion.

You see, when Mr. Fotheringay had arrested the rotation of the solid globe, he had made no stipulation concerning the trifling movables upon its surface. And the earth spins so fast that the surface at its equator is traveling at rather more than half that pace. So that the village, and Mr. Maydig, and Mr. Fotheringay, and everybody and everything had been jerked violently forward at about nine miles per second that is to say, much more violently than if they had been fired out of a cannon. And every human being, every living creature, every house, and every tree—all the world as we know it—had been so jerked and smashed and utterly destroyed. That was all.

These things Mr. Fotheringay did not, of course, fully appreciate. But he perceived that his miracle had miscarried, and with that a great disgust of miracles came upon him. He was in darkness now, for the clouds had swept together and blotted out his momentary glimpse of the moon, and the air was full of fitful struggling tortured wraiths of hail. A great roaring of wind and waters filled earth and sky, and, peering under his hand through the dust and sleet to windward, he saw by the play of the lightnings a vast wall of water pouring towards him.

"Maydig!" screamed Mr. Fotheringay's feeble voice amid the elemental uproar. "Here!—Maydig!

"Stop!" cried Mr. Fotheringay to the advancing water. "Oh, for goodness' sake, stop!

"Just a moment," said Mr. Fotheringay to the lightnings and thunder. "Stop just a moment while I collect my thoughts. . . . And now what shall I do?" he said. "What *shall* I do? Lord! I wish Maydig was about.

"I know," said Mr. Fotheringay. "And for goodness' sake let's have it right *this* time."

He remained on all fours, leaning against the wind, very intent to have everything right.

"Ah!" he said. "Let nothing what I'm going to order happen until I say 'Off!' . . . Lord! I wish I'd thought of that before!"

He lifted his little voice against the whirlwind, shouting louder and louder in the vain desire to hear himself speak. "Now then!—here goes! Mind about that what I said just now. In the first place, when all I've got to say is done, let me lose my miraculous power, let my will become just like anybody else's will, and all these dangerous miracles be stopped. I don't like them. I'd rather I didn't work 'em. Ever so much. That's the first thing. And the second is—let me be back just before the miracles begin; let everything be just as it was before that blessed lamp turned up. It's a big job, but it's the last. Have you got it? No more miracles, everything as it was—me back in the Long Dragon just before I drank my half pint. That's it! Yes."

He dug his fingers into the mould, closed his eyes, and said "Off!"

Everything became perfectly still. He perceived that he was standing erect.

"So *you* say," said a voice.

He opened his eyes. He was in the bar of the Long Dragon, arguing about miracles with Toddy Beamish. He had a vague sense of some great thing forgotten that instantaneously passed. You see, except for the loss of his miraculous power, everything was back as it had been; his mind and memory therefore were now just as they had been at the time when this story began. So that he knew absolutely nothing of all that is told here, knows nothing of all that is told here to this day. And among other things, of course, he still did not believe in miracles.

"I tell you that miracles, properly speaking, can't possibly happen," he said, "whatever you like to hold. And I'm prepared to prove it up to the hilt."

"That's what *you* think," said Toddy Beamish, and "Prove it if you can."

"Looky here, Mr. Beamish," said Mr. Fotheringay. "Let us clearly understand what a miracle is. It's something contrariwise to the course of nature done by power of Will . . ."

Spectre in Blue Doubleknit

by Bruce Bethke

As his eyes adjusted to the darkness, he found Richard and Louisa sprawled on the bed, asleep. Quietly, so as not to disturb them, he stepped out of the bedroom and wandered through the apartment, correlating.

The tattered green easy chair, the cigarette-scarred sofa, the disorganized heap of textbooks on the coffee table; good. The pint mason jar of marijuana, the pyramid of empty Schmidt "Sportspak" beer cans, the cold half-cup of coffee etching a ring on the top of the stereo speaker; all was exactly as he had pictured it. He headed for the kitchen, for the final test.

Blue mercury streetlight spilled through the uncurtained windows, allowing him to clearly read the date of the *Tribune* sports section lying on the radiator. May 6, 1975. Perfect. He'd manifested right on target.

He stepped back into the bedroom, and took a gentle moment to compare the dozing man to himself. The sleeper had a full head of thick, curly, brown hair, a smooth, clear, untroubled face, and a trim, muscular, one hundred seventy pound physique. His own body was another story; his hairline had receded clear back to the crown of his head, his ulcer was developing a resistance to Maalox, and he couldn't keep his weight under two forty on a bet.

A small twinge of sympathy passed through him as he looked down at the man on the bed. Twenty-two-year-old Richard Luck had such *possibilities* ahead of him. And he was about to toss them all away . . . That thought choked off the sympathy. He leapt up on the bed and kicked young Richard hard in the ribs.

His foot passed right through, of course.

With a modest sigh of disappointment, he lay down through the sleeper and started insinuating himself into the dream.

Richard and Carynne go to Marty's Deli for lunch, and as soon as they get inside the door he sees Louisa working behind the counter. He yells, "I can explain!" but she picks up that enormous knife she uses to slice the French bread, so he grabs Carynne's hand and starts running.

They run across the street, jump the fence, and start through the railroad tunnel, but when they get about halfway he sees his mother coming from the other end. "It's okay, Mom," he says, "I know what I'm doing." She just stands there blocking the end of the tunnel (which has become so narrow he's got to stoop to stand in it), and he can hear Louisa coming up behind, so he turns and drags Carynne down a side passage he hadn't noticed before. They emerge into the corridor by the physics classrooms in the basement of North Hall and round the corner to find the stairwell door locked from the other side, so Carynne pulls him into one of the dark classrooms and—my God, how'd she get to be so naked?—and pulls him tight against her smooth, cool skin, and pulls him down, and pulls him—

The fluorescent lights flare on; he and Carynne are entwined, naked, on the sofa in his parents' basement, and his father is standing there scowling. Except it isn't his father, it's the pudgy guy in the navy blue doubleknit suit! The pudgy guy walks over, picks up Richard's jeans off the floor, throws them at him, and says, "Wake up, dirtball. We need to talk."

"Dammit, you again? Bug off!"

"You can chase wet dreams later. This is important."

"Who *are* you?" Richard demands. "What are you doing here?" Carynne has vanished.

" 'Is it bigger than a breadbox?' " the pudgy guy mocks him. "What do you *think* I'm doing here? This is a premonition. I'm you from twenty years in the future."

"I'm going to look like *that* when I'm forty?" Richard wakes with a start, and finds himself drenched in cold sweat.

No, as Richard lay in the dark thinking about it, maybe he hadn't waked up. He was in his bedroom for sure, in his bed, staring at the ceiling; everything *seemed* real enough, but he was utterly unable to move. He believed the woman sleeping next to him was Louisa, but an effort to roll over and confirm that got him nowhere.

And then there was this curious sense of *detachment* he felt. He was lying on the bed, and at the same time lying under the bed among the old sneakers and dust bunnies, and sitting perched like a cat on the windowsill, and gently floating up near the ceiling, noting that the lintel moldings hadn't been cleaned in years. He thought his eyes were open, but the multiple viewpoints cast some doubt on that.

Deep in the back of his head, his rational daytime self panicked and started screaming something about being dead or paralyzed or at the very least psychotic, but Richard ignored the noise. His windowsill self (which was looking more like a cat with every passing moment) had spotted a sort of umbilical cord between his bedded and ceiling selves, and ambled over to investigate. The thought occurred to him then that if he could just get a window open, he'd be able to fly his ceiling self like a kite.

Whatever state his mind was in, it certainly wasn't awake.

"It's called lucid sleep," someone suggested, helpfully. "Your forebrain is awake, but your voluntary nervous system doesn't know that yet."

Richard managed to round up most of his attention and become aware of another presence in the room. A presence sitting on the foot of his bed, to be exact.

"Hello!" the spectre in the blue polyester suit said cheerfully.

With an unpleasant lack of startle reflex, Richard's eyes didn't snap open. "Omigod," Richard . . . *said*, for lack of a better word. His lips barely moved, no sound came out, and yet the thought was expressed. "Naw. Don't hallucinate like this from pot. Must be still dreaming." He turned his attention out to graze and tried to slide back into deep sleep.

"Stop it!" said the apparition. "Don't drag me back into dream-state again."

"Give me two good reasons," Richard mumbled.

"Lucid sleep is the only state I can reliably communicate with you in. If you go back to normal sleep I'm just a nightmare."

"A nightmare with lousy timing," Richard corrected. "I was finally going to score with Carynne."

"You want to go back to sleep? Never see me again?"

"Who, *me?*" Richard said, as sarcastically as possible. "Did *I* say that?"

The apparition leaned in close to bedded Richard's face. "Well, then get *this* through your little pea-sized brain, boy! You won't be rid of me until you hear me out. You don't know *half* the nightmare I can be!"

With the equivalent of a resigned sigh, Richard turned back from deep sleep. "Okay. Accepting—just for the moment—that this isn't some bizarre twist in the dream, how do you do it? I mean, you've been invading my sleep all week."

"Sympathetic resonance. My consciousness resonates inside your empty head."

"Insults from hallucinations I don't need," Richard snarled. The tiny flare of anger led to a twitch in his leg, which disturbed Louisa. She rolled a bit, *mmphed* something, and put an arm across Richard's chest.

The apparition bit his lip. "I'm pre-memory, okay? I'm an up-time projection of your own future consciousness. Look, it's all in the Muldoon book; read about it later. I can only hyperdynamize like this for about thirty minutes, so you'll excuse me if I get to the point."

"Aha!" Richard gleefully seized an idea. "*I* know where you come from. It's that silly parapsychology course, isn't it? I skipped the readings and now my subconscious is punishing me for it." He wished he were awake enough to resolutely cross his arms. "Well, I don't care if I get a Z-minus on the final. I got a B on the mid-term and an A on my paper, so I pass no matter what. I am *not* going to read any more of that garf; I've got a marketing final to worry about."

"Gah!" The pudgy spectre slapped himself on the forehead. "You *jerk!* Sure, there's so much fluff in the course it says *Do Not Remove Tag Under Penalty of Law* in the syllabus. Some of it is still true. If you—but no, all *you* can think about is Louisa's breasts and Carynne's tight jeans. *I* had to start studying projection all over again when I was thirty-five because *you* took such lousy notes. It took me six years to get here."

Louisa dragged an arm up, pushed a few strands of her long brown hair out of her face, and whimpered, "Whasmatter honey?" before nodding off again.

Richard focused on her, then on the spectre sitting across his knees. "Can she hear?" he whispered.

The pudgy man paled. "Jeez, I hope not. I'm supposed to be manifesting to you only. Maybe there's some spillover."

"Well, try to keep it down, will you?"

"Okay." They stared at each other in uneasy silence until Richard realized the older man was composing himself to deliver a lecture, just as Richard's father used to.

Richard quickly spoke first. "So you're my future, huh? How's IBM doing?" It had the desired effect; he totally blew away the older man's composure. "Y'see, I figure I can borrow another three grand at two points on my tuition loan and invest—"

"Kid!" the older man barked. "I came here to prevent the biggest mistake in your life. Not to turn a few lousy bucks."

"Slack off, okay?" Richard said defensively. "I mean, I'm having some trouble dealing with this, y'know? It's not every day my future pops in for a chat." Richard let his viewpoint drift back to the cat. He felt comfortable being a cat. "But I do know that if this were *really* happening, I wouldn't miss an opportunity like this. You sure you're my future?" The man just glared.

"Okay. Accepting for the sake of argument that you're who you say you are, don't you know that coming back is absurd? If you convince me to change my future, then the thing you came back to warn me about doesn't happen, so you don't—"

"I'm trying to save his life," the older man growled under his breath, "and he wants to argue jerk-off philosophy with me." He pointed at Richard and raised his voice. "Look, kid, every time you causality paradox I'll say branching alternate time-line. Personally I think you get premonitions from unchosen futures all the time; you're just too dimwitted to notice them. It took me five tries to get you lucid."

"But if this works, won't you disintegrate or something?"

"I don't know. And frankly I don't care."

Richard whistled low. "That bad, huh?" and watched as the pudgy man slowly, portentously, nodded. "There you go, getting all ominous again. You came *back* from the future, didn't you? That means the world doesn't get nuked into slag in the next twenty years. Hey, I feel better already!"

"Worse things can happen than the end of the world."

"You out of a job?" Richard suggested. "Economy collapse in the late eighties like Greenburg says it will?"

The older man angrily dug his ghost fingers into sleeping Richard's leg. "Is that all you want from the future? Money? Kid, your priorities are *all* screwed up. 'Am I successful?' Sure, I'm successful. I'm national sales manager for IMDC; I make—"

Richard interrupted. "Who?"

"Integrated Micro Data Corp. They don't exist yet."

"Damn." Cat/Richard twitched his tail with vexation. "And how much did you say you earn?" His interest perked up.

"For chrissakes, what difference does it make?!"

"I only ask," Richard pointed out, "because I want to know why a successful man wears such an ugly suit."

"It's part of the projection," the older man explained, patience struggling with exasperation. "I'm not physically here, of course. I can only travel by avatar—symbol—and my avatar is a sweaty guy in a cheap suit. It's not a true image; in the real world I wouldn't be caught dead wearing white patent leather loafers and a matching vest."

"*Sure*," said the cat, dubiously, "and—"

"Dammit, stop changing the subject! I'm trying to tell you about real happiness!"

"Ah," Richard said, with dawning comprehension. "Now we come to the point. You advise choosing spiritual fulfillment over material success, right? Thanks, I'll think it over, good night."

"Louisa's a nice girl. Marry her."

Richard licked a paw, rubbed his ear, and then sat in thoughtful silence. At last he spoke. "You traveled twenty years to tell me *that?*"

"She's a sweet kid. The two of you could be very happy."

"That's *it?*"

"No, there's one thing more. You're so worried about this marketing final, you've talked Carynne Reichmann into giving you some coaching this weekend. Break the date."

"But if I do that," Richard protested, "I'll flunk. And if I flunk marketing, how do I get to be a national sales manager?"

"Come off it," the older man said, annoyed. "You've had the hots for Carynne all year; this is just an excuse to take one last crack at her before she graduates."

Richard looked chagrined. "Okay, I admit I was dreaming about her. But hey, she's the original Snow Queen. Nothing will happen."

"Dickie boy," the older man said, clucking his tongue, "you forget who you're lying to. I *remember* what you're thinking. And right now, you're thinking that if you were getting somewhere with Carynne you'd toss Louisa out the door in a minute." The older man suddenly grabbed cat/Richard roughly by the neck, held him nose-to-nose, and spoke in low, dark tones. "*So get this straight, pinhead!* This Saturday, Carynne not only coaches you for the exam, but she also invites you into her bed. You'll come dragging your lethargic ass home Sunday at six in the morning to find Louisa already packed."

The cat stopped squirming. "Oh?"

"Of all the things you could possibly do in this universe, I promise you, you do *not* want to do that."

"Are you out of your mind?" Richard shrieked. "Carynne's beautiful! Brilliant! Everything I ever wanted in a woman!"

"Including selfish? Demanding? Manipulative?"

Richard fastened on an idea. "That's it. You're right about alternate time-lines; I'm the wrong past for you. *My* Carynne's nothing like—"

"Of course she isn't. Now."

Richard paused. "Okay, tell you what. If it turns out you're right, I'll dump her in a few years."

"Idiot!" the older man thundered, "in six months you marry her! In a year she pushes you into going back to school full-time—while holding down a full-time job—to get your MBA. In five years she's into leased BMW's and semiannual vacations in the Virgin Islands, neither of which you can afford; by the time you're thirty your hairline's back *here*," the older man karate-chopped himself on the crown of his head, "your stomach's in real trouble, and Carynne has realized you aren't half as ambitious as she is."

"So? Lots of people survive divorce."

"You, unfortunately, stay married. Always hoping things will improve, and always getting affection from her the same way Muffy gets dog yummies: only when you roll over and beg."

"*Muffy?*"

The older man dropped the cat on the bed. "Her lhasa apso."

"You mean one of those small, yapping . . . ? Eesh," said Richard, disgusted. He jumped down to the floor, sniffed at his self lying under the bed, then looked up at the older man and cocked his head quizzically. Somehow, no matter how hard he tried, he found it hard to accept such grim portents from a caricature of a salesman. "So it won't work, huh?"

"It can't work," the spectre explained. "You two are incompatible at the most primal level. I mean—look, you've got three avatars now, right? That's 'cause your life path isn't decided yet.

"That inert spud under the bed—that's *me*. Or rather what Carynne will make me out of. And that one up there," he gestured at the Richard floating near the ceiling, "I don't know what future he represents.

"But right now, your primary manifestation is as a cat. That's your favorite avatar; the tomcat.

"She can't stand cats unless they're neutered, declawed, and kept in the house. Even then she prefers docile, obedient, nearly asexual dogs. You're a cat person. She's a dog person. It's that basic."

Richard began pacing back and forth between the bed and the radiator, twitching his tail anxiously. "Look, there's got to be something redeeming about the marriage. Kids?" he suggested, hopefully.

"Two daughters who are carbon copies of their mother. They're into horses. You have any idea how much a ten-year-old who wants a horse can whine?"

"Friends, then?"

"Hers. Frank and Gordy are too plebeian for her tastes and you won't see them again after '77."

Richard looked up, into the older man's face. There was tremendous bitterness and inner-directed anger there, eating away at the man like a cancer. And yet, there was something else. A soft— wistfulness? Ignoring the cat for the moment, the older man had turned and was watching Louisa sleep. Hesitantly, tenderly, he reached out a ghost hand and touched her leg. She didn't stir. Quickly, as if she were a delicate treasure he feared his rude touch would ruin, he pulled his hand away and turned around, to find the cat looking straight into his eyes.

"Anyway, that's what I came here to tell you," the older man said softly. "It's your decision now." He turned to look at Louisa again. "I'll be snapping back to my own time in a minute or two."

That, at last, was what touched cat/Richard. For all the bluster, it was the brief, unguarded slice of tenderness that convinced Richard the older man was telling the truth. Unable to think of anything more comforting, he rubbed up against the man's legs. Older Richard noticed, reached down to scratch him behind the ears, and whispered, "Take good care of her, okay?" Before cat/Richard could answer, older Richard suddenly sat up straight, blanched white with pain, and clamped his fists to the sides of his head.

"What's wrong?" the cat mewed. "Can I help?"

"*Weird!*" gasped the older man. "Like—*hot maggots* in my brain! Snapback never felt like this be . . ." In that instant, both of them became aware of another presence in the room.

"I thought I'd find you here."

"Carynne!" older Richard shouted. Cat/Richard spun around to find a thin, deeply wrinkled, ascetic old woman wearing an elegant white dress and sitting stiffly erect in a Louis Quatorze armchair (which she had apparently brought with her), holding a lhasa apso in her lap. "And your little dog, too!" At that moment the dog spotted cat/Richard and, with a pugnacious yap, jumped out of the woman's arms.

"Muffy the fourth!" she commanded. "Heel!"

Instinctively, cat/Richard leapt up onto the bed, turned to face the dog, and let out his most vile and guttural hiss. The dog stopped short, considered the *very* sharp claws Richard had extended, and dutifully trotted back to Carynne. "I'm sorry," she said, addressing the cat. "Muffy's so excitable." She lifted the dog into her lap, then turned to older Richard. "Now, if you're done lying to this young man . . ."

"You can't be here!" older Richard gasped.

"Don't look so surprised, dear," the woman said. "If you can learn projection, I can."

"But—time transference only works between the same mind!"

"Dickie," she admonished, "as usual you're too stubborn to admit you're wrong. I *am* here; therefore I *can* be." She glanced at cat/Richard. "I only hope I'm in time."

"In time for what?" cat/Richard asked, suspiciously.

"I don't know what he's told you so far," Carynne explained, smiling, "but Dickie was going through a premature mid-life crisis when he started this projection business. Seems he had a habit of picking up teenage bimbos on his sales trips, and when his weight hit two fifty they started laughing in his face. Gave his poor little male ego a terrible shock."

Cat/Richard turned sharply on older Richard, forming the question.

"She isn't *my* Carynne," older Richard protested.

"I certainly am!" she countered.

"But you're so—"

"*Old?*" she completed. "Did you think you had a monopoly on projecting into your past? All this—" she pointed a long, polished fingernail at older Richard, "including *your* present, is *my* past!"

"How did you—"

"You hid your notes well, Dickie. I didn't find out about this projection nonsense until I went through your papers after you died."

"Died!" cat/Richard yowled.

"Don't listen to her," the older man said quickly. "She's trying to get you rattled."

"And so I've come back to provide some balance," Carynne continued, addressing the cat. "Not that it really matters what he tells you. He can't possibly succeed—causality paradox, you know—I'm just disappointed that he spent years trying."

"Kid?" the older man prompted, panic rising in his voice. Cat/Richard found himself wishing Carynne had flown in, cackling, on a broomstick; it would've made things so much easier. Instead, the glimpse of his own mortality had triggered a surge of guilt, and he was busy remembering just how convincingly he could lie to himself when he wanted something. "Listen, she's . . ." older Richard started, then paused when he saw the way the cat was glaring, first at him, then at Carynne.

"He's trying to decide who to believe," Carynne observed.

Older Richard turned on her. "You'll ruin *everything!*" he hissed. "You weren't satisfied with making *my* life miserable; you're trying to screw up all my *possible* lives." Closing his eyes, he sat up rigidly and grimaced with fierce concentration. "I won't let you do it," he whispered. "I'll force you out."

"Really, Dickie dear," Carynne said, shaking her head slowly, "I should think by now you'd know better than to try a contest of wills with me."

"I am restructuring the projection . . ." he muttered.

"And I'm still here," she said nonchalantly. "At the risk of reminding you of our sex life: are you finished?"

With a gasp, older Richard broke concentration and staggered to his feet, defiantly facing Carynne. "You think you've won, don't you?" he snarled. "I'll be back!"

"No, you won't," Carynne stated flatly.

"Stop me!"

Carynne shrugged. "If you insist. Dickie dear, do you understand how dreamstate time is purely subjective? I can control my projections far better than you ever could." She rapped her knuckles on the arm of the chair for emphasis. "In a month of real time I can haunt you for the rest of your sad little life, if you force it on me."

"*No!*" shouted cat/Richard. "Don't give in, Dickie!" He urgently tried to pull his selves together and focus all his awareness through the cat. "We can beat her! If we unite—"

"Goodbye, Dickie," Carynne smiled. A silvery umbilicus snaked

down from somewhere and started entwining older Richard. Cat/
Richard leapt at it, claws flailing, but the cord was unyielding as cold
marble. It fell about older Richard in heavy loops; he struggled
briefly, but when the end dropped down and the whole mass began
constricting, he gave up.

"*Dickie?*" the cat screamed.

"I'm sorry," came a muffled voice from inside the coils. "I can't
hold off snapback any longer." In the space of a few seconds, the
coils tightened to a mass the size of a fist and then abruptly vanished, leaving a momentary pucker in the air.

On the night of June 27th, 1995, Richard Luck woke up at two A.M.
with a start so sudden it disturbed his wife, Carynne.

"What's the matter, Dickie?" she asked.

"Oh . . . just had a *weird* dream."

"That's all right," she mumbled. Pulling him close, she gave him a
peck on the cheek, then rolled over and turned her back to him.
"Go back to sleep, dear. And no more dreaming about Louisa."

He was awake for hours, wondering.

"My, that was easy," Carynne said smugly. "Now, as for *you*," she
took a step towards cat/Richard, who crouched low, raised his
hackles, and bared his teeth. "Oh, very well. Go ahead and have
your little tantrum; you won't escape me, dear." She lifted the lhasa
apso into her arms and began spinning the same glossy cord about
herself, slipping into the coils with practiced ease. "See you Saturday!" she called out gaily.

Cat/Richard frantically nudged at his sleeping self, trying to wake
up. He had a feeling it was critically urgent that he wake up; he desperately needed to tell the whole story to his rational daytime self,
which was still asleep. If he could just remember every detail; if he
could just see Carynne with his waking eyes before she vanished—

As she spun the last loops about herself, Carynne cocked her head
at Louisa's sleeping form. "Dickie dear, you always had such cheap
taste in women. Whatever do you see in *her?*"

Cat/Richard was getting through. Slowly, his sleeping self was beginning to rouse. Slowly, *very* slowly, his daytime mind was grinding into gear. And then—

Carynne vanished. Richard sat up straight in bed. The disturbance woke Louisa. She rolled over, brushed a few strands of her long brown hair out of her face, and mumbled, "Whasmatter, honey? How come you're awake?"

"Damn cat was licking my face."

"Don't *have* a cat," Louisa noted.

"Then we'll get one. I want a cat."

"Silly boy," Louisa murmured. Richard realized that, as was often the case when he woke up in the middle of the night, he needed to go to the bathroom. He slid out of bed.

"Honey?" Louisa called out as he pulled on the terrycloth bathrobe they shared. "Come back to bed?"

"In a minute." He had this odd, nagging feeling in the back of his head, like there was something he needed to remember.

"Don't stay up late reading again. You need sleep, too."

"I know." Something *important*, and it was just beyond his grasp.

"Don't want to fall asleep during your marketing exam." He stopped short at the bedroom door. He *remembered.* Turning around, he came back to the bed, and kissed Louisa.

"Lou, sweetheart," he said gently, "I think it's time we talked about getting married."

"Inna morning, honey," she mumbled. Then, as the words soaked in, her eyes snapped wide open. "Did you say married?" she whispered. He nodded. Louisa threw her arms around Richard and hugged so hard his ribs ached. "I thought you'd *never* ask!"

Somewhere down the twisting braided streams of time, a different Richard began chuckling in his sleep again, which woke his wife one more time. It annoyed Carynne no end when it happened, but there was nothing she could do about it.

At that moment.

Poltergeist

by W. Sherwood Hartman

When Elaine and I found the Trotting Inn, it seemed to be exactly what we had been searching for. The building itself was old, but it seemed to be fairly sound. The kitchen was adequate and the equipment was in good shape. Of course, the bar was in need of redecorating and there were plenty of improvements that could be made, but we had plenty of time for that. The bar did a good day business and the evenings took care of themselves with the restaurant trade. We were close enough to Gettysburg to have the advantage of the summer tourist trade, and were surrounded by small towns that would give us enough business to carry us over during the off season. We were also close enough to Baltimore to be assured of a fresh supply of seafood, the specialty of the house. The owner wanted to retire and the price was reasonable. With a generous assist from the bank, we bought the place.

The first few weeks were pretty hectic. Elaine and I are retired show people and the transition into cook, waitress, and bartender wasn't easy, but the old owner stayed on to help until we got into the swing of things. After a month went by, we were on our own and things had moved into an easy routine. That's when we first heard it. . . .

As I said before, the Trotting Inn is an old building. There's a stairway from the kitchen that leads upstairs to an apartment, but many improvements were needed to make it livable so we decided to wait until after we had the business area refurbished to our tastes before we would undertake remodeling that area. After the first inspection, neither of us had been up there.

It was late on a Saturday night. The last customer had gone and I had locked up. Elaine was washing glasses back of the bar and I was cleaning up in the kitchen. We were both tired, and except for the soft sound of our labor, everything was quiet. Then, from above, there was a solid thump and a sound like an eerie gnome in the throes of agony. The groan faded into silence, but there was a shattering crash in the bar as Elaine dropped a tray of glasses. She spun around the corner into the kitchen and into my arms, shivering like a trapped rabbit. I'll admit I was a bit shaken myself, but I had to rationalize. We'd been busy that night, and it was possible that someone had wandered past me unnoticed in search of the men's room and had gone through the kitchen, up the back stairs, and had fallen asleep in one of the old beds up there. There's no outside entrance to the upstairs, so no one could be trying to break in.

I managed to calm Elaine, then turned on the lights in the stairway and went up. I entered the apartment expecting to find a drunk on the floor, but there was no one. I looked under the beds, in the closets; I searched the place thoroughly. It was empty. There was absolutely no one there, and I went downstairs to reassure Elaine.

We had cleaned up the broken glass behind the bar while I tried to explain that the noise must have been caused by a shift of the timbers in the old building, or that maybe the vibrations of the trucks passing on the highway had caused an old box to fall. Elaine finally had her nerves under control and we were laughing about the whole thing when we left. She got in the car and I switched the lights out inside. Then, just as I was about to turn the key in the lock, I heard the silliest giggle from upstairs that ever came out of nowhere. I locked the door and we went home.

The next three weeks were busy ones. We became acquainted with the local people and were happy with the way they accepted us. The Pennsylvania Dutch are easy to get along with if you don't try to press yourself on them. They like to be a little aggressive with their friendship, and will adopt an outsider like he's their own if he just stands back and waits. Things were working out real fine.

It was a Thursday afternoon when I heard it again. Elaine had gone to Hanover to shop and I was alone at the bar with Cy Rouser, one of the regulars. He lived his life on a farm about three miles east of the Inn. Now his two sons were running the place and he had time on his hands. He'd had two double shots of bourbon, two beers, and a pair of crab cakes for lunch, and was sitting at the end of the bar with his head in his hands, asleep, when I heard the second thump from upstairs.

Cy cocked his head toward the ceiling, grinned, and said, "That's our old buddy."

I started through the kitchen toward the stairs, but Cy called me back. "There's nobody up there," he said. "That's a poltergeist!"

I went back to the bar. "Cy, just exactly what is a poltergeist," I asked, "and what the hell is it doing upstairs over my barroom?"

"It ain't nothing to worry about. . . . It's been here ever since this place was built. My daddy used to tell me about it when I was just a little kid. A poltergeist ain't nothing but a friendly sort of a ghost. He don't bother nobody. He just likes to make a little noise once in a while to get some attention. You know, like he wants you to know he's there. . . . There ain't an inch of harm in a poltergeist!"

I tried to accept Cy's explanation, but it wasn't easy. The noises from above were baffling in their irregularity. It would be a quiet afternoon and sounds like rolling BB shot would tinkle across overhead. Then it would be a crowded Saturday night and the sounds from above would be like King Kong was wrestling with Superman. I had checked time after time, but nothing moved on the second floor. Even the dust lay static. I finally gave up and decided to live with it. I even stopped checking the second floor, and we began to use the stairway to store beer cases. Business was good and I wasn't about to let any silly ghost interfere with it, but it was still disconcerting to be watching a ball game in the afternoon on TV and have the sounds of a roller derby roar down the ceiling during the commercials.

The odd thing was that few of the customers, except for the regulars, noticed the noises. The regulars would cock their heads with a knowing smile and listen, while the others would continue eating or drinking as though nothing were amiss.

Then the thing started with the J. W. Dant bottle. Dant is a good sour mash whisky, but we have very few bourbon drinkers in the area and the bottle had never been opened. It stood on the top shelf of the back bar with the other slow moving whiskies and was dusted every Monday and Thursday.

I had opened up on a Tuesday morning and my first customer had asked for rye and soda. I put ice in the glass, poured a shot over it, reached under the bar for the soda—and came up with the bottle of J. W. Dant. My first thought was that Elaine was trying to be funny and had switched the bottles. The soda bottle was on the shelf where the Dant belonged. I put the Dant back on the shelf, and took the soda bottle back to the bar. Then there was a noise upstairs like a door slamming, giggling, and the rattle of tiny feet running across the floor. I heard them, but the customer didn't seem to hear a thing.

Kenny, my extra bartender, came in at eleven to help over the lunch hour, and I took a break to squeeze past the beer cases in the stairway and make my umpteenth inspection of the upstairs apartment. . . . It was like I figured. No one was there and nothing had moved. I walked through the deserted rooms mumbling to myself and scolding half out loud. Then, as I closed the door and started back downstairs, I heard the giggling again.

From there on, it turned into sort of a game. Most of the time the Dant bottle would be where it belonged, but then I would find it in the refrigerator. The next time it would be wedged behind some beer cases in the walk-in cooler. Then it was in the kitchen with the dinner plates. One morning I found it perched regally on top of the juke box. I found myself loudly berating my unseen tormentor and was usually answered with a tittering silence, although sometimes I seemed to get through and would be rewarded with a gentle thud from above, or a silly giggle.

After a while, the poltergeist seemed to tire of the game and several weeks went by with the Dant bottle staying in its normal place. I was honestly getting bored by the lack of activity. Then I opened up on a Saturday morning and found the bottle in the center of the bar, open and half empty, with a shot glass beside it and a chaser glass with an inch of water in the bottom. I yelled toward the ceiling, "I don't mind your silly games, but if you want to drink my whisky, drink bar whisky. This stuff's expensive!"

The whole upstairs exploded into a series of thumps and happy giggles. I didn't give it the satisfaction of going up to investigate. . . . A customer came in, and the upstairs was quiet for the rest of the day.

It was a busy Saturday and I had little time to contemplate the alcoholic apparition that resided above me. It was a tired one o'clock on Sunday morning when Elaine went home. Kenny had almost everything cleaned up and he left at one thirty. The few customers that were left gradually drifted out until I was left with two late drinkers, neither of whom seemed to be very talkative. I poured myself a nightcap and prepared to outwait them.

They were both strangers to me. The one at the right end of the bar was thin, in his middle thirties, and had a nasty scar under his left eye. The other one appeared to be younger and was built like a weight lifter.

The thin one finished his drink and nodded for a refill. Then he said, "Give us all a drink."

I gave him another, refilled the chunky one, and poured another for myself. Then, when I looked up, I found myself staring into the business end of a .38.

"Okay," the thin one said, "let's lock the place up. We don't want any more company tonight."

The tone of his voice and the deadly whiteness around the knuckles of the fist that held the revolver didn't leave any room for argument. He followed me into the kitchen and I turned the key in the lock of the back door. He stayed on my tail as I flipped the spring locks on the side door and the front. I turned off the outside lights and went back to the bar. The chunky one had a revolver in his hand, too. I was buttonholed.

"Look," I said, reacting as any normal coward would in a similar situation, "take whatever you want and leave. I'm not looking for any trouble."

"You hear that, Joe?" the tall one snickered to his buddy. "He wants us to leave. Ain't that the funniest?" Then he turned to me and I felt a shiver through my spine as I looked into his eyes. They were ice blue and had the chilling finality of an obituary column. "You don't mind if we finish our drink before we go, do you? We might want to stay around for a while."

The chunky one just grinned and they sat toying with their drinks. I poured myself another, figuring that if I were on the way out, I might as well ease the pain.

"Move away from the cash register," the thin one said, and I moved to the lower end of the bar near where he was seated. "Now get the money," he instructed his buddy.

The chunky one came back of the bar, took a paper bag from under the shelf, and started scooping the bills and change into it.

Then there was an explosive bang from upstairs like someone was slamming a door in anger. The chunky one froze at the register.

The thin one stared at the ceiling. Then he turned to me and his eyes were searing with hate and fear. "Okay, wise guy! Who's up there?"

I knew it was useless to tell the truth. "General Custer's ghost and a whole tribe of Indians!" I shouted.

"I'll damned soon find out, you nut!" he screeched at me as he jumped off the stool and went tearing back through the kitchen and up the stairs.

There followed an avalanche of beer cases and a smothered cry. The chunky one brushed by me, and the bottle of J. W. Dant fell off the top shelf just in time for me to catch it and smash it over Chunky's head.

As he slumped to the floor, I got his gun and stepped into the kitchen. All that was visible of the thin one was his hand and the gun. The rest was buried under cardboard shells and empty beer bottles. I stepped on his wrist, took his gun away, and called the state police.

It was about a month later when Elaine suggested that we remodel the upstairs apartment and live there in spite of old buddy, instead of driving back and forth from town. I rejected the idea as being too expensive but, in reality, I didn't want to lose the present tenant. . . .

Magic Nights

by Jas. R. Petrin

Being on a lower branch of the tree, Tom could see only the electric-yellow patch of wall over the curtain and a shadow drifting behind it. Ralph had a higher and better view, one foot on Tom's shoulder, stretched out along his own branch like a cat.

"The body," said Ralph, "must be old Mrs. Scharf, his mother. He's cut her all to pieces in the sink, and now he's stuffing the parts into his pockets."

"Why would he do that? Let me look."

But Ralph didn't budge. Tom could only watch the shadow, a movement of purple behind the screen. For a moment he had in his mind's eye a vision of Mr. Scharf the druggist in his wheezing, pink-faced jollity, stooping over his kitchen sink, red to the elbows, tucking body parts into his shirt and whistling.

"Why'd he do it?" Tom persisted. He was a visiting city cousin, and ignorant.

"She was a witch," said Ralph.

They rustled down out of the owl-shadowed midnight leaves, wrists and elbows all tree sap and scratches. Ralph had torn his trousers.

"I'll say a dog did it."

"It was black," Tom agreed.

"And as big as me. Now, come on. I'll show you the place where they all dance naked."

The two boys ran into the magic night, sailing their bodies like hawks over the grey grass, past the shadowed houses with their windows lit like eyes, past the school, past the church, white and straight, burning like a chimney lamp against the black New England woods. They jumped a low iron fence and walked among graves.

"This is creepy," Tom said.

"No, it isn't," Ralph replied. "It's safe. They don't bury witches in holy ground."

They sprang away on rubber soles, soft as cats.

But in the woods, at the end of the thin path that wound like a vein, near the heap of rusting moon-shadowed cars, a dewy meadow was deserted. No one was naked; no one danced.

They ran home.

It was Ralph's home actually. Ralph's and Aunt Mary's and Uncle Harry's. The boys leaped the three porch stairs and crashed through the door into the kitchen, and Aunt Mary wrestled Ralph out of his trousers, scolding all dogs and boys, then gave them ice cream to eat in the dark on the front porch swing.

"See that house?" said Ralph, pointing his spoon. "It's got bats."

"Where's Uncle?"

"He'll be late. He sees women. Mom's boiling."

Tom was doubtful. Aunt Mary might be warm, but never hot. She was short and full and comfortable, like a pillow. Soft as the cobwebs she pretended to find with her quick, whisking broom. Warm as the afghans she wove around every hard surface and sharp edge in the house.

"Do they fight?" Tom whispered.

"Dad does," Ralph said, "by himself." He pointed to a lamp-lit tree, bent at its waist like an old crooked man with a load of leaves on his back. "They hanged seven ladies there once." Then he added with reluctance, as though it pained him to admit it: "It was a mistake. None of them were witches."

They went in to bed. Hours later Tom awoke to hear Ralph's ragged breath, and Uncle downstairs thundering things and roaring so that the wall shook the book out of the casement to let the window fall down. Uncle might have been storming about the house all alone; Aunt Mary never made a peep; perhaps he'd killed her.

It was a terrible and wonderful thing to hear a drunken man roar in the night.

Tom and Ralph were up with the sun.

"Do you think we'll still be going," whispered Tom, "after last night?"

"Oh, sure, we never miss Cider Days Fair."

There was the belling of pots downstairs, the thump of the freezer door: Aunt Mary in her knitted slippers sculpting breakfast out of frozen blocks. And Uncle in the bathroom, whistling and yodeling under the shower. The boys ate like wolves, Uncle with laughs, growls, and winks, Aunt Mary with smiles so hard and thin you could have picked them up and whittled them with a knife.

They escaped to the car with Uncle. Couldn't get away quick enough from the sudden Eskimo arctic of Aunt Mary's kitchen and her bleak living room tundra.

Apple Cider Day!

The boys held their breath.

Marching bands, sack races, cotton candy, and frowning clowns. Three darts for a quarter, hit a balloon, win a prize. Spill a fat lady into water with a baseball. Toss a small ring around a large bottle, a large ball through a small hole, take any prize from *this* shelf. See the largest horse, almost, in the world. See a chicken spell its name. See old frowning farmers with thick silent wives, girls thin as celery, clutching coins. And an enormous plush bear on a tiny boy.

Roller coasters, mirror mazes, candy apples, wishing wells . . .

"But first," said Uncle, "I got to make a stop."

Ralph winked.

Uncle swerved the car in at Ashton's Music School, Lessons, $10.00 Per Hour. The boys craned their necks. They could just see the top of the ferris wheel, flying its candy cars above the barber shop roof. A huge voice woofed in the distance, loud-speakering them suddenly on a gust of music. Uncle gave them each ten dollars; and Tom nearly mentioned the ten dollars Aunt Mary had already given them, before Ralph kicked him.

"You can walk from here . . ." Uncle began, but the boys were already running. "Meet you later . . ." he echoed his voice down the empty street after them.

From the top of the stairs, Alice Ashton spotted Harold Martins' raw-boned body through the sheers and tingled. She drew the door open in her grandest manner, and he smiled his lopsided grin. He seemed slightly embarrassed.

"Is Loreen here, Ash?"

She pulled him gently in.

"Loreen is upstairs practicing her lesson. And I *won't* have you interrupting her."

It was an elegant hall, she liked to think, cool and shaded. A wide mahogany staircase, a grandmother clock doling out time with easy hollow ticks. Deep varnished silences. She knew Harold Martins from school days; she sometimes thought she might have married him if not for that prissy Mary Smith—what he'd ever seen in *her . . . !* And now he was chasing the college girls: Loreen James could be his daughter. Well, he'd soon learn Alice Ashton had other plans for him.

A bone-chilling moan issued from an upstairs room. Alice lifted herself under her white shift and said sweetly, "She just *murders* the saxophone, doesn't she?"

She led him into the drawing room, shutting out the sound with tall sliding doors. She was careful to pause under the huge, stuffed, glaring owl; she liked to have it behind her, wings half lifted, settling as though to seize her and carry her off; she felt it gave her an air of menace.

"You *will* have a whisky?"

He sat on the chair as though he might break it.

"Just a short one. I've brought the boys up to the fair." His eyes were fixed on the ceiling; you'd have thought his gaze could penetrate to Loreen James through the plaster.

Alice poured a strong one for him and a weak one for herself. She considered how to approach her subject.

"Bob Cole is leaving our group," she said finally.

He nodded. He might not have heard her. His thoughts were elsewhere in the house.

She went on.

"He took your place a year ago. Now he's been transferred out west. So we're left without our thirteen again, Harold."

Harold said nothing.

"We want you to come back."

Harold Martins smiled. He rumpled his hair before he spoke, a mannerism that had always attracted her—a little boy in a man's body.

"I got no time any more for that witchcraft stuff."

"You used to have time for it." She hesitated, then added: "And for me."

But his eyes were still on the ceiling.

"The coven thing was fun," he said, "for a while. But maybe I got tired of it." He hesitated, and then added, "Or maybe you just started getting too mean, Ash. At the beginning you said we'd only do white magic."

She could have reached out and clawed him.

"We aren't an entertainment," she snapped, "to amuse farm boys. What we do is serious business. Sometimes hard things must be done—punishments." She shook her head at him. "I'm sorry now I let you go. I should never have let you get away from us. You took an oath!"

"Bob Cole took an oath."

"That's different. He's not leaving by choice." She tightened her voice. "We must have our thirteen!"

Harold Martins still had his smile; but it was wilting. "I got no time, Ash. You can easy find somebody else."

"No."

She stood up. "I want you." She floated across the thick, silent carpet until she was standing over him. There was an especially loud wail from the room upstairs; even the sliding doors couldn't keep it out. She took his face in her hands. "I want you. . . ."

*   *   *

Steam tractors.

The boys lusted after them.

Bon-fired, black-smoked, and silver-breathed. Blaring their dino-
saur whistles and steel-cleating the ground, the monsters pistoned
by, crewed by snow-haired, tobacco-faced men who winked and
waved.

Ralph had spent nine, and Tom eight of the ten dollars Uncle
Harry had given them. They'd been whirled, swung, tossed, and
dropped. Cotton-candied, orange-popped, and red-stick-licoriced.
Tom had ridden a horse; Ralph, a camel. Neither of them had yet
been properly frightened.

They had reached the end of the midway and stood at the entrance to the House of Horrors. Ralph fingered his money.

"I bet it's a rip-off."

"Look at the pictures," Tom urged; "there's a vampire—"

"Wax," said Ralph.

"There's skeletons—"

"Sticks."

"And ghosts."

"Sheets."

Tom sighed. "Well," he said, "there's a witch."

"Okay," said Ralph.

Up a stair, through a curtain—blackness!

"Holy cow," said Ralph; "it's darker than the crawl hole under the
back of the church."

Down a ramp, round a corner, antenna-fingertips quivering,
like two human ants in a tunnel, moving with short, nervous
steps.

Pow!

A ghost on a stick exploded, shrieking.

"Yahhh!" The boys grabbed one another and jumped away into a
skeleton that plunged on a wire. "Help!" They blundered round a
corner. An air blast zapped them, gusting them up to a snap-open
curtain and a screeching fanged face. And a bat danced on their
heads.

They came to the witch under a blue light, gasping.

She was seated in the wall on a chair, dried-up and twisted, a crone. There was a peaked cap, broken-ended. A parsnip nose. Taloned, broom-strangling fingers, stripe-stockinged ankles sprouting thin as weeds out of buckled shoes. Sunken cheeks, bulbous eyes, warts . . . And a black cat perched on her shoulder as though on a fence.

"There's dust on that cat," whispered Ralph.

The witch flew at them, screaming.

They fled out into the sun.

The midway had not changed. There were still the pressing, laughing, suntanned people, the rides flying against the blue sky. And the ticket seller eyeing them impassively. They stopped to collect themselves, and walked off with dignity.

"That didn't even look like a witch," said Ralph.

"What does a witch look like, then?"

"Like Miss Ashton."

And suddenly here was Uncle Harry to end their afternoon, clapping their shoulders, joking and jostling them into the car, singing them back to the house, where Aunt Mary took them over with a dark look and a jar of liniment.

"They're burnt to a crisp!" she grumbled softly at Uncle. "Haven't you any sense at all?"

Alice Ashton was ready when Loreen James came down the stairs, one final wounded-saxophone wail still shivering the music room dust.

It had been close.

She had moved quickly in the basement room: a lamp in the magic circle; a consecration of salt and water; a summoning of the spirits. Through the circle she channeled the power of the twelve— not nearly as powerful as with the thirteen, of course, which is why she had decided to use her strongest spell.

And to choose from her most precious ingredients.

Hemlock, belladonna, arsenic, cyanide . . .

She had metered her selection carefully from the little pressed-tin boxes, and pestled them into a tincture . . .

She was waiting in the hall when Loreen came smiling down the stairs.

"I don't know where the afternoon went, Miss Ashton. You didn't come back. And I just kept on with page seventeen trying to get it right."

"I'm *so* sorry, my dear. But someone came to the door and I could *not* shake them off. Next lesson free, all right?" She stopped Loreen at the bottom stair. "Just let me have a look at that instrument, dear. It's making the most *unusual* sounds, and I'm sure it isn't you."

She had the case sprung in a moment, and the mouthpiece in her hand. "Well! No wonder. Just look at this reed, it *must* be replaced. I suspected as much and got another one out. Let me slip it in for you—there; try that just as soon as you get home."

"You shouldn't bother, Miss Ashton—"

"Oh, but I feel responsible. After all, Ashton Music is lending you this instrument. And even the best musicians can't get music out of a bad reed."

The door banged shut on Loreen James, and silence fell upon the house like a dark, settling dust. Alice watched the girl hurry down the walk, too full of life, too topped up with the stupid, naive cheeriness of youth. Bouncing bright hair, tight jeans, quick white runners flashing in the sun. . . .

And swinging at her thigh went the battered music case, gleaming on the inside with a grin of keys and buttons, and a lurking charm ready to lash out and strike like a bite.

"A night visit," Ralph said, "we got to do it. It's the only way to enjoy a fair." He added, as if it were a reason in itself, "We still got the money Mom gave us."

The weather had turned cooler, grey clouds tumbling over the town. They sat on the vacation-cleared steps of the school and chewed gum.

"Anyways," he continued, "I want to go through that haunted house again. I want to figure out how some of those spooky things work."

"I already figured them out," Tom said. "I think there must be treadles. Some sort of switches under the floor that make things pop out at you."

"You know that for sure?"

"Not for *sure*."

"Then it's settled. We go back to see if you're right. And we go tonight, okay?"

But Tom was staring hard at an elderly woman toiling by on the far side of the street with two sagging shopping bags that might have held bricks. He sucked in his breath.

"Say, Ralph, isn't that old Mrs. Scharf, the drugstore man's mother?"

Ralph jawed at his gum. "Yeah, it is."

The woman struggled on down the street.

"But I thought she was dead. That night, in the window—you said Mr. Scharf was cutting her up."

"He was."

There was a silence.

"But there she is," Tom said flatly.

Ralph shrugged. "I told you she was a witch, didn't I? I bet now she's cut *him* up, and she's carting him away in those bags." He snapped his gum and his eyes glazed over. "Just think," he said, "how great it'll be on the midway after dark, everything lit up like fireworks, everything bigger, brighter, busier. *That's* the time to take in the House of Horrors, with the dark breathing after you in those passages like a murderer. We got to go. We got to do it, Tom!"

Tom hugged his knees. "Aunt Mary's dead set against it."

Ralph snorted. "Mom worries too much. She figures we'd get robbed or beat up or something—nights is when the city folks come out here. But, Jeez, who'd ever catch *us* if we had half a step head start. We're going, and that's all there is to it."

"If Aunt Mary finds out . . ."

"She'll only find out if she looks in my room. And she never does *that*." He pointed. "See that old geezer there? He once served twenty years for murder—killed a tax man with a hammer."

They found Uncle in the back yard when they got home, sitting on a box, staring at the ground; he didn't even look up. Aunt Mary explained it to them, whispering grimly over a piecrust she was rolling out on the table. They looked at one another, then slipped up to Ralph's room, stocking-footed, and sat on the edge of the bed.

"I don't get it," said Tom. "Is this Loreen James related to your dad?—a cousin, or something?"

Ralph laughed thinly. "A kissing cousin, maybe. Don't you know anything about grownups?"

Tom thought. Then a sense of awareness slowly gripped him. "You mean Uncle Harry and that girl . . .?"

"I told you he saw girls, didn't I?"

Tom whistled. "Your poor dad—your poor *mom!*"

"Tonight," Ralph said, back in his own world. "We're going *to-night!*"

Alice Ashton slammed down the phone and felt her blood pressure shoot up a pound. Where was the saxophone mouthpiece? The instrument itself lay here before her, a long flash of gold in the velvet bed of its case.

Without a mouthpiece.

She had called the James house, waited on the phone while Mrs. James sent her boys scouring the place, had listened to the thump and bump of feet on the stairs while Mrs. James sobbed into the phone about her "little darling." The tiresome woman. Didn't she know about Harold Martins and the dark of the Beacon Theater? Or the car in the night on the River Road hill? The town cats knew more than she did.

The mouthpiece. Where was it? It still carried its spell. She had to find it.

She scowled up at the owl with its bat-spread wings, looking as though it knew precisely where to look but was being silent just out of spite. And another thing. She had better not wait. Now was the time to talk Harold Martins back into the fold. Now was when he'd be needing someone most.

She dialed.

But it wasn't Harold who answered—it was Mary. For a brief moment Alice was tempted to hang up the receiver without a word; she had done *that* before. But now, with the success of her spell, she felt bold. Mary's voice came feather-soft and paper-thin over the wires. A delicate voice, but one with a made-up mind behind it.

"No, Alice, I most certainly will *not* let you speak to my husband."

"But I only want to console him, Mary. Over his loss."

"He's got me for that." A so-soft voice, like dandelion seeds, floating.

"*You,* dear." Alice could not restrain her contempt. "He hasn't needed you for a long time, has he? Let *me* speak to him."

"I won't."

Alice felt her patience beginning to curdle.

"You're very bold now, aren't you dear? Now that Harold doesn't have his little Loreen to run to."

"He didn't have her anyway." A soft voice, but chill; like settling crystals of ice. "Loreen James visited me yesterday. She had just come from your place, she had her music case with her—"

Alice froze.

"—she sat right here on the sofa and told me how foolish she had been, and how sorry she was, and how she had decided to stay away from Harold for good. She was crying, and I believe she was truly sorry and that she meant every word of it."

Alice was dying to ask about the music case.

"Any *real* woman," she said, "would have slapped the little tramp silly, coming to you as bold as that."

"Any woman like you is what you mean, Alice. But I'm not like you. I don't pounce on people with my claws out."

"So," Alice said, "she told you all this nonsense, grabbed her music case and ran out the door, is that it?"

"Not at all. In fact, though I don't expect you to believe it, I think we became friends. We had a nice talk. I asked her about her school, about her music. She even took her saxophone out of its case to show me . . ."

Alice sucked in her breath.

". . . I asked her to play something for me . . ."

Alice pushed the phone into her ear so hard she hurt her head.

". . . she played some scales—she said it was all she had learned from you: I wasn't surprised about that—then we heard a car out back, I said it was Harold getting home, and she ran out of the front door and disappeared. Then later I heard how she . . ."

"And she left the instrument case?"

"Yes. And that's all you're worried about, isn't it? She left it and I sent it straight to her house."

"You should have sent it to me. It was mine. And there's a part missing, too—the mouthpiece. What'd you do with it?"

Mary Martins' voice got even softer now; and chillier.

"Is that so important? Don't you care a thing about that poor girl? She was your student, after all." There was a pause; then Mary said, "I *did* find a little part afterwards. It's in my purse. I'm going to send it along to Mrs. James."

A hunger ran away with Alice's voice: "You send it to me, do you hear? It's mine!"

She was sorry immediately. She could almost hear the suspicions crackle in the mousy little head at the end of the line. Finally, Mary said carefully, "I don't give anything to anyone that can't say please."

"But it's mine. You got to give it to me, Mary Martins. If you don't—"

Mary's voice came smiling down the line. "You'll what—cast a spell on me?"

So Mary knew about the coven. Of course, Harold would have told her. He was sworn to secrecy, and he had told her. But since she knew. . . .

"I will. I will cast a spell on you, Mary Martins. I'll . . ."

"Do it, then," Mary's voice crisped softly in the earpiece. "Go on. I dare you."

The challenge was infuriating—like being pricked by a needle. Alice replied with her lips drawn over her teeth, slinking her voice like a cat: "*You* can pretend to be brave, Mary Martins. But what about your family? Your boy?"

"You don't scare me at all with your make-believe," snapped Mary right back. "I know you too well, Alice Ashton—there's more bitch than witch about you!"

The phone banged down in Alice's ear.

Alice stood with the receiver still in her hand, stunned. It wasn't the language, she used that herself when it suited. But coming from Goodie Two-Shoes Martins, that one tame word was like a slap in the face.

Damn the woman. Alice slammed her own phone down so hard the bells rang. Her mind was already made up. She knew exactly what she was going to do. And no power on earth was going to keep her from it.

She stamped through the kitchen to the basement door, pounded down, down, down the stairs to her very private room, which she unlocked with a key on a thong around her neck. Mary Martins had scoffed at the thirteen. Mary Martins must have her come-uppance. . . .

The little room was a very special place; there was no other like it in a hundred miles. Alice had attended every sabbat in the area for the last ten years, and she ought to know.

In the center of the floor, beautifully painted by her own hand, was her circle, nine feet in diameter, marked with signs of the caballa: a lens to focus her power, a protection from the demons whom she often summoned to help in her work. From a deal table she took an incense burner, a container of salt, a chalice of water, and a dagger. All of this she took into the circle and placed on a tiny, low altar. Then she knelt in the circle herself and began her chant. . . .

She exhaled. The blood tingled in her fingers.

So now it was Mary Martins who stood in the way of the thirteen. She placed her dagger, *athame,* in the very center of the circle and lifted her hands. . . .

Mary Martins sat in her little parlor with her hands clenched tight in her lap. She sat without stirring, her slow breaths lifting, lifting, lifting her blouse. A beam of sunlight edged along the floor, trailing gold, orange, brown, then fading grey. Shadows gathered in the corners of the room.

Shadows.

She raised herself, finally, creaking the chair and the floor, crossing the room to the hall closet where she took from her purse a small object carefully wrapped in a plastic breadbag. This she studied carefully, thinking, thinking. . . .

Suddenly she recoiled as though the thing had bitten her. It fell to the floor. She watched it where it lay while a new comprehension came slowly over her.

She picked up the object gingerly, returned it to her purse, went into the kitchen, and thoroughly washed her hands.

Now to the door to snap-bang the locks into place. Now along the hall, past the empty kitchen to rattle the chain onto the back door. The old stairboards groaned her up to the second floor.

She looked in on Harold, sprawled on his bed fully dressed, drawing his breath in deep, heavy gasps as though the very act of sleep exhausted him.

Mary crossed the hall to her own room, then paused, went three more steps down the narrow passage and peeked into the boys' room.

An empty bed.

She stood for several long moments with her hand on the doorknob, then turned and went with certain, quick steps back down the stairs. She put on her coat, took her purse, let herself out of the house, carefully locking the door behind her.

"Isn't this more like it, though?" Ralph had to shout his words over the high-flying wind.

The ferris wheel had stopped. They swayed in a car at the top of the fair, the midway lights strewn below them like a handful of Christmas, the stars in the huge black bowl of the sky floating over the town like dust. Magic lay all around.

"I can see the post office," Ralph howled.

Tom pointed, "And the church."

"And the cars on First Street."

The wind shrieked, and tilted them.

"And—I can see your mom!" said Tom. He gripped Ralph's arm. "That *is* Aunt Mary, isn't it?"

An unmistakable plump female figure was hurrying towards the fairgrounds along the street, bowing against the night breeze, a purse like a sack gripped under one arm.

Tom felt Ralph stiffen. "Jeez, you're right! That *is* Mom. She must have checked my room." He bit his lip. "We got to get away. We can't let her catch us here. We got to get back to the house, get right to bed, tell her in the morning we just went out for a walk because we couldn't sleep—"

Tom broke in. "And who's that coming along behind her?"

Ralph looked. "That's Miss Ashton—the music teacher. Hey! Did you see that?"

For a second Aunt Mary had paused, turned quickly to glance behind her. And at that exact moment Miss Ashton had faded into a shop doorway.

The huge wheel lurched back to life and began rolling them downward.

"There's something weird going on," said Tom. He looked at Ralph, then at the ground lifting splashes of light up to them out of the dark. "Maybe we ought to find out what it is."

"How?"

Their car was on the ground, the operator tipping them out of their seats like delicate baggage.

Tom led the way to the back of a hot dog stand. "Aunt Mary's got to walk right by here if she comes in the gate."

Ralph swayed, and caught at a rope tying a tent to a spike. He was still looking back at the ferris wheel; it was moving again, drifting against the black sky like a burning circle.

"Here she comes!" hissed Tom, flattening himself against the stand.

They had hidden themselves just in time. Aunt Mary was approaching quickly along the midway, raking the squealing rides and the ticket-clutching lineups with her sharp eyes. They let her pass. Ralph would have stepped out after her, but Tom held him back.

"Look."

It was Miss Ashton. She had come into the fairground, too, right on the heels of Aunt Mary. She took no interest at all in the sights around her but walked with a purposeful, stalking stride. She kept one hand pressed to her side as though she were easing a pain.

Tom said, "That Miss Ashton is following your mother. Why would she do that?"

Ralph shrugged. "Let's find out."

This was a new and stimulating game. Tom could see his own excitement glowing in Ralph's eyes. It was like secret agents. Now, in the color and lights, in the crazy sounds, the pressing, laughing, fun-seeking people, they were suddenly caught up in something bigger than a stolen night out. They were putting one foot into the half-opened doorway of an adult world. Anything might happen. They expected it.

Along they went: Aunt Mary leading, scouring everything to her right and left; Miss Ashton hanging back, the one hand curiously pressed to her side; then the two boys, rubber-treading the packed earth, melting along in the wake of the women like two cats.

"Mom's looking for us," Ralph said. "That's plain."

"Yes," said Tom; "but what's Miss Ashton looking for?"

"She's got something in her hand. Some old roll of paper, or something."

"Yeah, or cloth."

Aunt Mary stopped; Miss Ashton stopped; the boys stopped.

Aunt Mary studied the Whirl-A-Way, plunging and hurtling its screaming prisoners in flashing steel cages through the waves of exploding music and the booming "Wanna go faster?" voice. The prisoners squealed "Yes-No," and the machine roared and flung them through the night wind, howling.

Aunt Mary trotted on, then stopped again, this time to scrutinize the Dodge-em car drivers. "Hey," said Ralph, "Miss Ashton's moving up. Look."

Miss Ashton seemed to have changed her strategy. No longer simply hanging back and following, she was creeping closer to Aunt Mary, taking advantage of the crowd. The Dodge-em cars crashed and buzzed, showering blue sparks. Miss Ashton was three, now two, now one person away when Aunt Mary spun on her heel and hurried on.

"I don't like it," said Tom. "Something awful's going to happen. We got to warn your Mom."

Ralph wasn't convinced.

"Wait a bit. It could be nothing. We can't give ourselves away for no reason. We can still beat Mom back home when she's ready to leave. *I* don't want to be grounded the rest of the summer if I can help it."

The crowd was thinning rapidly, diluted by the chill and the lateness of the hour. When they reached the House of Horrors, the once bustling midway was reduced to small knots of stragglers. Aunt Mary hurried faster, as if the House of Horrors was what she had been looking for all along. She paid her money and went straight in.

"She must have heard us talking about that place," Ralph said. "She figures we might be in there." He sucked in his breath. "And look at *her.*"

Miss Ashton had also bought a ticket, and was hurrying after Aunt Mary. She had discarded the cloth wrapping. There was a wink of light in her hand.

Both boys jumped forward at once. The idea of soft, vulnerable Aunt Mary being stalked in the bat-and-monster darkness was too much for them. They paid. They slipped through the entrance. And stopped.

There was someone standing a few feet ahead of them in the darkness, breathing. They could sense it. And somewhere ahead, a whisper of footsteps.

Farther on, something slammed like a door. There was a scream of wild laughter. Tom felt his heart jump under his collar and stay there: up ahead Aunt Mary must have just met the ghost. He felt the presence in front of them shift away into the passage. And again, farther on, a snap of wires like a tangling clothesline, a rattle like clothespins: the skeleton.

Tom searched for Ralph's sleeve, plucked at it, whispering, "You stick to Miss Ashton. I'll slip by her and warn Aunt Mary." He was moving before Ralph could argue.

Tom was glad of his rubber soles. The presence ahead of him could not move so silently, but went with a creak of wood floor and shoe leather and the tapping point force of a narrow heel. But the passage was narrow; it would not be an easy matter to slip by anyone unnoticed.

He formed his plan as he crept along. The screaming face ought to be next. He recalled it being lit with a flash of the brightest light, a light that could give him away. But if he kept to his right, flat up against the passage wall, he ought to be out of its beam, and Miss Ashton would probably reel back, momentarily blinded. In that instant after the light went out, with her pressed against the back of the passage, he might be able to duck by.

Air blasted his feet; he heard a cry right in front of him. He was so close to Miss Ashton, the air jet must have triggered once for both of them.

Forward, forward, easing along the floor of the passage, keeping as close as he dared to the presence before him. Soon, he thought, at any moment now, the screaming face will pounce. The flooring creaked. There was the sigh of a feathered breath.

Then, bam! The blinding light, the face, the wild scream! Tom threw himself against the right hand wall, twisting, darting silently by and on into the passage.

He went quickly now. Aunt Mary would be just ahead. Bats danced in his hair.

Not far now. The witch was close, the blue glow of her light just a few steps away. There was a shifting blackness in front of him. "Aunt Mary," he whispered. He caught up with her at the witch. "It's me Tom."

There was a scent of lilacs, a brush of cloth. He took Aunt Mary's sleeve. "Watch out for that Miss Ashton, she . . ."

A hand gripped his wrist like a clamp. A sharp breath hissed between thin, hard lips, and a terrible fear leaped within him as the blue light revealed the cold hard features of Miss Ashton where Aunt Mary's kindly face should be.

She growled like a cat. "You little—"

Her hand flew up. Cold steel flashed blue in the witch's light.

Tom's response was a reflex action.

He reached out his foot and stamped where the witch's treadle ought to be. The witch screeched and leaped. Tom yanked away. Miss Ashton went twisting down, hit the wall, the floor, groaned, and then sighed.

* * *

The sirening and strobing ambulance seemed a commonplace thing on the midway, its usual thunder stolen by the surroundings. The attendants, white-capped and jacketed, bundled their load out of the House of Horrors. The mound under the sheet seemed strangely small and fragile for the once bristling Miss Ashton.

There were fragments of conversation. ". . . must have fallen right on her own knife . . . what was she *doing* in there? . . ."

The boys stood on either side of Aunt Mary like guards. Tom tugged at her arm. "How did Miss Ashton get ahead of you in the passage?"

Her nervous voice pattered like a soft rain: "*I* knew she was following me. That's why I ducked into that haunted place—to get away. As soon as I got inside the entrance I stood back to let her go by me. *I* can take care of myself. . . ."

There was a multitude of questions.

The doctor was saying to a policeman: "I don't understand it. You can see that she fell on the knife—her hand was still gripping it. But it was a shallow wound, not normally a fatal one. . . ."

Aunt Mary touched his sleeve. "You'd better have a close look at that blade. I think you'll find something on it, something bad, some coating that shouldn't be there." She handed over the saxophone mouthpiece which she had in her purse, still carefully wrapped in its plastic bag. "And you'd better have a look at this, too."

She paused a moment, and added, "You all know me. You know where you can find me. My legs are shaking. I think I need a good liedown."

The policeman hesitated, then slowly nodded.

They walked Aunt Mary home.

And it was strange, Tom thought, how little magic there was in the streets this night at two o'clock in the morning.

Strange Prey

by George C. Chesbro

"It is most difficult to know to whom we are speaking; in this troubled world the Civilized and the Savage wear identical trappings." *Senator Thaag, speaking before the U.N. General Assembly.*

It was starting again; someone was near.

Victor Rafferty looked up from the milky-blue water in time to see a squat, balding man with a limp emerge from the locker room at the opposite end of the pool. The man knelt clumsily in the gutter and grunted as he splashed handfuls of the cold water into his armpits and across his hairy chest.

Rafferty frowned with displeasure and stared down into the water at his own legs with their large, jagged patches of fish-white scar tissue that registered neither heat nor cold. He knew, of course, that the athletic club was open to any of its members at any time; yet this man had chosen a piece of the afternoon that Victor had come to think of as his own. The pool was usually deserted at this hour, enabling Victor to swim endlessly back and forth rebuilding his damaged body, savoring the silence in his mind that came only when he was alone and at peace.

There wasn't any pain yet. The man was still too far away. Now there was only the familiar pressure in Victor's ears as if he were ascending in a plane, an agonizing buzzing sound that seemed to emanate from a vast, dark abyss somewhere behind his eyes.

The man was swimming in Victor's direction, struggling through the water with a ragged crawl. He drew closer, and Victor pressed his fingers hard against the chlorine-bleached tiles as the noise and pressure were suddenly transformed into a needle-strewn veil that seemed to float beneath his skull, lancing his brain as it closed around his mind. It is so much worse with strangers, he thought as he waited for knowledge of the man, which he knew would come next.

"Swimming," the man said, spewing water and blowing hard. He was hanging onto the edge of the pool, a few inches away from Victor. "Best all-'round conditioner there is. A man can't do enough of it."

Victor smiled and nodded through a haze of pain. The man pushed off the side and began to swim back toward the shallow end. Immediately the pain began to recede until finally there was only the residue of pressure and buzzing.

Rafferty knew the man was an accountant, suffered from hypertension, and had a headache that had been with him since early in the morning. He was also worried about his wife.

Madness, Victor thought grimly, rising and reaching for his towels.

He paused inside the locker room and stared at his naked image in one of the full-length mirrors that lined the walls. At forty, he was neither exceptionally handsome nor vain. It was not narcissism that held him motionless before the glass but rather fascination with the structure reflected there, the structure that housed his being; a body that should have been, by all the laws of probability, destroyed in the automobile accident four months ago. His hair was grayer now, and he was still too thin, but the swimming should remedy that; Roger had said so. At least he was alive.

But was he *well?*

Rafferty stepped forward so that his face was only a few inches from the glass. He reached up with his hand and slowly separated the hairs on the right side of his scalp to reveal a long, thread-thin scar that began an inch above the hairline and snaked down and along the side of his head and around to the base of his skull. He touched the wound, pressing on it with the tips of his fingers, first gently and then with increased pressure. There was no pain; there was hardly any sensation at all. Roger and his team had done a beautiful job of inserting the steel plate.

No, it was not the wound or the piece of metal that was causing the agony. He was fairly certain of that now. Other people; *they* were the source of his pain. In which case, Victor mused, he must indeed be going mad.

He stepped back but continued to gaze at his flat, scarred reflection. Perhaps it would have been better to die; better that than to suffer this ruptured consciousness that warped his senses and made even the close physical presence of his wife a fount of unbearable discomfort. Too, it was getting worse; his *awareness* of the man in the pool had been sharper, more distinct than ever before.

He knew now he should have told Roger about the pain and the images from the beginning. Why hadn't he? Victor wondered. Was it possible that he was so afraid of discovering the truth that he would wrap himself in his own silence before allowing himself to be told that his brain was permanently damaged . . . or that he was dying? Or was it a different fear, this ten-fingered hand that clawed at the inside of his stomach every time he even considered describing to anyone his symptoms?

Victor forced himself to walk away from the mirror. Then he dressed quickly. He lighted a cigarette and was not surprised to see that his hand was trembling. He was due in Roger's office in half an hour and he had decided to tell Roger everything, ignoring the possible consequences.

Victor wondered how the neurosurgeon would react when he was told his famous patient thought he could read minds.

It came as always; tongues of molten metal licking the scorched, exhausted sands of his mind; dagger thrusts that bled into a psychic pool of images and sounds that he could *feel* as well as hear as he approached the woman behind the desk.

"Dr. Burns will see you in a few moments," the receptionist said in her most professional tone. She'd spoken those words to him at least forty times in the last four months and her tone never changed. "If you'll be kind enough to go in and sit down . . ."

Victor thanked her and walked the few paces down the corridor into the large waiting room with its magenta walls and overstuffed, red leather chairs. He selected a magazine from a mahogany rack and tried to focus his attention on the lead article while waiting for the man who could hold the key to his sanity—or his life. He had barely enough time to finish the first paragraph before there was the soft click of a door opening and Victor looked up at the tall, lean frame of the man who had put his body back together after the accident. Roger was studying him through large, steel-rimmed eyeglasses that made his thin face seem all out of proportion.

"Come in, Vic," the doctor said at last, motioning Victor into a huge, booklined office. "It's good to see you; first interesting case I've had all day."

Victor strode quickly into the office, avoiding the other man's eyes. He automatically stripped to his shorts and sat down on the long, leather examination table. He studied Roger as the doctor glanced through the reams of charts and other papers that were the record of Victor's recovery.

He'd known Roger Burns for some time, even before the accident. In fact, he had designed the award-winning house in which Roger and his wife lived. He knew Roger to be—like many great men—lonely and estranged, the victim as well as possessor of prodigious skills. Victor could understand that. Still, he resented the cold, clinical detachment which Roger brought to this new doctor-patient relationship, an attitude which he knew was prompted by Roger's concern about his condition. Victor would have discerned this even without the flood of anxiety that flowed from the other man's mind; it was written in his eyes. He'd probably been talking to Pat.

"How was your walk?" Roger had risen from the desk and walked across the room to a huge bank of filing cabinets. He drew a bulging file from one of the sliding drawers and began clipping X-ray negatives along the sides of a huge fluoroscope suspended from the ceiling.

"I didn't walk."

Roger's eyes flicked sideward like a stroke from one of his scalpels. "You should walk. The exercise is good for you."

"I've been swimming."

Roger nodded his approval and walked toward Victor, who lay back on the table and closed his eyes against the sudden onrush of pain.

"Elizabeth is giving a cocktail party Friday evening for one of the new congressmen," Roger said, glancing back over his shoulder at one of the X-rays. "You and Pat be sure to be there. I'll need someone to talk to."

Victor grunted as the surgeon's long, deft fingers probed and pulled at the muscle and bone beneath the fresh scar tissue on his arms and legs. Roger was bent over him, following the path of the thin, bright beam of light that was lighting the interior of his eyes.

Victor reached out and touched a thought. "Why are you thinking that my intelligence may be impaired?"

There was a sudden wave of anxiety that flowed across his mind like a cold wave as Roger shut off the light and straightened up.

"What makes you think I consider that a possibility?" Roger's voice was too tight and controlled.

Victor stared hard into the other man's eyes, very conscious of the beads of sweat that were lining up like soldiers across his forehead. There would never be a better time. "Just guessing," Victor said at last. The words tasted bitter on his tongue and he felt empty inside. "What *do* you think?"

The light came back on and the examination continued. Victor fought to keep his mind away from the pain and the noises.

"You're a walking miracle," Roger said, resuming his probing, and Victor swallowed a bubble of hysterical laughter that had suddenly formed in his throat. "I don't have to tell you how lucky you are to be alive. How many men do you know who've had half their skull crushed and lived to worry about their intelligence?" He paused and seemed to be waiting for some reply. Victor said nothing.

"Your most serious injury was the damage to your brain," Roger continued matter-of-factly. "You're obviously aware of that."

"And?"

"I don't know. Really. There's so little that we actually know for certain about this kind of injury. It's still much too early to know for sure how any of your functions are going to be affected." Roger hesitated, trying to read the expression on Victor's face. "I'm not putting you off," he said very quietly. "I really don't know. Every rule in the book says that you should be dead or in the terminal stage of coma."

"I owe my life to you," Victor said evenly, noticing the slight flush that appeared high on the cheeks of the other man. In a moment it was gone. "I think there's something you're not telling me."

"Pat tells me that you seem . . . *distracted* lately." Roger had returned to his desk and was writing something on one of the charts in his folder. "She says you've become very absentminded. I understand you haven't even been . . . close . . . with her since the accident."

"You need a record of my love life?"

"No," Roger said, suddenly slapping the folder shut. "I need information. That is, I need information if I'm ever going to answer your questions. Have you lost the desire to make love?"

"No," Victor said, searching for the right words. How could he explain how it hurt his *mind* to be so close? "I've been . . . upset . . . worried. You can understand that." He hurried on, conscious of the rising note of impatience in his voice, eager to leave the subject of his relationship with his wife. "You must know what parts of my brain have been damaged. And you must know what happened to others with the same kind of injury."

Roger was preparing to take X-rays. Victor rose from the couch and walked to the machine.

"Much of the left cortex has been destroyed," Roger said. His voice was low, muffled by the lead shield and punctuated by the intermittent buzzing of the machine at Victor's head. "Usually, the patient dies. If not, there is almost always a loss of coordination and speech. For some reason that I don't pretend to understand, you don't seem to have suffered any appreciable loss of any kind. Of course there's no way of knowing what damage has been done farther down in the brain tissue."

"You mean I could drop dead at any moment. Or I could be losing my mind."

The machine continued to click, recording its invisible notes. "I can tell you this: neurosurgeons all over the world are following your case. You may or may not be the world's greatest architect, but you're certainly the leading medical phenomenon."

Victor swallowed hard. "I—I wasn't aware that many people knew anything about it."

Roger came out from behind the shield and repositioned the machine. "I haven't published anything yet although, eventually, I'd like to if you'll give your consent. I need your permission, of course. I'll need more time to run tests and chart your progress."

"How did it get so much publicity?"

Roger looked surprised. "Vic, there isn't a major city in the world that doesn't have one of your buildings. You're like public property. Then there was the fantastic way you recovered from the injuries. Didn't you suppose people would be interested?"

"It never occurred to me . . ." Victor's voice trailed off, stifled by the thought of a world watching his disintegration; cold, dispassionate men examining him like a worm wriggling beneath a microscope. The machine had stopped. "Roger, I think I can read people's minds."

His voice seemed swallowed up by the large room. There was the sharp click of a match as Roger lighted a cigarette. The surgeon's face was expressionless.

"I tell you I can *hear* people *thinking*," Victor said too loudly. He took a deep breath and tried to fight the panic he felt pounding at his senses like some gigantic fist. He searched Roger's face for some kind of emotion, but there was nothing; the other man was staring intently at a thin stream of smoke that flowed from his mouth. "It's true. I know it sounds crazy—maybe it *is* crazy—but I can feel you inside my mind right now."

"Can you tell me what I'm thinking?" Roger's tone was flat. He had not raised his eyes.

"It's not always like *that*," Victor said quietly. He knew . . . and then he didn't know; not for certain. He knew it seemed as if he had been challenged and was coming up empty. Still, he felt more relaxed and at peace than he had for months; at last he had invited someone else to peer into his private hell. "It's not always definite words or sounds. Sometimes it's just a jumble of sensations. But they're not a part of *me*. Can you understand that? It's like I'm listening in on other people's conversations with themselves!" Victor paused and waited until Roger's eyes were locked with his. His voice gathered strength. "Right now you're fascinated; you'd like to pinpoint the damaged area of my brain that's causing me to hallucinate. You don't believe a word I'm saying."

There was the slightest flicker of surprise and consternation in the doctor's eyes. It was quickly masked.

"Let's not worry about whether or not I believe you," Roger said. "At least not right now. It's obvious that you *believe* you're reading other people's thoughts, and that's all that's important. Why don't you describe these sensations?"

"I'm not sure exactly when it started," Victor said slowly, taking a cigarette from the pack on Roger's desk and carefully lighting it. His hand was steady. "A week, maybe two weeks after I got out of the hospital. I began getting these headaches; but they *weren't* headaches, not in the usual sense, and God knows I'd had enough real headaches to know the difference. And there were noises that would suddenly spring up from nowhere. Sometimes there were words, but mostly it was just noise, almost like . . . static. And it hurt.

"It took me a while to realize that I experienced the pain and the noises only when I was near other people. I'd walk up to people and immediately there'd be pressure in my ears and behind my eyes. I'd walk away and it would stop. Lately, I've *seen* whole strings of words in my mind, words and sounds all floating around in my head. And pain that I can't describe to you. And I *feel* things—emotions—that I know come from somebody else."

"Has there been any change in the *way* you feel these things?" Roger's voice was even.

"Yes. The impressions are stronger, and the pain is worse. The more I know, the more I hurt."

"And you think these sensations have something to do with the thought patterns of other people?"

"I don't know what else to think," Victor said hesitantly. He was conscious now, more than ever, of how sick and foolish he must sound. The words were coming harder; he was pushing them out of his throat. "A few minutes ago, while you were leaning over me on the table, I thought my head would split. I kept *feeling* the word, *intelligence*. Over and over again: *intelligence, intelligence*. In some way that I can't explain, I knew that was *your* thought. You were wondering how much my intellectual capacity had been impaired by the accident."

Victor watched Roger light another cigarette. Now it was the surgeon's hands that trembled.

"Go on."

"It's like the words have teeth. There's just no other way I can think of to describe it; they sit in my mind and they *bite*. And just before they come there's a kind of pressure, a buzzing . . . a *numb* feeling." Victor hesitated. "All right," he said at last, "you still don't think it's possible. For a moment there, you were almost convinced; you were thinking about the Russian claim that they have a woman who can read colors with her fingertips."

Again Roger's eyes registered surprise but he spoke without hesitation. "Let's be realistic," Roger said, leaning close, inundating Victor with his thoughts. "It's *most* important that we be realistic. You've survived a terrible injury and it's to be expected that there's going to be some residual pain. You must understand that the mind plays tricks, even in a healthy individual, and you're still far from well. You're going to have to give your body, and your mind, time to *heal*. That's what you have to think about, Victor; that and only that."

"Test me!" Victor was surprised at the vehemence in his voice. It had cost him a great deal to come to Roger with his fears. He would not now be denied; one way or the other he would know the truth. "If you're so sure I'm imagining this, test me!"

"Victor, as your doctor, I—"

"Do it as my friend! Roger, I *need* this! Have you ever read anything about ESP?"

"Well, naturally, I've read the literature. But I don't think—"

"Good! Then you know the tests are fairly simple as well as statistically reliable. There isn't that much work involved."

"It's not the work that I'm thinking about," Roger said. He was wavering now, torn by uncertainty that was clearly communicated to Victor. "Maybe next week."

"Tonight!" Victor had to struggle to keep from shouting. He was intoxicated with the vision of an end of his nightmare. "You won't help me to relax by forcing me to wait a week," Victor said quietly. "It won't be difficult to get the materials or set up the equipment. If I fail, well, I'll have all the time in the world to relax. Isn't that right, Roger?"

Victor gazed steadily back into the eyes of the tall man. "All right," Roger said, picking up Victor's folder and tucking it under his arm. "Tonight."

Victor paused in the lobby of the medical center and studied the knots of people moving past, crowding the sidewalk on the other side of the thick, glass doors. All his anger had been drained. In a few hours he would do battle with his fears in the neutral territory of a laboratory before the disinterested eyes of a man who believed he was hallucinating. It was all he asked. The tension and anxiety that had been steadily building over the long months was suddenly gone and in their place was an insatiable curiosity. Talking to Roger had brought him out of himself; his words had lanced the psychic wound that had festered in his silence. He was sure now that the sounds and images were real. Since he was not hallucinating, there was only one other possibility: he was telepathic.

Telepath; Victor rolled the word around in his mind, speaking it softly with equal parts fear and fascination. What if he could learn to control and interpret these sensations?

Victor pushed open the doors and strode out into the auburn glow of the late afternoon, plunging without hesitation into a small crowd of pedestrians who were waiting on the corner for the traffic light to change. Quickly, like a man pitching his body into an icy lake, Victor opened his mind and extended it out toward the man standing next to him. He remembered the time as a child when he had sought to prove his courage to a group of older boys by holding his arm over a campfire, holding it there until the soft down on his flesh had shriveled and fallen to the ground. It was like that now; his mind was suspended in the consciousness of another and he was burning. Still he hung on, struggling to stretch the words into sentences and trace the images and sounds to their source. A shaft of pain tore through him, erupting like a geyser.

Victor staggered back against a building, ignoring the frightened stares of the people at the crossing. The man whose mind he had touched was holding his head in his hands; he had dropped the briefcase he had been holding and was looking about him with a dazed expression. Victor pushed away from the stone facade and forced himself to walk the few paces to a phone booth which stood empty across the street. He half stumbled into the glass enclosure and slammed the door shut behind him.

Icy sweat had pasted his clothes to his body. Victor rested his head against the cold metal of the telephone and peered out from his sanctuary as he waited for the scream inside his head to subside. He had seen something inside the man's mind, something cold and dark which he did not understand and which frightened him; this time he had seen what before he had only felt.

I must practice, Victor thought; I must delve even deeper into this mysterious awareness which I now possess. Perhaps, in time, I could even learn to control the pain.

He hunted in his pockets for change, having decided to call Pat and tell her he would not be home for dinner, not until after he had seen Roger. Right now there was no time to waste; there was too much to learn.

Roger hesitated with his hand on the telephone as he tried to dispel a lingering uneasiness about the call he had decided to make. He finally picked up the receiver, dialed a number, and spoke in quiet earnestness for some minutes. When he had finished, he poured himself a tall drink from a bottle that had been a Christmas present and which had been around the office, unopened, for the past two years. He ground his knuckles into his eyes and groaned as pools of electric, liquid light darted and swam behind his eyelids.

Acting on an impulse, he had gone ahead and developed the latest series of X-rays, the set he had taken of Victor's skull earlier in the afternoon. He had not expected to find any significant change. He had been wrong. Now the entire surface of the large fluoroscope in his office was covered with negatives arranged in chronological order so as to provide, at a glance, a complete visual record of X-ray exposures taken over the past four months. Viewed in this manner, the effect was astounding.

On the left were the plates taken soon after Rafferty had been rushed to the hospital, more dead than alive. The carnage on the right side of the skull was indicated most vividly by small dots of light in a sea of gray, bits of bone imbedded deep in the tissue of the brain.

The next series of plates had been exposed three days later, after the marathon operation had been completed. The splinters of bone had been removed from the brain tissue and a metal plate inserted into the area where the skull had been pulverized. The rest of the exposures had been taken at two to three week intervals.

Now that he knew what he was looking for, Roger realized that the effect was evident, even in the early exposures: a tiny discoloration a few millimeters to the left of the injured area. Placed side by side, the plates offered conclusive evidence that the discolored region was rapidly increasing in size. It was almost as if the machine were not recording this area, but Roger had checked and rechecked the equipment and there was nothing wrong with it.

In the set of plates taken that afternoon the normal skull and brain tissue patterns were virtually nonexistent; the entire plate exploded in rays of light and dark emanating from that same tiny region just below the steel plate. It was as if the architect's brain had somehow been transformed into a power source strong enough to interfere with the X-rays—but that was impossible.

Roger licked his lips and swallowed hard, but there was no moisture left in his mouth. He turned off the fluoroscope and reached back for the wall switch before pouring himself another drink. In a few minutes there was the soft ring of chimes in the outer office. Roger glanced at his watch and rose to greet the first of the evening's two visitors.

Victor knew immediately that something had happened in the past few hours that made Roger change his mind; he could sense the excitement radiating from the mind of the neurosurgeon in great, undulating waves.

"Tell me again how you feel when you experience these sensations." Roger's voice was impassive, but his eyes glowed.

"Something like a second-grader trying to read *Ulysses*," Victor said easily. "You can recognize a few words but most of the time you haven't any idea what they mean."

His gaze swept the small anteroom where Roger had brought him. Shipping cartons, boxes of records, and obsolete equipment had been pushed back against the walls to make room for the two wooden tables that had been placed in the middle of the floor. Wedged between the tables and extending about four feet above their surfaces was a thin, plywood partition. On one table was what appeared to be a large stack of oversized playing cards, a pad, and a pencil. The other table was bare.

"I want you to sit here," Roger said, indicating a chair at one end of the empty table. He waited until Victor had seated himself. "I believe you may have been telling the truth this afternoon. Now I think we can find out for sure."

Victor felt as if he had been hit in the stomach. A few hours ago he would have given almost anything to hear Roger speak those words; now they stirred a reservoir of fear. He might have risen and left if it were not for the knowledge that, by doing so, he would be cutting himself off from the one person who might be able to return him to the world of normal sights and sounds.

"Let me show you what we're going to do," Roger said, fanning the cards out, face up, in front of Victor. They were pictures of farm animals. "I'm going to try to duplicate some of Duke University's experiments in parapsychology. There are figures on my pad which correspond to the pictures on the cards. Each time I turn over a card I'll signal with this," and Roger produced a small toy noisemaker from his pocket and pressed it several times. It emitted a series of distinct clicking noises. "You'll tell me whatever it is you see or feel: dog, horse, cat, or cow. At the end, we'll compute the number of correct responses. Any significant difference between your score and what is considered *chance* must be attributed to telepathy. It's as simple, or complex, as that."

"Fine. Just as long as it helps you to treat me."

"Victor," Roger said, shooting him a quick glance, "do you realize what it would mean for you to be proved telepathic?"

"Right now it means that I have a constant headache, occasional severe pain, and that I continually find myself knowing things about other people that I neither want, nor have the right, to know."

"Yes." Roger's voice was noncommittal. He disappeared behind the partition and Victor could hear him shuffling the cards.

It suddenly occurred to Victor that the other man was trying to hide something from him, concentrating hard on a set of words in what seemed an effort to mask an idea; the thought of *hiding* was floating in the other man's consciousness, soaring above and hovering over the other things on which he was concentrating. Why should Roger want to hide anything from him? Victor attempted to break through the curtain but Roger's will, and the pain, were too great. Victor let go and leaned back in the chair.

"Are you ready?"

"Ready."

Click.

". . . Dog." He said it with far more certainty than he felt; there was nothing there.

Click.

. . .

"You're waiting too long."

"I can't . . ."

"Your first reaction!"

Click.

Victor said nothing. There were no animal words in Roger's thoughts. The words that were there were scrambled and totally unrelated to one another. Why would Roger want to ruin his own experiment? Unless there were no words except those that sprang from his own shattered imagination; unless he had been right in the beginning to suspect he was on the verge of madness.

Clickclickclick.

. . .

"You're not responding, Victor! Tell me what animal you see! Tell me!"

Nerves shrieking, Victor sprang from his chair and stepped around the partition, slapping at the cards, strewing them over the table and floor. Sweat dripped from his forehead and splattered on the wooden surface, the sound clearly audible in the sudden silence. Victor stepped back quickly, profoundly embarrassed. Roger was studying him quietly.

"I—I can't see anything," Victor said, his voice shaking. "For God's sake, Roger, I . . . I'm very sorry."

"Let's try it once more."

Victor reached for his handkerchief and then stopped, his hand in mid-air; there was a new emotion in the other man, almost a sense of elation. He waited for Roger to look up, but the doctor seemed intent on rearranging the stack of cards, pointedly ignoring Victor's questioning gaze. Victor returned to his chair and sat down.

"Ready?"

"Ready," Victor said weakly, cupping his head in his hands. He suddenly felt very tired.

Click.

Victor slowly dropped his hands away from his head; his heart hammered. "Dog," he whispered.

Click.

"Cat."

Now the clicks came faster and faster, and each one was accompanied by a clear, startling, naked impression. It was *there!* Roger's mind was open and Victor barked out the words as the images came to him.

Click.

"Cow."

Click.

"Dog."

Clickclickclick.

"Cowcatdog."

Clickclickclickclick.

Finally the clicking stopped. Victor could feel Roger's mind begin to relax and he knew it was over. He sat very still, very conscious of his own breathing and the rising excitement in Roger as the results were tabulated. In a few moments the excitement had risen to a sharp peak of unrelieved tension. Victor looked up to find Roger standing over him, his facial muscles hanging loose in undisguised astonishment.

"One hundred percent," Roger said breathlessly, repeating the figure over and over as if unable to accept his own calculations. "Victor, you *can* read minds. You're telepathic to an almost unbelievable degree. Here, look at this!"

Victor glanced at the pad on which his responses had been recorded. On the first test he had scored about one correct answer in every four. *Chance.* On the second test all of the answers were circled in red; the marks grew darker and more unsteady as they proceeded down the page.

He looked up and was startled to find the neurosurgeon still staring at him. It was unnerving; the man's pupils were slightly dilated and his mouth worked back and forth. His thought patterns were strange and somehow unpleasant.

"Let me guess," Victor said tightly. "You're looking for antennae."

"I'm sorry," Roger said, stepping back a pace. "I was staring, wasn't I?"

"Yes."

"Well, you're a little hard to get used to. If you have any idea what this means . . ."

"I'd rather not get into that."

Roger flushed and Victor immediately felt ashamed. Were their situations reversed, he felt certain he would be the one staring.

"You were blocking me on the first test," Victor said easily. "Why?"

"Control." Roger's fingers were tracing a pattern up and down the columns of red circles. "I had the cards face down on the first run. I didn't know what they were myself. The second time . . . Well, you saw what happened the second time."

"Where do we go from here?" Victor shifted uneasily in his chair. He had the distinct impression that Roger was already thinking in terms of *application*.

"I wish I knew," Roger said. "I wish I knew."

Victor's head was splitting and the nervous sweat in his armpits was clammy. He concentrated on shutting out Roger's thoughts; he wanted nothing more than to go home and sleep, but first he needed some answers. "How?" Victor asked at last.

"How what?"

"How does all this happen? What's going on inside my brain?"
Roger tugged at his lip. "If I knew that, I'd be famous."

"You already are famous."

Roger grunted and continued to tug at his lip. When he finally
spoke, his tone was flat, his gaze fixed on some point at the far end of
the room.

"It's been estimated that during our entire lives we only use
fifteen to twenty percent of our total brain capacity," Roger said.
"Nobody really knows what happens with the other eighty. For all
we know, there may be a great source of power there, power that we
never use. We never have need to tap that power and so it atrophies
like an unused muscle. Maybe that power is there in reserve, to be
used by some future generation; or maybe it's simply the difference
between the ordinary man and the genius. It's just possible that in
your case the energy, or whatever you want to call what's happened
to you, was released as a result of the accident." Now Roger had
risen to his feet and was pacing, lost in thought, his voice a beacon
beckoning Victor to follow him through this thicket of ideas into
which he had wandered. He fumbled for a cigarette, finally found
one in a crumpled pack and lighted it. He couldn't sit down.

"We've always assumed brain damage to be disabling," Roger
continued, dragging heavily on his cigarette. "The brain controls
everything: coordination, thinking, reflexes. Different areas control
different functions and when one area has been damaged, its function is almost always lost.

"We always assume that our present condition is the best. It never
occurred to us that brain damage could be *beneficial* in any way."
Roger stopped and looked at Victor. "You've shown us how wrong
we were. Your injury somehow altered the function of your brain
cells, releasing a power like nothing that's ever been recorded." He
crushed out the cigarette. "I think evolution may have something to
do with it."

"*Evolution!*"

"Yes!" Roger fairly shouted. "Now follow me on this: there are
profound differences between the brain pans of, say, Neanderthal
and Cro-Magnon man. Yet they are direct descendants! True, the
changes took place over thousands of years; still, at least some

Neanderthals must have had the seeds of change within their genetic makeup, a cellular plan that would someday transform them into Cro-Magnon man."

"I'm not a superman," Victor said cautiously. "I'm all of the things everyone else is; no more and no less."

"That's not true," Roger said, his excitement undiminished. "You were gifted—apart from other men—even before the accident. Now you're telepathic." He paused for emphasis. "The Cro-Magnons' forebears were not obviously different from their fellows; they lived, ate, drank, fornicated, and died just like the others. The differences were too small to be seen, at least in their own lifetime. It must be the same with us; to generations of men a thousand years from now, *we* will seem like Neanderthals. And some of us—you, for instance—are their genetic forebears. If I'm right, a freak accident triggered a mechanism inside your brain that most men will not know for dozens of generations!"

"But how does it happen?" Victor lighted a cigarette, his moves slow and deliberate, his voice completely noncommittal.

"All *thinking* involves a release of energy. Electrical impulses are triggered by certain chemical reactions within the cells that we don't yet fully understand; it's precisely those impulses that we measure in an EEG."

Roger sat down suddenly and began drumming his fingers on the tabletop. "In your case, the cells have been altered to a degree where the nerve endings not only pick up your own impulses but other people's as well. We've always suspected that there was a certain amount of electrical radiation or *leak* from the brain, just as there is from any power source. Besides, there are quite a few recorded instances of telepathic communication—but never anything like this. It's just *fantastic*, Victor! I wonder if you realize just how unique you are?"

Victor was gently probing now, looking for the meaning behind the words, trying to determine just what Roger planned to do with his newly acquired knowledge. He gave up when he realized that the neurosurgeon was effectively, if unconsciously, blocking him.

"All right," Victor said, concentrating his attention on a water stain just over Roger's shoulder. "How do we stop it?"

Roger blinked rapidly as if just startled by a loud noise or awakened from a deep sleep. "Stop it?"

"That's what I said, stop it! Do you think I want to *stay* like this?" Aware that he was almost yelling, Victor dug his fingernails into the palms of his hands and took a deep breath. "I'm an architect," he continued more calmly. "I used to build things and that was all I ever asked out of life; it's all I ask now. If you had any idea . . . but you don't. There must be something you can do, an operation of some sort; I want it."

"That's impossible at this point," Roger replied, passing his hand over his eyes. His voice was now slurred with weariness. "To attempt any kind of operation now is out of the question; I wouldn't even know what I was supposed to be operating *on*. Besides, another operation now would probably kill you."

"There may not be *time*," Victor said, tapping his clenched fist gently but insistently on the table. "I tell you it's getting worse; each day I know more about people I've never met, strangers I pass on the street. And my head hurts. For God's sake, Roger, sometimes I wake up in the morning and I don't—"

"Have you considered the *implications* of this thing?" Roger seemed unaware of the fact that he had interrupted Victor. "You can read men's minds, know their innermost feelings! There are all sorts of—"

"I've thought about the implications and I don't like any of them."

"Police work; imagine, Victor! You would know beyond any doubt who was guilty and who was innocent . . ."

"Some sort of mental gestapo?"

". . . International relations, psychiatry . . ."

"Forget it, doctor," Victor murmured, half-rising. His voice was deadly soft. "If you won't help me, I'll find somebody else who will."

"I didn't say I wouldn't help you," Roger said, sobered by the intensity of Victor's tone. "I said I didn't think I *could* help you; at least, not yet, not until I know more. We'll have to conduct tests and *those* will be mostly guesswork. Even if I do operate, there's no way of knowing for sure whether it will do any good. That is, if it doesn't kill you."

"I'll take that chance. You can administer any test you want. The only thing I ask is that you do it quickly and that you keep this completely confidential."

"I'm afraid it's already too late for that, Mr. Rafferty."

Victor leaped to his feet, knocking over the chair. He turned in the direction of the voice and was startled to see a well-dressed woman standing behind him at an open door which he had assumed was a closet; now he could see the adjoining room beyond the door. The woman had been there all the time. She had seen and heard everything, and now Victor knew what Roger had been trying to hide.

Visual and mental images came at him in a rush: young and attractive but cold; high self-esteem, exaggerated sense of self-importance; fiercely competitive, slightly paranoid, habitually condescending. She concealed her nervousness well.

"Tell me, Mr. Rafferty," the woman continued, "don't you think the scientific community—your country—has a *right* to know about you?"

Victor turned slowly to Roger. "Who is she?" he asked very deliberately.

Roger's face was crimson. "Victor—Mr. Rafferty—I'd like you to meet Dr. Lewellyn, one of my colleagues."

"What the hell is she doing here?"

"Victor, I . . . I asked Dr. Lewellyn to observe. I value her opinion. I thought perhaps—"

"You had no right." Victor turned to face Dr. Lewellyn. "The answer to your question is *no*," he said tightly. "Neither you nor anyone else has any right to my life or my personal problems."

"Mr. Rafferty, I don't think you understand—"

"I mean it, Roger," Victor said, cutting her off, turning his back on her once again. "I expect this case to be handled with the utmost confidence. And I hold you responsible for this woman!" He hesitated, wondering why he suddenly felt so afraid. "If any word of this gets out, I'll deny the whole thing," Victor continued softly. "I'll make both of you look very foolish. Roger, I'll call you tomorrow. You can experiment with me all you want, but my condition *must* be kept secret. Is that clear?" He did not wait for an answer. Glancing once at Dr. Lewellyn, he walked quickly from the room.

"You've made a fantastic discovery, doctor," the woman said.

"Yes," Roger agreed, but there was no trace of his former enthusiasm.

"But he's terribly naive, don't you think? He must realize that we have certain obligations."

"I suppose so," the doctor said, crumpling the cards in his hands and studying their motions as they drifted lazily to the floor.

Pat Rafferty glanced up as her husband came through the door. She watched him for a moment, and her eyes clouded. "Victor," she said gently, "you smell like a brewery."

"I should," he said evenly. "I just drank a quart of scotch." He went quickly into the bathroom and splashed water over his face and neck. When he came back into the living room he was startled to find her standing in the same spot staring at him, her pale blue eyes rimmed with tears of hurt and confusion. Six years of marriage to the slight, blonde-haired woman had not dulled his love for her; if anything, the years had magnified his desire and need. It had been three days since the tests in Roger's laboratory and still he had not told Pat. It would have been hard enough, at the beginning, to tell her he feared for his sanity. Confirmation of his ability had only compounded his problem. How, he thought, does a man tell his wife she's married to a monster? "I'm not drunk," he said, turning away from her eyes. "I'm not even sure if it's possible for me to get drunk any more."

Pat continued to stare, dumbfounded at the words of this man who had, seemingly by intent, become a stranger to her. There was something in his eyes and voice that terrified her, robbed her of speech.

"You see," Victor continued, "I've made a remarkable discovery. If I drink enough, I can't hear other people thinking. I'm left *alone*. I . . ." Victor stopped, aware that his need had spoken the words his intellect would not. He turned away to hide his own tears of anguish. He did not flinch when he felt Pat's soft, cool fingers caressing the back of his neck. "I need your help," he murmured, turning and burying his face in his wife's hair.

Victor talked for hours, pausing only once when night fell and Pat rose to turn on the kitchen lights. He told her everything: the pain, his fear, the experiments in Roger's office. When he had finished, he drew himself up very straight and stared into her eyes. "Do you believe me?"

"I don't *know*, Victor. You've been acting so strangely for the past few months. I want to believe you, but . . ."

"The alcohol's worn off. Would you like me to demonstrate what I'm talking about?"

"I . . ."

"Think of a number. Go ahead; do as I say."

Victor held Pat's gaze and waited, probing, hunting for the numbers that he knew must eventually merge with the doubt and confusion he felt in her mind. When they came, he called them off with machine-gun rapidity, in a voice that never wavered. One by one he exposed every thought, every fleeting impression. He did not stop even when he felt the doubt replaced by panic. He could not escape the conviction that something terrible was about to happen. He needed Pat. Therefore, she must be convinced beyond any doubt that—

"*Stop!*" Pat's hands were over her eyes in a vain attempt to stem the tide of thick, heavy tears that streamed in great rivulets down her cheeks. "Stop it, Victor! Stop it! *Stop it!*"

Pat leaped from her chair and ran into the living room. Victor waited a few minutes and then followed. She was huddled on a far end of the sofa. He reached out to touch her but immediately stepped back as he felt her flesh quiver beneath his touch. In that moment he had felt what she felt and the knowledge seared him. He stepped farther into the darkness to hide his own tears. "I'm not a freak," he said quietly, and he turned away and headed back into the kitchen in an attempt to escape the sound of Pat's sobbing.

Her voice stopped him. "Forgive me, darling."

Victor stood silently, unwilling to trust his voice. He watched his wife sit up and brush away the tears from her face.

"I'm so ashamed," Pat continued in a voice that was steady. "I don't know what to say to you. All that time you were hurting so much . . . I *love* you so much, so very much . . ."

He went to her, folded her into his arms. They stayed that way for several minutes, each enjoying the renewed warmth and security in the touch of the other's body.

"You're afraid," Pat said at last.

"Yes."

"Why?"

Victor told her about Dr. Lewellyn.

"I still don't understand why you're afraid."

"They'll try to use me."

Pat pulled away just far enough to look up into Victor's eyes. "There's so much you could contribute, darling. Imagine what you could do in psychiatry, helping to diagnose patients. Think how much more scientists could learn from you about the human mind."

"They won't use me for those things," Victor said, surprised at the conviction in his voice. He had found the elusive source of his fear. "They'll use me for a weapon. They always do."

Pat was silent for long moments, her head buried once again in his neck. "We'll move away," she said at last.

"They'll follow."

"We'll change our names, start all over again."

"We'll see," Victor said, but he sensed that it was already too late.

Later, Victor lay back in the darkness and listened to Pat's troubled dreams. The orange-yellow glow of dawn trickled through the blinds of the bedroom window. He had not slept. If Roger was right, if his mind was, indeed, a window on man's future, what right *did* he have to keep that portal shuttered?

Pat was beginning to stir and Victor recognized the sharpening thought patterns that he had learned to identify as the bridge between sleep and consciousness. He slipped on his robe and went to the kitchen to make coffee. Pat joined him a few minutes later, kissed Victor lightly on the cheek and began preparing breakfast.

They ate in silence. Victor had poured a second cup of coffee and lighted a cigarette when the doorbell rang. He rose and kissed Pat full on the mouth, holding her close to him. He sensed, even before he had opened the door and looked into the man's mind, that the waiting was over.

He was a small man. His short arms and thin, frail body were in direct contrast to the strength Victor found in his mind. His face was pale and pockmarked, punctuated with a large nose that sloped at an angle as if it had been broken once and never properly set. He wore a thick topcoat and even now, in the gathering warmth of the morning, drew it around him and shivered as if he were cold.

"I'm Mr. Lippitt," the man said to Victor. "I think you know why I'm here."

"Come in," Victor said, surprised at the steadiness of his own voice. The man entered but politely refused Victor's invitation to sit. Victor glanced over his shoulder at Pat and waited until she had returned to the kitchen. "What do you want, Mr. Lippitt?"

The man suddenly thrust his hands into his pockets in a quick motion which served to break his wall of concentration. The dark eyes in the pale face riveted on Victor, measuring his reaction as he allowed his thoughts and knowledge to rush forth.

He's too strong, Victor thought; *too strong.* But he didn't react.

"If my information is correct," Mr. Lippitt said slowly, "you know what I'm thinking right now."

Victor returned the other man's gaze. He sensed pain, chronic discomfort that Mr. Lippitt went to great lengths to conceal. "Are you sure you have the right house?" For the briefest moment there was a flicker of amusement in Mr. Lippitt's eyes and Victor found that, in spite of himself, he liked the man.

"The people I represent believe you have a rather remarkable talent, Mr. Rafferty. Obviously, I'm not referring to your abilities as an architect. We know all about your interviews with Dr. Burns. We'd like to test and interview you ourselves. We would pay well for the privilege."

"No," Victor said evenly. "I don't wish to be tested or interviewed by anyone. Not anyone."

Mr. Lippitt's gaze was cold and steady. He hunched his shoulders deeper into his coat. "You understand that we could force you. We don't want that. Surely, you can see the necessity—"

"Well, I *can't* see the necessity!" Victor exploded. "What do you want from me?"

Lippitt's face registered genuine surprise. He drew his hand out from his pocket and gestured toward his head. "Don't you see?"

"I know who you work for," Victor said impatiently. "I can tell that you're not quite sure what to do with me and that I'm considered some kind of potential threat. The rest is very vague. Your training was very thorough; you're subconsciously blocking all sorts of information that you don't think I should have."

"You scored perfectly on a telepathic indicator test," Lippitt said, eyeing Victor curiously. "You can read thoughts like the rest of us read newspapers."

"It's not quite that simple."

"But it could be! I've heard the tapes of your conversations with Burns! You can control—" Mr. Lippitt paused and again Victor sensed his physical discomfort. When Lippitt spoke again his voice was softer and his breath whistled in his lungs. "We live in an age of technological terror. Both sides spend millions of dollars gathering information to assure themselves that they're not going to come out second best in any nuclear war."

"I'm not a spy, and I don't have the training or inclination to become one."

"Your mind makes conventional methods of espionage obsolete," Mr. Lippitt said, his eyes blazing. "Don't you see, Mr. Rafferty? You could gather more information in one hour spent at an embassy cocktail party than a team of experts could gather in a year! One drink with a foreign ambassador or general and you'd have the most valuable diplomatic and military information! There'd be no way for them to stop you. You'd know who was lying, what military moves were being considered, information that other men must risk their lives to get! In a way, you'd be the ultimate weapon. We would always be assured of having the most up-to-date and reliable—"

"Have I done anything wrong? Committed any crime?"

"No," Mr. Lippitt said, taken aback.

"Do you have the authority to arrest me?"

"No."

"Then my answer is still *no*," Victor said firmly. "I have a right as a citizen of this nation to be left alone."

"Have you considered your *duty* to this nation?"

"How would you know I was always telling the truth?"

"Ah, well . . . I don't have an answer for that; not now. I suppose, eventually, we would have to consider that."

"I don't want to work for you. I *won't* work for you."

Mr. Lippitt lighted a cigarette. Victor handed him an ashtray. Their eyes held steady.

"It's not that simple, Mr. Rafferty," Lippitt said. "It's just not that simple. No matter what you decided, you'd still need our protection."

"Protection?" The idea was there in Lippitt's mind but it was hazy and undefined.

"Our informant—"

"Dr. Lewellyn?"

"Dr. Lewellyn was more fervent than discreet," Mr. Lippitt said in a matter-of-fact tone that failed to conceal his embarrassment. "The channels she used to inform us of your existence were not, as we say, *secure*."

"You mean that in the spy business nothing stays a secret for very long."

"Not always," Mr. Lippitt said evenly, ignoring the other man's sarcasm. "But in this case we must assume that there's a possibility other powers may already know about you. If so, well, I think they'd go to great lengths to prevent you from working for us."

"They'd kill me?"

"Without a second thought. Unless, of course, they felt they could force you to work for them."

Victor was conscious of his wife moving about in the kitchen. "You'd have to eliminate every trace of my existence," he said. "Otherwise, I'd be useless to you. And what are you going to do with Pat? Maybe she wouldn't care to undergo plastic surgery. Certainly, I'd have to."

"We'd handle everything. Would you rather risk having her see you killed? Or they might torture her if they thought it would do them any good. You know, their methods can be quite effective. You might have a more difficult time explaining to them that you simply choose not to use your skills for a dirty business like spying."

Victor's head hurt from the prolonged contact with Lippitt. His entire body ached and throbbed with exhaustion. "What if I decide to take my chances?" He no longer made any effort to mask his anxiety.

"I'm afraid that would put *us* in a difficult position," Mr. Lippitt said slowly, for the first time looking away from Victor. "You see, if you weren't working for us, we'd have no way of being certain you weren't working for *them*. They wouldn't hesitate to kill your wife or anybody else if it would force you over to their side." Lippitt's eyes hardened. "Or they simply might offer you a million dollars. Sometimes it's as easy as that."

Victor flushed. "Either way, then *you'd* have to stop me."

"Yes."

"Then I'm trapped."

"I'm afraid so, Mr. Rafferty. I'm sorry that it has to be this way."

Victor rubbed his sweating palms against his shirt. He was seized with a sudden, almost overwhelming desire to strike out, to smash his fist into the white face that looked as if it would tear like paper. He clenched his fists, but his arms dropped back to his sides in a gesture of resignation. Lippitt was right; on a planet covered with nations strangling on their own words of deceit and treachery, he was the ultimate weapon. He could determine truth, and he sensed that absolute truth and certainty would be a most dangerous possession in the hands of the wrong men. Had Hitler known the frailties of the men he fought, he would have ruled the world. On the other hand, a telepath could have prevented Pearl Harbor.

"Can I have some time to think about it?"

"What is there to think about?"

"Dignity. Allow me the dignity of believing I still have some freedom of choice."

Mr. Lippitt looked at Victor strangely for a moment before drawing a card from his pocket and handing it to him. "You can reach me at this number, any time of the day or night. Call me when you've . . . reached your decision." He paused at the door, turned and looked at Victor in the same odd manner. "I meant what I said, Mr. Rafferty. I am sorry that it has to be this way."

"So am I," said Victor.

The door clicked shut behind Victor with a terrible certainty, muffling Pat's sobs, punctuating a decision Victor knew could not be reversed. There was no turning back once he had begun running. Never again could he be trusted, but he would be free.

Somewhere in the United States there had to be a place where he and Pat could lose their identities and start over, perhaps a small town in the south or the west. Victor knew he must find that place and find it quickly. Then he would send for Pat. Perhaps it was, as he suspected, a futile gesture, but it was something he had to attempt, the only alternative to imprisonment in a world of uniforms, security checks, and identity cards. He knew, too, that he must conserve his strength; already his arm ached from the weight of his single suitcase.

He knew there was something wrong the moment he stepped down from the porch. Victor felt the man's presence even before he spoke.

"Please stop right there, Mr. Rafferty."

Victor froze; he knew there was no sense in trying to run. Even without the suitcase, which he needed because it contained his bank book and credit cards, he realized that his physical condition would never enable him to outrun the guard. He turned and stared into a pair of cold, gray eyes. The man was short and stocky, very well dressed, with close-cropped blond hair. Victor felt the man's mind coiled like a steel spring.

"Who the hell are you?" Victor snapped, his frustration forming meaningless words. He already knew the answer: Lippitt's man.

"I'm sorry, sir. I must ask you to come with me."

"Your boss told me I'd have time to think things over."

"I'm sorry, sir, but I have my instructions. I was told to bring you with me if it looked like you were trying to leave. Will you follow me, please?"

Victor shifted his weight back on one foot and then lurched

forward, sending the suitcase swinging in an arc toward the man's head. The guard stepped easily aside, allowing the weight of the suitcase to carry Victor around until he was off balance. He moved with the grace of a dancer, stepping behind Victor, knocking the suitcase to the ground and twisting Victor's arm up behind his back gently but firmly, so that the responsibility for any pain would be Victor's if he attempted to struggle.

Victor acted instinctively, throwing back his head and closing his eyes in fierce concentration. He probed, ignoring the blinding pain, searching for some fear or anxiety in the guard's mind that he could touch and *grab hold of* with his own. There was something there, dark and shapeless, rough and rattling with death. Victor strained, probing harder and deeper, obsessed with the need to escape.

Now the guard was making strange, guttural sounds deep in his throat. Victor felt steel-hard fingers at his neck, pressing, searching for the nerve centers at the base of his skull. He was inside the guard's mind and there was pain there that he was causing; still the man would not let go. Victor probed still deeper, wrenching the sensations, magnifying the pain.

Then the fingers were no longer around his neck. Victor turned in time to see the man sink to the ground. The guard was moaning softly, writhing on the ground and gripping his head in his hands. The moaning stopped. The guard twitched and then lay still.

Victor knelt down beside the guard and was immediately aware of yet another presence. He threw himself to one side and missed the full force of a blow delivered by a second, larger man who must have been positioned at the rear of the house. The second man tripped over the first and sprawled on the flagstone walk.

This time it was Victor who attacked, swinging around and stepping close to the second guard who was just springing to his feet. There was already pain in the other man as a result of his fall, fear and uncertainty at the sight of his prostrate partner. Victor seized on both thoughts and concentrated, thrusting deep. The man slumped to the sidewalk without a sound.

Victor reached for his suitcase and looked up into the face of Pat, who had run out onto the porch at the sounds of the struggle. Her eyes wide with fear, the woman had jammed her knuckles into her mouth so that only her mind screamed in terror and ripped at Victor's consciousness. Victor threw aside the suitcase, turned and ran, away from the fallen men, away from the horror in his wife's mind.

Roger Burns was certain he'd turned off the lights in his office and laboratory. Even if he'd forgotten, the cleaning woman would have remembered. He'd had no way of knowing that sleeplessness and excitement over the Rafferty file would bring him back here to his office in the middle of the night. Now, someone had broken into the building. There was no other explanation for the shaft of light that leaked out from beneath his office door into the darkness.

Roger's hand rested on the doorknob. He knew he should call the police, yet the only phone was the one on the other side of the door. He could not wake up a neighbor at three o'clock in the morning, the nearest pay booth was three blocks away, and he did not want the intruder to escape. He was outraged at the thought of someone rifling through his highly confidential files, if that was it.

Anger triumphed over reason. Roger burst into the room and then stopped short, frozen into immobility by the sudden realization that the two men in the office were no ordinary burglars and that he had stumbled into a situation he was totally incapable of handling.

The light came from the fluoroscope. One man, an individual Roger had seen a few times at Washington cocktail parties, was taking photographs of Victor Rafferty's X-rays. The other had been microfilming files that Roger knew must also be Victor's. This man now had a revolver in his hand. The long, thick silencer made it seem ridiculously out of proportion, like a toy rifle.

Roger raised one arm and the gun kicked. There was a soft, chugging sound and a small, round, white hole opened in Roger's forehead, then quickly filled with blood.

* * *

Victor sat in a booth at the rear of the coffee shop, toying nervously with a cup of muddy brown coffee and staring at the front page of the newspaper he had spread out before him. He felt numb, dazed with guilt; the stories seemed to leap from the page, stabbing at his senses with twin fingers of accusation. So, Victor thought, I am responsible for the deaths of two men.

He was sure Roger had been murdered because of him; the guard, a man who had merely been doing his job, he had killed himself.

Some enterprising reporter had outwitted the dozen policemen outside his home with a telephoto lens. The picture showed the dead man on the walk. The second guard was just rising to his feet. Mr. Lippitt was standing off to one side, obviously unaware that the photograph was being taken. The picture had been captioned with a single, large question mark.

The waiter, an elderly man with dirty fingernails and a soiled apron, kept glancing in his direction. Victor wearily signaled for another cup. The waiter came to the table and wiped his hands on his shirt.

"Coffee," Victor said, not looking up.

The waiter pointed to the unfinished cup on the table. "You don't look so good, pal," he said. "Maybe you oughta get some food in your stomach."

"I'm all right," Victor said, aware that he sounded defensive. "You can get me some bacon and eggs. And orange juice."

The waiter swiped at the table with a damp rag and then shuffled off, mumbling to himself. Victor reached out for the sugar bowl and began rolling it back and forth between his hands. With the suitcase gone, he had little money and no place to go. In any case, Mr. Lippitt would have all the airports and bus terminals watched. It was too late to do anything and so it didn't bother him that he was too tired to think clearly; there was nothing left to think about. He wondered if they'd shoot him on sight.

He could still feel the *texture* of the guards' minds as he had entered them to twist and hurt; he could see their bodies lying on the ground. Most of all, he remembered the expression of sheer horror on Pat's face.

Victor stopped spinning the sugar bowl. He had been staring at it and it had suddenly come to him that he was seeing the object in an entirely different way, with more than his vision. He *saw* the glass he was touching with his hands; at the same time he could *feel* the mirror image of the bowl somewhere in his brain, elusive, ephemeral, and yet seemingly real enough to be grasped.

Victor slowly took his hands away from the bowl and touched the image in his mind.

The pain was greater than any he had ever known. Victor immediately released the image and gripped the edges of the table in an effort not to lose consciousness. The pain passed in a few moments, gradually ebbing away. He opened his eyes but did not have enough time to evaluate what had happened. The waiter, approaching his table with a tray of food, tripped over a loose linoleum tile. The tray and its contents came hurtling through the air. Victor reacted instinctively in an effort to protect his only set of clothes; he reached out and pushed at the tray with his mind. At that instant Victor felt his body bathed in searing fire. The walls and ceiling tilted at an odd angle and the floor rushed up to smash into his face.

The waiter stared, dumbfounded. His startled gaze shifted rapidly back and forth between the unconscious man on the floor and the eggstains on his apron. Something was wrong, he thought, something besides the man on the floor; there was something out of place. The old man's slow mind struggled with the problem of the flying tray and food as he hurried to call the police and an ambulance.

Now only the memory of the pain remained, like the lingering, fuzzy morning taste of too many cigarettes. Victor's mind and senses were clear at last, cleansed of their blinding crust of panic by the shock of coma. The sour, antiseptic smell in his nostrils told him he was in a hospital; the dull throb in his skull told him he was not alone. Victor kept his eyes closed and lay very still.

He recalled the incident in the coffee shop very clearly and he knew what had happened. He had seen the word in the textbooks: *telekinesis,* the theoretical ability to move objects by the intense focusing of thought energy. Except that telekinesis was no longer theoretical; he could do it. No matter that the crippling pain made it highly improbable that he could ever use it effectively; the very fact that he had exhibited the power made him that much more desirable, or dangerous, in the eyes of Mr. Lippitt and whoever had killed Roger Burns. Perhaps they had already decided that the risks of using him were too great. He had run. He had killed a man. He was a criminal. They could easily shut him away in some prison for the rest of his life to make sure, if he didn't work for them, he wouldn't work for anyone else.

In the meantime, Pat was in terrible danger. Whoever had killed Roger would be after her next; Mr. Lippitt had said as much. They would torture her, kill her, if they thought it could lead them to him. Victor was sure Mr. Lippitt had assigned men to guard her but that couldn't last forever. No, Victor reflected, he was endangering Pat by the very fact that he was alive.

The guard testified to the fact that he was caught. Probably the police or the hospital had called his home, and Mr. Lippitt would certainly have the phone tapped. Victor was surprised the thin man in the overcoat wasn't already at his bedside.

His was a prison with no doors and windows, a killing trap that was sucking his wife in to die with him, a problem with no solution—except one; only one. It was, as yet, only the embryo of an idea. First, he must escape the hospital.

"I'm feeling very well now," Victor said loudly, sitting up quickly and swinging his legs over the side of the bed. "Maybe you can tell me where my clothes are."

The policeman sat up as if stabbed with a pin. Startled, he fumbled for his gun and finally managed to point it in Victor's direction, but the asking of the question had been enough to implant the answer in the policeman's mind. Victor probed gently; the policeman was very tired; and his clothes were in the white closet at the far end of the room.

"You might as well just lay back there, mister," the policeman said, releasing the safety on his pistol as an afterthought. "I'm not even supposed to let you go to the head without keepin' an eye on you."

Victor crossed his legs on the bed. His lungs ached from the tension, but he managed to feign innocence. "Well, do you mind telling me why?" He must put the policeman off guard and there wasn't much time.

The policeman eyed Victor suspiciously. "I'm not supposed to talk about it."

Victor began to probe deeper and then stopped, sickened by the memory of the man he had killed outside his home. In that moment he knew he would not kill another innocent man, even if it meant his own death. Then, how?

" . . . damned silly."

"What's that?"

The policeman hesitated, and Victor probed, gently magnifying the frustration he found in the other man's mind. He smiled disarmingly. "I didn't hear what you said."

"I didn't say . . . Oh, hell, this whole thing is silly. Some little guy claims you turned a plate of eggs around in the air without touchin' them. 'Fore ya know it, I'm pullin' this extra babysittin' duty."

"That does sound pretty silly." Then he knows for certain, Victor thought; Mr. Lippitt knows I am telekinetic.

"Mind you, I was just on my way out the *door* when I pull this duty. As if that wasn't enough, I'm catchin' a few winks and this creep comes in and belts me in the mouth! He *hits* me, mind you! Weird little guy in an overcoat! Must be eighty degrees in here and this guy's wearin' an overcoat! I'd have killed any other guy did that and this creep's a *little* guy. But his eyes; I never seen eyes like that. Crazy, if ya know what I mean. Man, ya don't mess with a guy that's got eyes like that." The policeman sneezed and Victor sat very still. "Anyway, this guy says he'll have my job *and* my pension if I fall asleep again. Just like that! No, sir! Ya don't mess with a guy like that. And get this, he takes the key and locks me *in* here! He's gotta be some kind of big shot or he wouldn't dare do somethin' like that. Says he's gotta go someplace and he'll be right back." The man rubbed his nose and lips with an oversized red handkerchief, then blew hard into it and repeated the process. "I think he's some kind of spy," the policeman continued, studying Victor through narrowed eyelids. "I think maybe you're a spy, too. Spies are always makin' up screwy stories. Call 'em *cover* stories. See it all the time in the movies."

Victor choked back the strained, hollow laughter in his throat. "Did he say where he was going?"

The hand with the gun had relaxed. Now it tightened again and the barrel leveled on Victor's stomach. "You ask too many questions," the policeman snapped. "I ain't even supposed to talk to you. Maybe you're a *Russky* spy. Yeah, for all I know you're some kind of commie."

"It's all a mistake," Victor said very quietly, eyeing the gun. "I asked where the man went because I'm anxious for him to get back. I'm sure everything will be straightened out when he gets here. It's just too bad you had to get dragged into it, particularly when you didn't sleep much last night."

"Hey, how'd you know I didn't get much sack time?"

"Your eyes look tired. You were probably out playing poker with some of the fellas."

"Sonuvagun, you know you're right? Dropped twenty bucks and my wife's gonna be screamin' at me for a week!"

Victor began to concentrate on a single strand of thought. "You must be very tired," he said, accenting each word, caressing the other man's weariness. "You should sleep." The policeman yawned and stretched, and Victor glanced toward the door. Mr. Lippitt could enter the room at any time; he'd have other men with him. "It's all a mistake. You're free to go to sleep, to rest."

"I . . . can't do that." The man was fighting to keep his head up. The gun had fallen on the floor and he looked at it with a dazed expression.

"It's all right. You can sleep. Go to sleep."

The policeman looked at Victor with a mixture of bewilderment and fear and then slumped in his chair. Victor quickly eased him onto the floor before going to the cabinet and taking out his clothes. He dressed quickly and stepped close to the locked door. He bent down and looked at the lock, breathing a sigh of relief; it was a relatively simple, interlocking bolt type with which he was quite familiar.

Victor knew he must not think of his fear or the pain which was to come, but only of the consequences of failure. He sat on the floor and closed his eyes. He rested his head against the door, summoning up in his mind an image of the moving parts of the lock, each spring, each separate component. He knew he must duplicate his feat in the coffee shop; he must control the image in his mind so as to move the tiny metal bars in the door. Pat's life, and probably his own, depended on it.

The pain came in great, sweeping, hot waves, as it had in the coffee shop, and Victor recognized the wet, dark patches behind his eyes as the face of death. He could feel his fingernails breaking and bleeding as he pushed them into the wood, defying the agony. The lock *must* turn. His blood surged through his body, bloating the veins and arteries in his face and neck to the point where Victor knew, in a few seconds at most, they must burst.

The lock clicked.

Physically exhausted, Victor slumped to the floor. He sucked greedily at the cool drafts of air wafting in beneath the door as he waited for the fire in his head to cool. At last he rose and opened the door far enough to look out into the corridor. Empty; Mr. Lippitt had thought the locked door would be enough.

The policeman was beginning to stir. Victor hurriedly found the man's wallet and took out the money he needed. Then, summoning up his last reserves of strength, he stepped out into the hallway and headed for the emergency exit.

Pat Rafferty opened her eyes and stared into the darkness. She did not have to look at the luminous dial on the alarm clock to know it was the middle of the night; and there was someone in the room with her. "Victor?" She said it like a prayer.

"Yes," came the whispered reply. "Don't be frightened and don't turn on the light. I want to make love to you."

Pat felt a shiver run through her body. The voice was Victor's but it was different somehow, flat and sad. Resigned. His hand was on her body.

"Victor, I can't—"

"Don't think that, darling. Please love me. I need you now."

She felt her desire mount as Victor pressed his mouth against hers; his closeness and the need of her own body swept away her fears and she reached out to pull him down alongside her. In a few minutes they lay, spent and exhausted, in each other's arms; but Victor rose almost immediately and began dressing.

"Victor, please come and lie down again."

"I can't, darling. There isn't much time. I have to go."

Pat rubbed her eyes. Everything seemed so unreal. "How did you get in? There are men all around the house."

"I have my own built-in radar system," Victor said. "I can tell where they are." He moved closer to the bed so that Pat could just make out his shape in the darkness. She raised her arms but Victor moved back out of her reach. "I had to take the chance," he continued. "I had to see you to tell you I've always loved you. You see, I have to do something . . . terrible. There's no way to make you understand. I had to see you this one last time to say goodbye."

"Goodbye? Victor, I don't understand. Why . . . ?" She was suddenly aware of a numb, *thick* sensation in her forehead. Her ears were buzzing. "Victor," Pat murmured, "I feel so strange . . ."

"I know, darling," Victor said. His voice was halting as if he were choking on tears. "I know. Goodbye."

He stood in the darkness for a long moment, staring at the still figure on the bed. Once he started to walk toward her and then stopped. Finally he turned and went back the way he had come.

Mr. Lippitt sat at his desk in the specially heated office. His feet were propped up on his desk and he held a steaming glass of tea in his hand. His frail body was enclosed in a thick, bulky sweater buttoned to the mid-point of his chest. He sipped at his tea and stared off into space. He regretted the fact that the order had gone out to kill Victor Rafferty.

But what else could one do with such a man save kill him? Lippitt thought. He can read thoughts, move objects, and he can kill, all without lifting a finger. The military potential of such a man is too great ever to risk its possible use by a foreign power. Unlike the atom, there is only one Victor Rafferty, and whoever commands his allegiance possesses a terrible weapon, a deadly skill that was silent and could be used over and over again undetected, with virtually no risk to its user. I had always prided myself as a good judge of character, Lippitt thought. I would have sworn to Rafferty's decency and patriotism. Then why had he run?

Mr. Lippitt was interrupted in his thoughts by the buzz of the intercom. "Yes?"

"There's a message on an outside line, sir. I've already scrambled the circuit. Should I put him through?"

Mr. Lippitt's feet came down hard on the floor, jarring the desk and its contents, spilling the tea over a stack of multicolored, cross-indexed documents Lippitt had spent the day ignoring. He waited until he was sure he had regained control of himself and then picked up the receiver. "All right," Mr. Lippitt said, "cut him in."

There was a soft, whirring sound in the line, an automatic signaling device signifying that the scrambling device had been activated. "Lippitt here."

"He's in New York City," said the voice on the other end of the line. "He has a research lab in the Mason Foundry. He's hiding there. What are your instructions?"

Mr. Lippitt bent over and picked up the overturned glass. "What's your code name?"

"Vector Three," came the easy reply.

"Of course," Mr. Lippitt said, fingering the glass. "And I suppose that's where you are? The Mason Foundry?"

"Of course."

Mr. Lippitt hung up and shoved the revolver beneath his sweater, inside his waistband along the hard ridge of his spine. He jabbed at the intercom.

"Yes, sir?" came the quick reply.

"I want a jet to New York, *now*," Mr. Lippitt barked at the startled secretary. "Arrange for helicopter and limousine connections. All top priority."

Mr. Lippitt was not surprised to find no agent waiting for him outside the building; neither was he surprised to find Victor Rafferty waiting for him inside.

"Come in," Victor said, leveling a pistol at Mr. Lippitt's forehead and motioning him to a chair across the booklined executive office. "You look as if you expected me."

Mr. Lippitt shrugged. "You picked the wrong man's brain. Vector Three left for France two days ago."

"Then why did you come?"

"May I have a cigarette?" Victor threw a pack of cigarettes across the room and Mr. Lippitt purposely let them fall to the carpet. He bent over, freeing the revolver. He was certain his speed was sufficient to draw and kill Rafferty before the other man could even pull the trigger. He sat back up in the chair and lighted the cigarette. "I was curious," Mr. Lippitt said casually. "I don't think you meant to kill that man. If I did, I'd have had this place surrounded with troops. Why did you run?"

"I don't think I could make you understand."

"That's too bad. You see, having you around is like living with an H-bomb; whether it's ticking or not, it still makes you uncomfortable."

"Now you're beginning to understand."

Mr. Lippitt glanced around the room, fascinated by the many models of buildings Victor had designed, relying on the properties of the high-tension steel alloy developed by the foundry. Strange, he thought, how buildings had never interested me before. He rose and walked across the room to examine one of the models more closely; he could feel the gun aimed at the back of his neck.

"So, what are you going to do?" Mr. Lippitt asked.

"I've already been contacted and all the arrangements have been made. I leave for Russia tonight."

"That means you'll have to kill me."

"Yes."

Mr. Lippitt turned to face Victor. "Why? I mean, why defect?" He no longer made any effort to hide the emotion in his voice. "I wouldn't have thought you were a traitor."

Anger flickered in Victor's eyes, then quickly faded. "You forced me to do what I'm doing," Victor said. "An H-bomb! That's what you compared me to, right? To you and your people—"

"They're your people, too."

"All right, *people!* To people, I'm nothing more than a weapon! Did it ever occur to you I might want to lead my own life?"

"We've already been over that. Without us, you and your wife would either be killed or kidnapped. We wouldn't want you to be killed; we couldn't allow you to be kidnapped."

"Exactly. So it boils down to this: since my life is no longer my own anyway, the only thing I can do is choose the side which can best provide protection for Pat and myself. That means a communist country. By definition, a police state can provide more protection than a non-police state. Since I wouldn't be *free* in either country, I have to pick the country where I would be *safe*. Their very lack of freedom guarantees my life and Pat's."

"Very logical."

"Oh, there's money, too. I won't deny that. As long as I have to live out my life in virtual captivity, I may as well be comfortable. I've been assured of . . . many things. You don't operate that way, do you?"

Mr. Lippitt ground out his cigarette and immediately lighted another. He regretted not killing Rafferty when he had the chance. "No, we don't. Unfortunately, our budget forces us to rely on patriotism."

Victor said nothing. Mr. Lippitt watched the other man rise and walk toward him. He tensed, waiting for exactly the right moment to drop to the floor and grab for his gun. He knew it would be very difficult now, for Rafferty was close and the element of surprise was gone. Yet, he knew he must not fail; he was the only remaining barrier between Rafferty and the Russians.

"Out the door," Victor said, prodding Mr. Lippitt with the gun. "Left and up the stairs. Walk slowly."

"Don't be melodramatic. Why not just shoot me here?"

"I want to show you something. If you prefer, I'll shoot you now."

There was something strange in the other man's voice, Mr. Lippitt noted, an element that he could not identify. In any event, he realized he would stand little chance if he made his move now. He walked ahead and through the door. The barrel of Rafferty's pistol was pressed against his spine, no more than an inch above the stock of Lippitt's revolver.

The stairway led to a long, narrow corridor. Mr. Lippitt walked slowly, the echo of his footsteps out of phase with those of the man behind him. He said, "It's quiet. Where is everybody?"

"There's no shift on Saturday," Victor said tightly. "There's only the watchman. I put him to sleep."

"You can do that?"

"You know I can."

"Just making conversation." Mr. Lippitt hesitated. "There is such a thing as *lesser evil* in the world, Rafferty. We need you on our side. Think about it."

"I'm sorry," Victor said. He reached out and grabbed Mr. Lippitt's shoulder. "In there."

Mr. Lippitt pushed through the door on his left marked RE-STRICTED. He found himself on a very narrow catwalk overlooking a row of smelting furnaces. The cover hatches of the furnaces were open, and Mr. Lippitt looked down into a liquid, metal sea that moved with a life of its own, its silver-brown crust buckling and bursting, belching huge bubbles of hot, acrid gas. The air was thick, heavy with its burden of heat.

"You wanted to show me where you were going to dump my body," Mr. Lippitt said.

"Yes."

Mr. Lippitt watched Victor's eyes. He could not understand why the other man had not been able to probe his thoughts and discover the existence of the gun. Perhaps he had not felt the need; the reports had mentioned the pain linked with the act. In any case, Mr. Lippitt thought, Rafferty will be dead the moment he blinks or looks away for even a fraction of a second. "You're going to do very well in your chosen profession," Mr. Lippitt said, steeling himself for the move he knew he would have only one chance to make. "People tend to trust you, give you the benefit of the doubt. You have a very disarming air about you."

"That's not all I wanted to show you," Victor said.

Lippitt's muscles tensed but his hand remained perfectly still. When he did go for the gun it would be in one fluid, incredibly explosive motion.

"I want to show you what might have been if things were different," Victor said.

Mr. Lippitt said nothing. It seemed to him that Rafferty was relaxing, letting down his guard. Also, he judged that the angle of the gun would allow him to get off at least one shot, even if he were hit, and one shot was all he needed. Still, he waited.

"You're cold," Victor said suddenly. "You can't even feel the heat from those furnaces."

"What?"

"I said, you're cold. You're always cold. You've been cold for the past twenty years. That's why your mind is so strong. You can't block out the memories so you control and discipline yourself to the point where they no longer make any difference, but still you can't feel any warmth."

"Don't," Mr. Lippitt said, his voice scarcely a whisper.

"You can't forget the Nazis and their ice baths. They put you in the water and they left you there for hours. You shook so much you thought your bones would break. You remember how they laughed at you when you cried; you remember how they laughed at you when you begged them to kill you."

"You stay out of my mind! Stop it!" Mr. Lippitt's voice was quivering with rage.

"It takes enormous courage to keep going in the face of memories like that," Victor continued easily. "All those coats, all those overheated rooms; none of it does any good. We're alike, you and I. Both of us suffer agony others can't begin to understand. That's why you broke all the rules and came here alone, even when you knew I'd be waiting for you; you were reluctant to see them kill me."

"You devil," Mr. Lippitt said through tightly clenched teeth. "You play with people, don't you?"

"There's nothing wrong with your body, you know. That healed long ago. The Nazis are gone. You don't have to be cold any more."

There was something soothing and hypnotic about Rafferty's voice. Mr. Lippitt struggled to clear his mind as he fought against the pervading warmth spreading through his body, fought it and yet embraced it as a father his dead child returned to life.

"It's a trick," the thin man said, startled to find his eyes brimming with tears.

"No," Victor said quietly, insistently. "I'm not putting the warmth

in your body; it was always there. I'm simply helping you to feel it.
Forget the water. All that happened a long time ago. You can be
warm. Let yourself be warm."

"No!"

"Yes! Let me into your mind, Lippitt. Trust me. Let me convince
you."

Mr. Lippitt closed his eyes, surrendering to the strange, golden
warmth lighting the dark, frozen recesses of his soul. He thought of
all the years he had spent in the prison of his memory, immersed in
the water that was sucking away his life . . .

"You don't feel cold any more."

"No," Mr. Lippitt whispered. Now the tears were flowing freely
down his cheeks. "I don't feel cold any more."

"Why don't you test it? Take off your coat."

Mr. Lippitt slowly removed his heavy overcoat. Now the revolver
was within easy reach. "I'm sorry," he said. "I'm grateful to you, but
no man should have that kind of power."

"Not unless he can use it wisely," Victor replied, raising the hand
with the gun. The hammer clicked back with the soft, assured sound
of finely-tooled metal. "The demonstration is over."

Mr. Lippitt dropped to his knees and rolled over on his side,
clawing for the gun in his waistband. Years of experience and training had transformed him into a precision killing instrument, the
movements of which must be measured in milliseconds. Still, inside
Mr. Lippitt's mind, it was all slow motion, as in a nightmare; he
drifted through the air and bounced on the concrete, the gun
appearing miraculously in his hand and aimed at Victor Rafferty's
heart, but there was something pulling at the gun, an invisible force
that he could feel writhing like a snake in the metal. Steel bands had
wrapped about his head and were squeezing, crushing his brain. He
pulled the trigger twice, then peered through a mist of pain as
Victor Rafferty threw out his arms and toppled over the guard rail,
his body arching grotesquely as the pull of gravity snapped his legs
over after his body and he fell through space to land with a muffled,
crackling splash in the soft inferno below. It was the last thing Mr.
Lippitt saw before sinking down into a black void laced with the
smell of gunsmoke.

The barrel of the revolver was still warm, leading Mr. Lippitt to conclude that he couldn't have been unconscious more than a few minutes. He lurched to his feet and, supporting himself on the guard rail, stared down into the pit where Victor had fallen; the slag continued to belch and bubble. There was no trace of the other man, not even the smell of burnt flesh. So, he reflected, he had killed the man who had cured him. No matter that there was no choice; for the rest of his life, even as he savored the warmth of the sun on his body, he would remember this day and welcome his own approaching death; he had simply traded one nightmare for another.

He paused at the foot of the stairs and, after a moment's hesitation, entered one of the offices. He picked up a telephone and dialed one of the outside lines to the agency.

"Good afternoon," came the cheery voice, "this is—"

"This is Mr. Lippitt. The fox is dead."

There was a long silence on the other end of the line. When the woman spoke again, her voice was punctuated by heavy breathing.

"Sir, this is an outside line. If you'll wait for just a moment—"

"This is an emergency," Lippitt said slowly. "Fox is dead. Fox is *dead.*"

He hung up before the frightened woman had time to reply. He reasoned that the others would be suspicious at first, at least until they'd had time to check their sources for the code words. Besides, he'd make sure that certain information was leaked. That, he decided, should keep them away from the woman. He lighted a cigarette, then picked up the phone again to call the Rafferty home.

I'm here to see Mr. Thaag.

The Civilized and the Savage. He'd been a guest of the General Assembly the day Senator Thaag had made that speech. He'd never met the man. That should make things easier.

Some men would kill for a tattered tribal banner. Their imagination sets with the sun, their world ends at the horizon. Others travel the planet, whisper many tongues, and find only the face of their brother.

The Civilized and the Savage. How does one tell the difference? He could tell the difference.

May I have your name, sir?

Nagel. John Nagel.

Or any other name. It didn't make any difference. His real name had died with his old identity. It was all there in the two-column obituary in the *Times*. Everything in his past had died back in the foundry with the image he had planted in Mr. Lippitt's mind. Eventually, he would need a new appearance, a new manner and personality. For now, John Nagel would have to get along with tinted contact lenses, false beard, and an exaggerated limp.

He'd miss Pat; he'd ache for her. But his "death" had been her only guarantee of life.

I'm sorry, sir, but your name is not on the appointment list. Are you expected?

He would lean close, make contact with her mind. She must be convinced of his *importance*. The secretary would disappear for a few minutes, then reappear, smiling.

The Secretary General will see you now.

He was not sure what would happen next; he would have to wait until he could get close to Thaag and explore his mind. Even then, he was not sure what he would be looking for; perhaps, simply, a man he could trust.

Victor Rafferty went over his plan once more in his mind. Satisfied, he began walking slowly across the United Nations Plaza toward the massive glass and stone obelisk rising up from New York's East River. He stopped and looked up into the bright, sun-splashed day; a breeze was blowing and the multitude of flags strained against their stanchions, painting a line across the sky.

Love at Second Sight

by Patricia Moyes

Of course the ways of Fate are utterly illogical: otherwise, what possible excuse could Providence have had for picking Bridie Donovan, of all people, on whom to bestow the priceless gift of prophetic dreams? And not just any old prophetic dreams, mind you, but the first three horses in the Derby—one, two, three, just like that.

When you consider the number of earnest and hardworking sportsmen in Dublin, when you think of the patient hours they spend studying form, and the wear and tear to their vocal chords as they discuss the merits of various runners in bars all up and down the city, it makes you weep to think of such an unparalleled blessing being thrown away on a chit of a girl, who'd never so much as bet sixpence on a raffle ticket.

She was a pretty enough little thing, to be sure, with her black hair and blue eyes and creamy skin. I'd often thought so, in a vague sort of way, since she came to work in the office. Perhaps I'd better explain about the office. It's a small import-export firm that I inherited from my father a couple of years ago, much to the disgust of several uncles, who considered that at twenty-five I wasn't capable of running a bath, let alone a business.

I think I can say I proved them wrong. I'm no financial genius, but I managed to keep the place ticking over, and none of the customers complained. There were just the five of us in the office. Me, in my private room, signing letters and directing policy, which generally meant doing the crossword puzzle and studying form. My three clerks—Murphy, Regan, and O'Grady—in the big office where the real work was done. And Bridie, flitting in and out with cups of tea from the little cubicle where she sat with her typewriter. It was a nice, cosy little setup, and we all enjoyed it.

Now, I'm not pretending that everything I'm going to tell you is first-hand because of course I wasn't there for all of it—in fact, as you'll see, I don't really come into the story at all. But I've heard it told so often that I feel I can take a little poetic license. So here goes.

Well, it was on the morning of Derby Day, and we were all hard at work. I had the *Irish Times and Sporting Life* out on my desk, and I was putting in some hours of concentrated study. Next door, Murphy, Regan, and O'Grady had just about every newspaper in Dublin between them, and Regan had brought his form book. They hadn't reached the arguing stage: it was more like the quiet, reverent atmosphere you get at the start of a prayer meeting. They didn't even look up when Bridie came in. Nor did they react when she said, as she hung up her coat, "I had the strangest dream last night, so I did."

Bridie wasn't worried about getting no answer. She was used to talking to herself on Big Race days. So as she combed her hair and powdered her nose and took the cover off her typewriter, she prattled gaily on.

"I was in this great fairground, see, like the one my auntie took me to in Connemara, with coconut shies and swings and bounce-the-lady-out-of-bed and all of it. But the one thing I'd set my heart on—in my dream, this is—was to ride on the roundabout. You never saw such hobbyhorses, all painted in red and blue and gold and yellow, with manes made of real horsehair and real eyes that were alive and tails that swished so that they'd have taken the flies off the creatures, if there'd been any flies. Beside the roundabout was a funny little man, like a pixie. So I asked him how much was it for a ride, as I hadn't but sixpence in my pocket. And he said, 'For you, Bridie Donovan, it's nothing at all. Now, which horse do you fancy?' I said it was all the same to me, and he said, 'Surely you'll be wanting the winner?' "

At the word "winner," Murphy did look up for a moment. He's a little man with red hair and a sharp face, like a weasel. "What's this about a winner?" he asked.

"It's nothing at all, only Bridie's nonsense," said Regan, who's tall and broad and dark as the devil.

"You may call it nonsense, Mr. Regan," said Bridie, with spirit, "but indeed he did give me the winner. And the next two after it."

"What do you mean, gave you the winner?" O'Grady demanded. O'Grady's a plump man in his forties, with soft fair hair like a baby's, and going bald fast.

Bridie closed her eyes. "I can hear him now," she said. "He said, 'The first is red as roses, and the second is yellow as corn, and the third is blue as the sea. The first is from the fire, and the second is from the earth, and the third is from the air.'"

There was a silence. Then O'Grady said, "Would you say all that over again?"

Bridie said it again.

"Well, it's a remarkable thing," said O'Grady. "I don't know if you fellows realize that there's a horse called Flame Flower running today, and another called Cornstalk, and a third by the name of Blue Gull."

"Sure, and none of them in the least interesting," said Murphy.

"Cornstalk might be worth a small investment, if the price were right," said Regan. "I suppose your friend didn't give you the SP by any chance?"

There was a general laugh at this, but finally O'Grady said, "I'll have a tanner each way on each of them, just for luck. You never can tell."

I don't need to tell you, of course, that Flame Flower romped home at 20-1, with Cornstalk second at 100-8, and Blue Gull third at 7-2. O'Grady netted over fourteen bob profit on his six tanners, although he went down the drain with the rest of us on the favorite. However, as you can imagine, it was not the amount won that caused the sensation but the fact that Bridie should turn out to have these sensational powers, which had clearly been bestowed by heaven for the purpose of making the fortunes of Messrs. O'Grady, Murphy, and Regan.

That evening, after the office, the three of them took Bridie out to

a public house and bought her a bottle of Guinness—the first time
such a thing had happened in all her nineteen years, for she lived
with an aunt who was teetotal to a fault.

"Now, Bridie," said O'Grady, "you're to go to sleep tonight with a
pencil and paper under your pillow and in the morning you're to
write down what you've dreamt. Every detail, mind. And you're to
tell nobody but us three."

"You want to find that fairground man again," Murphy added.
"And when you do, take some trouble to cultivate him. Wish him
good morning, or good evening, as may be appropriate, and thank
him for his help."

"You might tell him we're sorry we didn't take his first message
more seriously," said Regan. "I wouldn't like him to think we'd
ignored him, and him taking all that trouble."

Well, Bridie found herself back in the fairground that night in her
dreams, and she met the little attendant, who was as civil as could
be, and she gave him Regan's message, which seemed to please him.
He took her over to the hoop-la stall, and the first ring she threw
encircled a diamond brooch made in the shape of a dart. O'Grady,
Regan, and Murphy scraped up a fiver between them to put on
Bright Arrow in the three thirty, and netted fifty quid.

The next night the fairground attendant took her to the sideshows
and pointed out a magnificent lion in a small cage. The syndicate put
the whole of the kitty on Noble Captive in the four o'clock, which
came in at three to one, so that meant fifty quid for each of them—
although Murphy, who was acting as treasurer, advised them to
leave it all with him for the next day's investment.

How long this would have gone on nobody knows because on the
third day the syndicate made their big mistake. They grew too
greedy, and forgot their manners.

Regan started it by demanding that Bridie ask the man for the
starting prices of the horses he gave them. Murphy went further,
and said she should tell him that they wanted odds of at least ten to
one on all his selections. O'Grady added that the first time he'd
given them the second and third as well, and that he thought the
service was slipping.

That night Bridie, being an honest and straightforward girl, repeated to the fairground attendant what the trio had said. The little man suddenly stopped smiling.

"Oh, so that's the way of it, is it?" he said. "And what are you getting out of all this, Bridie Donovan?"

"Nothing," says Bridie.

"Not even a tanner to keep for yourself?"

"Not a thing," says Bridie.

"Is that so?" says the man. "Well, you shall. I've got something good for your friends tonight. Step this way."

The following morning, Bridie turned up with her notebook as usual, and the syndicate could see that there were several pages of it closely written in Bridie's clear hand. Their spirits rose.

"Come on now, my dear," said Murphy. "Did you tell him what we said?"

"I did that," said Bridie demurely, "and he said he had a good thing for you."

"Let's have it, then," said Regan.

Bridie consulted her notes. "Last night," she said, "he took me to the big circus tent. There was a beautiful lady in pink tights riding round the ring on two horses, standing up with one foot on each of them. One of the horses was a chestnut, and the other was a big black creature. The lady had a sash on her, with the name Joan embroidered on it in red."

"Now there's a funny thing," said Murphy. "There doesn't seem to be any sort of a horse running with a name to fit to that."

"Then," Bridie went on, "the lady climbed down and kissed the black horse and pinned a red rose on its bridle. But the chestnut trotted off to the stables, where there was a little fat donkey nibbling away at some hay. The donkey didn't seem to realize that he wasn't getting his fair share because the chestnut was stealing all the hay from the other side of the manger."

"That's a very odd dream," said O'Grady, studying the lists of runners. "I can't see a horse to fit that."

"Last of all," said Bridie, "the donkey went off to where the black horse was, and he brayed at the top of his lungs, so that all the animals came running. They all started kicking the black horse, and biting it . . . and then I woke up."

"I make no sense of that at all," said Regan. "You'd better tell your man not to set us such riddles in future. We want the names quite clearly."

"There's one name that's clear, and that's Joan," said O'Grady. Then he looked at Murphy, and said, "Your wife's called Joan, isn't she, Murphy?" And then he looked at Regan, the big black fellow, and most pointedly he looked at the red rose that Regan wore in his buttonhole.

At that, Murphy gave a sort of howl. "So that's the way of it, is it?" he yelled, rushing at Regan. "Riding in double harness, is she, and kissing you and giving you roses!"

"Why couldn't you keep your big useless mouth shut?" Regan bellowed at O'Grady. "You're the fat donkey, all right!"

"So I'm the donkey, am I?" shouted O'Grady to Murphy. "In that case, what about the hay you're stealing from my manger? Who made you treasurer anyway?"

Well, as you can imagine, by this time there was a fine fight going on, with everyone at everyone else's throat, and swearing and shouting and eyes being blacked and windows broken. When it got too loud, I thought I'd better take a hand, so I came out of my office.

I suppose I must have seen the three men because it was difficult to miss them, but frankly I didn't notice. What I did see was Bridie, cowering up in a corner, terrified and crying, and I realized quite suddenly that here was the girl I'd been waiting for all my life.

"You're fired, all of you!" I shouted to Murphy, Regan, and O'Grady. They didn't hear me, of course. They were throwing chairs by then. I walked over to Bridie and picked her up in my arms and carried her out of the office.

We've been married nearly a year now, and it's coming up to Derby Day again. I did mention it in passing to Bridie, but she just smiled and told me she didn't dream at all these days. Perhaps it's just as well.

The Misfits

by Jane Rice

The Pritchetts' side street environs of timeworn porch houses were all alike, except for a personal touch here and there—a flamingo yard ornament, a yucca plant, a border of conch shells, a horseshoe nailed above the door of a weary garage. The residents, too, had a certain sameness, but in every neighborhood there are a few eccentrics. Misfits. The Pritchetts themselves could have been termed prime examples.

Reticent, thick-spectacled Elmo Pritchett, though seldom seen, had acquired an image of always being slightly singed around the edges for the reason that his inventive endeavors had earned a reputation for self-destructing in a flurry of pyrotechnics. Nothing to get alarmed about, repetition having borne out the trickle-down across back yard fences that Elmo's ventures, like Elmo, weren't going to set anything on fire. The neighborhood consensus was that he was nuts and that his unassuming, sparrowy little wife, Lottie, had her work cut out for her.

Not that Lottie Pritchett minded. She was convinced that someday Elmo's preoccupation with interstitial space, whatever that was, would cool and he would begin to invent novelty gadgets, and then the shoe would be on the other foot. Meanwhile, she considered her part-time job as a clerk in a shopping center hardware store a godsend that enabled her to augment the shrinking royalties Elmo derived from earlier patents for machine tools that were fast becoming obsolete.

Lottie Pritchett might not be much to look at, or listen to, but she knew how to make ends meet.

However, neighborhood-wise, the consensus was that Lottie was likewise nuts, for the reason that she never threw anything away and, as a consequence—

"—couldn't begin to count the odds and ends of chinaware, the knickknacks, the boxes of gewgaws. Balls of yarn. Goldfish," Annie Biggs told her new neighbor Roxine (call me Roxie) Moore, across their mutual back yard fence, to alert her quick-in-a-hurry as to what to expect of the Pritchetts, who lived on the other side of the Moores, across the opposite fence.

"Boxes of *goldfish?*" The penciled Moore eyebrows arched as far as they would go.

Annie, noting that one of call-me-Roxie's earrings had a pearl missing, set the record straight about the goldfish, which were alive and thriving in their numerous bowls along with a sprinkling of snails and wee turtles.

"I suppose it's her way of compensating for not having had a family," Annie said, thinking that call-me-Roxie's scoop-neck sundress didn't leave much to the imagination, for someone with such a generous upper story. "Not that that's anything against her," she amended hurriedly, some deepdown instinct notifying her that it was highly unlikely call-me-Roxie, despite her endowments, had produced any offspring either.

"I know many's the time, if I'd had my druthers, I'd have stopped at five." Annie gave a light conspiratorial laugh to indicate that her Matt had been some boy-o in his heyday.

She hesitated. Took the plunge. "Just you and the mister?"

"And Jewel," Roxine Moore added absently, her attention having wandered to Annie's hollyhocks.

Annie, who had named her three daughters Opal, Pearl, and Ruby, felt her heart beginning to thaw towards this showy replacement for Mary Murphy, her previous next door sidekick, who, having become increasingly forgetful and prone to "sinking spells," had been packed up willynilly by an officious daughter and whisked off before you could say whipperstitch.

"Jewel," Annie repeated. "What a lovely name. And somewhat of a coincidence, you might say. I named my first three girls Opal, Pearl, and—"

"Clint calls her Jocko," Roxine Moore went on, her tone revealing this was becoming a bone of contention.

Annie, who had been a slow learner and had suffered the nickname "Ninny" until she'd blossomed out in junior high, elevated her own eyebrows in silent commentary on "Clint's" lack of sensitivity. One eyebrow lowered a notch. By the same token, maybe Jewel was the kind who, these days, "monkeyed around" and, in between, came home to roost. Sophie Carrico's son Jack, who was on the rebound, would be a sitting duck if Jewel was in his age bracket.

"Nicknames come and go," Annie said. And, innocently, "How old is she?"

"She'll be a year in September." Roxine reached across the fence, pulled a blossom from one of the hollyhocks, and regarded it curiously.

"A year," Annie echoed, thinking *that must've come as an almighty surprise.*

"I'd like to have another one," Roxine Moore said, using the hollyhock flower to flick a ladybug from her upper arm, "but Clint says nix to that. He says as far as he's concerned one is one too many. He'd sell Jewel in a minute, if I'd let him."

Annie, thinking possibly she hadn't heard correctly, bleated, "*Sell* her?"

"Ummmm. But I'm not about to give in. Not yet. And if he does, without my say-so, it's going to be goodbye Charley and I don't mean maybe." She tucked the flower behind an ear. The penciled brows lifted in query. "Do you have a kitty?"

Back in her kitchen, Annie Biggs put the kettle on for a mid-morning break. "Name's Moore," she said to her husband, who was up on a stepladder giving the ceiling a coat of paint. "Roxine and Clint, which don't sound like names you'd be baptized with. Just the both of them, which might could be why they moved in without much to speak of in the way of furniture, even if they do have a brass bed. Though, if you ask me, in my opinion they get repossessed a lot."

She got down the sugar bowl, two mugs, and a box of tea bags. "Unless I miss my guess from here to Okeechobee, they aren't hitting it off too good. She has this cat she dotes on and he uses it for an excuse to get her goat. He sounds like he might could have a mean streak in him."

She placed a tea bag in each mug. Observed, "I wish they'd quit using plastic strings and go back to string strings. I'm gong to try a different brand next time." She held the box at arm's length to read the brand name, as if the tea had been foisted off on her by an unscrupulous grocer. "There was this purple-green bruise on the inside of her arm and how're you going to knock up against something with the inside of your arm?"

Annie pursed her lips, reflecting on call-me-Roxie's complete lack of interest in Opal and Pearl, much less Ruby, and the decorative use of the hollyhock flower that had been appropriated without so much as a by-your-leave. "She's short on manners and long on splash."

She sniffed, sampling the air. "If you ask me, Elmo Pritchett is trying to invent a substitute for brimstone."

She switched on the radio, flipped the dial to a quartet of gospel singers. "Water's on the boil. You want plain or jelly doughnut? *Matt*, I'm *talking* to you."

Elmo Pritchett emerged, coughing and slapping at himself, from the outside entrance to his basement workshop.

Forewarned by Annie Biggs as to Elmo's occupational hazards, Roxine pretended to be oblivious. Heading for her back steps, her cat cradled in her arms, she glimpsed a movement at her kitchen window. The shadow of a smile twitched a corner of her mouth. Every once in a while she had to make Clint sit up and take notice and, after their last go-round, now was a golden opportunity. With Jewel for conversational openers, this Pritchett individual would be a pushover.

She changed her course and approached their front fence. "Are you all right?"

Elmo, his coughing beginning to subside, nodded that he was all right.

"Are you sure?" She let a note of concern seep into her voice.

Elmo nodded that he was sure. Mulling over the possibility that he had miscalculated the force of gravity on light, thereby negating prismatic inversion as a primary factor in the fusion of dimension, he administered a final slap here and there.

Roxine gave an exaggerated sigh of relief. "Well, you certainly gave *me* a scare. Oh, I'm your new neighbor. Me and my hubby, that is. We're the Moores. Clint and Roxine . . . Roxie for short." She tightened her grip on Jewel, who was becoming restive. "And this is a third Moore. Jewel's her name."

She hoisted Jewel a trifle higher and waited for Elmo Pritchett to say, "Hi there, Jewel," and ask what kind of a cat Jewel was. Everybody always did, usually. When she replied, "Siamese," more often than not those of the masculine gender who weren't in any hurry to terminate the encounter generally kidded, "Where's the other one?" Jewel was practically a foolproof ice breaker.

Elmo Pritchett contemplated the middle distance, as if harkening to a distant drummer.

"A third more joules?" he murmured. The myopic eyes behind the thick glasses became mere squints. His speculative "Hah" acknowledged a fresh hypothesis. The proportionate mass, if *extensive*, would necessitate greater force to counteract inertia. . . . Therefore, induction would *require* more energy per unit volume. At the terminus of gravitational acceleration it might work. Worth the try!

He focused in on Roxine Moore, and before she could collect her wits or discern his intent, he advanced to the fence and grasped her shoulders. "Yes! Yes!" He emphasized each exuberant "Yes!" with an equally exuberant shake.

Jewel, having taken advantage of the opportunity to abandon ship the instant Elmo took over, padded up the Moores' kitchen steps, jumped on the screen door, and, in seeming emulation of what was transpiring down by the fence, shook the screen back and forth, undeterred by a spate of expletives from the interior.

* * *

"What was all that about?" Clint Moore inquired in a tone of bored indifference.

Roxine suppressed a smile, finished wiping her shoulders with a damp tea towel, tossed the towel on the counter. "Don't ask me. I'll say this, he's not the usual."

"You can say that again." Clint Moore retrieved the towel, pulled it taut, aimed it at Jewel's flank.

"I'll say *this* again, if you ever pop her one it's goodbye Charley and I don't mean maybe," Roxine told him, dealing out each word as if it were a face card and she was daring him to up the ante. She shooed Jewel out of the kitchen, saying, "Go find a sunny windowsill, honeybun, before you're obliged to give somebody cat scratch fever." And, to Clint, "Don't *you* go getting *your* back up, hear?"

She settled her sundress. Gave her hair a push. Remembered the flower. Discovered she'd lost it.

"Me? Get my back up? Over a four-eyes in Charlie Chaplin pants? Don't make me laugh."

"He may not be a dude—" she paused just long enough to convey the idea that in her opinion Clint was one and that this was the extent of his accomplishments "—but he's no dumb bunny."

"What's that supposed to mean? I am?"

"You said it. I didn't. If the shoe fits, wear it."

"Now you listen here—"

"Don't you now-you-listen-here me, Clinton *Lewellyn* Moore."

Annie Biggs turned down the gospel singers and listened to the escalating Moores. "See, I told you," she said. "Unless I miss my guess from here to St. Patrick's Day, they spell trouble with a capital T."

"Could be," Matt replied around a mouthful of dunked doughnut. He gave an appreciative chuckle. "With a big rig like her, no telling what." Realizing his mistake, he choked down his mouthful with a too quick swallow of hot tea.

"Don't be biting off more than you can chew," Annie admonished. Except for the innuendo, she might have been chiding him for his table manners.

"She may turn out to be a nice addition to the neighborhood," Matt said defensively.

"I wouldn't bet the rent." Annie's retort was amiable but her eyes were gimlets.

Elmo Pritchett, delving now and then into his rag box, proceeded to make a careful inspection of the elliptical contraption that was bolted to the basement floor and resembled a pipefitter's nightmare. When he was satisfied no real damage had been done—making slight readjustments here and there as he went along—both his bladder and his stomach refused to be denied longer. One needed emptying, the other filling . . . the latter supplying the additional input that if this was Friday—and it felt like a Friday—Lottie would've left him what she called "a duke's mixture" for lunch. Friday was sweep-the-icebox day. When his ship came in, one of the first things they would dispense with was "a duke's mixture."

He patted his invention as if to assure it that the latest setback had been of minor importance. That success was but a hairsbreadth away. That, due to a fluke of circumstance, they were about to snatch victory from the jaws of another defeat. One hundred fourteen other defeats to be exact. No matter. One hundred fifteen was the turning point. He could feel it in his bones. His goal was in sight. This was it!

An unbidden memory surfaced of a bright fall afternoon and a football field. Jim McCready, the squad captain, who was built along the lines of a Mack truck, gave him a man-to-man whack on the butt and said, "This is it, buddy." And, with the score tied and seconds to go in the final quarter of the Big Game, he—Elmo Pritchett—braced himself to kick for a last-ditch try at a field goal. The whistle blew and—with the stadium going wild and Maybeth Lorrimer, in her cheerleader outfit, shrieking his name—he swept forward. The toe of his boot connected squarely with the pigskin and, as the sweet elixir of triumph permeated his whole being, the dream exploded and he found himself on the floor, beside his desk in physics class, rubbing his head and going "wha . . . wha . . . wha . . ." to the unrestrained hilarity of everybody in the classroom with the exception of Miss Jenkins, the teacher, who dismissed Maybeth Lorrimer and Jim McCready from the room until they could pull themselves together—an unfortunate choice of words that increased rather than diminished the mirth. And, right there, he had decided that one day he'd make each and every one of them say, *We knew him when.*

Not that that obtained any more. Not after all these years.

A wistful expression shadowed his countenance.

Still, it would be nice to show up at a class reunion. Just once. Be pointed out. Overhear—*There he is! That's him!*

His eyes dimmed with an unexpected film of tears. He blinked them away. Put his soiled rags to soak. About to go upstairs, he hesitated. Squared his shoulders. Walked to his machine and bestowed a flathanded whap.

"Team," he said.

He about-faced and, ignoring his tingling fingers, mounted the stairs singing "The Strife Is O'er" in a reedy falsetto.

In the basement, not far from the spot where Elmo's whap had landed, a gauge quivered. Activated. Began a quickening metronomic movement. In swift succession a variety of devices triggered into play. There was a *thrum*, and a tremorous hum began to emanate from what had become a working machine.

A thrust of iridescent light as thin as a needle shot into existence and steadily increased in brilliance. Where its tip bored into empty space, an amorphous swirl appeared, grew rapidly in size, and, like a magician's trick conjured out of nowhere by a blinding wand of light, became an aperture. Murky. Cavelike.

The hum altered in pitch. The wand wavered. A chromatic phosphorescence danced among the machine's maze of fittings. The dark opening whirlpooled and silently imploded. The light vanished. A burst of incandescence disintegrated into a shower of sparks that cascaded harmlessly to the cement floor. The hum ceased.

Somewhere upstairs a toilet flushed, and ran until the handle was jiggled. A tap was turned on and off. Elmo, his voice again lifted in song, wended his way kitchenwards.

At Pleet-Holder Hardware, as the afternoon wore on towards closing time, Lottie Pritchett stationed herself advantageously in order to be prepared for the surge of last minute customers trying to get a jump on Saturday, a predictable influx that left the other clerks unenthusiastic despite the WE AIM TO PLEASE machine-stitched in pea green on the breast pocket of their tan jackets.

Not so, Lottie. She knew which side her bread was buttered on, and who kept it buttered, and she had developed a nose for those she perceived as the butterers. She moved in now on a definite Positive—double chin, voile dress patterned with teeny-tiny rose-buds, sensible shoes, "invisible" hairnet, bakery box from Hei-nemann's next door, roundhead door key already in hand to speed the process of having a duplicate made, wherever the means to this end was located in among everything else.

Lottie's solicitous "May I help you, ma'am?" startled her prospective customer, who had been completely unaware of Lottie's presence.

Lottie took pains to make sure the duplicate was perfect, laying aside the first attempt as not quite smooth enough. "We aim to please, even if it costs us," she said. The implication being that the new key was virtually a giveaway. She fostered this concept of Pleet-Holder as a purveyor of freebies, if you took advantage of an opportunity, by providing her customer with a ready pencil and a slip to fill out for the prize that was given each month to the lucky entrant whose name was drawn.

"I have a hunch it could be a pretty china teapot like that one over there with the gilt trim."

Mission accomplished, she reclaimed the pencil from Mrs. Rufus B. Hobbs of 342 Maple Street, wished her a nice weekend, directed her towards the drawing box, and awaited the approach of a Possible whom she assessed as one of the growing number of "swinging singles" who subsisted on frozen pot pies, never defrosted their refrigerators or tidied their bureau drawers. No loose change in the customary places, but plenty of cheese and a variety of crackers, that Perrier water Elmo called H-two-O-and-then-some, tube socks galore, maybe a hotel ashtray from somewhere far off to add to her collection . . . it was amazing how many people stole ashtrays from hotels.

Her "I have a hunch this month it could be beer glasses, like those packaged ones there" produced the desired result. And her "Have a nice weekend" evoked the gratuitous information that he was going to the beach and, on second thought, maybe she'd better make him a couple more keys.

Lordy, Lottie thought, young people these days! She'd surely had a liberal education, in many ways, since the day several years ago when it had dawned on her that if she could somehow acquire a small, nondescript car she could solve her increasingly worrisome budgetary problems, slick as a whistle, without disturbing Elmo's peace of mind one iota.

Occasionally, but not very often, she wondered if the original owner had been taught a lesson about leaving his car keys in the ignition.

Long before the store closed she had garnered, and unobtrusively tagged and pocketed, three more "imperfects." Ample. She knew from experience that these, plus those she had accumulated on her other half days, would fill the gaps her weekly wages wouldn't cover. She had learned how to pick and choose and the persons she selected weren't Pleet-Holder regulars, so she wasn't being disloyal. Furthermore, she made it a point of honor not to take undue advantage, nor throw away a nickel's worth . . . as Elmo said, Waste-Not-Want-Not was her middle name.

Dear, innocent, guileless, unsuspecting Elmo.

Her brown eyes grew limpid. Instead of waiting until tomorrow to investigate Mrs. Rufus B. Hobbs' bakery box, she'd go ahead and splurge on two lemon tarts for a grand finale to the sweep-the-icebox casserole. Elmo loved lemon tarts. Savoring the aftertaste of the last squashy bite, he'd say, "When my ship comes in, we'll have these every day for breakfast."

And she would say, lightly thumping the table for emphasis, "On a silver platter."

And he would reach over and give her fingers a tender squeeze.

Elmo emitted a replete sigh. "When my ship comes in, we'll have these every day for breakfast."

"On a silver platter," Lottie responded, giving the table an affirmative thump.

Instead of tenderly squeezing her fingers, Elmo, too, gave the table an affirmative thump. "I wasn't going to say anything until I was absolutely sure," he said, impulsively. "But I am absolutely sure. It came to me out of the blue. Lottie—" He broke off to fumble through his pockets for notations.

"You've an idea for a novelty item," Lottie hazarded hopefully.

Elmo stared blankly at the dilapidated whatever it was he had dredged up from a pocket. Remembered he had left his calculations in the bathroom when he'd gone up to wash before supper.

"What is it?" Lottie inquired, and answered her own question as she took it from him. "It's a hollyhock flower. Or what's left of one." She returned her puzzled regard to Elmo. "I don't understand."

"Hollyhock flower," Elmo echoed, peering at what she held. His face brightened. "Oh. Yes. That's what she had behind an ear. It fell off while I was giving her a shake. I must have picked it up without thinking, while I was thinking about what I was thinking about."

"She?"

"A woman."

"What woman?"

"I don't know. She was just there, across the fence, in Mary Murphy's back yard."

"The new neighbors," Lottie said, enlightened. And, in mild reproof, "Elmo, you don't shake hands like you're trying to get water from a pump."

"I didn't shake hands with her. She was holding a cat."

"But you said—" She contemplated Elmo in disbelief. "Elmo—?"

"I got carried away," Elmo said, sheepishly.

"You . . . shook her? You mean . . . you *shook* her?"

"She was talking a blue streak and suddenly I—"

"Elmo!" Lottie drew a deep breath, said, as if she were speaking to a small boy, "You'll have to make amends, Elmo."

"All right. Listen, Lottie—"

"I hope she'll be nice about it. How did she act?"

Elmo thought. Again his face brightened. "On the order of Mae West," he said. "Remember Mae West?" He made a descriptive, fulsome gesture with both hands. "She was sort of a cross between Mae West and Dorothy Lamour. Remember Dorothy Lamour? Always had a blossom behind an ear. Wore a sarong."

"This woman was wearing a *sarong*?"

"No. But there wasn't much to it." He probed his memory to drum up a clearer image for Lottie's benefit. "She had orange hair and pale green eyelids."

"She sounds . . . different."

Mentally comparing the newcomer to Mary Murphy, Elmo said, "She is." Perplexed at how far he had strayed from his initial subject, he began anew. "Lottie, guess what!"

"What?" Lottie brushed a stray crumb to and fro with the flimsy remains of the flower.

Elmo's excitement ebbed. What if he were wrong? He wasn't . . . but what if he were? Better that he wait. One day soon, very soon, he would simply call up the basement stairs for her to come down, that he had something to show her. And, while she stood stockstill in open-mouthed astonishment at his *fait accompli*, he'd say . . . he'd say . . .

"I fixed the bulb in the toilet tank," he said.

Ella Zimmer inched back a curtain as Roxine Moore appeared in response to a summoning toot from a yellow compact driven by her husband.

"There they are," Ella informed Jake Zimmer. "Going gallivanting already from the looks of her. Our car beats theirs, even if theirs *is* yellow."

Jake Zimmer cast an obliging glance over the top of his newspaper.

Ella said, "From what I can see of him, he's a dead ringer for a store dummy."

"Well, *her* assets are sure above the national average," Jake Zimmer said. He lowered his paper to gawk openly. Said, "Hoo boy."

"Fly-by-nights," Annie Biggs declared under her breath to the African violet, on her parlor windowsill, that she had been inspecting for mites. "Here today and gone tomorrow." Her gaze veered to her front steps and her husband's broad back, which she also seemed to be inspecting for mites as—watching Roxine Moore ease herself into the small car, one leg at a time—he let the match he'd struck to light his pipe burn down to his fingers.

For the same reason Jack Carrico, hosing his van, inadvertently drenched brass-lunged little Amelia Grubb, who was playing hopscotch on the sidewalk.

Faces were everywhere in evidence as the Moores drove off, leaving a visible wake of blue exhaust.

By the time Saturday was in full sway the news had traveled, almost by osmosis, that the Moores were misfits. Especially her.

As a rule, Lottie's Saturday morning excursions gave her a perky, mischievous uplift. Once she had ascertained that the coast was clear, as it usually was (what with housewives engaged in a mass invasion of supermarkets, and husbands assembling on golf courses, and singles fleeing their habitats like lemmings to engage in the latest "in" pursuits), a sort of while-the-cat-is-away-the-mice-will-play feeling took hold and made her forays seem more of a frolic than an economic necessity.

Today, however, her heart wasn't in it. Even the discovery that Mrs. Rufus B. Hobbs had an aquarium—from which she extracted a mottled goldfish, with the aid of Mrs. Rufus B. Hobbs' wire strainer and a Mason jar—failed to enliven her spirits.

Ordinarily, after she had made her modest acquisitions from the kitchen shelves of those she had chosen as benefactors, and had generated a reasonable amount of change from a sugar bowl, or a coffee can, or whatever, and had acquired an extra or two . . . socks, toothpaste, scouring powder, rags . . . and selected a souvenir, she would breathe a departing "thank you" in the direction of the ceiling. Now, as she lifted her eyes, the underlying cause of her lackluster attitude welled to the surface.

"He's been smitten and doesn't know it," she blazed. And, fiercely, "We mustn't allow it!"

Her eyes snapping, her color rising, a determined jut to the delicate line of her chin, she resembled an undersized Valkyrie about to yank a spear from her shopping bag. The resemblance dwindled and died.

"But how?" she beseeched. "How?"

The answer came to hand, literally, at her last stop when, inspecting the contents of a dresser drawer, she came upon a strategically padded girdle, a pair of falsies, and a strapless bra. The phrase *All's fair in love and war* zipped through her mind with the speed of light. An adjacent dressing table provided the rest of the paraphernalia.

Her posture behind the wheel of her car was triumphant as she rattled homewards.

Careful not to disturb Elmo, who, judging from the profound silence in the basement, was deep in concentration, she stowed away the perishables. Set two frozen pot pies on a cookie sheet and put them to bake. Transferred the goldfish to an isolated bowl in the parlor with only an artificial seahorse for company, until she could be sure it was a perfectly healthy specimen and fit for a suitable berth with some of its peers.

Only then did she succumb to the temptation for a sneak preview of her "new look."

When, presently, she stood back to contemplate her handiwork, pivoting to appraise the shapely, mirrored stranger whose powdered countenance was lined with mascara, eyeliner and shadow, blusher and lip rouge, she was astounded at the transformation she had wrought. She fluffed out her hair. Yielding to the larky feel of the moment, she improvised a sarong from a half slip she redeemed from the basket of mending beside her sewing rocker. Struck a pose.

Below, the basement door leading to the kitchen relayed its familiar creak. Elmo's voice, calling her name, had an urgent ring.

Forgetful of her appearance, knowing only that Elmo was in distress, Lottie dropped her stance and raced downstairs, her heart pounding.

Elmo's aspect had also undergone a drastic change. He was bedraggled, dirty, malodorous, and in pain. "My back's gone out again," he said as if that explained everything, including the red smear of lipstick on his mouth.

Bit by bit, while she maneuvered him into a chair, and loosened his belt, and wiped his face, and removed a watermelon seed from his hair, and fetched him a glass of water, Lottie extracted the gist of what had happened to him.

He had found himself unable to fix his mind on rechecking some recent calculations, due to the fact that having to make amends was like an uninvited guest standing at his side interfering with his computations, until, totally distracted, he decided to go ahead and make amends and get them over with. Whereupon he had acted accordingly, taking the quickest route via the alley. About to open Mary Murphy's former back gate he had stepped on a wad of something sticky and while he was scraping the sole of his shoe with a plastic fork that had been lying nearby, the rubbish men drove up and began heaving away and, in the process, dumped a cat out of a garbage can into their vehicle.

Because of his proximity they assumed the cat was his cat and had waxed vociferous. They didn't take dead critters, they informed him in no uncertain terms, and when he responded that their assumption was incorrect, that the creature wasn't his and wasn't defunct or it wouldn't have taken possession of a fish head, they took umbrage at his use of the words assumption, creature, and defunct, and the big fellow said, "Awright, egghead. Let's *you* get it the hell outta there, an' I be glad to *ass*ist you."

Before he knew what was happening, Elmo said, he found himself in close juxtaposition to the cat, who evidently feared the fish head was in jeopardy and became aggressive.

An involuntary shudder accompanied the recollection.

"Oh, *no.*" Lottie protested, horrified at the scene he had evoked.

"Fortunately, there was a splayed broom within grasp and I managed to fetch the creature a swipe with it, at which juncture my back went out and I could do no more."

"Oh, you poor dear. Those dreadful men! That awful cat!"

"Yes. If its owner hadn't arrived when she did, no telling what the outcome might have been."

"Whose cat was it?"

"Hers."

"Hers? Oh. *Hers.*"

As if responding to a cue, a questing "Helloo-oo?" floated up from the basement.

Elmo said, "That's—" A spasm of pain rendered him speechless.

"Her," Lottie finished. She patted his cheek, said, "I'll attend to it," the angle of her chin belying her level tone.

The purpose of Roxine Moore's unexpected visit was self-evident. "They got creamed in the hassle," she said, handing over the wreckage of Elmo's spectacles. Introducing herself, she continued non-stop. "You must be his wife. I guess he's told you what happened and how he went to the rescue. That was the sweetest thing! After how he, you know, like leaped at the breach to save Jewel, he's ace high in my book. Tell him if he ever wants a favor all he has to do is ask, hear?"

She gave Lottie's attire a quick once-over. "Well, I won't keep you. I wouldn't have barged in like I did, even if the door *is* wide open, if I'd known you were in dishabille."

Her gaze drifted to Elmo's ellipsoid creation. "I heard your hubby invented," she said, as if her concept of an inventor had been dashed. "Is that thingamajig one?" She arched an analytical eyebrow. "It *has* to be. What's it for?"

Lottie tried to find her voice and failed. Her benefactors had a tendency to meld in retrospect, but she possessed total recall when it came to Mrs. Clinton L. Moore.

Mrs. Clinton L. Moore had had a door key duplicated in January and had bought a fake rock to hide it under, volunteering the explanation that she had accidentally locked herself out the day before, when she'd stepped outside in her kimono to see if there was any mail.

"If it hadn't been for the super coming along when he did, I'd have been in a real pinch," she said, with a reflective half smile at the word "pinch."

In response to Lottie's "I have a hunch" stratagem, she quipped, "I've got a hunch I'm spinning my wheels, but what the hell when you got nothing to lose."

Lottie had classified her as a Possible. Elmo doted on the type of deli fare that leaned heavily on mandarin oranges, marshmallow whip, coconut, and maraschino cherries and went by such interchangeable euphemisms as Tahiti Delight and Hawaiian Surprise . . . and Mrs. Clinton L. Moore looked as if she lived on treats of this ilk.

Reconnoitering the former Moore place of residence, in a past-its-prime pseudo-Spanish complex in need of restuccoing, Lottie had very nearly changed her mind. However, since she was there she had gone ahead with her original plan, secure in the knowledge that her disguise—a drab headscarf, sunglasses, and a paper shopping bag with a display of carrot tops for window dressing—rendered her invisible. She was a nobody-anybody returning from an anywhere supermarket. Not worth a second glance.

She had forgotten whether Tahiti Delight or an equivalent had been available, but she recalled her decision, based on the skimpy furnishings and an untidy pile of bills, not to pick out a souvenir. Fair was fair.

The thing she *really* remembered, though—and wouldn't forget in a thousand years—was the incident at the storage closet.

She had gone down a short, dark hall to investigate the closet, thinking it might be a source of supply for some rags for Elmo. She had opened the door, and congealed.

Standing amid the clutter was a scantily clad and barely recognizable Mrs. Clinton L. Moore, in a provocative pose.

Momentarily, she had been too paralyzed to move and then, in a wild surge of panic, had tried to escape and stumbled over a half grown cat. The cat, seeking a haven, had skittered between her feet and into the closet before it bounded off, while Mrs. Clinton L. Moore slid sideways and, stiff as a board, came to rest at an impossible tilt with her head against a dead possum suspended from a hook.

The possum turned into an old muff and she perceived that Mrs. Clinton L. Moore was a replica of a younger self. A cutout of the sort used by questionable theaters to entice male passersby. A memento of a time when she'd been "a drawing card"?

Concealed under the torn lining of the muff was a cache of greenbacks. Replacing the money intact, Lottie hoped the Moores wouldn't ever be burgled. To a practiced eye, the muff might as well be transparent.

The recollection dissolved as Roxine Moore, misinterpreting Lottie's silence, said, "Excuse me for being nosy. Can't say I blame you for keeping mum, what with all the sharpies ready to knock off anything and everything at the drop of a hat. Anyhoo, I hope he sells whatever it is for big bucks. Couldn't happen to a nicer guy. Tell him that Clint, my hubby, is a used car salesman off and on, and he does this."

Before Lottie realized her intention Roxine Moore went to the machine and gave it a kick.

"Then," Roxine went on, "he'll say, 'This baby is put together. What I mean is p-u-t to-*gether*,' like that. Clint says you don't have to work yourself blue in the gills on an iffy deal if you have a punch line for a clincher. And speaking of blue in the gills, honey, I don't want to step on your toes but I used to be in show biz and, take it from me, that shade of face powder doesn't do a lick for sallow skin tones like yours. Same goes for that blueblue*blue* eye shadow and the frost lipstick. You could improve your touch with mascara, too. Spiky is tacky. Black in particular. You don't want to look like a poop, if you'll pardon the expression, you want to look like, you know, you're center stage. Just say the word and I'll be glad to give you some pointers, but right now I'd better get a move on. I left Clint trying to get a handle on tonight's dog races and Jewel is liable to meow and get blamed for throwing him off the track. Ha ha. I, personally, go for hunches myself. Clint thinks hunches are for the birds. From where I sit, that's why he's in a slump, and why I've socked away close to what it takes to get a neck lift. But that's for me to know and him to find out."

She gave Lottie a wink. "Men. What they don't know won't hurt 'em. Right?"

She waggled a handful of fingers, said, "Well, bye-bye. Enjoyed our chat," and took her departure, leaving a shaken Lottie and the lifeless vestiges of the scintillating personality she had donned so briefly with such a high heart.

Unwittingly, Mrs. Clinton L. Moore had done her a favor. She rubbed off her ersatz complexion with a rag from Elmo's box. Not that it made any difference. Without his spectacles Elmo couldn't see boo. In the fluster, she hadn't noticed they weren't in their accustomed position. Lucky for her they'd been smashed.

She picked up Elmo's shattered glasses, held them by their mangled ear pieces. . . . She was manning Elmo's machine, zinging blueblue*blue* darts at a bulls-eye painted on a far wall, when Mrs. Clinton L. Moore sauntered in through the outside door and inquired, "Where's Ellllmo?"

"None of your beeswax," she replied and, swiveling the machine, she accelerated the power. There was a flash . . . falling sprinkle of charred—

The *pies*. She scurried up the basement steps to salvage what hadn't bubbled over, without observing that a gauge had begun to oscillate on Elmo's "thingamajig."

In rapid order the various devices triggered over. Synchronized. A *thrum*, more sensed than heard, focalized into a hum no louder than the drone of a bee. An attenuated stab of prismatic light materialized. Elongated. Began to glow with increasing intensity. Where it seemingly drilled into thin air a nebulous whirl appeared. The whirl deepened. Gained quickly in size and dimension. Steadied. Suddenly coalesced into a definite cavelike entrance. Beyond the periphery of the opening lay an impalpable darkness as thick as fur. There was no hint of what might be within.

For a full minute the materialization held its position, solidly, in space before the hum fluctuated. The needle of light vacillated. The aperture yawned. The light vanished. A flickering luminescence glimmered here and there. The hum ceased. A lone, spiraling spark winked out and, once again, the machine was inoperative.

Lottie left The Optical Place with a sinking heart. Prices had skyrocketed since the last time. She had barely been able to cover the minimum payment now required, and she was going to have to come up with the balance, cash on the barrelhead, by Saturday when Elmo's glasses would be ready. And she was going to be eighty-seven dollars short. The rainy day savings she had stashed in a ball of yarn had recently been depleted by what the garage mechanic had called a ring job and unless she resorted to outright *stealing* when she did her Saturday shopping. . . .

Unthinkable! Stealing implied victims, and she had never victimized anyone in her entire life. The items she acquired on her Saturday sorties, and the dibbles and dabbles she withdrew from sugar bowls and jelly jars and so forth, certainly hadn't *victimized* anybody. As for her souvenirs, they were merely trinkets and trifles that had caught her fancy, collected as a kind of memorabilia, in a spirit of fun.

What to do?

A yard sale was too risky. Someone might turn up out of nowhere, as had Mrs. Clinton L. Moore, and recognize an inconsequential fiddle-faddle, and the fat would be in the fire. By the same reasoning, a pawn-broker was out of the question. Her one involvement with a loan company had cost her more in the long run than the amount of the original loan. Mr. Osgood, the manager of Pleet-Holder, had an inflexible rule against borrowing on wages. Although she was friendly with her neighbors, neither she nor Elmo was gregarious by nature and had kept to themselves. To approach, say, Annie Biggs or Ella Zimmer with a request for a loan of eighty-seven dollars would be an embarrassment of gargantuan proportions. Besides, a sum of this magnitude would be a subject for discussion with whoever's respective husband, and if the final decision was no, her mortification would be doubled and trebled and forevermore.

What to do?

As the week wore on and the sight of Elmo, forlorn and at a loss, tugged more and more at her heartstrings, she cast her eyes ceilingwards so often that one of her cohorts at the hardware store ventured the conjecture that she might need glasses. A suggestion she had very nearly answered with a wail.

And then, on Friday, as she was about to despair, Annie Biggs unknowingly pointed out the means by which she could acquire the necessary wherewithal.

"Get a load of that," she said to Lottie, flapping a hand at an empty cat food tin and a banana skin lying beside the Moore's garbage can. "And unless I miss my guess from here to Tarpon

Springs, that's only the beginning. After the tonguelashing she gave the rubbish men over that cat of hers, they'll have it in for the alley . . . bashed in trash cans . . . litter blowing around. . . . She had a nerve, laying them out to cool like she did. Her cat wasn't their lookout."

Annie knuckled her hands on her hips, gave vent to the underlying cause of her considerable ire. "I don't want to sound begrudging but you know what she did? She came over to borrow some sugar while I was in the bathtub, and Matt got down the box of superfine I had earmarked for an angel food and she took the whole box. I didn't find out until I'd gone ahead and separated the whites from the yolks. Twelve eggs! Who wouldn't raise the roof! But from how Himself stomped out, you'd think I'd denied aid to the starving."

She warmed to her subject. "She's a troublemaker is what she is. Remember when Jack Carrico doused little Amelia with the hose? I saw how it happened and none of it *would've* happened if Guess Who hadn't been all legs getting into that yellow excuse they have for a car. And you know Jack. Anyhow, the Grubbs and Jack got *that* falling out patched up, thanks to Sophie who hates hard feelings like the devil hates holy water. So, yesterday, if little Amelia didn't go and throw a rock at Jack's van and put a dent in that hula scene he had painted on it in enamel. Ike Grubb says a dent in the Kohinoor diamond wouldn't cost what Jack wants to have his dent ironed out and re-enameled. And Jack says if Ike won't pay off he'll take him to small-claims court. Sophie is a wreck.

"And they're not the only ones on the outs. Jake Zimmer put his foot in his mouth with some comment—" Annie jerked her thumb at the Moores' house, to indicate who had caused the comment "—and Ella is fit to be tied. Come to think of it, if it hadn't been for that cat, your husband wouldn't have hurt his back. How's he coming along?"

Conquering a momentary urge to blurt out her own dilemma, Lottie explained Elmo's predicament.

"There you are!" Annie Biggs said, vindicated. "The neighborhood was normal as corned beef and cabbage until she showed up.

She's the key to the whole kaboodle. If you ask me, little Amelia threw her rock at the wrong target."

The fake rock stood out like a gray ghost among the half-sunken, weathered ones in Mary Murphy's rock garden, which was beginning to have a neglected aspect. Lottie ceased pretending she was scraping out a flowerpot and returned to her kitchen to find that Elmo had blundered into a door and given himself a bloody nose.

That settled it. Cracking ice to staunch the flow of Elmo's blood, she dismissed any lingering qualms. Tonight, after Elmo had retired early—as he'd been doing to bring a merciful close to another do-nothing day—and while the Moores were at the dog track, she would don her black coat. Go out through the basement. Keep close to the fence. Slip through the alley into the Moores' back yard. Remove the key from beneath the rock. Use it. Extract the eighty-seven dollars—Elmo's just recompense—from Mrs. Clinton L. Moore's neck-lift funds hidden in the muff.

It was simple as pie. Her spirits rose. The worry lines between her brows smoothed . . . only to reappear as the question surfaced phoenix-like from the ashes of her anxiety . . . *what if the key wasn't there?*

The key was there.

What if it was some other key? What if it didn't fit?

It fit.

As she pocketed the key and stepped over the threshold, a vague feline shape crossed her path. Even as she thought *cat*, her knees threatened to betray her. With a stubborn exercise of will she proceeded on to the storage closet, located, as was hers, in a recess under the stairs.

Please, let the muff be there.

She turned the doorknob, switched on her pencil flashlight, directed its dim beam into the cubicle.

The muff was there, dangling by its wrist cord from a nail. In the uncertain glow its dead possum quality was eerie. A frazzled feather duster looked as though it might come alive and cock-a-doodle-do.

The come-hither smile on the cardboard countenance of the cutout seemed to hint at a secret.

What if the money had been hidden elsewhere?

The money was there . . . in fives, tens, and twenties.

She counted out eighty-five dollars, decided it was better to have two dollars less than Elmo was entitled to, rather than three dollars more, and retain a clear conscience. Tomorrow, when she did her Saturday shopping, she would make up the difference, and forego a keepsake to pay back.

She stowed her windfall in her coat pocket, replaced the remainder in the muff, restored the muff to its nail, extinguished the flashlight. And froze.

The warbly, Danny-boy tenor of Matt Biggs, seeking his doorstep, broke in mid-note and he swore happily and with bleary eloquence as he stumbled, charting a course up the front steps of the lookalike house she was standing in.

She had a mental picture of what would ensue. Curtains edged aside. Observation posts established. Annie emerging like a sloop in a high wind. The picture altered. Somehow, she, Lottie Pritchett, had been detected . . . apprehended . . . was being led, handcuffed, to a summoned police car . . . neighbors lined the walk . . . sotto voce comments expressed shocked amazement . . . no one paid any attention to her perfectly logical explanation . . . little Amelia hefted a rock . . . Elmo tried to intervene and was pummeled. . . .

Lottie fled.

Safe in her own house, thankful she had had the foresight to leave the basement door cracked for a fast re-entry, and reassured by the peaceful snore drifting to her ears that Elmo had not roused, she hurriedly divested herself of her coat and put it away.

The money was safe where it was. Get to bed. Skip the preliminaries and just get to bed before she keeled over from emotional exhaustion.

She wakened to find the room pale with daybreak. Still muzzy with sleep, she automatically stretched out an arm to defeat the alarm, remembered it was Saturday. The events of the previous night swarmed in. She was out of the woods! Her worries were over! She sat bolt upright and hugged her knees, relishing a moment of pure joy. Beside her, Elmo shifted position, murmured an unintelligible equation, subsided.

Ordinarily on Saturdays she allowed herself an extra half hour to hover between sleep and waking but, now, she slipped out of bed and stole down the stairs in her nightgown and bare feet to resurrect her bonanza for the sheer pleasure of verifying her achievement. Halfway down she slowed to a snail's pace.

A partially unraveled ball of pink yarn lay on the hall runner. Had it been there last night? Had she overlooked it in her hurry, in the dark? How had it gotten there?

Quickening her descent, she nabbed the ball and wound up the raveling as she went to the doorway of the parlor, a room which long since had acquired an atmosphere normally associated with flea markets. Even as her eyes took in the scattered balls of yarn spilled from an overturned basket, and located the inconspicuous gray one that served as her savings bank, she came to the conclusion Elmo had walked in his sleep, as he sometimes did after a sweep-the-icebox casserole. Had he accidentally strayed into the parlor, or had his subconscious led him there to check their cash reserve . . . a reserve that, awake, he had trustingly believed was plenty for the simple reason that she had told him so. What if, sound asleep, he had put the remaining bills somewhere else? Her eyes flew about the jam-packed room. *It might take her weeks. . . .*

She scooped up the ball of gray wool.

The bills were there.

She cleared a place next to a fishbowl and counted to be sure. Gave a sigh of relief. Zeroed in on the fishbowl and its sole occupant, the artificial seahorse.

The mottled goldfish was gone.

The thought that maybe *she* had walked in her sleep slithered into her mind. Had last night's escapade been a dream? What if there was a goldfish in her coat pocket instead of the muff money! Within seconds she had jabbed a shaking hand into the coat pocket.

The muff money was there.

She was home free. The goldfish was inconsequential. Inevitably, after three days, it would make its whereabouts known. She riffled the bills happily, dislodging a small object which hit the floor with a clink.

Mystified, she stooped and with a sinking sensation in the pit of her stomach picked up the key. In her precipitate flight she had failed to replace the key.

If its loss was discovered, the Moore woman would make a bee-line for the muff. After that there'd be the police . . . and, after that, it wouldn't be long before the connection between herself, Pleet-Holder, the key machine, and the fake rock was established beyond the shadow of a doubt.

Once more, little Amelia drew back her throwing arm. . . .

The hounds rounded the far turn in a pack in close pursuit of the mechanical rabbit, and began to gain ground. The distance between the dogs and the lure shortened dramatically. The gap closed. The lead dog lunged. There was a scrap. A pileup. Aghast, she saw the thing they were tearing to pieces was her muff. Her money was flying in all directions.

Roxine Moore came awake with an indrawn gasp, to find the bedroom pearly with early morning light. Clint stirred, mumbled an incoherent series of syllables, and burrowed into his pillow.

Roxine Moore edged out of bed, slid her feet into scuffs, shrugged on her kimono, went quietly into the bathroom, and exhumed her last night's winnings from inside her shower cap.

With what she had salted away in the muff she could get going on a neck lift, pronto. Thanks to Elmo Pritchett. Funny how her comment about him being ace high in her book had sprung to mind, like he was standing at her elbow pointing a broom at a surefire winner. Ace High. Ace High had been a skinny, undersized scroot with the trembles. Nevertheless, she'd plunged, without letting on to Clint. And she'd *kept* her mouth shut.

Three twenty-two was shaping up to be a lady-luck address, right off the reel, even if it was a low-end street. Like she'd told Clint when she saw the advertisement in the FOR RENTS, three-two-two added up to seven, which was lucky in anybody's language, except for crapshooters, and Clint was more of a pool player . . . her birthday was March twenty-second . . . they'd be married going on two years come February third . . . plus they could swing the rent.

As Lottie had done, Roxine betook herself downstairs for the sheer pleasure of verifying her achievement.

She gave the cutout a cursory glance, noting that in posture and costume it was showing its age. The flirty pose was almost quaint, and the skimpy garb no longer daring. Worse, it revealed an era and it wouldn't take a CPA to figure out how old she was.

Relieving the muff of its contents she went on to the kitchen, where, calling softly *kittykittykitty*, she poured canned milk into a saucer and sat down at the table with a glass of tomato juice to prolong the flush of the moment by separating the money according to denomination.

Meanwhile, Lottie, dressed and ready—the key in her apron pocket, a measuring cup in her hand—left by her kitchen door. A housewife short on sugar going to borrow some for breakfast from a next door neighbor. She would tarry at the rock garden ostensibly to tie a loose shoelace and, her real purpose fulfilled, would go on to the back door. All open and aboveboard, if she were noticed. Should either of the Moores be up and about, which was doubtful, could they spare half a cup of sugar? If her knock went unanswered she would go on to Annie's for the sake of verisimilitude. In less than five minutes she would be out from under and back in her own kitchen.

She selected a clear space between two puffy clouds that were in the process of turning from pink to white and firmed her resolve. There was nothing worse than a scared prayer.

Thank You for coming to my assistance.

Her rehearsed plan went smoothly. Mary Murphy's back gate yielded without complaint. So far as she could tell she was unobserved. There was no mistaking the fake rock. She almost bestowed a preliminary pat when she leaned over to go through the motions of tying her shoelace.

In that instant, however, the prevailing hush was sundered by a cry of fury issuing full force from the larynx of Roxine Moore.

"YOU THIEVING SONOFABITCH!"

Lottie fled.

The accelerating furor brought the sleep-frowzed neighborhood to its collective feet and kept the onlookers at their stations until Clint Moore, who obviously had dressed in haste under adverse conditions, made an ignominious getaway in the yellow compact.

Those whose curiosity had led them outside withdrew. And Lottie, at her kitchen window, steeled herself. It was now or never.

"I'm going over there," she said to Elmo, who had appeared carrying a flashlight, under the impression an emergency had developed and that a flashlight might be useful.

"She could've been hurt," Lottie said, trying to sound perturbed.

"I'll go with you."

"That cat will have it in for you. Why don't you make some coffee—" she crossed her fingers under the cover of her apron "—in case I bring her here." With that she left, before she caved in and confessed just to rid herself of the increasingly heavy feeling that a great cold stone lay between her shoulder blades. Whoever had penned the lines *A fearful soul, alas, alack/Bears a bully on his back* had known what he was talking about. She wondered, fleetingly, what had bullied him and if he'd have swapped with her.

She opened Mary Murphy's back gate with outward aplomb. This time, if she were seen, she was a neighborhood version of Mother Teresa going to the aid of a leper. When she bent, to tie the shoelace, she had the key in readiness . . . and dropped it as Annie Biggs rose up from behind the fence.

Lottie, undone, followed suit.

"Didn't mean to scare you," Annie apologized, leaning her forearms companionably on the top board. "I figured since I was out here anyway I might as well pull a few weeds. What's that you've got?"

Numbly, Lottie handed over the rock she found she was holding, as if she were Alice in Wonderland complying to a request from her counterpart on the other side of the Looking Glass.

"It was out of kilter," she said.

Annie said, "It won't be the only one." She inspected the rock. "I'll declare. I'd forgot all about this. It's a phony," she explained. "There's a place underneath to hide an extra key in. See? Key's gone, but there's where it fits. I got it out of a catalogue for Mary Murphy's birthday. She was always misplacing her door key."

Annie gave a sad little laugh. "She was getting pretty absent-minded. Bless her heart. I expect she forgot what this was for. Or that it was there. Or, more'n likely, got hustled off before she had any say-so. That daughter of hers was a pistol."

She twitched a nod in the direction of the Moores' back door. "And unless I miss my guess from here to the moon, we've got us a whole shooting gallery rolled into one. That was a humdinger, wasn't it? If we're going to have that for a steady diet, the neighborhood is in a fix. I knew they were misfits from the min—" Her countenance registered belated bafflement . . . what was Lottie doing on the wrong side of the fence?

"I thought she might be hurt," Lottie said, fielding the question before Annie asked.

"If she is, I'm a monkey's uncle," Annie retorted. "He was running like the devil was after him." She cocked her head, listening. "Isn't that her I hear calling her cat." It was a statement, not an inquiry. Roxine Moore wasn't hurt a whit.

Annie considered the rock. "No reason on earth why I shouldn't have this," she said, "on account of I'm the one who paid for it. Right?" The query was purely rhetorical and, remarking that she'd better go tend to Matt, who had a head as big as the inside of Jonah's whale, she ambled off with the rock and a vague impression of Lottie Pritchett as being a mouth breather.

Jewel was missing.

Roxine Moore, disheveled and spent, discovered she really didn't give a hoot. If Jewel was out in the alley chewing on something awful, let her. If Clint had grabbed her, like for a hostage if the car didn't start, so what? Lately, Jewel had been acting slinky and hateful. Only yesterday she'd showed her claws and gone *yowrrrr* when she'd been routed out from behind the fridge.

She had more on her mind to think about than where Jewel was. Like how, as of right this minute, she'd had it with Clint. If he'd taken the whole wad it wouldn't have been as lowdown as his sneaking two tens, three twenties, and a five. The two-bit, sticky-fingered bastard! The weasel! If he thought she'd be here when he slunk in, beer-sorry and thinking to make up the way he knew how to do best. . . .

Roxine Moore's eyes began to shine. Welllll, why not add some incentive. The cardboard cutie pie in the storage closet wasn't all that antique, in a dim light, if you were half plotzed. With an artful arrangement of pillows and the sheet pulled up, he'd go for it. And for the rest of his pea-picking life a brass bed would set his clock back, but good. Serve him right! Why she'd picked him for number three, over George Smedley, she'd never know. Even if George was short. Short didn't amount to a nickel's worth of sawdust, if the fellow could saw wood.

And she wasn't dead yet.

She hoisted the glass of tomato juice as though in response to a toast from an imaginary tablemate.

"It's good to *be* back," she said.

By the time Lottie returned from her Saturday shopping, it was common knowledge that Roxine Moore had departed in a taxi, with two suitcases, a garment bag, several pocketbooks slung from a shoulder, a couple of coats flung over an arm, and no cat.

Annie Biggs imparted this information across the fence to Lottie, tailoring the circumstances to fit her conclusions.

"He sold the cat," she declared, gesturing authoritatively with her trimming clippers. "That's what the fracas was about. She wasn't calling her cat, she was bemoaning its loss. She told me, her own self, he wanted to sell it and that she'd give him the pitch if he did, and he did, and she's done it."

"Over a cat," Lottie said, thinking she'd seldom heard such welcome news. It was true that all burdens were lifted from you if you but *believed*.

"I expect the cat was only the tip of the iceberg," Annie said. "Unless I miss my guess from here to the First National Bank, he'll bow out when the rent comes due." She wiped her forehead with a wrist, leaving an earthy smear. "I might make him an offer for that brass bed, if he's willing, and doesn't want an arm and a leg for it. And if it's paid for," she amended, as an afterthought. "My, you two sure do eat a lot of carrots."

"They're supposed to benefit the eyes," Lottie said.

"When does he get his specs?"

"We're going in to get them after lunch."

"Well, don't let me keep you. Run along." And, in a burst of camaraderie, "The neighborhood isn't the same without a smell or two, no offense intended."

"None taken," Lottie said, happily. "None taken whatsoever."

Lottie Pritchett had her peculiarities, Annie thought, watching her tote her shopping bags up her kitchen steps, but she was a nice little person. Trustworthy. Not a devious bone in her body.

Elmo Pritchett, his sight restored, his inactivity at an end, descended the basement stairs and would have enfolded his machine in loving arms had his arms been of sufficient length. Relatively speaking, a week was a lifetime when, with nothing else to do but think, your cogitations had taken an unexpected direction that had led to some sobering conclusions.

One. By opening the field of interstitial space, he might be raising the lid of a Pandora's box . . . unknown viruses could be freed, germs, bacteria, dreadful plagues, hideous diseases. . . . Perhaps there were inhabitants worse than rats, more prolific than roaches . . . evil. . . .

Two. The extent of interstitial space could very well be beyond the realm of imagination. The dimensions might be completely different from those that governed the present concept of area as three-dimensional. Ultimately, strobic dependency would be eliminated, leading to rapid exploration. Dissensions would arise over territorial claims. The result would be wars and more wars and, with the advance of ever more deadly weaponry, the annihilation of mankind.

Three. Should none of these assumptions be valid and interstitial space prove to be a benign environment, the exploitation thereof was an unqualified certainty. Inevitably, this marvel he had

wrought, this brainchild that had been aborning for so many fruit-
less years, would be prostituted by greed merchants, despoilers,
outright crooks. Eventually, interstitial space would be exactly the
same as here.

And he wasn't going to permit any of this to happen. He had
wrestled with his scruples, in a vain attempt to justify his master-
work, and had lost each and every bout. Truth was absolute. And
the truth was . . . face it . . . he'd been obsessed. At Lottie's ex-
pense. No more. There was plenty of room for prosaic inventions
that filled a need. As Lottie kept hinting.

Lottie.

Lottie had been a brick. She deserved the biggest silver platter
he could find, and anything else she fancied. As soon as he dis-
mantled this . . . face it . . . Frankenstein creation, he would begin
work on a flexible flashlight, magnetic glue, a spray-on-peel-off
bandage. . . .

He went to his tool bench, selected a wrench, returned to the
machine, and, walking beside it, ran a gentle hand along its length.

"It is best that I not know," he said softly, as if clarifying a moot
point to a colleague. He swallowed the lump that swelled in his
throat, and applied the wrench to a joining.

The rings resisted his efforts. After several hard raps with the
wrench in futile attempt to loosen the coupling, he cast about for
his oil can. Scanning the laden shelves lining the walls, he told
himself that from here on in he was going to have a place for
everything and keep everything in its proper place, even though
such methodical practices more or less eliminated the fortuitous
happenstance. At least for him. His modus operandi had been a far
cry from the ordered world of microchips and processors, and how
those people did what they did was a mystery to him. One he had
no desire to solve. As of today, simplicity was the watchword . . .
easy-free nuts and bolts— BUY PRITCHETT'S E-Z FREES—a permanent faucet washer, a sonic ear plug to circumvent tinnitus, although, as of the moment, he found a faint persistent hum a
pleasant improvement over the crickety clicking that customarily
beset him.

In the act of taking down the oil can, he grew still, his gaze riveted on an apothecary jar whose glassy surface reflected a hairline streak of prismatic light.

He wheeled about. Sucking in his breath. The oil can fell from his nerveless clasp.

Wide-eyed and incredulous, he approached the dark opening a careful step at a time, lest any untoward motion have an adverse effect on the unwavering needle of light, and, bending slowly, he strained to see within. Was there a pulsing, frondlike movement? Or was this a variance in the consistency of the woolly blackness that blocked depth perception?

A stifled sneeze from the vicinity of the stairs told him that Lottie was there. Too late, he made a backward motion for her to stay where she was.

"You've done it," Lottie whispered, at his elbow.

From the corner of his eye she seemed a stranger. A trespasser, bringing him the flashlight he had left in the kitchen. A meddler, with her apron bunched in one thin birdbone hand, giving her nose a wipe. An intruder, who was an unwelcome reminder of the noble resolutions he had entertained.

When she smothered a second sneeze, he would have throttled her to prevent a third. . . . However, the brilliant prismatic needle remained as stable as if embedded in stone.

He began to relax. There was no need for alarm. The machine was producing its own energy density. Evidently the rap with the wrench had been the catalyst, which indicated a slight malfunction in the time-varying magnetic field, a simple problem of small import. He couldn't have cared less. His theory, that interstitial space existed, had become a proven actuality. Lottie had recognized the salient thing. *He had done it.*

His animosity waned. She would neither want him to jettison a breakthrough of this immensity nor allow him to. He took the flashlight from her and, switching it on, played the beam over the cavelike opening. Like fur, he thought. Thick, black fur.

Lottie gulped, audibly. "Elmo, you're not going in there, are you?" she asked in a parched voice.

He straightened. Eased his back. "No," he said. "No. I'm satisfied. I've done what I set out to do. Once the news hits—" with a

thumb and forefinger he depicted the sweep of the banner headlines "—there will be an endless stream of eager volunteers."

He turned towards her with a jubilant smile. Spread his arms.
Said, "I could do with a hug."

These were Elmo Pritchett's last words.

Before he could perceive her intention, Lottie snatched the flashlight from him and clobbered him with it.

He staggered, off balance, stupefied, instinctively trying to protect his spectacles, and Lottie, exerting all her strength, gave him a
shove that sent him reeling and floundering into the dark aperture.

For a split second she had an impression that something sluggish
stirred at the bottom edge. Otherwise there was no indication of any
break in the enveloping blackness as Elmo passed through.

He did not reappear.

Lottie angled away, attempting to marshall the thoughts that had
been leaping like squirrels ever since she had come to a halt on the
basement stairs, dumbstruck at the sight of this terrible hole in
the air. She had known from the way Elmo was calmly perusing the
shelves that the hole had evolved while his back was turned. If a
black, hairy spider the size of a bucket had crawled out and crept
towards him, she couldn't have screamed if she'd wanted to . . . and,
standing there, unobserved, the realization came to her—as if from
a distance—that she wouldn't have screamed anyway.

In the process of making do, from week to week, she had fashioned a secret life for herself . . . a life she had come to enjoy and, as
the wife of a celebrity, would have to forego. She would be expected
to dress up, pour tea at social functions, be on committees with
people who didn't know a Phillips screwdriver from a roofing nail,
attend luncheons and dinners, listen to speeches, stand in reception
lines until the bunion plaguing her left big toe howled like a ban-
shee for the merciful comfort of her old flats with the slit in the
proper spot, and smile until her head ached beneath its tortured
beauty salon hairdo. . . .

She would be a misfit, no matter what. And Elmo? Judging from
his recent performance, he would be putty in the hands of flashy
women, who were out there by the dozens.

She backed into Elmo's rag box, nearly fell, and before she could regain her footing a supple, black, hairy appendage emerged and brushed her cheek. Beating at it with the flashlight, she heard shrieking.

Jewel, galvanized by the assault on her tail, scrambled from the box and—desperate for some peace and quiet in which to undergo her rapidly approaching motherhood—sought refuge in the cave-like recess, and was gone.

Lottie discovered that it was she who was shrieking.

She regained her composure.

Gathered her wits.

So a cat, undoubtedly the one she had encountered last night, the same one that had caused all the trouble to begin with, was the explanation for the lost goldfish and the strewn balls of yarn. Good riddance. It had gotten its comeuppance.

As for Elmo . . . well, thanks to her, he was in a position to satisfy his curiosity about interstitial space to his heart's content. He had become a veritable Robinson Crusoe. Only better off. Robinson Crusoe hadn't had a cat.

Keeping a wary eye on the yawning cavity into which Elmo and the cat had disappeared, she availed herself of a hammer and went to work. The results were immediate and gratifying. She waited out the accompanying rain of sparks in the protective lee of the furnace, slapping at fiery vagrants with her apron but keeping the hammer at the ready—though any further action was hardly probable.

As for Elmo's absence, nobody would miss him if his presence was projected from time to time. A string of firecrackers now and then. Once in a while a noxious odor—burning chicken feathers would do nicely. On a dreary day a brief appearance in a pair of Elmo's baggy pants, his draggled raincoat, and old slouch hat. An "Elmo says" dropped on occasion in casual chitchat over the fence . . . and she might as well begin her program without delay, dropping an "Elmo says" in the ear of Annie Biggs, who sounded in a dither and was at the door.

"Coming," she answered. "*Coming.*" She eliminated a last twirling spark, went to greet Annie, and called over her shoulder as she opened the door, "It's Annie Biggs, Elmo. Is it all right to let her in?" And, to Annie, "You'd better not. His mice escaped and they're all over everywhere."

"*Mice*," Annie bleated, retreating. "Good Lord! I thought I heard you screaming! No wonder!"

"One of them jumped off a shelf and almost went down my neck." Lottie joined Annie outside. Eased the door to.

"They're white mice. Elmo says they're not the least bit germy."

"Mice are mice," Annie asserted, continuing her retreat. "All you need is one mama mouse loose in the walls. I once spent ten dollars on traps and cheese and made two novenas to get rid of the things. Tell Elmo I don't want to be ugly but I'll hold him responsible if what I hope doesn't happen happens."

"I'll tell him," Lottie said, with an understanding nod. "And thanks for coming, even if it was a false alarm."

"You're entirely welcome," Annie said, her tone conveying the message that, henceforth, Lottie was on her own. She marched off to settle her nerves with a mug of tea and to alert Sophie Carrico and Ella Zimmer as to Elmo Pritchett's latest fiasco. The man was a born klutz, and Lottie was a saint on earth who deserved to go to heaven in a basket without any stopovers.

Lottie, preparing to settle her own nerves with a cup of tea, wondered what a novena was. Decided it was a pious method of presenting a request by beating around the bush instead of going directly to the Top. To each his own. If you didn't ask for the impossible, you generally got what was coming to you.

Without thinking, she took down two cups. Stood there, bereft. She was going to miss Elmo. For the time being, she would have to keep a stiff upper lip. Sooner or later other matters would take precedence, would supplant her feeling of loss. Hopefully sooner. *Please. Oh, please!*

The shrilling whistle of the tea kettle masked the creak of the basement door as it was slowly pushed open behind her.

The Masque of the Red Death

by Edgar Allan Poe

The "Red Death" had long devastated the country. No pestilence had ever been so fatal, or so hideous. Blood was its Avatar and its seal—the redness and the horror of blood. There were sharp pains, and sudden dizziness, and then profuse bleeding at the pores, with dissolution. The scarlet stains upon the body and especially upon the face of the victim, were the pest ban which shut him out from the aid and from the sympathy of his fellowmen. And the whole seizure, progress, and termination of the disease were the incidents of half an hour.

But the Prince Prospero was happy and dauntless and sagacious. When his dominions were half depopulated, he summoned to his presence a thousand hale and lighthearted friends from among the knights and dames of his court, and with these retired to the deep seclusion of one of his castellated abbeys. This was an extensive and magnificent structure, the creation of the prince's own eccentric yet august taste. A strong and lofty wall girdled it in. This wall had gates of iron. The courtiers, having entered, brought furnaces and massy hammers and welded the bolts. They resolved to leave means neither of ingress nor egress to the sudden impulses of despair or of frenzy from within. The abbey was amply provisioned. With such precautions the courtiers might bid defiance to contagion. The external world could take care of itself. In the meantime it was folly to grieve, or to think. The prince had provided all the appliances of pleasure. There were buffoons, there were improvisatori, there were ballet dancers, there were musicians, there was Beauty, there was wine. All these and security were within. Without was the "Red Death."

It was toward the close of the fifth or sixth month of his seclusion, and while the pestilence raged most furiously abroad, that the Prince Prospero entertained his thousand friends at a masked ball of the most unusual magnificence.

It was a voluptuous scene, that masquerade. But first let me tell of the rooms in which it was held. There were seven—an imperial suite. In many palaces, however, such suites form a long and straight vista, while the folding doors slide back nearly to the walls on either hand, so that the view of the whole extent is scarcely impeded. Here the case was very different as might have been expected from the duke's love of the bizarre. The apartments were so irregularly disposed that the vision embraced but little more than one at a time. There was a sharp turn at every twenty or thirty yards, and at each turn a novel effect. To the right and left, in the middle of each wall, a tall and narrow gothic window looked out upon a closed corridor which pursued the windings of the suite. These windows were of stained glass whose color varied in accordance with the prevailing hue of the decorations of the chamber into which it opened. That at the eastern extremity was hung, for example, in blue—and vividly blue were its windows. The second chamber was purple in its ornaments and tapestries, and here the panes were purple. The third was green throughout, and so were the casements. The fourth was furnished and lighted with orange—the fifth with white—the sixth with violet. The seventh apartment was closely shrouded in black velvet tapestries that hung all over the ceiling and down the walls, falling in heavy folds upon a carpet of the same material and hue. But in this chamber only, the color of the windows failed to correspond with the decorations. The panes here were scarlet—a deep blood color. Now in no one of the seven apartments was there any lamp or candelabrum, amid the profusion of golden ornaments that lay scattered to and fro or depended from the roof. There was no light of any kind emanating from lamp or candle within the suite of chambers. But in the corridors that followed the suite, there stood, opposite to each window, a heavy tripod, bearing a brazier of fire, that projected its rays through the tinted glass and so glaringly illumined the room. And thus were produced a multitude of gaudy and fantastic appearances. But in the western or black chamber the effect of the firelight that streamed upon the dark hangings through the blood-tinted panes was ghastly in the extreme, and produced so wild a look upon the countenances of those who entered that there were few of the company bold enough to set foot within its precincts at all.

It was in this apartment, also, that there stood against the western wall a gigantic clock of ebony. Its pendulum swung to and fro with a dull, heavy, monotonous clang; and when the minute hand made the circuit of the face, and the hour was to be stricken, there came from the brazen lungs of the clock a sound which was clear and loud and deep and exceedingly musical, but of so peculiar a note and emphasis that, at each lapse of an hour, the musicians of the orchestra were constrained to pause, momentarily, in their performance, to hearken to the sound; and thus the waltzers perforce ceased their evolutions; and there was a brief disconcert of the whole gay company; and while the chimes of the clock yet rang, it was observed that the giddiest grew pale, and the more aged and sedate passed their hands over their brows as if in confused reverie or meditation. But when the echoes had fully ceased, a light laughter at once pervaded the assembly; the musicians looked at each other and smiled as if at their own nervousness and folly, and made whispering vows, each to the other, that the next chiming of the clock should produce in them no similar emotion; and then, after the lapse of sixty minutes (which embrace three thousand and six hundred seconds of the Time that flies), there came yet another chiming of the clock, and then were the same disconcert and tremulousness and meditation as before.

But in spite of these things, it was a gay and magnificent revel. The tastes of the duke were peculiar. He had a fine eye for colors and effects. He disregarded the *decora* of mere fashion. His plans were bold and fiery, and his conceptions glowed with barbaric lustre. There are some who would have thought him mad. His followers felt that he was not. It was necessary to hear and see and touch him to be *sure* that he was not.

He had directed, in great part, the movable embellishments of the seven chambers upon occasion of this great *fête*; and it was his own guiding taste which had given character to the masqueraders. Be sure they were grotesque. There were much glare and glitter and piquancy and phantasm—much of what has been since seen in *Hernani*. There were arabesque figures with unsuited limbs and appointments. There were delirious fancies such as the madman fashions. There were much of the beautiful, much of the wanton, much of the bizarre, something of the terrible, and not a little of that which might have excited disgust. To and fro in the seven chambers there stalked, in fact, a multitude of dreams. And these—the dreams—writhed in and about, taking hue from the rooms, and causing the wild music of the orchestra to seem as the echo of their steps. And, anon, there strikes the ebony clock which stands in the hall of the velvet. And then, for a moment, all is still, and all is silent save the voice of the clock. The dreams are stiff-frozen as they stand. But the echoes of the chime die away—they have endured but an instant—and a light, half-subdued laughter floats after them as they depart. And now again the music swells, and the dreams live, and writhe to and fro more merrily than ever, taking hue from the many-tinted windows through which stream the rays from the tripods. But to the chamber which lies most westwardly of the seven there are now none of the maskers who venture; for the night is waning away; and there flows a ruddier light through the blood-colored panes; and the blackness of the sable drapery appalls; and to him whose foot falls upon the sable carpet, there comes from the near clock of ebony a muffled peal more solemnly emphatic than any which reaches *their* ears who indulge in the more remote gaieties of the other apartments.

But these other apartments were densely crowded, and in them beat feverishly the heart of life. And the revel went whirlingly on, until at length there commenced the sounding of midnight upon the clock. And then the music ceased, as I have told; and the evolutions of the waltzers were quieted; and there was an uneasy cessation of all things as before. But now there were twelve strokes to be sounded by the bell of the clock; and thus it happened, perhaps, that more of thought crept, with more of time, into the meditations of the thoughtful among those who revelled. And thus too, it happened, perhaps, that before the last echoes of the last chime had utterly sunk into silence, there were many individuals in the crowd who had found leisure to become aware of the presence of a masked figure which had arrested the attention of no single individual before. And the rumor of this new presence having spread itself whisperingly around, there arose at length from the whole company a buzz, or murmur, expressive of disapprobation and surprise—then, finally, of terror, of horror, and of disgust.

In an assembly of phantasms such as I have painted, it may well be supposed that no ordinary appearance could have excited such sensation. In truth, the masquerade license of the night was nearly unlimited; but the figure in question had out-Heroded Herod, and gone beyond the bounds of even the prince's indefinite decorum. There are chords in the hearts of the most reckless which cannot be touched without emotion. Even with the utterly lost, to whom life and death are equally jests, there are matters of which no jest can be made. The whole company, indeed, seemed now deeply to feel that in the costume and bearing of the stranger neither wit nor propriety existed. The figure was tall and gaunt, and shrouded from head to foot in the habiliments of the grave. The mask which concealed the visage was made so nearly to resemble the countenance of a stiffened corpse that the closest scrutiny must have had difficulty in detecting the cheat. And yet all this might have been endured, if not approved, by the mad revellers around. But the mummer had gone so far as to assume the type of the Red Death. His vesture was dabbled in *blood*—and his broad brow, with all the features of the face, was besprinkled with the scarlet horror.

When the eyes of Prince Prospero fell upon this spectral image (which, with a slow and solemn movement, as if more fully to sustain its role, stalked to and fro among the waltzers), he was seen to be convulsed in the first moment with a strong shudder either of terror or distaste; but in the next, his brow reddened with rage.

"Who dares—" he demanded hoarsely of the courtiers who stood near him "—who dares insult us with this blasphemous mockery? Seize him and unmask him—that we may know whom we have to hang, at sunrise, from the battlements!"

It was in the eastern or blue chamber in which stood the Prince Prospero as he uttered these words. They rang throughout the seven rooms loudly and clearly, for the prince was a bold and robust man, and the music had become hushed at the waving of his hand.

It was in the blue room where stood the prince, with a group of pale courtiers by his side. At first, as he spoke, there was a slight rushing movement of this group in the direction of the intruder, who at the moment was also near at hand, and now, with deliberate and stately step, made closer approach to the speaker. But from a certain nameless awe with which the mad assumptions of the mummer had inspired the whole party, there were found none who put forth hand to seize him; so that, unimpeded, he passed within a yard of the prince's person; and, while the vast assembly, as if with one impulse, shrank from the centers of the rooms to the walls, he made his way uninterruptedly, but with the same solemn and measured step which had distinguished him from the first, through the blue chamber to the purple—through the purple to the green—through the green to the orange—through this again to the white—and even thence to the violet, ere a decided movement had been made to arrest him. It was then, however, that the Prince Prospero, maddening with rage and the shame of his own momentary cowardice, rushed hurriedly through the six chambers, while none followed him on account of a deadly terror that had seized upon all. He bore aloft a drawn dagger, and had approached, in rapid impetuosity, to within three or four feet of the retreating figure, when the latter, having attained the extremity of the velvet apartment, turned suddenly and confronted his pursuer. There was a sharp cry—and the dagger dropped gleaming upon the sable carpet, upon which, instantly afterward, fell prostrate in death the Prince Prospero. Then, summoning the wild courage of despair, a throng of the revellers at once threw themselves into the black apartment, and, seizing the mummer, whose tall figure stood erect and motionless within the shadow of the ebony clock, gasped in unutterable horror at finding the grave cerements and corpselike mask, which they handled with so violent a rudeness, untenanted by any tangible form.

And now was acknowledged the presence of the Red Death. He

had come like a thief in the night. And one by one dropped the revellers in the blood-bedewed halls of their revel, and died each in the despairing posture of his fall. And the life of the ebony clock went out with that of the last of the gay. And the flames of the tripods expired. And Darkness and Decay and the Red Death held illimitable dominion over all.

Catechism for Granma

by Charles M. Saplak

I'll go to Hell for sure.

You go to Hell if you hate your granma, and I sure as Hell hate mine, and Granpaw, too. I wonder about Hell, about the fire and all, and remember the time I burnt all the skin off three knuckles of my left hand on the stove at school. Boy, that hurt bad.

Right now, though, thinking about Hell ain't so bad, because I think about how cold I am. When I started out down here, I was just chilly, but if you're chilly long enough you're cold, and I been down here in this cellar long enough—all day! I never thought my own granny would put me here. I've never heard of a granny as mean as her!

Let me start at the beginning. For the first nine years of my life I never knew Granma and Granpaw Toschar except as the funny couple in a picture on Mama's dresser. You couldn't tell much in that picture except that Granpaw was skinny and sitting down with his hat in his hand, and Granma looked skinnier and stood up with her hand on his shoulder. I never really thought too much about them being alive, although Mama would cry over their picture and told me sometimes that they were still in "Checkoswowokkeeha," which is where all old folks live, because Papa calls it the Old Country.

When Papa and I sit on the porch, he puffs his pipe and tells me to be proud of "Checkoswowokkeeha." Once I told him that when the boys at school called me dumb Pollack or dumb Bohunk I blacked their eyes, but when they called me dumb Check I just twisted their arms and put them in the dirt, and we were friends afterwards. Papa smiled at that.

I never told Papa that when the big fat nuns take rulers to my hands and call me Pollack I sneak in at lunch and break their chalk into dustpiles.

Then about two months ago Mama got a letter, and danced around saying that her Nana and Poppy were moving to a farm outside of Wheeling. Papa just puffed his pipe and asked why aren't they coming here first, and I think he didn't want them to come but felt that it made us look bad because they weren't coming to stay with us. I don't think Papa ever feels just one thing at a time, like Mama when she dances or cries feels one thing at a time, which is probably why Papa never laughs or cries.

I didn't think this would make any difference to me, but one day Mama came out to meet me when I was coming home from school and told me I was going to stay with Granma and Granpaw Toschar when school was out, and wasn't I happy? I should have known by then it was going to be trouble because Mama was smiling so big and I knew deep down that the last thing I wanted was to go to the house of Granma and Granpaw near Wheeling.

By that time I had beat every boy in school on the playground, and beat most at reading and doing numbers, and they didn't call me "dumb" anything. They even wanted me to play baseball with them all summer and I wanted to.

More than one thousand times I asked Mama to not go, and more than one thousand times I asked why Papa and Mama could not come along.

More than one thousand times Mama said that Papa had to work in the mines so long as they had the work, and she had to clean houses for the citizens in town so long as they wanted her to, that if she asked to go for a long time, they would not want her back to work.

So I left school that last day and carried home ribbons for best in arithmetic and best in handwriting, and a rosary of glass beads for saying the most catechism. With these prizes and a whole summer ahead of me I should have been happy, but all I could think of was a summer with the skinny people in that faded picture.

Mama packed me up with almost all the clothes I owned and made me take the ribbons and rosary from school. I didn't care one bit whether Granma or Granpaw saw the ribbons. I felt like crying or asking again to not go, but somehow, when Papa stood there puffing his pipe and looking at me, I knew that he wouldn't cry or ask not to go, so I shouldn't either.

Finally Papa walked with me to town and left me with Mr. Brammer. Before Papa left I thought for sure I would cry, but Papa reached into his pocket and pulled out a pocket knife, which he gave me. He said not to tell Mama or Granma that I had it, and I think that made it twice as much fun to have.

I don't really know how long it took for our wagon to get here. All I really remember is that the whole way up Mr. Brammer chewed on a big black plug of tobacco. The night of the first day we camped beside a lake. On the second day he offered me some tobacco from his plug and I cut it with the new pocket knife. I got so sick I had to lie in the back of the wagon, and Mr. Brammer laughed so much tears ran down his fat cheeks.

Toward the evening of the second day Mr. Brammer stopped the wagon and pointed down a long red-dog road. He started throwing my bags out of the wagon and said that my grandparents lived down that road, and that he would take me all the way except he still had to get to Wheeling, and my Papa hadn't paid him that much.

I thought for a long time about the possibility of running away right then, but I remembered Papa's knife and found myself walking down that noisy gravel road. Before I knew it I was here.

I guess I had pictured that Granma and Granpaw would come running out to hug me and make a big fuss and take me in where they had a big meal fixed and that she would pinch my face and that he would want to mess up my hair. I'd seen other boys with their grandparents.

But as I came up on the big house with the big porch and the weedy yard, nobody came out. After a while I knocked on the door, but there was still no answer. I would have yelled, but I was too scared. I wasn't worried about the neighbors; all the way down the gravel road after Mr. Brammer let me off, I never saw any sign of anyone living out here, nor any branches in the road. I didn't think to wonder about why they lived so far away from everyone else.

I didn't know what to do. I felt lost and was mad at Mama and Papa for ever sending me away. It never came to my mind that I should just walk right in, so I sat down on the steps of the porch and curled up against the big pillowcase full of clothes I carried.

I must have fallen asleep. The next thing I knew, Granma and Granpaw were on the porch with me, Granma lifting me up, Granpaw carrying the bags. I could only see them by the dim light coming from the windows of the house because the sun had already gone down. They didn't come out and give me the big hellos like I pictured; they didn't even come out and wake me up, they just picked me up and carried me into the house.

Inside the parlor, they sat me down in a dusty chair, then sat across from me on their couch to have a look at me. My heart was in my throat and I was scared to talk. While they looked at me, I was looking at them.

They were the same people from the picture, but older and even skinnier. You don't often see people that skinny. They only had one little kerosene lamp burning in the whole living room, and that was burning really low. In that orange light I couldn't see a lot of details, but they looked sick somehow.

One more thing, but it's hard to say. The picture Mama had was black and white and grey. Now I was seeing them in real life, and they looked as pasty as ever, like their faces were drinking up the light and color from that kerosene lamp.

It wasn't long before the questions began. What about Mama? How much did we have to eat? Did Papa work? A thousand questions, most of which I couldn't answer. I never thought about this until now, but most old people I know can't talk without funny sounds on everything they say, because they're used to talking in Old Country talk. Not Granma and Granpaw, though. They spoke American perfectly . . . I guess they're really smart because some old people have been here years and only talk Old Country.

We must have sat there for hours, them asking about a thousand questions. They didn't ask anything about school or my friends, but couldn't hear enough about how often Mama went to church and what I remembered about what the priest says at church. They also couldn't ask enough about how much I play and what I eat. I didn't really know what to tell them, but they would ask question after question about food, even asking about what sort of pots and pans Mama cooks with.

Because they didn't ask anything about school I almost forgot to tell them what Mama made me promise I'd tell them. When I got a chance to talk I piped up about the ribbons I had in school. I took them out to show, and to tell the truth, Granma and Granpaw didn't make the fuss over them that I was afraid of. Then I told them about the prize I got for catechism reciting, which was of course the little rosary with the purple glass beads. I dug around in my pillowcase until I found the little wooden box.

It's hard to explain the next part. When I opened up the box, both Granma and Granpaw, who were pasty-faced anyway, went solid white. I mean, I thought I could see through 'em. Granpaw started sputtering and Granma jumped up and closed her hand around both the box and my hand, shutting the box. Her hand was like a big bony spider, but it was *strong*.

Granma took the box and said that she wanted to look at it awhile, after I went to bed. Granpaw, who still looked so white I could swear he was clear, said that's a good idea, and he picked up my things and took them all to a bedroom upstairs.

The only light downstairs was that one kerosene lamp, and the only light upstairs was what moonlight spilled in through the windows, but I could see that their house wasn't like Mama keeps our house. For one thing, Mama believes that the more pictures and pillows and lace doilies she can keep in the house, the better. Granma's house had furniture, but just a little furniture, and none of the extras. Another thing, my Mama keeps the house clean. Way too clean, as a matter of fact. Granma's house was dusty and smelled like the basement of our house. Even in that dim light I could see it was messy.

The room Granpaw showed me to was small and had a bed, a chair, a dresser, and one tiny window, about one foot from the ceiling. He dumped my things on the bed, then left without a word, closing the door behind him.

I think that at that moment I came the closest to crying as anytime during the whole deal. Right now back home my friends were probably running wild. They were coming up on a summer of swimming, baseball, and picking blackberries to earn dimes for the picture show. Meanwhile I was in the middle of nowhere just outside of Wheeling living with two strange old pasty-faced skeletons who were nothing like Mama said they would be. I thought about running away, and came real close to doing it.

The only thing that stopped me was the fact that when I crept over to the door and turned the knob, I found that it was locked. If I hadn't been afraid of making enough noise to wake up Granma and Granpaw, I would have tried to bust the door open.

I even thought about pushing the dresser over to where I could climb up on it and get to the little window where the moonlight was streaming in, but I realized that it was way too small to climb through.

Since there was no way out, I decided to just go to bed. I didn't even take my clothes off, but got under the musty old covers and tried to go to sleep.

As bothered as I was by everything, I couldn't go to sleep. I did something then that I never do at home. I tried to go to sleep by reciting lessons in my head.

I went through the presidents and the state capitals, multiplication tables and even practiced handwriting in my mind. Still I couldn't sleep, so I tried reciting some of the catechism lessons the nuns liked to beat into us so much.

After about five minutes of that, the door flew open and Granma stood there, moonlight shining on a face that was uglier than any I'd ever seen. She said that I was talking too loudly and that it was keeping Granpaw awake, and that he didn't feel good anyway, so I had to stop. I just croaked a weak, "Yes, Granma," and she shut the door.

If I live to be one hundred I'll never forget that face.

I hadn't even known that I'd been talking out loud.

* * *

I guess I got to sleep eventually, but I don't know how. I can't remember my dreams, but I know that they were filled with snakes and rats and graveyards and bones. I think I remember tossing and turning and kicking at the covers because I felt like they were holding me to the bed and strangling me.

The moonlight had faded from the room and the sun wasn't up yet when the door opened again. At first I didn't see anybody there and wanted to sit up and say something but just couldn't get up. It was like I was still asleep and dreaming that I was awake, but thought that I was dreaming. I couldn't tell my arms and legs what to do.

Then Granma and Granpaw came into the room. It wasn't like they were walking, but just standing straight up and floating, like they were in a dream, too.

Granma pulled back the covers and Granpaw picked me up. They took me down the stairs and out through the front door. All this time I couldn't move. I was surprised that they were able to carry me, but I'd already seen how strong Granma could be when she shut up my rosary case.

We went down the front steps, floating more than walking. We went to a door by the side of the house and they took me down some stone stairs and dropped me on the floor. Then they left. I could hear them behind the closed door for what seemed like five minutes, locking the door and making sure that it was shut up tight. All this time I just lay on the dirt floor, unable to get up. Then it all faded, like nightmares do.

I woke up and sunlight was coming through little cracks in the storm door. The room I'm in smells terrible, like wormy dirt. I've been down here most of the day.

I think they put me here because they know that I could have kicked open that door to the bedroom. The door down here is thick and the locks are too strong. There's no window and no other door.

I don't know what they want to do with me, but I don't think it's anything good. I felt my way around down here and found that it's a kind of cellar. There are shelves of jars of stuff that Granma probably canned herself.

I got hungry after my first couple of hours down here and decided to open up one of the jars to get something to eat. It was too dark to see what was in it.

When I finally got one open and put it to my lips I threw up. I knew what the stuff was because last summer I cut my hand on a hatchet and sucked on the cut like I'd seen people do.

I don't hate Mama or Papa for sending me here because they didn't know. I don't hate Mr. Brammer for sending me down the road alone, because even if he had brought me all the way he probably would have just left me at the porch and I'd still be here now.

I do hate Granma and Granpaw, though. I hate them a lot. Even if they aren't the same people that Mama remembered, even if they aren't the same people from the picture, they're still Granma and Granpaw, so I'll probably go to Hell.

But I've got that knife that Papa gave me. I've broken down a shelf and stomped it until it splintered, and I'm working one of the big long splinters into a good point with this knife. Working on it warms me up, even though the cellar here is cool. My hands are full of splinters, but I'm not crying about it.

They'll be back for me. Granma and Granpaw are strong, but I'm strong, too, and I've whipped boys older than me and bigger than me. I'm also fast and they're probably going to be very surprised when they open the door and I'm not sitting in the dirt crying, but standing here waiting with my sharp sticks. I can also shout out my catechism lessons so loud that their ears ring while they try to grab me.

Maybe I'll go to Hell for this, but if I do, I'm taking somebody else along.

Separate Vacations

by Maggie Wagner-Hankins

"I can't believe after thirty-five years of marriage you want to take separate vacations." His voice was a hurt whine as he focused on the flyer she had handed him about the ranch.

"It's not exactly—separate vacations."

"Well, I don't know what else you'd call it. We won't be together. We won't even see each other the whole time we're there."

That was true. In fact, it was the main selling point as far as Grace was concerned. Five glorious days of no Harold to analyze every word she spoke, to shadow every step she took. No Harold breathing down her neck or looking over her shoulder to see what she was doing (which was never much of anything anyway, because what could a person do when she hadn't even a smidgen of privacy in her life?).

"I don't know how you'll manage, Grace. Really, what if something happens? What if you get—well—mauled by some wild beast? What then?"

"I won't be mauled. The people at the ranch assured me it's perfectly safe. It's a totally controlled experience. And just think, you won't have any responsibilities; you won't even have to *think* about what I'm doing. You can just relax and be free to experience it. Doesn't that appeal to you?"

Of course that first part wouldn't appeal to him. She shouldn't have even mentioned his not having to think about what she was doing. What else was his life for? But maybe he'd focus on the rest of it—the relaxation, the freedom.

He lay back in his recliner and screwed up his face as if considering it, while Grace waited, acting unconcerned about his response.
It wouldn't do to appear too eager, or he'd pick her brain to pieces
on the whys of it. "Well, I don't know," he finally said, "it might be
okay. But then again, it might be just asking for trouble."

"Well, think about it, won't you? Look some more at the flyer. I'm
going to start supper."

Harold touched a spot on his recliner and was immediately enclosed in a six foot square Plexiglas box. Grace knew he was setting
the dials for a spring shower in the woods with a light breeze. Lately
that was his favorite, a good sign. It meant he craved relaxation. And
his choosing a natural setting rather than one of the indoor ones—
the concert hall, for instance, or a big band dance lounge or sauna—
gave her hope that the trip to the transference ranch would strike
just the right chord in him.

As she was preparing the vegetables (Harold would only eat two
kinds now, baby carrots and brocciflower; tonight it was carrots),
his voice came to her through the intercom. She heard rain in the
background. He must have increased the intensity on the spring
shower.

"What are you cooking?"

"The same thing I always cook on Tuesdays. Spaghetti with mush-
room sauce, baby carrots, and raisin Jell-O on the side." Harold was
a vegetarian. That was okay. A lot of people were these days, and she
had gotten used to cooking meatless meals. When she got really
desperate for beef, she'd go to the cafe across town and have an old
fashioned hamburger.

"Did you pay the power bill today?"

It was a totally idiotic question, she knew, and yet he had asked it
on such a regular basis over the years that it sounded almost natural,
like saying good morning to the neighbors or bless you when someone sneezed.

"Of course. When have I missed paying the power bill on Tuesdays? I called it in at nine o'clock, if you want to check the log."

"Your sarcasm really gets to me, Grace, and there's no reason for
it. I'm just making sure."

"I thought you were relaxing. Do you want to come out here and stand with me while I fix dinner so you can be sure I put enough pepper on the carrots?"

There was no answer, but she could sense him, still hovering over her via the intercom connecting his environmental stimulation chamber with her kitchen.

I *am* getting sarcastic, aren't I? she thought, allowing herself a smile. At least he couldn't see her.

It was the flyer that was causing it. Just the act of sending for it had emboldened her a little. She daydreamed about the possibilities a vacation like this offered, envisioned herself at the ranch, strong and free. She had never really stood up to Harold's hovering, pestering ways before, but had accepted as just his way his need for total supervision of her every move, his insistence on dissecting every comment she made.

A wife's duty was to put up with her husband, and a husband's was to put up with his wife. It was practically written in black and white in the contract. And if there was more putting up with required of one spouse than the other, well, that was just, as Harold sometimes said, tough titmouse. Things had changed since the old days when nobody put up with anything and marriages lasted an average of eleven months. She was almost as proud as Harold that their marriage had lasted so long, particularly since they hadn't really loved each other for the last thirty years, and felt it was a tribute to her patience and her ability to adapt to less than pleasant circumstances.

But now the opportunity of a short period of freedom from him was right in front of her, and she wasn't about to give it up without some effort.

Just the thought of roaming the simulated jungle environment on the ranch sent a tingle through her, filling her with a foretaste of the power enjoyed by the powerful animals that hunted there.

Maybe the vacation could even do something for Harold, like help him gain a wider perspective on life. He was far too concerned with the tiny little closed up world he had created for himself.

She poured them both milk and thought about the options the ranch offered. There was no doubt which plan she would choose when they got down to making their choices. She had always loved cats—the graceful way they moved, the sinuous power barely concealed beneath their sleek coats.

That was one thing she didn't have to worry about with Harold—that he would choose the same plan she did. He hated cats. Hadn't he had both of hers put to sleep when she was out shopping, right after they were married? It was so cruel of him she'd almost filed for an annulment, but he'd talked his way out of it using some half-baked excuse about an allergy from his mother's side, and had gone on and on about how disgusting they were, killing innocent little animals for food whenever they got the chance, no matter how much cat food they got in their bowls every day. No, she could almost predict which plan he'd select if he agreed to the trip at all. He'd be herbivorous, and a runner.

"In my youth I could run like a young gazelle." How many times had he said those words. She'd been tempted to make a sampler of it in her folk arts class. Wouldn't it look great, hanging on the wall over their bed? *In my youth I could run like a young gazelle.*

Well, he wasn't a young gazelle any more. He was a middle-aged moose with a paunch and jowls. Still, she knew he looked back on those days as his best. They probably had been. Too bad they'd been over around the time they got married.

Yes, she was pretty sure he'd opt for something in the deer family, something swift and lean and light on its feet. And, glory to God in the highest, they'd be miles apart. She let out a deep, wistful sigh. As she might have expected, Harold's voice asked into the air just over her head, "You tired, Grace?" Of course he hadn't turned off the intercom. She couldn't even sigh in privacy.

In bed that night, she brought it up again.

"You know, if we sign up now, we get a twenty percent discount. It's their founder's day celebration."

"I don't know, Grace. I just don't know if we ought to. It's a lot of money."

"We can afford it. It won't cost a cent more than that furniture we were planning to buy for the rec room, and we can certainly wait another year or two on that. The kids never come any more anyway, so who's there to use it?" She didn't add, it's because of you, Mr. Buttinski, that they stay away, because, first of all, there was no point sticking a knife in him and twisting, and second of all, he wouldn't believe it anyway. He thought all fathers told their grown children where they should go to dinner on their anniversaries and what color socks to buy the kids.

"I don't know, Grace."

"Picture it, Harold. You, a young gazelle, prancing through a meadow of tall grass, the wind in your face, the scent of clean, sweet air in your distended nostrils." She felt him settle into the mattress, a smile begrudgingly playing across his face.

He opened his eyes and looked at her. "Are you sure this is safe?"

"Harold, they've been doing it for years. It's perfectly safe. The Phillers did it two years ago, and they said it was a wonderful experience."

"What if you stay stuck in the animal?"

"Harold, you aren't *in* an animal. You *become* an animal. It's something to do with rearranging your molecules—Jerry Philler could explain it more scientifically. But you just get in the box and you become whatever it is you want to become."

"I don't know. It sounds kind of unnatural to me. How can they do that?"

"I don't know. How can they send someone back into the past? But they've done it. They're *scientists*, Harold. They can do practically anything now. This is probably nothing to them."

He grunted and rolled over. "I'll think about it."

They lay there awhile in silence. She knew from the absence of his snore that he was still awake. Maybe he was envisioning himself leaping through a field of tall grass.

"Harold?"

"Yeah?"

"What would you be? If we did it, I mean?"

"That's easy. Can't you guess?"

"I can guess. A gazelle."

"You got it." A minute later he said, "Grace?"

"Hmmm?"

"What about you? You wouldn't change your mind, would you, and be a gazelle with me?"

And have you critiquing every prance I made? Concerning yourself over the quality of every blade of grass I chose to nibble? she thought. Not on your life. But she only answered, "I don't think so, dear. I really do have my heart set on being something in the cat family."

"That's a shame. We won't be able to get near each other. Or will we?"

"I don't think so. They say when you make the transference, you get the same instincts, in a watered down version I imagine, that the real animals have. They could never keep the cats anywhere near the game animals."

Thank God.

"I suppose not. It's too bad, though. Also too bad we haven't worked harder on the mental telepathy stuff. It'd be nice to be able to know what's going on with each other, don't you think?"

"Um-hmmm. But it's only for five days. I think we can stand to be in suspense that long. Afterward you can tell me all about your experience, and I'll tell you about mine."

"I guess. I still don't like it very well, though. It really is almost like taking separate vacations."

She smiled into the darkness. The words *separate vacations* floated through her mind as she drifted off to sleep, still smiling.

"Grace, we'll do it. By God, we'll do it!" He slammed the flyer onto the breakfast table, affirming his commitment.

"You dreamed of being a gazelle, didn't you?"

He smiled self-consciously. "I have to admit I did."

"I thought so. You were making little running movements during the night, and you kept doing sniffing things with your nose."

"Well, I guess that helped me make up my mind. Say, what's that on your blouse?"

She was so elated that she didn't even resent his scrutiny this morning. "Some strawberry jam I spilled on it."

"Here, let me see if I can get it out for you—"

"Harold, I'll take *care* of it. Now, why don't you sit down and enjoy your breakfast. I'll call the agency after we eat and book our places at the ranch."

"What did *you* dream last night?" he asked, scooting up to the table and tucking his napkin under his chin. He laid another across his lap. Harold didn't like food on his clothes. Or anyone else's, for that matter. "Did you dream about being a pussycat?"

Did I ever, she thought. But it's nothing I'd care to share with you. It was far too lovely to talk about in ordinary language. "No, I don't recall dreaming anything."

It had been so wonderful she had resisted waking up for as long as possible. She could still feel the way her shoulder and thigh muscles worked as she moved through the jungle and out onto the grassy plain in search of food, could feel the tension in her body as she prepared to spring, could recall the joyous abandon in running on all fours in great, long, reaching strides.

"This toast isn't our usual bread, is it?"

She blinked and came back to the present.

"No, dear. It's a new brand. I thought I'd try it. Don't you like it?"

"It's all right. I just noticed it has a little different flavor. Try it and tell me what you think it has that the other doesn't."

She tried a bite, just to appease him, and could tell no difference. "I don't know."

"Oh, well, I guess it's not really important," he said, not sounding convinced.

Are any of the things you think about important? she wanted to ask. Oh, it would be so wonderful to be in that other world. For the first time, she wondered what would happen if she never came back—if she just stayed out there in the far recesses of the ranch and they never found her to put her back in the box and change her into herself again.

But of course they would find her. It was a big place but not that big, not for a full grown tiger. She'd need to eat. They could find her by following the trail of dead game she would have sustained herself on. Or maybe they would even close down for a bit and remove the food supply until she gave herself up.

It was a nice dream, though.

"You know," Harold said, practically mirroring her thoughts, "I wonder if anyone ever just stays like that. You know, someone with a lot of money who could afford to live out there as an animal non-stop."

"I don't know. It doesn't seem like it would be too healthy. Their longest plan is ten days. I imagine anything over that might cause some kind of structural damage or maybe even mental problems or something."

"Probably just as well. We were born people, and we ought to stay people. Animals can't even talk. But I was just thinking that there are some people who'd probably be better off as animals. You know, like Burt Rossner. He's such a pigheaded person to deal with, hates everyone, he'd probably be just as happy to be turned into a mule or something and live out in a pasture."

"I suppose."

"What're you going to do today?"

"Oh, I don't know. I have some shopping to do. For Stephanie's new baby." Stephanie was their neighbor. She'd just had a baby girl, and Grace loved buying things for her.

"Think I'll go along," Harold announced. "Keep you company."

"Oh, you really don't need to, dear. I'm just going to be looking at baby things."

"That's okay. Maybe I can help. It never hurts to have another opinion on things, does it?"

This was the biggest drawback to their both being retired. Before, she'd at least been able to get away from him at work, and if she was in the mood to shop by herself, she'd just stop on her way home. But now none of Harold's time was spoken for. He was available twenty-four hours a day to serve as her shadow.

"All right. But now I think I'll call the agency about our reservations."

"Good idea." Harold jumped up. "I'll just pick up the extension, so you don't have to repeat the whole conversation to me afterwards." He settled himself at the kitchen phone station while she went in to her desk and called the number on the flyer.

*　　*　　*

The ranch was huge—thousands and thousands of acres, all sectioned off to approximate an incredible array of natural environments and wildlife habitats.

Their special service rep explained as much as she could about the animals they wished to become, and gave them each a personality analysis to be sure there was nothing in their natures that would make their choices unsuitable. Grace passed with flying colors.

So did Harold, the gazelle. His area, Grace was pleased to note, was at least a mile from where she would be roaming, and was separated from hers by a road with electric fences on each side. There was no way Harold would be able to get near her, even if for some reason he decided to try to find her while they were still in their animal forms. He'd had an electric shock when he was a boy, and he still worried that it had left lasting damage to his psyche and certain other parts of him.

The thought of five whole days of peace, freedom, and privacy elated her so that she was filled with a sudden tenderness toward Harold. When they kissed and said their goodbyes, just prior to their final phase of instruction before the transference took place, she felt almost guilty about her eagerness to get away from him. Seeing his reluctance to part with her, she gave him an extra kiss and a pat on the shoulder and said, "Bye, honey. You have a great time. I'll see you right here on Wednesday."

"Honey," he called after her, "did you give the kids the number for this place?"

"Yes, Harold."

"Good. Never know when they might need something. Oh, and did you—"

"Yes, yes, Harold, I did all those things. Now let's don't keep these nice people waiting while we go down the checklist again. I'll see you soon."

She noted, looking back as she was driven away toward her embarkation point, that Harold already looked rather deerlike, his big brown eyes trailing the truck as if he had just one more question to ask her.

Bye, Harold. Enjoy your grass. Already the preliminary enzyme they'd given her to stimulate tigerlike instincts in her was taking effect. She found herself craving a hamburger as she hadn't in a year.

It was incredible. Unreal. Sometimes, not very often but a few times during that first day in her new surroundings, she almost forgot she was a human being. But then she'd remember Harold. The funny thing was, when she thought about him now she thought of him as a gazelle, and she was almost embarrassed to realize that she envisioned him more as a snack than as a husband. Thank goodness he was miles away.

Most of the time she just let herself go, living in the moment as most animals surely did. She saw things differently, not just because her eye level was different or because she was walking on four legs or because she was so much bigger than she'd been before. Things had a new relationship to one another, and she was very aware of each one's importance in maintaining the delicate balance of the relationship. The grass, the ground, the sky, the insects buzzing around her face, the wind, the animals she killed for food, she herself—all were part of one big whole, pieces of a puzzle that fit perfectly and precisely together. She felt at home against the earth, not as a landlord but as a part of it.

It was the freedom, too. There was no one to keep track of her moves, to caution her, to advise her. She had her instinct and her common sense (one of the human aspects, along with her memory when she chose to use it, that had been left to her in the trans-ference) to direct her actions. Occasionally she'd catch sight of one of the ranch hands, just making sure things were okay. But they didn't pester. They didn't encroach on her territory. They just let her be. They let her live in peace.

She'd thought it might bother her to kill animals for food, but the fact that she had omnivorous tastes had convinced the analysts that she'd have no problem, once she was injected with the tiger per-sonality enzyme. Someone like Harold wouldn't have been able to handle it. His natural revulsion toward eating meat would have set up a resistance to the enzyme, and he'd have been a very hungry, very crazy tiger by the time he was turned back into human form.

But then they'd never have let Harold become a meat-eating animal. They were very careful about things like that.

The first animal she killed was an injured deer. She felt a fleeting surprise that she felt no guilt over the act. The animal's body was food, just as one day her body would be food for something, whether vultures or insects or just the earth that would nourish itself from her flesh. And so when she killed the deer (quickly and cleanly, she was pleased to note, and not bunglingly as she might have expected for her first try), the act seemed as natural as breathing in and out. She ate as much as she could and spent the afternoon lolling in the sun.

Stretching was a particularly enjoyable pastime during these days. So was lying there, watching the world happen around her. She also enjoyed growling, purring, and grooming herself.

By the fifth day, she had managed to put Harold and most of the rest of her human life almost entirely out of her mind. She knew, somewhere in the back of her head, that something was drawing to a close, that she should be preparing for something, but she didn't give it too much thought.

She was hungry.

Getting up and stretching, she loped off in search of something to eat. She'd tried some small mammals, but they didn't satisfy her as a larger animal did. Maybe there would be another deer in the area. There was game to be had, but it wasn't abundant. She had to work for it. She'd been told that up front, and it didn't bother her. But today she had put off exerting the effort to find food until her hunger had grown acute, so now, when she noticed an animal running almost straight for her despite her being so obviously visible, it didn't occur to her to wonder why it was acting in such a careless manner. If the animal was that stupid, she'd just go ahead and eat it without a chase. She flexed her muscles while it bounded eagerly up to her.

Not until after it was dead and she was devouring its left shoulder did she notice the strange odor about it. Some trace of her human senses was able to supply a name for it that was unfamiliar to her tiger self. *Burnt.* The animal smelled burnt, or singed. Singed hair, that was it.

She looked at the gazelle and noticed a dark, blackened patch of hair on its flank, and another on its neck, as if it had bumped into something hot.

I should be remembering something, she thought as she continued eating.

"Mrs. Harrison, I'm afraid we're having a little trouble locating your husband," the service rep said. Grace was in the recovery room, once again in human form and waiting for her mental, emotional, and instinctual chemistry to catch up with the physical.

The impact of the representative's words on her wasn't as severe as she'd expected it to be. She felt almost calm. "Is it possible," she asked carefully, "that he could have gotten out?"

"Oh, highly unlikely. The whole range is fenced by electrical barbed wire. Even if he'd tried, he'd have gotten a bad enough burn to send him back."

"Could he have jumped the fence? I mean, if he was a really strong, healthy gazelle?"

"I—suppose it's—possible. But again, it's highly unlikely. And why would anyone want to? If your husband had wanted to terminate the experience, he could have come to the embarkation station. All guests are told about this. It's stressed so that no matter how 'in character' they are, they could hardly ever forget it." It was true. Grace had always had the thought in the back of her head that if she was finding the experience disagreeable in any way, she could go back to where she had entered the habitat and they would immediately return her to normal.

"Anyone who could make it past all the hindrances we have up would have to be very determined," said the rep. Grace thought about the time Harold had flown alone through a major ice storm just so he could be with her when she gave Stephanie's baby shower, in order not to miss out on any of the details.

And the time he had masqueraded as a woman because her ladies' club luncheon had been females only and he hadn't wanted her to miss him.

"I'm sure they would," Grace reassured the woman. "And I'm

sure you'll find my husband. He must have just wandered off some-place. By the way, can I ask you a question?"

"Sure."

"Would a guest's body go back to its original form sooner or later without intervention from you, or would he remain in the animal form until you 'deprogrammed' him?"

"I suppose you're asking because you're wondering if, in case your husband is out there wandering around lost, he'll change back into his human form so we can spot him easier."

"Yes, that's why I'm asking."

"Well, the body would eventually go back on its own, but it would be a slow and probably not too pleasant experience. But I have every confidence that we'll find your husband long before that could hap-pen to him. I'm guessing we'll locate him in a matter of a few hours."

"I'm sure you will. Now I have another question. It's just curiosity—this is all so fascinating. What if," she asked delicately, "one of your guests, heaven forbid, of course, should die while in animal form? Would they be transformed immediately back into human form, or would they just waste away as an animal?"

"Mrs. Harrison! I hope you're not assuming—"

"Of course not. It's a hypothetical question. I'm a writer, you see, and I'm just naturally curious about things."

"Well, in that case," the rep said, still looking uncomfortable, "I suppose the—departed person would maintain the animal form for as long as it took for—the remains to—"

"Rot?" Grace asked. The service representative nodded and looked more uncomfortable still.

"Well, I'll tell you what," said Grace, getting up, feeling almost like herself again, "I think I'll just go on home now. My children will be wondering how everything went, and I need to take care of some business. My husband would want me to do that. He's so picky about things' being done right and on time. You just call me when you find out anything, and I'll keep the home fires burning until he turns up."

"If that's the way you want it, Mrs. Harrison. I feel terrible about this, but I'm sure it'll all be cleared up in no time. I can't understand—"

"Oh, don't give it a thought. Harold was probably enjoying himself so much that he couldn't stand the thought of its ending so soon. You know, in his youth he could run like a young gazelle. He's probably just finding it hard to give up."

Grace made a mental note, as she drove away, to stop by the market and buy some ground beef. Maybe the kids would like to bring their families over for hamburgers this evening.

The Bottle Imp

by Robert Louis Stevenson

*Note. Any student of that very unliterary product, the
English drama of the early part of the century, will here
recognize the name and the root idea of a piece once
rendered popular by the redoubtable B. Smith. The root idea
is there and identical, and yet I believe I have made it a new
thing. And the fact that the tale has been designed and
written for a Polynesian audience may lend it some
extraneous interest nearer home.*

R.L.S.

There was a man of the island of Hawaii, whom I shall call Keawe;
for the truth is, he still lives, and his name must be kept secret; but
the place of his birth was not far from Honaunau, where the bones of
Keawe the Great lie hidden in a cave. This man was poor, brave, and
active; he could read and write like a schoolmaster; he was a first-
rate mariner besides, sailed for some time in the island steamers,
and steered a whaleboat on the Hamakua coast. At length it came to
Keawe's mind to have a sight of the great world and foreign cities,
and he shipped on a vessel bound to San Francisco.

This is a fine town, with a fine harbor, and rich people uncount-
able; and, in particular, there is one hill which is covered with
palaces. Upon this hill Keawe was one day taking a walk, with his
pocket full of money, viewing the great house upon either hand with

pleasure. "What fine houses these are!" he was thinking, "and how happy must these people be who dwell in them, and take no care for the morrow!" The thought was in his mind when he came abreast of a house that was smaller than some others, but all finished and beautiful like a toy; the steps of that house shone like silver, and the borders of the garden bloomed like garlands, and the windows were bright like diamonds; and Keawe stopped and wondered at the excellence of all he saw. So stopping, he was aware of a man that looked forth upon him through a window, so clear, that Keawe could see him as you see a fish in a pool upon the reef. The man was elderly, with a bald head and a black beard; and his face was heavy with sorrow, and he bitterly sighed. And the truth of it is, that as Keawe looked in upon the man, and the man looked out upon Keawe, each envied the other.

All of a sudden the man smiled and nodded, and beckoned Keawe to enter, and met him at the door of the house.

"This is a fine house of mine," said the man, and bitterly sighed. "Would you not care to view the chambers?"

So he led Keawe all over it, from the cellar to the roof, and there was nothing there that was not perfect of its kind, and Keawe was astonished.

"Truly," said Keawe, "this is a beautiful house; if I lived in the like of it, I should be laughing all day long. How comes it, then, that you should be sighing?"

"There is no reason," said the man, "why you should not have a house in all points similar to this, and finer, if you wish. You have some money, I suppose?"

"I have fifty dollars," said Keawe; "but a home like this will cost more than fifty dollars."

The man made a computation. "I am sorry you have no more," said he, "for it may raise you trouble in the future, but it shall be yours at fifty dollars."

"The house?" said Keawe.

"No, not the house," replied the man; "but the bottle. For, I must tell you, although I appear to you so rich and fortunate, all my fortune, and this house itself and its garden, came out of a bottle not much bigger than a pint. This is it."

And he opened a lockfast place, and took out a round-bellied bottle with a long neck; the glass of it was white like milk, with changing rainbow colors in the grain. Withinsides something obscurely moved, like a shadow and a fire.

"This is the bottle," said the man; and, when Keawe laughed, "You do not believe me?" he added. "Try, then, for yourself. See if you can break it."

So Keawe took the bottle up and dashed it on the floor till he was weary; but it jumped on the floor like a child's ball, and was not injured. "This is a strange thing," said Keawe. "For by the touch of it, as well as by the look, the bottle should be glass."

"Of glass it is," replied the man, sighing more heavily than ever; "but the glass of it was tempered in the flames of hell. An imp lives in it, and that is the shadow we behold there moving; or, so I suppose. If any man buys this bottle the imp is at his command; all that he desires—love, fame, money, houses like this house, ay, a city like this city—all are his at the word uttered. Napoleon had this bottle, and by it he grew to be the king of the world; but he sold it at the last and fell. Captain Cook had this bottle, and by it he found his way to so many islands; but he, too, sold it, and was slain upon Hawaii. For, once it is sold, the power goes and the protection; and unless a man remain content with what he has, ill will befall him."

"And yet you talk of selling it yourself?" Keawe said.

"I have all I wish, and I am growing elderly," replied the man. "There is one thing the imp cannot do—he cannot prolong life; and it would not be fair to conceal from you there is a drawback to the bottle; for if a man die before he sells it, he must burn in hell forever."

"To be sure, that is a drawback and no mistake," cried Keawe. "I would not meddle with the thing. I can do without a house, thank God; but there is one thing I could not be doing with one particle, and that is to be damned."

"Dear man, you must not run away from things," returned the man. "All you have to do is to use the power of the imp in moderation, and then sell it to someone else, as I do to you, and finish your life in comfort."

"Well, I observe two things," said Keawe. "All the time you keep sighing like a maid in love, that is one; and, for the other, you sell this bottle very cheap."

"I have told you already why I sigh," said the man. "It is because I fear my health is breaking up; and, as you said yourself, to die and go to the devil is a pity for anyone. As for why I sell so cheap, I must explain to you there is a peculiarity about the bottle. Long ago, when the devil brought it first upon earth, it was extremely expensive, and was sold first of all to Prester John for many millions of dollars; but it cannot be sold at all, unless sold at a loss. If you sell it for as much as you paid for it, back it comes to you again like a homing pigeon. It follows that the price has kept falling in these centuries, and the bottle is now remarkably cheap. I bought it myself from one of my great neighbors on this hill, and the price I paid was only ninety dollars. I could sell it for as high as eighty-nine dollars and ninety-nine cents, but not a penny dearer, or back the thing must come to me. Now, about this there are two bothers. First, when you offer a bottle so singular for eighty-odd dollars, people suppose you to be jesting. And second—but there is no hurry about that—and I need not go into it. Only remember it must be coined money that you sell it for."

"How am I to know that this is all true?" asked Keawe.

"Some of it you can try at once," replied the man. "Give me your fifty dollars, take the bottle, and wish your fifty dollars back into your pocket. If that does not happen, I pledge you my honor I will cry off the bargain and restore your money."

"You are not deceiving me?" said Keawe.

The man bound himself with a great oath.

"Well, I will risk that much," said Keawe, "for that can do no harm," and he paid over his money to the man, and the man handed him the bottle.

"Imp of the bottle," said Keawe, "I want my fifty dollars back." And sure enough, he had scarce said the word before his pocket was as heavy as ever.

"To be sure this is a wonderful bottle," said Keawe.

"And now good morning to you, my fine fellow, and the devil go with you for me," said the man.

"Hold on," said Keawe, "I don't want any more of this fun. Here, take your bottle back."

"You have bought it for less than I paid for it," replied the man, rubbing his hands. "It is yours now; and for my part, I am only concerned to see the back of you." And with that he rang for his Chinese servant, and had Keawe shown out of the house.

Now, when Keawe was in the street, with the bottle under his arm, he began to think. "If all is true about this bottle, I may have made a losing bargain," thinks he. "But, perhaps the man was only fooling me." The first thing he did was to count his money; the sum was exact—forty-nine dollars American money, and one Chili piece. "That looks like the truth," said Keawe. "Now I will try another part."

The streets in that part of the city were as clean as a ship's decks, and though it was noon, there were no passengers. Keawe set the bottle in the gutter and walked away. Twice he looked back, and there was the milky, round-bellied bottle where he left it. A third time he looked back, and turned a corner; but he had scarce done so, when something knocked upon his elbow, and behold! It was the long neck sticking up; and, as for the rounded belly, it was jammed into the pocket of his pilot-coat.

"And that looks like the truth," said Keawe.

The next thing he did was to buy a corkscrew in a shop, and go apart into a secret place in the fields. And there he tried to draw the cork, but as often as he put the screw in, out it came again, and the cork as whole as ever.

"This is some new sort of cork," said Keawe, and all at once he began to shake and sweat, for he was afraid of that bottle.

On his way back to the portside he saw a shop where a man sold shells and clubs from the wild islands, old heathen deities, old coined money, pictures from China and Japan, and all manner of things that sailors bring in their sea chests. And here he had an idea. So he went in and offered the bottle for a hundred dollars. The man of the shop laughed at him at first, and offered him five; but, indeed, it was a curious bottle, such glass was never blown in any human glassworks, so prettily the colors shone under the milky white, and so strangely the shadow hovered in the midst; so, after he had disputed awhile after the manner of his kind, the shopman gave

Keawe sixty silver dollars for the thing and set it on a shelf in the midst of his window.

"Now," said Keawe, "I have sold that for sixty which I bought for fifty—or, to say truth, a little less, because one of my dollars was from Chili. Now I shall know the truth upon another point."

So he went back on board his ship, and when he opened his chest, there was the bottle, and had come more quickly than himself. Now Keawe had a mate on board whose name was Lopaka.

"What ails you?" said Lopaka, "that you stare in your chest?"

They were alone in the ship's forecastle, and Keawe bound him to secrecy, and told all.

"This is a very strange affair," said Lopaka; "and I fear you will be in trouble about this bottle. But there is one point very clear—that you are sure of the trouble, and you had better have the profit in the bargain. Make up your mind what you want with it; give the order, and if it is done as you desire, I will buy the bottle myself; for I have an idea of my own to get a schooner, and go trading through the islands."

"That is not my idea," said Keawe; "but to have a beautiful house and garden on the Kona Coast, where I was born, the sun shining in at the doors, flowers in the garden, glass in the windows, pictures on the walls, and toys and fine carpets on the tables, for all the world like the house I was in this day—only a story higher, and with balconies all about like the king's palace; and to live there without care and make merry with my friends and relatives."

"Well," said Lopaka, "let us carry it back with us to Hawaii; and if all comes true, as you suppose, I will buy the bottle, as I said, and ask a schooner."

Upon that they were agreed, and it was not long before the ship returned to Honolulu, carrying Keawe and Lopaka, and the bottle. They were scarce come ashore when they met a friend upon the beach, who began at once to condole with Keawe.

"I do not know what I am to be condoled about," said Keawe.

"Is it possible that you have not heard," said the friend, "your uncle—that good old man—is dead, and your cousin—that beautiful boy—was drowned at sea?"

Keawe was filled with sorrow, and, beginning to weep and to

lament, he forgot about the bottle. But Lopaka was thinking to himself, and presently, when Keawe's grief was a little abated, "I have been thinking," said Lopaka, "had not your uncle lands in Hawaii, in the district of Kau?"

"No," said Keawe, "not in Kau: they are on the mountainside—a little by south Hookena."

"These lands will now be yours?" asked Lopaka.

"And so they will," says Keawe, and began again to lament for his relatives.

"No," said Lopaka, "do not lament at present. I have a thought in my mind. How if this should be the doing of the bottle? For here is the place ready for your house."

"If this be so," cried Keawe, "it is a very ill way to serve me by killing my relatives. But it may be, indeed; for it was in just such a station that I saw the house with my mind's eye."

"The house, however, is not yet built," said Lopaka.

"No, nor like to be!" said Keawe; "for though my uncle has some coffee and ava and bananas, it will not be more than will keep me in comfort; and the rest of that land is the black lava."

"Let us go to the lawyer," said Lopaka; "I have still this idea in my mind."

Now, when they came to the lawyer's, it appeared Keawe's uncle had grown monstrous rich in the last days, and there was a fund of money.

"And here is the money for the house!" cried Lopaka.

"If you are thinking of a new house," said the lawyer, "here is the card of a new architect, of whom they tell me great things."

"Better and better!" cried Lopaka. "Here is all made plain for us. Let us continue to obey orders."

So they went to the architect, and he had drawings of a house on his table.

"You want something out of the way," said the architect. "How do you like this?" and he handed a drawing to Keawe.

Now, when Keawe set eyes on the drawing, he cried out aloud, for it was the picture of his thought exactly drawn.

"I am in for this house," thought he. "Little as I like the way it comes to me, I am in for it now, and I may as well take the good along with the evil."

So he told the architect all that he wished, and how he would have that house furnished, and about the pictures on the walls and the knickknacks on the tables; and he asked the man plainly for how much he would undertake the whole affair.

The architect put many questions, and took his pen and made a computation; and when he had done he named the very sum that Keawe had inherited.

Lopaka and Keawe looked at one another and nodded.

"It is quite clear," thought Keawe, "that I am to have this house, whether or no. It comes from the devil, and I fear I will get little good by that; and of one thing I am sure, I will make no wishes as long as I have this bottle. But with the house I am saddled; and I may as well take the good along with the evil."

So he made his terms with the architect, and they signed a paper; and Keawe and Lopaka took ship again and sailed to Australia; for it was concluded between them they should not interfere at all, but leave the architect and the bottle imp to build and to adorn that house at their own pleasure.

The voyage was a good voyage, only all the time Keawe was holding in his breath, for he had sworn he would utter no more wishes, and take no more favors, from the devil. The time was up when they got back. The architect told them that the house was ready, and Keawe and Lopaka took a passage in the *Hall*, and went down Kona way to view the house, and see if all had been done fitly according to the thought that was in Keawe's mind.

Now, the house stood on the mountainside, visible to ships. Above, the forest ran up into the clouds of rain; below, the dark lava fell in cliffs, where the kings of old lay buried. A garden bloomed about that house with every hue of flowers; and there was an orchard of papaia on the one hand and an orchard of herdprint on the other, and right in front, toward the sea, a ship's mast had been rigged up and bore a flag. As for the house, it was three stories high, with great chambers and broad balconies on each. The windows were of glass, so excellent that it was as clear as water and as bright as day. All manner of furniture adorned the chambers. Pictures hung upon the walls in golden frames—pictures of ships, and men fighting, and of the most beautiful women, and of singular places;

nowhere in the world are there pictures of so bright a color as those Keawe found hanging in his house. As for the knickknacks they were extraordinarily fine: chiming clocks and musical boxes, little men with nodding heads, books filled with pictures, weapons of price from all quarters of the world, and the most elegant puzzles to entertain the leisure of a solitary man. And as no one would care to live in such chambers, only to walk through and view them, the balconies were made so broad that a whole town might have lived upon them in delight; and Keawe knew not which to prefer, whether the back porch, where you get the land breeze, and looked upon the orchards and the flowers, or the front balcony, where you could drink the wind of the sea, and look down the steep wall of the mountain and see the *Hall* going by once a week or so between Hookena and the hills of Pele, or the schooners plying up the coast for wood and ava and bananas.

When they had viewed all, Keawe and Lopaka sat on the porch.

"Well," said Lopaka, "is it all as you designed?"

"Words cannot utter it," said Keawe. "It is better than I dreamed, and I am sick with satisfaction."

"There is but one thing to consider," said Lopaka, "all this may be quite natural, and the bottle imp have nothing whatever to say to it. If I were to buy the bottle, and got no schooner after all, I should have put my hand in the fire for nothing. I gave you my word, I know; but yet I think you would not grudge me one more proof."

"I have sworn I would take no more favors," said Keawe. "I have gone already deep enough."

"This is no favor I am thinking of," replied Lopaka. "It is only to see the imp himself. There is nothing to be gained by that, and so nothing to be ashamed of, and yet, if I once saw him, I should be sure of the whole matter. So indulge me so far, and let me see the imp; and, after that, here is the money in my hand, and I will buy it."

"There is only one thing I am afraid of," said Keawe. "The imp may be very ugly to view, and if you once set eyes upon him you might be very undesirous of the bottle."

"I am a man of my word," said Lopaka. "And here is the money betwixt us."

"Very well," replied Keawe, "I have a curiosity myself. So come, let us have one look at you, Mr. Imp."

Now as soon as that was said, the imp looked out of the bottle, and in again, swift as a lizard; and there sat Keawe and Lopaka turned to stone. The night had quite come, before either found a thought to say or voice to say it with; and then Lopaka pushed the money over and took the bottle.

"I am a man of my word," said he, "and had need to be so, or I would not touch the bottle with my foot. Well, I shall get my schooner and a dollar or two for my pocket; and then I will be rid of this devil as fast as I can. For to tell you the plain truth, the look of him has cast me down."

"Lopaka," said Keawe, "do not you think any worse of me than you can help; I know it is night, and the roads bad, and the pass by the tombs an ill place to go by so late, but I declare since I have seen that little face, I cannot eat or sleep or pray till it is gone from me. I will give you a lantern, and a basket to put the bottle in, and any picture or fine thing in all my house that takes your fancy; and be gone at once, and go sleep at Hookena with Nahinu."

"Keawe," said Lopaka, "many a man would take this ill; above all, when I am doing you a turn so friendly, as to keep my word and buy the bottle; and for that matter, the night and the dark, and the way by the tombs, must be all tenfold more dangerous to a man with such a sin upon his conscience, and such a bottle under his arm. But for my part, I am so extremely terrified myself, I have not the heart to blame you. Here I go, then; and I pray God you may be happy in your house, and I fortunate with my schooner, and both get to heaven in the end in spite of the devil and his bottle."

So Lopaka went down the mountain; and Keawe stood in his front balcony, and listened to the clink of the horse's shoes, and watched the lantern go shining down the path, and along the cliff of caves where the old dead are buried; and all the time he trembled and clasped his hands, and prayed for his friend, and gave glory to God that he himself was escaped out of that trouble.

But the next day came very brightly, and that new house of his was so delightful to behold that he forgot his terrors. One day followed another, and Keawe dwelt there in perpetual joy. He had his place

on the back porch; it was there he ate and lived, and read the stories
in the Honolulu newspapers; but when anyone came by they would
go in and view the chambers and the pictures. And the fame of the
house went far and wide; it was called Ka-Hale Nui—the Great
House—in all Kona; and sometimes the Bright House, for Keawe
kept a Chinaman, who was all day dusting and furbishing; and the
glass, and the gilt, and the fine stuffs, and the pictures, shone as
bright as the morning. As for Keawe himself, he could not walk in
the chambers without singing, his heart was so enlarged; and when
ships sailed by upon the sea, he would fly his colors on the mast.

So time went by, until one day Keawe went upon a visit as far as
Kailua to certain of his friends. There he was feasted; and left as soon
as he could the next morning, and rode hard, for he was impatient to
behold his beautiful house; and, besides, the night then coming on
was the night in which the dead of old days go abroad on the sides of
Kona; and having already meddled with the devil, he was the more
chary of meeting with the dead. A little beyond Honaunau, looking
far ahead, he was aware of a woman bathing in the edge of the sea;
and she seemed a well-grown girl, but he thought no more of it.
Then he saw her white shift flutter as she put it on, and then her red
holoku; and by the time he came abreast of her she was done with
her toilet, and had come up from the sea, and stood by the sidetrack
in her red holoku, and she was all freshened with the bath, and her
eyes shone and were kind. Now Keawe no sooner beheld her than
he drew rein.

"I thought I knew everyone in this country," said he. "How comes
it that I do not know you?"

"I am Kokua, daughter of Kiano," said the girl, "and I have just
returned from Oahu. Who are you?"

"I will tell you who I am in a little," said Keawe, dismounting
from his horse, "but not now. For I have a thought in my mind, and
if you knew who I was, you might have heard of me, and would not
give me a true answer. But tell me, first of all, one thing: are you
married?"

At this Kokua laughed out aloud. "It is you who ask questions,"
she said. "Are you married yourself?"

"Indeed, Kokua, I am not," replied Keawe, "and never thought to be until this hour. But here is the plain truth. I have met you here at the roadside, and I saw your eyes, which are like the stars, and my heart went to you as swift as a bird. And so now, if you want none of me, say so, and I will go on to my own place; but if you think me no worse than any other young man, say so, too, and I will turn aside to your father's for the night, and tomorrow I will talk with the good man."

Kokua said never a word, but she looked at the sea and laughed.

"Kokua," said Keawe, "if you say nothing, I will take that for the good answer; so let us be stepping to your father's door."

She went on ahead of him, still without speech; only sometimes she glanced back and glanced away again, and she kept the strings of her hat in her mouth.

Now, when they had come to the door, Kiano came out on his veranda and cried out and welcomed Keawe by name. At that the girl looked down, for the fame of the great house had come to her ears; and, to be sure, it was a great temptation. All that evening they were very merry together; and the girl was as bold as brass under the eyes of her parents, and made a mark of Keawe, for she had a quick wit. The next day he had a word with Kiano, and found the girl alone.

"Kokua," said he, "you made a mark of me all the evening; and it is still time to bid me go. I would not tell you who I was, because I have so fine a house, and I feared you would think too much of that house and too little of the man that loves you. Now you know all, and if you wish to have seen the last of me, say so at once."

"No," said Kokua, but this time she did not laugh, nor did Keawe ask for more.

This was the wooing of Keawe; things had gone quickly; but so an arrow goes, and the ball of a rifle swifter still, and yet both may strike the target. Things had gone fast, but they had gone far also, and the thought of Keawe rang in the maiden's head; she heard his voice in the breath of the surf upon the lava, and for this young man that she had seen but twice she would have left father and mother and her native islands. As for Keawe himself, his horse flew up the path of the mountain under the cliff of tombs, and the sound of the hoofs, and the sound of Keawe singing to himself for pleasure, echoed in the caverns of the dead. He came to the Bright House, and still he was singing. He sat and ate in the broad balcony, and the Chinaman wondered at his master, to hear how he sang between the mouthfuls. The sun went down into the sea, and the night came; and Keawe walked the balconies by lamplight, high on the mountains, and the voice of his singing startled men on ships.

"Here am I now upon my high place," he said to himself. "Life may be no better; this is the mountain top; and all shelves about me toward the worse. For the first time I will light up the chambers, and bathe in my fine bath with the hot water and the cold, and sleep above in the bed of my bridal chamber."

So the Chinaman had word, and he must rise from sleep and light the furnaces; and as he walked below, beside the boilers, he heard his master singing and rejoicing above him in the lighted chambers. When the water began to be hot the Chinaman cried to his master: and Keawe went into the bathroom; and the Chinaman heard him sing as he filled the marble basin; and heard him sing, and the singing broken, as he undressed; until of a sudden, the song ceased. The Chinaman listened, and listened; he called up the house to Keawe to ask if all were well, and Keawe answered him "Yes," and bade him go to bed; but there was no more singing in the Bright House; and all night long the Chinaman heard his master's feet go round and round the balconies without repose.

Now, the truth of it was this: as Keawe undressed for his bath, he spied upon his flesh a patch like a patch of lichen on a rock, and it was then that he stopped singing. For he knew the likeness of that patch, and knew that he was fallen in the Chinese Evil.

Now, it's a sad thing for any man to fall into this sickness. And it would be a sad thing for anyone to leave a house so beautiful and so commodious, and depart from all his friends to the north coast of Molokai, between the mighty cliff and the sea breakers. But what was that to the case of the man Keawe, he who had met his love but yesterday, and won her but that morning, and now saw all his hopes break, in a moment, like a piece of glass?

Awhile he sat upon the edge of the bath, then sprang, with a cry, and ran outside; and to and fro, along the balcony, like one despairing.

"Very willingly could I leave Hawaii, the home of my fathers," Keawe was thinking. "Very lightly could I leave my house, the high-placed, the many-windowed, here upon the mountains. Very bravely could I go to Molokai, to Kalaupapa by the cliffs, to live with the smitten and to sleep there, far from my fathers. But what wrong have I done, what sin lies upon my soul, that I should have encountered Kokua coming cool from the sea water in the evening? Kokua, the soul ensnarer! Kokua, the light of my life! Her may I never wed, her may I look upon no longer, her may I no more handle with my loving hand; and it is for this, it is for you, O Kokua, that I pour my lamentations!"

Now you are to observe what sort of a man Keawe was, for he might have dwelt there in the Bright House for years, and no one been the wiser of his sickness; but he reckoned nothing of that, if he must lose Kokua. And again he might have wed Kokua even as he was; and so many would have done, because they have the souls of pigs; but Keawe loved the maiden manfully, and he would do her no hurt and bring her in no danger.

A little beyond the midst of the night, there came in his mind the recollection of that bottle. He went round to the back porch, and called to memory the day when the devil had looked forth; and at the thought ice ran in his veins.

"A dreadful thing is the bottle," thought Keawe, "and dreadful is the imp, and it is a dreadful thing to risk the flames of hell. But what other hope have I to cure my sickness or to wed Kokua? What!" he thought, "would I beard the devil once, only to get me a house, and not face him again to win Kokua?"

Thereupon he called to mind it was the next day the *Hall* went by on her return to Honolulu. "There must I go first," he thought, "and see Lopaka. For the best hope that I have now is to find that same bottle I was so pleased to be rid of."

Never a wink could he sleep; the food stuck in his throat; but he sent a letter to Kiano, and about the time when the steamer would be coming, rode down beside the cliff of the tombs. It rained; his horse went heavily; he looked up at the black mouths of the caves, and he envied the dead that slept there and were done with trouble; and called to mind how he had galloped by the day before, and was astonished. So he came down to Hookena, and there was all the country gathered for the steamer as usual. In the shed before the store they sat and jested and passed the news; but there was no matter of speech in Keawe's bosom, and he sat in their midst and looked without on the rain falling on the houses, and the surf beating among the rocks, and the sighs rose in his throat.

"Keawe of the Bright House is out of spirits," said one to another. Indeed, and so he was, and little wonder.

Then the *Hall* came, and the whaleboat carried him on board. The after part of the ship was full of Haoles—whites—who had been to visit the volcano, as their custom is; and the midst was crowded with Kanakas, and the forepart with wild bulls from Hilo and horses from Kau; but Keawe sat apart from all in his sorrow, and watched for the house of Kiano. There it sat low upon the shore in the black rocks, and shaded by the coron palms, and there by the door was a red holoku, no greater than a fly, and going to and fro with a fly's business. "Ah, queen of my heart," he cried, "I'll venture my dear soul to win you!"

Soon after darkness fell and the cabins were lit up, and the Haoles sat and played at the cards and drank whisky as their custom is; but Keawe walked the deck all night; and all the next day, as they steamed under the lea of Maui or Molokai, he was still pacing to and fro like a wild animal in a menagerie.

Toward evening they passed Diamond Head, and came to the pier of Honolulu. Keawe stepped out among the crowd and began to ask for Lopaka. It seemed that he had become the owner of a schooner—none better in the islands—and was gone upon an adventure as far as Pola-Pola or Kahiki; so there was no help to be looked for from Lopaka. Keawe called to mind a friend of his, a lawyer in the town (I must not tell his name), and inquired of him. They said he was grown suddenly rich, and had a fine new house upon Waikiki shore; and this put a thought in Keawe's head, and he called a hack and drove to the lawyer's house.

The house was all brand new, and the trees in the garden no greater than walking sticks, and the lawyer, when he came, had the air of a man well pleased. "What can I do to serve you?"

"You are a friend of Lopaka's," replied Keawe, "and Lopaka purchased from me a certain piece of goods that I thought you might enable me to trace."

The lawyer's face became very dark. "I do not profess to misunderstand you, Mr. Keawe," said he, "though this is an ugly business to be stirring in. You may be sure I know nothing, but yet I have a guess, and if you would apply in a certain quarter I think you might have news."

And he named the name of a man, which, again, I had better not repeat. So it was for days, and Keawe went from one to another, finding everywhere new clothes and carriages, and fine new houses and men everywhere in great contentment, although, to be sure, when he hinted at his business their faces would cloud over.

"No doubt I am upon the track," thought Keawe. "These new clothes and carriages are all the gifts of the little imp, and these glad faces of men who have taken their profit and got rid of the accursed thing in safety. When I see pale cheeks and hear sighing, I shall know that I am near the bottle."

So it befell at last that he was recommended to a Haole in Beritania Street. When he came to the door, about the hour of the evening meal, there were the usual marks of the new house, and the young garden, and the electric light shining in the windows; but when the owner came, a shock of hope and fear ran through Keawe; for here was a young man, white as a corpse, and black about the eyes, the hair shedding from his head, and such a look in his countenance as a man may have when he is waiting for the gallows.

"Here it is, to be sure," thought Keawe, and so with this man he noways veiled his errand. "I am come to buy the bottle," said he.

At the word, the young Haole of Beritania Street reeled against the wall.

"The bottle!" he gasped. "To buy the bottle!" Then he seemed to choke, and seizing Keawe by the arm, carried him into a room and poured out wine in two glasses.

"Here is my respects," said Keawe, who had been much about with Haoles in his time. "Yes," he added, "I am come to buy the bottle. What is the price by now?"

At that word the young man let his glass slip through his fingers, and looked upon Keawe like a ghost.

"The price," says he; "the price! You do not know the price?"

"It is for that I am asking you," returned Keawe. "But why are you so much concerned? Is there anything wrong about the price?"

"It has dropped a great deal in value since your time, Mr. Keawe," said the young man, stammering.

"Well, well, I shall have the less to pay for it," says Keawe. "How much did it cost you?"

The young man was as white as a sheet. "Two cents," said he.

"What?" cried Keawe, "two cents? Why, then, you can only sell it for one. And he who buys it-" The words died upon Keawe's tongue; he who bought it could never sell it again, the bottle and the bottle imp must abide with him until he died, and when he died must carry him to the red end of hell.

The young man of Beritania Street fell upon his knees. "For God's sake, buy it!" he cried. "You can have all my fortune in the bargain. I was mad when I bought it at that price. I had embezzled money at my store; I was lost else; I must have gone to jail."

"Poor creature," said Keawe, "you would risk your soul upon so desperate an adventure, and to avoid the proper punishment of your own disgrace; and you think I could hesitate with love in front of me. Give me the bottle, and the change which I make sure you have all ready. Here is a five-cent piece."

It was as Keawe supposed; the young man had the change ready in a drawer; the bottle changed hands, and Keawe's fingers were no sooner clasped upon the stalk than he had breathed his wish to be a clean man. And, sure enough, when he got home to his room, and stripped himself before a glass, his flesh was whole like an infant's. And here was the strange thing: he had no sooner seen this miracle than his mind was changed within him, and he cared naught for the Chinese Evil, and little enough for Kokua; and had but the one thought, that here he was bound to the bottle imp for time and for eternity, and had no better hope but to be a cinder forever in the flames of hell. Away ahead of him he saw them blaze with his mind's eye, and his soul shrank, and darkness fell upon the light.

When Keawe came to himself a little, he was aware it was the night when the band played at the hotel. Thither he went, because he feared to be alone; and there, among happy faces, walked to and fro, and heard the tunes go up and down, and saw Berger beat the measure, and all the while he heard the flames crackle, and saw the red fire burning in the bottomless pit. Of a sudden the band played Hiki-ao-ao; that was a song that he had sung with Kokua, and at the strain courage returned to him.

"It is done now," he thought, "and once more let me take the good along with the evil."

So it befell that he returned to Hawaii by the first steamer, and as soon as it could be managed he was wedded to Kokua, and carried her up the mountainside to the Bright House.

Now it was so with these two, that when they were together Keawe's heart was stilled; but as soon as he was alone he fell into a brooding horror, and heard the flames crackle, and saw the red fire burn in the bottomless pit. The girl, indeed, had come to him wholly; her heart leaped in her side at the sight of him, her hand clung to his; and she was so fashioned, from the hair upon her head to the nails upon her toes, that none could see her without joy. She was pleasant in her nature. She had the good word always. Full of song she was, and went to and fro in the Bright House, the brightest thing in its three stories, caroling like the birds. And Keawe beheld and heard her with delight, and then must shrink upon one side, and weep and groan to think upon the price that he had paid for her; and then he must dry his eyes, and wash his face, and go and sit with her on the broad balconies, joining in her songs, and, with a sick spirit, answering her smiles.

There came a day when her feet began to be heavy and her songs more rare; and now it was not Keawe only that would weep apart, with the whole width of the Bright House betwixt. Keawe was so sunk in his despair, he scarce observed the change, and was only glad he had more hours to sit alone and brood upon his destiny, and was not so frequently condemned to pull a smiling face on a sick heart. But one day, coming softly through the house, he heard the sound of a child sobbing, and there was Kokua rolling her face upon the balcony floor, and weeping like the lost.

"You do well to weep in this house, Kokua," he said. "And yet I would give the head off my body that you (at least) might have been happy."

"Happy!" she cried. "Keawe, when you lived alone in your Bright House you were the word of the island for a happy man; laughter and song were in your mouth, and your face was as bright as the sunrise. Then you wedded poor Kokua; and the good God knows what is amiss in her—but from that day you have not smiled. Oh!" she cried, "what ails me? I thought I was pretty, and I knew I loved him. What ails me, that I throw this cloud upon my husband?"

"Poor Kokua," said Keawe. He sat down by her side, and sought to take her hand; but that she plucked away. "Poor Kokua," he said, again. "My poor child—my pretty. And I had thought all this while to spare you! Well, you shall know all. Then, at least, you will pity poor Keawe; then you will understand how much he loved you in the past—that he dared hell for your possession—and how much he loves you still (the poor condemned one), that he can yet call up a smile when he beholds you."

With that, he told her all, even from the beginning.

"You have done this for me?" she cried. "Ah, well, then what do I care!" and she clasped and wept upon him.

"Ah, child!" said Keawe, "and yet, when I consider of the fire of hell, I care a good deal!"

"Never tell me," said she, "no man can be lost because he loved Kokua, and no other fault. I tell you, Keawe, I shall save you with these hands, or perish in your company. What! you loved me and gave your soul, and you think I will not die to save you in return?"

"Ah, my dear, you might die a hundred times, and what difference would that make," he cried, "except to leave me lonely till the time comes of my damnation?"

"You know nothing," said she. "I was educated in a school in Honolulu; I am no common girl. And I tell you I shall save my lover. What is this you say about a cent? But all the world is not America. In England they have a piece they call a farthing, which is about a half a cent. Ah! sorrow!" she cried, "that makes it scarcely better, for the buyer must be lost, and we shall find none so brave as my Keawe! But, then, there is France; they have a small coin there which they call a centime, and these go five to the cent or thereabout. We could not do better. Keawe, let us go to the French islands; let us go to Tahiti, as fast as ships can bear us. There we have four centimes, three centimes, two centimes, one centime, four possible sales to come and go on; and two of us to push the bargain. Come, my Keawe! kiss me, and banish care. Kokua will defend you."

"Gift of God!" he cried. "I cannot think that God will punish me for desiring aught so good! Be it as you will, then, take me where you please; I put my life and my salvation in your hands."

Early the next day Kokua was about her preparations. She took Keawe's chest that he went with sailoring; and first she put the bottle in a corner, and then packed it with the richest of their clothes and the bravest of the knickknacks in the house. "For," said she, "we must seem to be rich folks, or who will believe in the bottle?"

All the time of her preparation she was as gay as a bird; only when she looked upon Keawe the tears would spring in her eye, and she must run and kiss him. As for Keawe, a weight was off his soul; now that he had his secret shared, and some hope in front of him, he seemed like a new man, his feet went lightly on the earth, and his breath was good to him again. Yet was terror still at his elbow, and ever and again, as the wind blows out a taper, hope died in him, and he saw the flames toss and the red fire burn in hell.

It was given out in the country they were gone pleasuring to the States, which was thought a strange thing, and yet not so strange as the truth, if any could have guessed it. So they went to Honolulu in the *Hall*, and thence in the *Umatilla* to San Francisco with a crowd of Haoles, and at San Francisco took their passage by the mail brigantine, the *Tropic Bird*, for Papeete, the chief place of the French in the south islands. Thither they came, after a pleasant voyage, on a fair day of the trade wind, and saw the reef with the surf breaking and Motuiti with its palms, and the schooner riding within-side, and the white houses of the town low down along the shore among green trees, and overhead the mountains and the clouds of Tahiti, the wise island.

It was judged the most wise to hire a house, which they did accordingly, opposite the British consul's, to make a great parade of money, and themselves conspicuous with carriages and horses. This it was very easy to do, so long as they had the bottle in their possession; for Kokua was more bold than Keawe, and, whenever she had a mind, called on the imp for twenty or a hundred dollars. At this rate they soon grew to be remarked in the town; and the strangers from Hawaii, their riding and their driving, the fine holokus, and the rich lace of Kokua, became the matter of much talk.

They got on well after the first with the Tahitian language, which is indeed like to the Hawaiian, with a change of certain letters; and as soon as they had any freedom of speech, began to push the bottle. You are to consider it was not an easy subject to introduce; it was not easy to persuade people you are in earnest, when you offer to sell them for four centimes the spring of health and riches inexhaustible. It was necessary besides to explain the dangers of the bottle; and either people disbelieved the whole thing and laughed, or they thought the more of the darker part, became overcast with gravity, and drew away from Keawe and Kokua, as from persons who had dealings with the devil. So far from gaining ground, these two began to find they were avoided in the town; the children ran away from them screaming, a thing intolerable to Kokua; Catholics crossed themselves as they went by; and all persons began with one accord to disengage themselves from their advances.

Depression fell upon their spirits. They would sit at night in their new house, after a day's weariness, and not exchange one word, or the silence would be broken by Kokua bursting suddenly into sobs. Sometimes they would pray together; sometimes they would have the bottle out upon the floor, and sit all evening watching how the shadow hovered in the midst. At such times they would be afraid to go to rest. It was long ere slumber came to them, and, if either dozed off, it would be to wake and find the other silently weeping in the dark, or, perhaps, to wake alone, the other having fled from the house and the neighborhood of that bottle, to pace under the bananas in the little garden, or to wander on the beach by moonlight.

One night it was so when Kokua awoke. Keawe was gone. She felt in the bed and his place was cold. Then fear fell upon her, and she sat up in bed. A little moonshine filtered through the shutters. The room was bright, and she could spy the bottle on the floor. Outside it blew high, the great trees of the avenue cried aloud, and the fallen leaves rattled in the veranda. In the midst of this Kokua was aware of another sound; whether of a beast or of a man she could scarce tell, but it was as sad as death, and cut her to the soul. Softly she arose, set the door ajar, and looked forth into the moonlit yard. There, under the bananas, lay Keawe, his mouth in the dust, and as he lay he moaned.

It was Kokua's first thought to run forward and console him; her second potently withheld her. Keawe had borne himself before his wife like a brave man; it became her little in the hour of weakness to intrude upon his shame. With the thought she drew back into the house.

"Heaven," she thought, "how careless have I been—how weak! It is he, not I, that stands in this eternal peril; it was he, not I, that took the curse upon his soul. It is for my sake, and for the love of a creature of so little worth and such poor help, that he now beholds so close to him the flames of hell—ay, and smells the smoke of it, lying without there in the wind and moonlight. Am I so dull of spirit that never till now I have surmised my duty, or have I seen it before and turned aside? But now, at least, I take up my soul in both the hands of my affection; now I say farewell to the white steps of heaven and the waiting faces of my friends. A love for a love, and let mine be equaled with Keawe's! A soul for a soul, and be it mine to perish!"

She was a deft woman with her hands, and was soon apparelled. She took in her hands the change—the precious centimes they kept ever at their side; for this coin is little used, and they had made provision at a government office. When she was forth in the avenue clouds came on the wind, and the moon was blackened. The town slept, and she knew not whither to turn till she heard one coughing in the shadow of the trees.

"Old man," said Kokua, "what do you here abroad in the cold night?"

The old man could scarce express himself for coughing, but she made out that he was old and poor, and a stranger in the island.

"Will you do me a service?" said Kokua. "As one stranger to another, and as an old man to a younger woman, will you help a daughter of Hawaii?"

"Ah," said the old man. "So you are the witch from the eight islands, and even my old soul you seek to entangle. But I have heard of you, and defy your wickedness."

"Sit down here," said Kokua, "and let me tell you a tale." And she told him the story of Keawe from the beginning to the end.

"And now," said she, "I am his wife, whom he bought with his soul's welfare. And what should I do? If I went to him myself and offered to buy it, he will refuse. But if you go, he will sell it eagerly; I will await you here; you will buy it for four centimes, and I will buy it again for three. And the Lord strengthen a poor girl!"

"If you meant falsely," said the old man, "I think God would strike you dead."

"He would!" cried Kokua. "Be sure he would. I could not be so treacherous, God would not suffer it."

"Give me the four centimes and await me here," said the old man.

Now, when Kokua stood alone in the street, her spirit died. The wind roared in the trees, and it seemed to her the rushing of the flames of hell; the shadows towered in the light of the street lamp, and they seemed to her the snatching hands of evil ones. If she had had the strength, she must have run away, and if she had had the breath she must have screamed aloud; but, in truth, she could do neither, and stood and trembled in the avenue, like an affrighted child.

Then she saw the old man returning, and he had the bottle in his hand.

"I have done your bidding," said he, "I left your husband weeping like a child; tonight he will sleep easy." And he held the bottle forth.

"Before you give it me," Kokua panted, "take the good with the evil—ask to be delivered from your cough."

"I am an old man," replied the other, "and too near the gate of the grave to take a favor from the devil. But what is this? Why do you not take the bottle? Do you hesitate?"

"Not hesitate!" cried Kokua. "I am only weak. Give me a moment. It is my hand resists, my flesh shrinks back from the accursed thing. One moment only!"

The old man looked upon Kokua kindly. "Poor child!" said he, "you fear: your soul misgives you. Well, let me keep it, I am old, and can never more be happy in this world, and as for the next—"

"Give it me!" gasped Kokua. "There is your money. Do you think I am so base as that? Give me the bottle."

"God bless you, child," said the old man.

Kokua concealed the bottle under her holoku, said farewell to the old man, and walked all along the avenue, she cared not whither. For all roads were now the same to her, and led equally to hell. Sometimes she walked, and sometimes ran; sometimes she screamed out loud in the night, and sometimes lay by the wayside in the dust and wept. All that she had heard of hell came back to her; she saw the flames blaze, and she smelled the smoke, and her flesh withered on the coals.

Near day she came to her mind again, and returned to the house. It was even as the old man said—Keawe slumbered like a child. Kokua stood and gazed upon his face.

"Now, my husband," said she, "it is your turn to sleep. When you wake it will be your turn to sing and laugh. But for poor Kokua, alas! that meant no evil—for poor Kokua no more sleep, no more singing, no more delight, whether in earth or Heaven."

With that she lay down in the bed by his side, and her misery was so extreme that she fell in a deep slumber instantly.

Late in the morning her husband woke her and gave her the good news. It seemed he was silly with delight, for he paid no heed to her distress, ill though she dissembled it. The words stuck in her mouth, it mattered not; Keawe did the speaking. She ate not a bite, but who was to observe it? For Keawe cleared the dish. Kokua saw and heard him, like some strange thing in a dream; there were times when she forgot or doubted, and put her hands to her brow; to know herself doomed and hear her husband babble, seemed so monstrous.

All the while Keawe was eating and talking, and planning the time of their return, and thanking her for saving him, and fondling her, and calling her the true helper after all. He laughed at the old man that was fool enough to buy that bottle.

"A worthy old man he seemed," Keawe said. "But no one can judge by appearances. For why did the old reprobate require the bottle?"

"My husband," said Kokua, humbly, "his purpose may have been good."

Keawe laughed like an angry man.

"Fiddle-de-dee!" cried Keawe. "An old rogue, I tell you; and an old ass to boot. For the bottle was hard enough to sell at four centimes; and at three it will be quite impossible. The margin is not broad enough, the thing begins to smell of scorching—brrr!" said he, and shuddered. "It is true I bought it myself at a cent, when I knew not there were smaller coins. I was a fool for my pains; there will never be found another, and whoever has that bottle will carry it to the pit."

"O my husband!" said Kokua. "Is it not a terrible thing to save oneself by the eternal ruin of another? It seems to me I could not laugh. I would be humbled. I would be filled with melancholy. I would pray for the poor holder."

Then Keawe, because he felt the truth of what she said, grew the more angry. "Heighty-teighty!" cried he. "You may be filled with melancholy if you please. It is not the mind of a good wife. If you thought at all of me, you would sit shamed."

Thereupon he went out, and Kokua was alone.

What chance had she to sell that bottle at two centimes? None, she perceived. And if she had any, here was her husband hurrying her away to a country where there was nothing lower than a cent. And here—on the morrow of her sacrifice—was her husband leaving her and blaming her.

She would not even try to profit by what time she had, but sat in the house, and now had the bottle out and viewed it with unutterable fear, and now, with loathing, hid it out of sight.

By and by, Keawe came back, and would have her take a drive.

"My husband, I am ill," she said. "I am out of heart. Excuse me, I can take no pleasure."

Then was Keawe more wroth than ever. With her, because he thought she was brooding over the case of the old man; and with himself because he thought she was right, and was ashamed to be so happy.

"This is your truth," cried he, "and this is your affection! Your husband is just saved from eternal ruin, which he encountered for the love of you—and you can take no pleasure! Kokua, you have a disloyal heart."

He went forth again furious, and wandered in the town all day. He met friends, and drank with them; they hired a carriage and drove into the country, and there drank again. All the time, Keawe was ill at ease, because he was taking this pastime while his wife was sad, and because he knew in his heart that she was more right than he; and the knowledge made him drink the deeper.

Now, there was an old brutal Haole drinking with him, one that had been a boatswain of a whaler—a runaway, a digger in gold mines, and convict in prisons. He had a low mind and a foul mouth; he loved to drink and see others drunk; and he pressed the glass upon Keawe. Soon there was no more money in the company.

"Here, you!" says the boatswain, "you are rich, you have been always saying. You have a bottle or some foolishness."

"Yes," says Keawe, "I am rich; I will go back and get some money from my wife, who keeps it."

"That's a bad idea, mate," said the boatswain. "Never you trust a petticoat with dollars. They're all as false as water; you keep an eye on her."

Now, this word struck in Keawe's mind; for he was muddled with what he had been drinking.

"I should not wonder but she was false, indeed," thought he. "Why else should she be so cast down at my release? But I will show her I am not the man to be fooled. I will catch her in the act."

Accordingly, when they were back in town, Keawe bade the boatswain wait for him at the corner, by the old calaboose, and went forward up the avenue alone to the door of his house. The night had come again; there was a light within, but never a sound; and Keawe crept about the corner, opened the back door softly, and looked in.

There was Kokua on the floor, the lamp at her side; before her was a milk-white bottle, with a round belly and a long neck; and as she viewed it, Kokua wrung her hands.

A long time Keawe stood and looked in the doorway. At first he was struck stupid; and then fear fell upon him that the bargain had been made amiss, and the bottle had come back to him as it came in San Francisco; and at that his knees were loosened, and the fumes of the wine departed from his head like mists off a river in the morning. And then he had another thought; and it was a strange one, that made his cheeks to burn.

"I must make sure of this," thought he.

So he closed the door, and went softly round the corner again, and then came noisily in, as though he were but now returned. And, lo! by the time he opened the front door no bottle was to be seen; and Kokua sat in a chair and started up like one awakened out of sleep.

"I have been drinking all day and making merry," said Keawe. "I have been with good companions, and now I only come back for money, and return to drink and carouse with them again."

Both his face and voice were as stern as judgment, but Kokua was too troubled to observe.

"You do well to use your own, my husband," said she, and her words trembled.

"Oh, I do well in all things," said Keawe, and he went straight to the chest and took out money. But he looked besides in the corner where they kept the bottle, and there was no bottle there.

At that the chest heaved upon the floor like a sea billow, and the house spun about him like a wreath of smoke, for he saw she was lost now, and there was no escape. "It is what I feared," he thought. "It is she who has bought it."

And then he came to himself a little and rose up; but the sweat streamed on his face as thick as the rain and as cold as the well water.

"Kokua," said he, "I said to you today what ill became me. Now I return to carouse with my jolly companions," and at that he laughed a little quietly. "I will take more pleasure in the cup if you forgive me."

She clasped his knees in a moment; she kissed his knees with flowing tears. "Oh," she cried, "I asked but a kind word!"

"Let us never one think hardly of the other," said Keawe, and was gone out of the house.

Now, the money that Keawe had taken was only some of that store of centime pieces they had laid in at their arrival. It was very sure he had no mind to be drinking. His wife had given her soul for him, now he must give his for hers; no other thought was in the world with him.

At the corner, by the old calaboose, there was the boatswain waiting.

"My wife has the bottle," said Keawe, "and, unless you help me to recover it, there can be no more money and no more liquor to-night."

"You do not mean to say you are serious about that bottle?" cried the boatswain.

"There is the lamp," said Keawe. "Do I look as if I was jesting?"

"That is so," said the boatswain. "You look as serious as a ghost."

"Well, then," said Keawe, "here are two centimes; you must go to my wife in the house, and offer her these for the bottle, which (if I am not much mistaken) she will give you instantly. Bring it to me here, and I will buy it back from you for one; for that is the law with this bottle, that it still must be sold for a less sum. But whatever you do, never breathe a word to her that you have come from me."

"Mate, I wonder are you making a fool of me?" asked the boatswain.

"It will do you no harm if I am," returned Keawe.

"That is so, mate," said the boatswain.

"And if you doubt me," added Keawe, "you can try. As soon as you are clear of the house, wish to have your pocket full of money, or a bottle of the best rum, or what you please, and you will see the virtue of the thing."

"Very well, Keawe," says the boatswain. "I will try; but if you are having your fun out of me, I will take my fun out of you with a belaying pin."

So the whaler man went off up the avenue; and Keawe stood and waited. It was near the same spot where Kokua had waited the night before; but Keawe was more resolved, and never faltered in his purpose; only his soul was bitter with despair.

It seemed a long time he had to wait before he heard a voice singing in the darkness of the avenue. He knew the voice to be the boatswain's; but it was strange how drunken it appeared upon a sudden.

Next the man himself came stumbling into the light of the lamp. He had the devil's bottle buttoned in his coat; another bottle was in his hand; and even as he came in view he raised it to his mouth and drank.

"You have it," said Keawe. "I see that."

"Hands off!" cried the boatswain, jumping back. "Take a step near me, and I'll smash your mouth. You thought you could make a cat's paw of me, did you?"

"What do you mean?" cried Keawe.

"Mean?" cried the boatswain. "This is a pretty good bottle, this is; that's what I mean. How I got it for two centimes I can't make out; but I am sure you sha'n't have it for one."

"You mean you won't sell?" gasped Keawe.

"No sir," cried the boatswain. "But I'll give you a drink of the rum, if you like."

"I tell you," said Keawe, "the man who has that bottle goes to hell."

"I reckon I'm going anyway," returned the sailor; "and this bottle's the best thing to go with I've struck yet. No, sir!" he cried again, "this is my bottle now, and you can go and fish for another."

"Can this be true?" Keawe cried. "For your own sake, I beseech you, sell it me!"

"I don't value any of your talk," replied the boatswain. "You thought I was a flat, now you see I'm not; and there's an end. If you won't have a swallow of the rum, I'll have one myself. Here's your health, and good night to you!"

So off he went down the avenue toward town, and there goes the bottle out of the story.

But Keawe ran to Kokua light as the wind; and great was their joy that night; and great, since then, has been the peace of all their days in the Bright House.

Extra Cheese, and I Have Your Coupon

by Dan Crawford

Business was in a lull at eight on that summer Saturday at Pizza Steve's. Not that sales at Pizza Steve's were ever something to make the Fortune 500 tremble. The joint was a closet office, a kitchen, and a garage. The garage was the cleanest part.

Pizza Steve's loyal fleet of drivers sat behind their trio of fifth-hand vans, fortifying themselves for the work ahead, if any. "What *is* this?" demanded Avery, around a mouthful of whatever had prompted the question.

"It's Steve's new brainstorm, Tropical Storm Pizza," said Jim. "Anchovy and pineapple, I think."

"Tropical Storm?" said Mary Pat. "Not really?"

"Believe it," said Avery. "Tastes like a week of bad weather."

Jim opened his mouth to speak or eat, but before he could do either, an obnoxious buzzer rattled the garage. "I'm up, right?" he said.

"You were here when I got here," said Avery.

Jim nodded and, taking his plate of rapidly cooling Tropical Storm, strolled toward the kitchen. About a yard from the door, he stopped at a large crack in the garage wall and dumped the plate down inside.

"Don't let Steve see you doing that again," Mary Pat called. "He says it attracts bugs."

"I'm ready for him." Jim reached into his Pizza Steve wind-breaker and brought out a box labeled "Lyle's No-Buggy."

"You'll need more than that for these roaches," said Avery.

"It's not for the roaches," Jim told them. "It's to carry around in my pocket and show Steve." He tucked the sealed box back into his pocket, and moved on into the kitchen.

"Whatcha got?" he asked Valencia, behind the counter.

"Two deliveries out on Leckey Avenue North," she told him, pushing two of the off-orange Pizza Steve boxes across to him.

Jim grimaced. Leckey Avenue was a crackerbox/basketball hoop development, all families and small tips unless you happened to get a man whose wife was out of town for the weekend. But he shrugged and hauled the little boxes out to his truck.

He tried the radio, just on the off chance that it was alive today. It had worked on three trips of the last forty, but there was always hope he'd bring in some station loud enough to drown out the rattling of the loose doors. So far, these doors had never fallen off while he was in motion, but there was no reason to think they wouldn't.

The clunker was so noisy that he had been on the road for nearly five minutes before he realized there was someone else there. He caught the motion behind him to the left and almost turned to look.

But he had his instructions. Steve couldn't afford insurance, so he told all his drivers how to behave in these situations. Jim kept his eyes squarely on the road as he said, "I've only got twenty in change. It's all yours, and take as much pizza as you want."

"That's not what I want."

Something in the voice made him look, despite instructions. Something in the eyes made him say, "Wh-who are you?"

The little man blinked once. "Some call me Death."

Jim believed it; you could tell by the eyes. Certainly there was nothing in the face or that weeny little mustache. And that necktie had to be a clip-on.

But the eyes were more than human. "Death," said Jim. It took him a few seconds to think of any reason such a being would be in his pizza truck.

Jim had the same reaction anyone would on seeing the Great Eventually become the Big Fat Right Now. "Why me? Why today?"

"That's not my department." A clipboard appeared in the little man's hands, and he raised the top sheet. "But you're on the schedule, so you have to go."

"When?" asked Jim. "How?"

The man nodded and flipped through the sheets on the board. "Says here you will be hit head-on by a large truck as you drive down Cullen Boulevard or Towner Street."

"You mean I get hit by a truck either way?" Jim demanded.

"Probably."

The exit for Cullen Boulevard, the shorter route to Leckey, was coming up, so this was a matter of some urgency. "What 'probably'? You mean there's a way out? I can live?"

"That's not the way I'd bet," said the supernatural being. "There's always an out, but it's a billion-to-one shot. And if you figure it out, six otherwise unscheduled people will have to die instead of you. Naturally, that's a lot of extra work, so it's better if you just meet your destiny and that truck."

Jim let the exit for Cullen go right by. "Come on. Can't you even give me a hint?"

"I could get called on the carpet for just coming to see you this early," the man told him. "But since the odds are so much against your surviving, I figured there was no harm."

"But . . ." He could always turn around and just go back. His life was worth more than his job, surely. Maybe a quick U-turn was his one chance. U-turn?

"If I don't hit the truck, I'll live?" Jim demanded.

"Well, not forever," said his passenger. "Seventy-five years, tops."

"Is that all?" Jim demanded.

"All right, make it ninety," the man replied, slapping the papers back down on his clipboard. "You won't get it."

The antiquated delivery truck had reached the exit to Towner. Jim studied the traffic carefully; he wasn't sure whether the ramp counted. He started up and, since there was no one coming down the ramp at him, he wrenched the steering wheel around, praying that the doors wouldn't pick this minute to pull free.

"Oh, I say!" protested his passenger as the truck sped down Towner backwards.

"Let's see someone hit me head-on now," Jim retorted. "How about those ninety years?"

The man was scowling at his clipboard. "Now I have to take six other people instead."

"Not my worry," said Jim.

"I'd have expected you to take that attitude," snapped the man. "Good day, sir!" And he simply faded away.

Jim did not let his guard down for all that. He drove backward all the way out to Leckey, and he was careful to drive backward all the way back down Cullen on the return trip. The highway patrol was fortunately patrolling elsewhere, for all Jim's concentration was required to get the rattletrap along the roads in reverse without complete collapse. He unbuttoned his shirt and tossed the windbreaker in the back.

"If we survive this," he promised the truck, "I swear I'll take you out tomorrow and *wash* you."

They did survive, but when Jim went to work the next day, his truck was not to be seen.

"Hey, where's the clunker?" he asked Avery.

Avery started for the kitchen without a word. "What's with him?" Jim asked Mary Pat.

She didn't answer that. "Steve wants to see you in back," she said.

He shrugged. "So I'll turn around." Mary Pat didn't laugh.

So Jim made his way to the little office, stepping carefully so as not to slide in the grease. Through the open back door, he spotted the patrol car. Somebody must have spied him on Cullen and gotten his license number.

"They said you wanted to see me," he told Steve, trying to ignore the two large policemen and the man in the suit. Surely driving backward down the highway didn't rate a man in a suit. Anyway, Avery and Mary Pat could testify he hadn't been drinking.

"Mr. Cloke?" said the man in the suit.

Jim sighed. "Yes, sir?"

"Mr. Cloke," the man said, reaching for something on the floor, "four people died last night, and two more are in critical condition.

They show similar symptoms, but the only thing these six people have in common besides that is that they'd all had pizza from Pizza Steve's last night, all delivered by the same truck. The truck in which we found this."

He raised a plastic bag in which had been sealed a box labeled "Lyle's No-Buggy." From where he stood, Jim could see that the top of the box was missing.

He had two thoughts simultaneously. One was that the man in the truck might have been Death and might have been some other supernatural. The other was that his deal for ninety years might not turn out to be the best bargain he'd ever made.

It Ain't Necessarily So

by Terry Black

Fruitcake.

It wasn't a word Prudence often used to describe her husband—but like a pair of extra large bluejeans, it seemed to fit a little more each day.

That was why she wanted him to see Miss Krantz, not a psychiatrist but a *psychologist;* all she did was make you talk about your troubles until they didn't seem quite so bad. No muss, no fuss, no mood-shifting compounds—just a warm, relaxed conversation, what was the harm in *that?*

Even so, it took the seven labors of Hercules to get Randall to make the appointment. And now here he was *breaking* it, he was blitzed with work, he had three feature stories due by four P.M., perhaps another time for Miss What's-Her-Name—

Prudence sensed a window closing, a chance disappearing. So she did what any half-hysterical spouse with a hubby going rapidly bonkers would do in her place:

She bundled Miss Krantz into a taxi, and took *her* to see *him.*

The *Daily Snoop* had its editorial offices in an ancient Gothic high-rise on West 63rd, shoehorned between a parking structure and a place that sold foul-smelling submarine sandwiches.

Prudence hated the place, both in form and function. She disliked the brooding grayness of its half-century-old façade, weatherworn and studded with gargoyles; but she *really* hated the muckmonger-ing newsrag they published there, a tabloid of such infamy it made the *National Enquirer* look like Pulitzer bait.

Unfortunately, her husband's reporting skills couldn't have found a better home.

ELVIS HAUNTS MY WALK-IN WARDROBE, screamed a lami-nated headline on display in the lobby. GAY-BASHING PSYCHIC CASTRATES GHOST OF LIBERACE.

"Your husband . . . *works* here?" asked Miss Krantz, gaping at the decor. She was short and prim, in a colorless wool dress; she fit into this garish lobby like a brussels sprout in a Winchell's Donut Shop.

Instead of answering, Prudence borrowed the house phone from a yawning receptionist and stabbed four buttons.

"Randall Morton," said her husband.

"It's me, with a little surprise," Prudence explained, hoping her impertinence wouldn't land them in divorce court. "Since you couldn't get away to see Miss Krantz, well—I decided to bring her here."

"She's *here?* In this building?"

"It'll only take a minute," said Prudence. "And I *know* it'll make you feel better."

She pictured him counting to ten. On six he blurted, "Honey, I can't! I've got to do twelve column inches on Hitler's brain, then a piece on the three-headed baby and that new cholesterol diet—"

"Fifteen minutes. Time it. You'll be fresher after a break anyway."

Randall sighed. "All right, come on up. But don't dawdle—take the express elevator."

Prudence dropped the phone, grabbed Miss Krantz, and led her into the ancient and unreliable high-speed elevator. They had to share it with two cub reporters and a buck-toothed gofer, toting a trayful of hoagies. The sandwiches smelled like a maggots' nursery.

"Thirteen, please," said Prudence.

Miss Krantz winced. "I thought they didn't have thirteenth floors in buildings."

"They do in this place, lady," the gofer snorted.

After a moment, the elevator grumbled upwards, like an old man roused from sleep. Maybe it's my imagination, Prudence thought—probably it is—but I'd swear this thing is *swaying* from side to side . . .

Nonsense, she decided. I'm always overreacting, just like Randall says. He won't respect me until I learn to get a grip on things.

She glanced around, expecting to find her sudden terror unmirrored in the faces of her companions. But for the first time, Prudence's phobia was universal; *everyone* seemed panicked, especially when the elevator bucked like a bronco and lurched leftward, with a sickening *ssscrape*—

And the lights went out, with a CRASH-BANG-SNAP! straight from her worst waking nightmare—

And incredibly, impossibly, no one would ever believe it but it was happening here and now, to *me*, thought Prudence, the elevator snapped its couplings and started to falllll

(this can't be right, said a tiny voice that was not her own, I can't die, I'm the person watching all this, I'm the one it all happens to, I can't die)

. . . but they *were* falling, and when they finally hit bottom they hit HARD; she hoped to perish quickly but wasn't granted that privilege—

Randall Morton sat bolt upright, clawing at his temples.

It's happening again, he realized, the visions are back, worse than ever before. Jesus, they made you want to curl up and die . . .

His phone was ringing. Slowly it dawned on him that he should answer it. I have to, he thought; I have to pretend I'm normal.

"Randall Morton," he told the phone.

"It's me," said his wife, "with a little surprise. Since you couldn't get away to see Miss Krantz, well—I thought I'd bring her here."

"She's . . . here?"

"It'll only take a minute. And I'm sure it'll make you feel better."

Normally Randall would have read her the riot act: all the work he had to do, the looming deadlines, the sheer futility of seeing a shrink—

He couldn't. The vision was still too fresh, the images too horrible.

"Okay," he said. "Come on up." He started to hang up, thought better of it, and added, "Don't dawdle—take the express elevator."

Prudence dropped the phone, grabbed Miss Krantz, and led her into the high-speed elevator. They had to share it with two cub reporters and a buck-toothed golfer, with a trayful of hoagies.

"Thirteen, please," said Prudence.

Miss Krantz winced. "I thought they didn't have thirteenth floors in buildings."

"They do in this place, lady," the gofer snorted.

After a moment, the elevator grumbled upwards. Maybe it's my imagination, Prudence thought—probably it is—but I'd swear this thing is *swaying* from side to side . . .

Nonsense, she decided. I'm always overreacting to things, just like Randall says.

She glanced around, expecting to find her sudden terror unmirrored in the faces of her companions. And she was right, of course; the others all had that bored, elevator stare, unmoved by the mild jolting, veterans of this bumpy ride. One of the cub reporters pulled out a pack of Juicy Fruit gum.

"Thirteenth floor," said the gofer, as the doors slid open.

Prudence composed herself and led Miss Krantz through a crowded bullpen, past a rabbit warren of chattering typewriters (just like in the movies, she thought), past chainsmoking reporters and perpetually ringing telephones, to a cubicle even more cramped and squalid than its neighbors.

"Hi, honey," said Randall Morton. "Come in, sit down."

Morton's invitation was easier said than done, but Randall unearthed a chair from under a trashheap of red-lined pages and Prudence sat on his desk top.

"This is Miss Krantz," Prudence began. "She's an expert on all forms of . . . uh, unusual behavior."

Randall winced at the awkward euphemism. "No offense, Miss Krantz—but I doubt if you've ever seen anything quite like *me* before."

"Nonsense, Mr. Morton." Miss Krantz folded her perfect hands. "One benefit of therapy is to show the patient that his problems are not terribly different from—"

"Oh, I'm different," Randall broke in. "You want a f'rinstance? Just a moment ago I had a vision that you and my wife were killed in the elevator, coming up here. Killed horribly."

Miss Krantz hesitated. "Well . . . since that didn't happen, I guess you're not much good at foretelling the future."

"Quite the contrary," Randall shot back. His eyes twinkled with a manic gleam. "You see, I'm not like most psychics. My polarity's wrong, or something. I only see what's *not* going to happen."

"Come now, Mr. Morton—"

"I mean it! Nothing I've seen has *ever* come true."

"Well, what's so strange about that? Lots of people imagine things that don't take place."

Morton shook his head. "But they're right *some* of the time. With me it's different. If I predict something, you can bet your life savings *against* it. Why do you think I wanted you on that elevator? When I saw you getting pulverized, I figured it was the safest place on earth."

Miss Krantz drew a sharp breath.

"But if I have a vision that everything's fine, *then* I worry. Like last year, I had this flash about not getting my taxes audited—"

"Stop and think a moment, Mr. Morton," Miss Krantz interrupted. She leaned forward, framing her words carefully. "How many things *don't* happen every day? Cars don't explode, murders aren't committed, planes don't fall out of the sky—"

"Gorillas don't give tuba lessons. Housewives don't see the face of Jesus in their mashed potatoes. Aliens don't dine at the White House." Randall slapped the front page of the *Daily Snoop's* latest edition. "Don't you see? They're headlines, every one of 'em!"

He ran his finger down the page.

"Famed psychic's head explodes. Bigfoot monsters living on welfare. Woman gets abortion, is haunted by fetus."

"What are you saying?" asked Miss Krantz.

"I'm saying the public doesn't *want* real stories. They're too boring. They'd rather find out what *didn't* happen—and somehow, I've developed this thing in my subconscious that shows exactly that."

"So you're sort of . . . an antipsychic?"

"Yeah. And it makes me crazy. I don't *want* to know what's not going to happen. It's none of my business."

There was an awkward silence, as the psychologist considered her next words. She was still pondering when a bearded face poked around the doorjamb.

"Hey, Morton," said the newcomer, obviously a fellow journalist, "how do you spell 'alcoholic'?"

Randall groaned. "For God's sake, Bruce, look it up."

"I haven't got a dictionary."

"Take mine."

Randall pitched him a hardbound *Webster's*, but Bruce didn't leave. He just stood there in the hallway, thumbing pages, mouthing words. Occasionally his eyes would roll up into his head, as he considered some new lexicological insight.

"Uh . . . Bruce," Randall said at last, "do you mind? This is kind of personal."

Bruce turned another page. "Hang on, I only need one more word. 'Venereal,' as in venereal disease."

"You're writing a celebrity profile," Randall realized.

"That's right." Bruce copied something out of the dictionary. "Who do you think the celebrity should be?"

The phone rang. Randall got it and heard his boss bellowing, "Morton! Get down here yesterday, and drag Bonzo with you."

"Yes, Mr. Cheswick." Randall turned to his wife and Miss Krantz and said, "Sorry, gang, we're wanted in surgery. See you another time."

Prudence tried to stop him, but he was already sailing past her, towing Bruce by the shirtsleeve. She sighed helplessly.

"I guess we'll have to do this another time," she told Miss Krantz.

"That's all right," said the therapist, rising to leave. "But this time, let's take the stairs."

Chester Cheswick sat in his chair, overflowing it, drumming his blunt fingers on a tearsheet from last week's paper. He didn't look happy.

"Good afternoon, gentlemen," he told Bruce and Randall, fixing

them with a steel-gray stare. Randall was reminded of George S.
Patton, dressing down his troops.

"I'll get right to the point," Cheswick continued, turning his gaze
on Randall. "Morton, that piece on elephant zombies is the most
preposterous piece of poppycock to cross my desk in twenty-five
years."

"Sorry, sir . . ."

"Keep up the good work." He turned to Bruce. "Billings, you're
fired."

Bruce Billings' jaw fell open. He looked like a ventriloquist's
dummy left unattended. "But . . . but why?"

"Because your stories are insulting and slanderous, full of brutal
slurs based on flimsy, undocumented evidence."

"I thought you *liked* that!"

"Not any more. I changed my mind when this paper was served
with a ten million dollar libel suit from Burt Murphy, darling
of the Superbowl and veteran of half a hundred Lite Beer commercials."

Billings swallowed hard. "I only said he *might* be gay, I didn't say
he *was*."

"You, on the other hand, are definitely fired." Cheswick pressed a
button and mumbled something; a big guard came in, cradling a
truncheon. "Goodbye, Mr. Billings. Best of luck in another market."

"You bastard," Bruce blurted, taking a half step forward. "You'll
pay for this, you wait—"

Cheswick waited for Bruce to depart, at the guard's none-too-
gentle insistence. Then he folded his hands and turned toward
Randall, in a philosophical mood.

"Did you know today's my birthday, Morton? This afternoon I'll
be sixty." He shook his head, as if counting the years. "You'd think
I'd have learned to keep the deadbeats off the payroll."

Randall shrugged. "Can I go now, sir?"

"Poor Bruce," said Prudence, without surprise, when he told her
the news that evening. "I guess his time was up."

Randall sat back in his reclining chair. "I figured it was coming. Last week I had a dream that Cheswick made him vice-president."

"You and your dreams again." Gently Prudence massaged his neck. "Are you going to call Miss Krantz?"

"I don't know," said Randall. He reached for his paper—a *real* paper, the *Times*, with honest-to-God news—and started flipping pages. "I'm still not—hey, what's *this?*"

He pointed to an article on an inside page. It read:

NEWSPAPER TYCOON NOT KILLED WHEN BOMB FAILS TO EXPLODE
by Dennis Boyd, *Times Staff Writer*

Publishing giant Chester Cheswick was not declared dead on arrival today at County General Hospital, after a bomb failed to explode in his face at precisely 4:00 P.M.

Non-grieving relatives expressed no regrets, and made no plans for a funeral this coming Saturday.

"Well, that's peculiar," said Prudence, frowning. "Why make such a fuss over something that *didn't* happen?"

"They wouldn't," Randall realized, his eyebrows rising. "Unless . . . unless . . . *oh my God—*"

Randall Morton sat bolt upright, clawing at his temples.

It had happened again, he knew instantly. It was all another dream—but a frighteningly *specific* one. If his vision was right (or, rather, if it was wrong) then his boss would be blown to bits at precisely four P.M.

He checked his watch. Three forty-nine, and counting.

For a moment he sat paralyzed. Should he evacuate the building? Run like hell and save himself? How could he explain that everyone was in danger because he'd seen the future, and it looked *fine?*

Call him. Call Cheswick.

Randall fumbled with the phone, managed to hunt-and-peck the right extension, and listened for eight agonizing rings before he concluded that the boss and his secretary were elsewhere.

But where?

He bolted out of his seat, his deadlines forgotten, and sprinted down the hall. He turned a corner and broadsided a secretary, sending a stack of papers and two cups of cream-and-sugar coffee flying.

"Where's Cheswick?" he blurted. "I've got to see him—"

"The only thing *you're* going to see is a severance check," snapped the secretary, dabbing futilely at the stains on her blouse, "if you ever—"

But Randall was already past her, zigzagging down the corridor toward the glass-fronted office labeled CHESTER CHESWICK, PUBLISHER.

He burst in, saw no one (what did you *expect?* he thought) and found nothing, not a clue, not a memo, not a hastily scribbled hint as to where the newspaper magnate might be facing his doom.

"Where's Cheswick?" he cried, buttonholing a copyboy. But all he got was a puzzled frown.

He checked his watch. Three fifty-one—no, three fifty-*two*, it changed as he looked at it.

Where *was* the old idiot?

Suddenly Randall had an inspiration. He backtracked, found the door marked MEN'S ROOM and flung himself inside. But Cheswick was nowhere to be seen; the only occupant was Bruce Billings, wiping his hands on a paper towel.

"What's the problem?" asked Bruce, seeing Morton's crazed expression.

Randall could contain himself no longer. "A bomb is gonna blow up and kill Mr. Cheswick in less than eight minutes! *That's* my problem!"

He expected disbelief. But instead of skepticism, Bruce got angry.

"Dammit," he snapped, "how did *you* find out?"

Randall started to explain, then did a double-take. "Wait a minute," he demanded. "How come you believe me, when nobody else does?"

Bruce didn't answer. Instead he sprang for the door. Randall made a grab but got only a handful of shirt, it tore away ɑ̵ ̶d Billings was free—

—just as the door swung inward right into Billings' face, *thwack-*ing him between the eyes. Bruce went down like a condemned building, out cold.

"Excuse me," said a junior somebody, poking round the door.

Randall grabbed Bruce by his shirt front, trying to hoist him back up into consciousness. Bruce had planted the bomb; he wanted revenge for getting bounced, and he was going to get it in about ninety seconds—

"*Where's the bomb?*" Randall asked hopelessly.

But Bruce was past caring. Morton let go and the would-be killer's head hit the floor.

That's when Randall heard it.

It was soft, muffled, barely audible; he might never have noticed if his senses hadn't been sharpened to pin-drop sensitivity by the force of desperation. But he *did* hear it: the unmistakable strains of *Happy Birthday,* coming from the lunchroom.

He almost made it.

Randall raced through the *Daily Snoop* building with impossible speed; he stole only one glance at his wristwatch, long enough to realize he was down to seconds now: 3:59:42, 3:59:43—

(What if the bomb isn't synchronized to your watch, what if it's off just a little, maybe a little bit early?)

He burst into the lunchroom on the line, "Happy *Birth-*day, dear Chester . . ." to find Chester Cheswick surrounded by his best-loved employees, posed beside a magnificent layer cake, with a buttercream likeness of Cheswick's craggy features—

The bomb was in the cake. Randall *knew* it somehow. He could have proved it, if only he'd had time to reach through the gobby frosting and pull it out in time to disarm it.

But he didn't.

The bomb went off when he was halfway there. Cheswick died instantly, Randall a moment later, and everyone else in the crowded lunchroom either right away or soon thereafter, of multiple burns, contusions, and trauma.

The *Daily Snoop* did not go out of business, however; in the aftermath of Cheswick's demise it was swallowed up by Rupert Murdoch, who saw its circulation and sales climb forty percent over the next three years.

Prudence got a check from the insurance company, a big check, but it was some time before she could bring herself to cash it—

Randall Morton gasped, clawing at his temples.

It had happened again, yet again, there was no end to these damned visions. But now that it was over, where was he, and *when* was he . . . ?

"Morton!" growled Cheswick, in his most ferocious baritone. "What are you doing here?"

Randall opened his eyes.

He was standing in the lunchroom. Chester Cheswick was surrounded by his best-loved employees, posed beside a magnificent layer cake, with a buttercream likeness of Cheswick's craggy features.

Randall's watch read four o'clock exactly.

He pounced. He plunged both hands into the gobby frosting, obliterating Chester's profile, snowplowing the sugary mess between his fingers until he found it, clutched it, yanked it free: four sticks of dynamite and a detonator, wired to an egg timer.

He pulled the wires free. The timer went *bzzzzzzt!* but nothing else happened.

For a moment, no one said anything.

Then Cheswick goggled and cried, "My God, that's a *bomb!* Someone tried to blow me up!"

"Bruce Billings," said Randall, feeling suddenly very tired. "You'll find him in the men's room. Take some aspirin and an ice bucket."

Randall didn't expect his wife to believe it all, but she did—after it showed up on the evening news. Over dinner he tried to fill in the details.

"Don't you see?" he asked, through a forkful of meatloaf. "When I finally dreamed I *couldn't* stop the bomb, that meant I *could*. And not a moment too soon."

Prudence toyed with her stringbeans. "Was Cheswick grateful?"

"Are you kidding? He's a new man! He didn't even make me pay for his birthday cake."

Prudence pushed her plate away, with an air of resignation. "So what's next?" she asked, not wanting to hear his answer. "Are you going to join the circus? Use your powers for the good of mankind?"

Randall smiled—a good smile, warm and confident. "I don't *have* any powers. Not any more."

Prudence frowned.

"I'm cured," he insisted. "It's gone. Whatever gave me those crazy dreams is out of my head, forever. Don't ask me how I know. I just . . . *feel* it, somehow." He took a final bite of meatloaf. "From now on, my life's going to be perfectly, wonderfully *boring*."

And in spite of herself, without quite knowing if she believed him or not, Prudence took his hand. She smiled—

Randall Morton sat bolt upright, clawing at his temples.

Prudence was watching him curiously; on the plate before him was a half-eaten serving of meatloaf.

He thought, *here we go again—*

The Undertaker's Wedding

by Chet Williamson

It's a shame you children never knew your grandpa. Oh, he was such a gentle man. Problem was, people confused his gentleness with sneakiness, I couldn't tell you why. Maybe not sneakiness exactly, but more like cowing, is that the word? Like a cowed animal always looking for somebody to hit it. He was shy, that was all, and gentle. And because of that people thought he was less than he was. Why, in other towns you'd have your undertakers being well thought of, town council members, maybe even mayors like over in Willow Creek, even if it *was* just for two years. But not here in town, not for Grandpa.

I suspect some folks thought he never should've been an undertaker, quiet and shy as he was. Nowadays so many undertakers are big, hearty, happy men with red faces and big hands that grab you when you shake 'em, like what they're doing had nothing to do with death. Oh, at the funerals they look serious and make their mouths go straight, but on the street you'd think they were salesmen from how most of them act.

Grandpa, he wasn't like that. He was gentle, he said to me once that his were the last hands to touch them on the earth, and he wanted their last memories of this place to be good because if they went to Heaven they might tell the Lord of the kindnesses they'd had here and he might not be so hard on us. If they went to the other place, well, then those poor souls'd value Grandpa's last kindnesses all the more. In fact, he said it was the bad 'uns needed his gentleness most of all, since they'd most of them had so little shown to them when they were alive.

But nobody knew he thought like that, not even me. Oh, I giggled with the other girls, and as hard as any of 'em when he'd walk by on the street, or when he sat near some of us in church. Only in church, of course, we couldn't giggle, could only make little faces at each other. It *was* funny at first, and a little scary. Sometimes we'd giggle loud just so's he could hear us, and he'd stick his head down between his shoulders and scurry away. And maybe one of the girls would say, "You better not let him hear you laugh, or he'll come to your house some night and *drag you away!*" And surely that'd make us giggle all the more, at the thought of the quiet, creepy old undertaker trying to do that, when we knew he'd jump if you said boo to him. It wasn't *him* that made it scary, but what he did when we'd think about it, burying people, getting them all ready and having to undress them and wash them and dress them and put them in their coffins. It didn't seem nice, it just seemed scary. And that's why, even when we were laughing, we still felt a little funny, leastways I did.

I don't like to say that I was special or any nicer, but after a while it wasn't much fun for me to laugh at him at all. It didn't seem right somehow, or maybe I just grew up a little faster than the others. But one May day we were all coming out of the soda parlor on Market Street—it's long gone now—and he was walking by. Well, some of the others started to giggle, and he turned red right off. And I just thought, he looks so nice, and he did, with a pressed white shirt and dark trousers and a pretty blue bow tie, his hair just so, like he'd come from the barber shop, and I could smell some nice aftershave lotion that smelled so cool in that hot sun. So I shushed the others real sharp, and they shut up fast. But the shush I made was so loud it startled him, and he stopped dead in his tracks and just looked at me like I'd been shushing him. He looked in that second just like a little boy looking up at his ma, ready to do whatever she asked. But of course I *hadn't* been shushing him, so I just smiled and nodded, not knowing what else to do. Then he smiled, such a tiny little smile like he thought a bigger one would break his face, and he gave a little nod back at me, and kept walking.

Well, the other girls had a heyday with that. They giggled at first, then when he was gone they laughed fit to bust, and started singing, "Emmy's got a boyfriend, Emmy's got a boyfriend," and dancing in a circle around me. Then they laughed some more, and one of them said, "You be careful, Emmy, I hear he got real *cold* hands." I just got mad then and walked away, deciding I wasn't going to make no more fun of him. Why, he'd *smiled* at me, and smiled real nice, too.

The next time I saw the girls, they acted funny, like I might be mad at them. I was a little, I guess, but they said no more about the day before and neither did I, so we were friends again, and I sort of forgot about the whole thing.

That's why it was a big surprise, a few days later, when my daddy told me the undertaker'd come to see him in the store where he clerked, and asked for permission to come calling on me. Surprise, did I say? Why, I fairly flew into a frazzle when I heard, and when my daddy told me he'd said it was all right, I near cried. "Now, Emmy," my daddy said, patting my shoulder, "don't take on so. He's just coming to call, nothing more. If you don't like him, you don't have to see him again, I promise." I guess I must have looked pretty scared, because he went on. "He's a good man, Emmy. A quiet man, but a good'un."

I just nodded. He was coming Friday night, and I didn't say nothing to my chums about it, didn't want them to find out if I could help it. That day I was so nervous I couldn't eat a bite for supper, just sat at the table and watched my mother and daddy eat. Mother looked near as scared as me, though she was getting some food down. Only my daddy seemed like normal, and he'd look at me and give me a smile that told me not to worry, but I did, and I don't really know about what.

Along about seven o'clock he came up the walk, carrying a bunch of flowers. They were awfully pretty, and I got a little choked up, since this was the first time I'd ever had a caller and flowers, not being one of the prettiest girls in town. But then the idea hit me so queer, of an undertaker bringing flowers, and I knew it was stupid, but all I could think of was where he'd *got* them from. I still feel bad today when I think of how that nasty thought got into my head, like a harsh word you can never take back. He must have seen what was in my mind when he handed them to me because his face looked like I'd just cut him with a knife, and he was trying hard not to let the pain show. But I made myself smile, and took the flowers, and gave them to Mother, who looked a little queasy as she took them, but I don't think he noticed.

Thank the Lord my daddy had taken the evening off from clerking at the dry goods, for he did most of the talking, asking Grandpa whether he thought that rain was going to come, and what he thought of the Athletics' chances, and whether they'd ever get a dam built up at French Creek. And Grandpa answered him soft and polite. It was the first time I'd ever heard him speak, and I was surprised at what a deep low voice he had, when I'd expected a high little peep. Not that he was small—he was a medium-sized man, I suppose—but he was just so shy and scary that you'd have thought he'd have the same kind of voice. Oh, it was shy, but low and real full, like I thought Lawrence Tibbett would sound if I'd ever heard him talk instead of sing.

After a while of talking, Daddy looked at me and smiled and then looked at my mother and said as how it was time to leave the young folks alone for a spell to get acquainted. Well, that froze me a little, though not as cold as it would've before we'd all chatted for a while. So Mother and Daddy left us alone in our little front parlor and went back into the kitchen, where I could hear Daddy turning the pages of the newspaper and Mother saying things real low every once in a long while.

For the longest time Grandpa and I just sat there, he on the old wing chair, me across the room in a side chair with Mother's needlework on the seat and back. Neither one of us said a word, and finally he cleared his throat and said as how it was a real pleasure to be able to come and call on me, and he was wondering if I enjoyed the moving pictures. I allowed as how I did, and then he asked me if I would be interested in accompanying him—that's the word he used, *accompanying*—to the U.S. Theater the next night to see *The Old Homestead*. He told me it was a very respectable picture, and that Pastor Myers had seen it and said it was very good.

I didn't want to go, not really, but right then and there I was just so flustered that I didn't know how to make up a lie. Boys just didn't ask me out, not even boys I didn't want to go out with, and I had no experience with such things. So I just nodded and said all right, and he got the sweetest, happiest smile on his face that right off I was *glad* I'd said yes. Then he just talked a little more about the movie and took a little handout thing the theater gave away about it and handed it to me to keep, and I allowed that it looked like a good picture and we just sat there again until he remarked how late it was getting, and said he'd best be going. So I called Mother and Daddy out and we all said our goodnights.

After he was gone, I didn't say anything to them and they asked me no questions, just eyed me, my mother worried-looking, Daddy smiling, and I excused myself and went upstairs.

Once I realized what I'd done, I got sort of panicked. I knew that my friends would be at the pictures, some of them anyway, and by next morning it'd be all over town that I'd been out with the undertaker. *Everybody'd* know at the service. And what about the service—would he expect me to sit with him? I had such foolish, awful dreams that night, I can still remember. Dreamt I was at the pictures with Grandpa, but the movie wasn't a real movie—it was Grandpa working, getting the dead ready for burial. And all around me my friends were watching and smiling at me and saying what a fine job he was doing, and though I couldn't bear to watch the screen, I couldn't *not* watch, either. Then Grandpa took my hand in the dark theater, and it was cold, so cold I woke up, to find my own hand grabbing the cool brass bedpost.

Next morning I told my daddy that I'd been asked out and said yes, but I wasn't sure I wanted to go. He said to me, well, you said you would, didn't you? And I allowed as how I had, and he said, well then, you should. Mother took my side, but Daddy said if she said she would, then she should. Next time just say no if you don't want to. You've got a mouth, so start to use it. Then he spoke less sharp and touched a hand to my cheek. He's a kind man, Emmy, he said. He said, he won't hurt you at all, but you be careful so's not to hurt him.

I knew he was right about going, and that night Grandpa came by for me and we went to the pictures. I didn't see anyone I knew when we went in, and I felt ashamed that I was glad of it. The movie was good. It was the first time I ever heard Grandpa laugh, and such a sweet laugh he had, like music. He never touched my hand once, nor put an arm around me.

When the show was over and the lights came on, I saw Mandy Dawson sitting two rows back with her fellow, looking at me like the cat that just ate the bird, and I knew she'd start spreading the news that very night. There was something in her look that right then made me mad, made me think the hell with what *they* think. I know that's no language for a lady, but that's what went through my head, and when Grandpa asked if I'd like a soda, I smiled and said yes, and we went in the soda parlor and sat at a bright table in front where any nosy parker could see us, and talked about the movie and a lot more, and we *both* smiled that night.

Next morning I sat with him in church, and I think it surprised my mother as much as it did my friends. Oh, they gave me the dirt at first, but once they knew that I'd see who I *wanted* to see, they left me be quick enough. Some of them left me be for good, though my best friends stuck by me—Marion and Dorothy and Katie. In fact, they confessed that they'd always thought Grandpa was sort of cute, no matter what he did.

He and I didn't talk about that for the longest time, even though we started going together regular. He lived above the funeral parlor, and of course I never went over there anyway, that just wasn't done. When we'd have plans to do something, and someone would die and he'd have to hold the service and all, he'd just say he was sorry but we couldn't go to so and so because he was needed. That's what he'd say, he was needed. And I'd know, and it would be all right. But we never talked about it directly. Leastways, not till he asked me to marry him.

We'd been going out together for maybe five months when he'd got up the nerve. It was October, and we'd just been on a hayride with the church, and he was walking me home, and he stopped right on the corner of Orange Street and Washington, and he asked me if I'd consider being his wife. It was pretty chilly that October, but that wasn't why I shivered so. And don't go thinking I shivered because it was the *undertaker* asking me to wed him. I shivered because marrying him had been all I'd been thinking about since we went to the soda parlor after that first picture. I loved that man sure enough, but if you'd told me I'd be feeling that way six months earlier, I'd've called you crazy.

But I didn't say yes right away. Maybe I would've if he'd let me go, but straightaway after he asked me he told me to take my time and think about it. I said I would, but I smiled so, and kissed him on the cheek, that he knew fairly well what my answer would be. Once we got to my house we didn't go straight in but sat on the porch swing in that autumn chill and talked real low so's my mother and daddy wouldn't hear.

He told me a lot about himself I'd never heard before, how he'd become an undertaker because his daddy had been one and it was the only thing he'd been taught, how his daddy had died when he was nineteen and he'd taken over the undertaking parlor but folks were hesitant to trust their dead to someone that young so he had a hard few years. He never made many friends because he was too busy working at odd jobs he had to do to be able to live. When the Spanish-American War came along, he enlisted, and when he came back to town, folks were more likely to use his services because, he said, then folks thought he was a man since he'd been to war. And he shook his head, his eyes real sad.

He didn't say anything for a while. Then he said he liked what he did, and made no apology to any man for it. It was something that had to be done, just like doctoring or governing, or being a fireman or policeman, something that helped folks. It was then he told me what I said before, about kindness and gentleness being the last things done to them, and I got a little bit weepy when he said that, thinking what a scary old monster we girls had made him out to be. Last, he told me how old he was. Forty. I was nineteen. But it didn't matter any. I told him I'd marry him, and then I kissed him on the lips for the first time. They were warm and dry and soft, just the way I'd always thought a husband's lips should be.

The next day he asked Daddy for my hand, and Daddy said yes. By that time Mother knew Grandpa well enough to know what a good man I was getting. But even I didn't know how good he really was. I found out that winter.

It was a monstrous cold winter. We had our first big snow in mid-

November, and it must have been two feet deep at least. It never got warm enough to melt it until early March, so snow piled on top of snow, and it just got deeper and deeper. The roads stayed open, though. Seemed every time you looked, the Hastings boys were out plowing them. Don't know how much the town paid them that winter, but the next spring both Dick and Bob started new houses. Grandpa had a hard time, too. The ground was frozen solid, and the Hastings boys, who also dug the graves at the Upper and Lower Dellfield cemeteries, nearly doubled their price because of it. Grandpa once told me he'd probably paid for their chimneys that winter. He wouldn't pass on the extra price to his customers, though. Claimed that a loved one's death was bad luck enough, so the freeze was *his* bad luck.

But it wasn't because of the snows alone that folks remembered that winter. Twenty years later you'd mention that winter and folks'd say wasn't that the year Roy Stoller got killed trying to rob the feed store? It wasn't often that things like that would happen, even in *Lower* Dellfield. First shooting death, my daddy said, since Amos Martin accidentally killed his cousin Wilbur when they were hunting back in '03. I don't think it surprised anyone, though, leastways not anyone who knew about Roy Stoller. Roy was a bad'un, no two ways about it. He just seemed doomed for something like that to happen. His daddy was mostly no-account, and his mother died when he was born. Roy quit his schooling when he was only ten to help his daddy try to pull some harvest out of that scrubby ten acres they called a farm. Now, I expect, that ten acres would fetch a fair price, but back then it was worthless. After old Mr. Stoller died, Roy gave up farming and just lived there in the farmhouse, tending a little vegetable patch and keeping mostly to himself, except when he'd come into town for supplies, or to drink at Rohrer's Tavern. Nobody knew for sure where he got the money he needed, but there'd been some talk of insurance money on his daddy, and some folks said he stole. They were proved right, of course. He spent a few days in jail, on and off, especially after drinking nights, mostly from picking fights in the tavern. Had no friends, none at all. People didn't like him much and seemed to stay away.

A couple of weeks after Christmas he broke into the feed store through a back window. He didn't know Mr. Wenger was working late in his office, and Mr. Wenger surprised him with a pistol. Roy Stoller had a gun, too, and shot first but missed. Then Mr. Wenger shot Roy right in the head. The doc said he was dead before he hit the floor.

There were no relatives and no estate to speak of, so the county was supposed to pay a local undertaker fifty dollars to bury him. The sheriff took him to Frank Weyden first, but Weyden wouldn't do it—said it'd be bad for his business, handling criminals. But Grandpa said he'd take Roy, and next day when he told me he'd done it I didn't like it, but I didn't say anything except something about the fifty dollars being a small price to get for tarnishing his business.

He got real serious then, as near to mad as I'd ever seen him before or since, and told me that no matter what folks'd done, it wasn't ours to judge them once they were dead, but rather to give them as much dignity and kindness as we could, for they'd be judged quick enough by someone far higher. Then he said Roy Stoller'd never had a chance for anything in his life, and how he was more to be pitied than anything else. His words made me feel pretty small, though I was still concerned with what other folks might think. But that didn't bother Grandpa in the least, and he even gave back to the county what was left of the fifty dollars after he'd paid his costs on the coffin and the gravedigging. I won't profit off an unfortunate, he said, and nobody was more unfortunate than Roy Stoller. Grandpa put him next to his daddy, in the Lower Dellfield Cemetery. At the funeral, there was just him and me and the Negro pastor from the Baptist church over in West Davis. The Dellfield ministers were all busy that day, so they said.

We got married in early February, a week after my twentieth birthday. We hadn't had snow for almost two weeks, and the sun was shining bright as anything. The temperature was just below freezing, and after the winter we'd been through, it felt like the South Seas. It was just a small wedding. I only invited my closest friends and their families. Since Grandpa had no real friends to speak of, I made sure Mother had the two ushers seat some of the guests on the groom's side. Grandpa looked handsome, and the mirror told me I was as pretty as I was ever going to be, and it was a nice wedding. Although at the end of the vows, when we said till death us do part, I got that funny feeling again—it just came over me—and I wondered if I died first, if he'd take care of me, make me ready for the grave.

It was a dark thought, and it had no place at a happy thing like a wedding, so right then I drove it out of my head. But I thought about it for a long time afterwards.

We had the reception in the church basement, and my daddy and mother were both happy but teary-eyed. Grandpa was chattering away with the guests and members of the wedding, just like he'd never been shy in his life, and I remember thinking, well Jiminy Christmas, this man should've got married a long time ago. Some of the people there that day became his friends for life.

I'd asked him and asked him where we were to go on our honeymoon, but he wouldn't tell me. A surprise, was all he'd say. But no Niagara Falls, or anything like that. Somewhere that we can *keep*, he whispered, and I just couldn't work out what he meant.

After the reception we went back to my daddy's house to pick up my suitcase, and then we climbed into Grandpa's Model T, and off we went, out of Upper Dellfield, and through Lower Dellfield, then up into the hills north of here, which surprised me. All the cities and towns of any size are all east and south, but we headed north instead. I said as how I hoped we'd get to where we were going before too long, as night was coming on and the sky had turned dark like there was snow coming. Don't worry, he told me, we're almost there now. And sure enough in another mile he turned the car up this dirt road smack dab through the woods. It looked like it had just been plowed that day, for you could see the brown earth in patches through the snow. Looks like the Hastings boys made it, he said, and I asked him just what was going on here, and he said you'll see.

Finally we came to a spot where the lane ended and the trees got too thick for an automobile to pass. We walk from here, he said, and lifted me out of the car. Then he takes two pairs of snowshoes from the back of the Model T, and I just looked at him. He asked me if I'd ever walked on them before, and of course I hadn't, so he showed me how. I was still asking him what it was all about but he wouldn't tell me, just picked up my suitcase and his and asked me to follow him. Whither thou goest, he said, and laughed.

By that time it was nearly dark, and it had started to snow as well, big wet flakes that looked like white leaves falling in the dusk. We followed a little trail through the trees, and I could see other snowshoe tracks, so I asked whose they were. Grandpa said they were his.

It was just light enough so we didn't need a lantern when we got to the cabin. It was in a little open space in the woods, and a small stream solid with ice was next to it. It was the prettiest little building I'd ever seen, made of light brown logs. There was a black shingle roof and a green door and shutters, and mostly covered with snow as it was, it looked like something from a fairy tale. I felt Grandpa's arm around my shoulders, and he asked me if I liked it. There was no doubt of that. I thought there couldn't have been a better place in the world for two people who loved each other to be alone. He told me his father had built it years before, but after he died Grandpa rented it to an old trapper who finally had to give up his line that past year because of his legs and move in with relatives. Grandpa'd been coming up here for months fixing it up as a surprise for me.

I hugged him hard and told him I couldn't wait to see inside, so we tramped the rest of the way through the snow, which was falling thicker now, and went inside and lit a lantern. It was beautiful. He'd put curtains at all the windows and hung some pictures on the walls. At one end was a little table with two chairs, a dry sink, and a woodstove, with cupboards full of dishes and food. There were three chairs and a fireplace in the middle of the room, and at the other end was a chest of drawers and a bed behind a big red curtain he'd rigged up so as to give me my privacy. But right then I didn't want any privacy, not from him anyway. I hugged him and kissed him and said as how it would be a wonderful honeymoon, and he laughed that gentle low laugh and said it would be if we didn't freeze first.

He took the lantern over to the big open fireplace and touched a match to the kindling he'd got ready before. It caught fast and started crackling and popping for fair. It must have been a pine knot or something like it that cracked so loud and threw a hot spark into the lantern, but at the time I could've sworn it was a bomb. The lantern just exploded—I didn't see it, just heard it—and when I turned around and looked, Grandpa was falling over like a big tree, and fire was jumping all over the wooden floor. I didn't bother to scream, but yanked down the curtain and started beating out the fire with it. It didn't take long, and then I looked at Grandpa. He'd been scarcely singed, but a piece of that thick, heavy glass from the lantern's base had hit him right on the temple, cutting him open and making him bleed something fierce. He wasn't conscious, either.

I ripped a hunk out of my slip and tried to stop the blood, but it kept coming, slow and steady, and I knew that I had to get him to a doctor fast. I thought of dragging him out to the car on a blanket, but even if I could do it, the jolting might do him worse than leaving him be.

We had only the one lantern, so by the light of the fire I lit some candles, then pressed down on Grandpa's cut and tried to think. It was dark as pitch now, and the snow was falling so thick and the wind blowing so hard it seemed the cabin's roof might blow clean off. There was no way I could get him out, and I wondered if I could find the way out myself, and bring back help. I thought as how that was the only way I could save him, so I put some logs on the fire to keep him warm, tied a bandage tight around his head, bundled myself up as much as I could, and went outside on the snowshoes.

I hadn't gone twenty yards before I knew it was impossible. Even if the trail had been plain in front of me, I couldn't have seen it. So I turned around and made my way back to the cabin, following the little glow of the fire through the windows. Grandpa was no better, still unconscious, though the bleeding had slowed a little. But his breathing was real funny, and I don't mind telling you children I was scared more than I'd ever been, being purely certain he'd die before I could ever get out and maybe bring back somebody the next day.

All I could do was sit there on the floor, holding his poor bleeding head in my lap, and pray. I prayed that night like Jesus must have prayed in the garden. And I'm not sure if God heard me or not, but I know something did. For sometime in that long night, I heard through the wind a knocking on the cabin door. No footsteps on the boards of the porch, but just a knocking. Three times, real slow-like.

I didn't even think. I just ran to the door and flung it open, and I saw Roy Stoller standing there on the porch.

I knew it was him. I'd seen his face before, and it looked fairly as it must have when he was alive. You'll remember the winter had been cold and the ground was frozen. So what was under the ground stayed frozen, too. I could still see the little mark in his forehead where Grandpa had closed up the bullet hole. And the firelight was bright enough that I recognized the old suit of Grandpa's that he'd dressed him in.

I didn't scream. I think I was too scared to. I just stepped back, and Roy Stoller walked into the cabin, went over to Grandpa, and picked him up as lightly as if he were a child. Then he walked to the cabin door with him, and turned and looked at me, like he was waiting. And something in his dead face told me that it was *good* he wanted to do, not bad. So I bundled up again and put on the snowshoes, and though it took all my courage to do it, I wrapped a blanket around Grandpa as he lay in Roy Stoller's arms. Then Roy Stoller walked out the door into the storm, and I followed him.

He didn't glow or nothing, and he didn't talk at all, but I had no trouble following him, even though I couldn't see him. It was like there was some kind of warmth coming from him, and I just followed it. Before too long we were at the car, and Roy Stoller put Grandpa in the back. I just stood there, not knowing what to do next. I'd never driven a car, only ridden in one since I'd been going with Grandpa. So Roy Stoller got it started right up and got in the driver's side, while I climbed into the back with Grandpa. I wondered how we'd get through the snow—about a foot had fallen, and you couldn't even see the lane we'd come in on—but that didn't worry Roy Stoller none. The automobile just seemed to drift over the snow, and when I looked behind, I couldn't see any tracks we'd made.

We drove for what seemed like ages, passing nary another automobile, though that snow was so thick we wouldn't have seen another car's lights even if anyone had been foolish enough to be out that night. Finally the Model T slowed down and just *floated* to a stop, and I swear I could feel it and us sink slowly and softly into the deep snow on the ground. Roy Stoller didn't do anything, just sat there looking out into the night like he'd done all he could. I looked out to the right and saw a dim light glowing, so I climbed out of the car and walked through the snow toward it. I was just amazed when I saw where I was—right in the middle of town, and that glowing light was a lamp in Doc Farnsworth's window.

I pounded on the door till Doc's wife opened it and called her husband down from upstairs. I took him by the hand and led him out to the automobile, not even wondering what Doc would do when he saw dead Roy Stoller sitting behind the wheel, only worrying about Grandpa and wanting to get him into the warm as quick as could be. But Roy Stoller wasn't in the car anyway, and when Doc was hauling Grandpa up onto his shoulders, I looked out into the dark but couldn't see him anywhere. There was no tracks of his walking away, either, though even if there had been the wind might've blown them away just that quick. But I don't think there were.

You children all know that Grandpa *didn't* die. He came to the next day, and Doc said it'd been a good thing I got Grandpa to him when I did, that he just might have bled to death. It was peculiar. From the second Roy Stoller picked Grandpa up in his arms, the bleeding stopped. But soon as Doc took him from the car, I could see it had started again. Of course Doc got it stopped fast once we were inside. He knew how.

When Grandpa woke up and realized where he was, he asked me how I did it, how I got him back to town, and so I told him about Roy Stoller. I wasn't sure, and I'm still not sure to this day, whether he believed me or not because he smiled a smile that could've meant he thought I was seeing things, or likewise it might've been a smile he smiled because he knew he'd been right about the way he thought about and treated the dead folks.

A few days later, when he was up and around and the snow had long since stopped, we went down to the Lower Dellfield Cemetery and looked at Roy Stoller's grave. It was under the snow same as the rest, and when Grandpa brushed the snow away to see the earth beneath, it looked like any fresh grave, with no sign that anything'd come out of it. But still, that wasn't proof that something hadn't.

There was nothing else at the grave—no piece of the blanket I'd wrapped around Grandpa or any of the clues you'd expect to find in a real old fashioned ghost story. Just the snow and the hard earth. I left some flowers I'd brought along. Roses. They looked real pretty on the white snow. And I hoped as we walked away that maybe what Roy Stoller'd done that night would help to make up for the bad he'd done when he was alive. The more I thought about it, the more I was sure that it should just plumb *erase* that badness, wipe it away. For all he'd done, Roy Stoller'd never *killed* anybody, but he did save a life, and I was mighty thankful to him for it.

I was thankful, too, that Grandpa was the man he was, that he'd done good for Roy Stoller from his heart. At first I'd thought that what he'd said about kindness to the dead was nice but foolish. But now I know better. It wasn't ever too late to be kind. And you can be kind even to people's memories, and it might be known to them, and appreciated. Grandpa taught me that lesson. He taught me other things, too, and he taught me good. Why, you children can just look at yourselves if you don't believe me.

Oh, I hope you don't mind me calling you children, but that's how I think of you, especially since Grandpa and I never had any of our own. It just seemed natural for us to call *you* our children. After all, we care for you, comfort you, lay you down in your last sleep.

There now. All finished, and all ready. That wasn't bad, was it? I just wish Grandpa was still alive to see how peaceful you look. Yes, peaceful. I may not be the best or the fanciest undertaker in these parts, but I dare hope to say I'm the most gentle.

Ash

by Charles Garvie

Ashley had sworn that he'd come back. It was the last thing he'd said as Wishart pushed him out of the window, and although Wishart wasn't the superstitious type, he'd had him cremated anyway. Just in case.

But it seemed as if he needn't have worried. Ashley seemed quite content to stay under his rose tree in the Garden of Remembrance, and never did the soft swish of ashy feet sound in Wishart's hallway or pace past his bolted door. Until he began to court Elinor again.

Elinor had been Wishart's girl at university back in '82, but of recent years she had been more taken with the charms of elder brother Ashley and his rancid Porsche. Even though the car phone kept ringing every time they went out together.

But it hadn't been any good. Elinor had fallen for the thirty-five thousand per annum and the second house in Brighton, and Wishart had been forced to do the sporting and gentlemanly thing and push his sod of a brother out of the window. Which hadn't been at all easy.

However, once he'd finally managed to spin a yarn good enough to lure the lout round to his flat in Battersea, it had been quite easy to convince him that there was a wounded bird on the ledge and that he, Wishart, was too scared of heights to go out and get it. After that it had been, more or less, plain sailing. Less in the sense that Ashley had hung on tenaciously to his fat life and Wishart had had to be very careful just how he whacked his brother's grasping little fingers with the walking stick, but more once the deed was done and the police and public had swallowed, hook, line, and sinker, his story of Ashley's fatal accident whilst trying to save the life of a tiny fledgling sparrow. The fat greaseball had even made it to the front page of the local paper. Still Wishart was cautious.

But his fears seemed groundless until the Fatal First Night he brought Elinor round to the flat. They had been to a concert at the South Bank—Elinor's first Public Appearance, as the saying goes, since the death of her fiancé—and she had confided to him over coffee that she really needed to get out more and that she was glad to have an old friend like him to rely on. So Wishart's heart sang. And then sank as he saw the delicate flakes of ash fluttering against the windowpane.

Wishart froze. Despite the central heating. But there was no denying it. Snowflake-cute and bobbing like a syncopated defector from *Fantasia* it fluttered and pirouetted against the neon-pierced velvet of the night sky. Ash. Ashley's ash.

Wishart pulled himself together, drew the curtains, and closed his mind.

But he slipped up three weeks later when, bowled over with excitement because she'd let him kiss her cheek when he escorted her home the previous night, he was too busy putting on his kid gloves to notice that he'd not only left the curtains open but the window as well.

And it had been quite a descent from Seventh Heaven when one moment they'd been kissing passionately on the settee and the next some gentle gossamer-floating-thing had lightly stroked his cheek and drifted daintily onto his lap.

He'd screamed. No, let's be honest here. He'd yelled his head off and cried like a baby. And it had taken the puzzled Elinor almost ten minutes to finally quiet him down and another half hour to get back to where they had left off on the couch.

But the Grand Finale came two weeks later when she rose from the settee and, taking his hand, smiled her Little-Girl-Lost smile and asked coyly where the bedroom was. And, with Wishart's heart doing rapid-succession press-ups, they glided through the open door and floated down onto the snowy white bedspread which was, of course, covered in a fine white flour-light dusting of—all together now—ash.

It was the straw the camel dreads and Wishart went berserk, screaming and wailing and clutching at Elinor's skirt and burying his face in her lap as she tried to comfort him. And then, of course, the fool went and blurted out the whole sordid story.

But she took it calmly and patted and there-there'd him at all the appropriate places, and when he was done she went and got her handbag for tissues to dab his eyes with. And they sat there like that for some time while he sobbed and she crooned fairy tales (yes, fairy tales—this was one screwed-up lady) in his ear to console him.

"There now, there now," she soothed. "Dry your eyes and Elinor will tell you a story. A sad story that happened long, long ago. Listen . . .

"Once upon a time there lived a Beautiful Maiden who loved a Scholar, but as the Scholar was never likely to rise beyond the village of Battersea, the Maiden decided to marry the Fat Prince, confident that once she had his fortune some misfortune would befall him. However, unbeknownst to her, the Scholar, inflamed with jealousy, slew the Fat Prince before the Maiden could lay claim to his loot, and can you guess what the Maiden did to the silly Scholar when he finally spilled the beans, Wishart?"

But there was no glittering star prize behind the red and gold dappled curtains for solving this particular little conundrum, and the disgustingly convenient crime writer's standby with the mother-of-pearl handle which had appeared in her hand gave the game away even before the roar of the explosion seared his eardrums.

In fact, the blast was so loud that under normal circumstances grumpy old Mr. Peterson from next door would have been shuffling over to moan about the noise, but as he was sitting at his kitchen table writing an irate letter to the factory at the bottom of the road at the time, he missed the whole show.

Their damned incinerator had developed the filthy habit of blowing ash through his front windows and he wasn't standing for it. After all, if everybody just threw their ash around unchecked, it wouldn't be long before people were suffocating in the damn stuff and dropping dead because of it. And, believe you me, *he* wasn't going to end up being found dead in his living room after fighting the last war for a cleaner place to live.

But, unfortunately, the Fates were working from a different script, and even as his pen flew over the Basildon Bond, Elinor was easing up the latch on his front door and creeping stealthily up behind him.

Not that she had any real need to get rid of the old fool, of course, because he'd heard nothing and didn't know she existed anyway. But Elinor was a methodical worker and just liked to be sure of everything. After all, that was the trouble with the world today, wasn't it? You never *could* be sure that some maniac with a gun wasn't going to walk in off the street and mow down two innocent, unconnected people. Or even, for that matter, that a truck wouldn't career blindly off the road and strike a hurrying girl because the driver got dust in his eyes. Or maybe even ash?

The Horror of the Heights

by Arthur Conan Doyle

The idea that the extraordinary narrative which has been called the Joyce-Armstrong Fragment is an elaborate practical joke evolved by some unknown person, cursed by a perverted and sinister sense of humor, has now been abandoned by all who have examined the matter. The most macabre and imaginative of plotters would hesitate before linking his morbid fancies with the unquestioned and tragic facts which reinforce the statement. Though the assertions contained in it are amazing and even monstrous, it is nonetheless forcing itself upon the general intelligence that they are true, and that we must readjust our ideas to the new situation. This world of ours appears to be separated by a slight and precarious margin of safety from a most singular and unexpected danger. I will endeavor in this narrative, which reproduces the original document in its necessarily somewhat fragmentary form, to lay before the reader the whole of the facts up to date, prefacing my statement by saying that, if there be any who doubt the narrative of Joyce-Armstrong, there can be no question at all as to the facts concerning Lieutenant Myrtle, R.N., and Mr. Hay Connor, who undoubtedly met their end in the manner described.

The Joyce-Armstrong Fragment was found in the field which is called Lower Haycock, lying one mile to the westward of the village of Withyham, upon the Kent and Sussex border. It was on the fifteenth September last that an agricultural laborer, James Flynn, in the employment of Mathew Dodd, farmer, of the Chauntry

Farm, Withyham, perceived a briar pipe lying near the footpath which skirts the hedge in Lower Haycock. A few paces farther on he picked up a pair of broken binocular glasses. Finally, among some nettles in the ditch, he caught sight of a flat, canvas-backed book, which proved to be a notebook with detachable leaves, some of which had come loose and were fluttering along the base of the hedge. These he collected, but some, including the first, were never recovered, and leave a deplorable hiatus in this all-important statement. The notebook was taken by the laborer to his master, who in turn showed it to Dr. J. H. Atherton, of Hartfield. This gentleman at once recognized the need for an expert examination, and the manuscript was forwarded to the Aero Club in London, where it now lies.

The first two pages of the manuscript are missing. There is also one torn away at the end of the narrative, though none of these affect the general coherence of the story. It is conjectured that the missing opening is concerned with the record of Mr. Joyce-Armstrong's qualifications as an aeronaut, which can be gathered from other sources and are admitted to be unsurpassed among the air pilots of England. For many years he has been looked upon as among the most daring and the most intellectual of flying men, a combination which has enabled him to both invent and test several new devices, including the common gyroscopic attachment which is known by his name. The main body of the manuscript is written neatly in ink, but the last few lines are in pencil and are so ragged as to be hardly legible—exactly, in fact, as they might be expected to appear if they were scribbled off hurriedly from the seat of a moving aeroplane. There are, it may be added, several stains, both on the last page and on the outside cover, which have been pronounced by the Home Office experts to be blood—probably human and certainly mammalian. The fact that something closely resembling the organism of malaria was discovered in this blood, and that Joyce-Armstrong is known to have suffered from intermittent fever, is a remarkable example of the new weapons which modern science has placed in the hands of our detectives.

And now a word as to the personality of the author of this epoch-making statement. Joyce-Armstrong, according to the few friends who really knew something of the man, was a poet and a dreamer, as well as a mechanic and an inventor. He was a man of considerable wealth, much of which he had spent in the pursuit of his aeronautical hobby. He had four private aeroplanes in his hangars near Devizes, and is said to have made no fewer than one hundred and seventy ascents in the course of last year. He was a retiring man with dark moods, in which he would avoid the society of his fellows. Captain Dangerfield, who knew him better than anyone, says that there were times when his eccentricity threatened to develop into something more serious. His habit of carrying a shotgun with him in his aeroplane was one manifestation of it.

Another was the morbid effect which the fall of Lieutenant Myrtle had upon his mind. Myrtle, who was attempting the height record, fell from an altitude of something over thirty thousand feet. Horrible to narrate, his head was entirely obliterated, though his body and limbs preserved their configuration. At every gathering of airmen, Joyce-Armstrong, according to Dangerfield, would ask, with an enigmatic smile: "And where, pray, is Myrtle's head?"

On another occasion after dinner, at the mess of the Flying School on Salisbury Plain, he started a debate as to what will be the most permanent danger which airmen will have to encounter. Having listened to successive opinions as to air pockets, faulty construction, and over-banking, he ended by shrugging his shoulders and refusing to put forward his own views, though he gave the impression that they differed from many advanced by his companions.

It is worth remarking that after his own complete disappearance it was found that his private affairs were arranged with a precision which may show that he had a strong premonition of disaster. With these essential explanations I will now give the narrative exactly as it stands, beginning at page three of the bloodsoaked notebook:

"Nevertheless, when I dined at Rheims with Coselli and Gustav Raymond I found that neither of them was aware of any particular danger in the higher layers of the atmosphere. I did not actually say what was in my thoughts, but I got so near to it that if they had any corresponding idea they could not have failed to express it. But then they are two empty, vainglorious fellows with no thought beyond seeing their silly names in the newspaper. It is interesting to note that neither of them had ever been much beyond the twenty thousand foot level. Of course, men have been higher than this both in balloons and in the ascent of mountains. It must be well above the point that the aeroplane enters the danger zone—always presuming that my premonitions are correct.

"Aeroplaning has been with us now for more than twenty years, and one might well ask: Why should this peril be only revealing itself in our day? The answer is obvious. In the old days of weak engines, when a hundred horsepower Gnome or Green was considered ample for every need, the flights were very restricted. Now that three hundred horsepower is the rule rather than the exception, visits to the upper layers have become easier and more common. Some of us can remember how, in our youth, Garros made a worldwide reputation by attaining nineteen thousand feet, and it was considered a remarkable achievement to fly over the Alps. Our standard now has been immeasurably raised, and there are twenty high flights for one in former years. Many of them have been undertaken with impunity. The thirty thousand foot level has been reached time after time with no discomfort beyond cold and asthma. What does this prove? A visitor might descend upon this planet a thousand times and never see a tiger. Yet tigers exist, and if he chanced to come down into a jungle he might be devoured. There are jungles of the upper air, and there are worse things than tigers which inhabit them. I believe in time they will map these jungles accurately out. Even at the present moment I could name two of them. One of them lies over the Pau-Biarritz district of France. Another is just over my head as I write here in my house in Wiltshire. I rather think there is a third in the Homburg-Wiesbaden district.

"It was the disappearance of the airmen that first set me thinking. Of course, everyone said that they had fallen into the sea, but that did not satisfy me at all. First, there was Verrier in France; his machine was found near Bayonne, but they never got his body. There was the case of Baxter also, who vanished, though his engine and some of the iron fixings were found in a wood in Leicestershire.

In that case, Dr. Middleton, of Amesbury, who was watching the flight with a telescope, declares that just before the clouds obscured the view he saw the machine, which was at an enormous height, suddenly rise perpendicularly upwards in a succession of jerks in a manner that he would have thought to be impossible. That was the last seen of Baxter. There was a correspondence in the papers, but it never led to anything. There were several other similar cases, and then there was the death of Hay Connor. What a cackle there was about an unsolved mystery of the air, and what columns in the halfpenny papers, and yet how little was ever done to get to the bottom of the business! He came down in a tremendous volplané from an unknown height. He never got off his machine and died in his pilot's seat. Died of what? 'Heart disease,' said the doctors. Rubbish! Hay Connor's heart was as sound as mine is. What did Venables say? Venables was the only man who was at his side when he died. He said that he was shivering and looked like a man who had been badly scared. 'Died of fright,' said Venables, but could not imagine what he was frightened about. Only said one word to Venables, which sounded like 'Monstrous.' They could make nothing of that at the inquest. But I could make something of it. Monsters! That was the last word of poor Harry Hay Connor. And he *did* die of fright, just as Venables thought.

"And then there was Myrtle's head. Do you really believe—does anybody really believe—that a man's head could be driven clean into his body by the force of a fall? Well, perhaps it may be possible, but I, for one, have never believed that it was so with Myrtle. And the grease upon his clothes—'all slimy with grease,' said somebody at the inquest. Queer that nobody got thinking after that! I did—but, then, I had been thinking for a good long time. I've made three ascents—how Dangerfield used to chaff me about my shotgun—but I've never been high enough. Now, with this new, light Paul Veroner machine and its one hundred and seventy-five Robur, I should easily touch the thirty thousand tomorrow. I'll have a shot at the record. Maybe I shall have a shot at something else as well. Of course it's dangerous. If a fellow wants to avoid danger, he had best keep out of flying altogether and subside finally into flannel slippers and a dressing gown. But I'll visit the air-jungle tomorrow—and if there's anything there I shall know it. If I return, I'll find myself a bit of a celebrity. If I don't this notebook may explain what I am trying to do, and how I lost my life in doing it. But no drivel about accidents or mysteries, if *you* please.

"I chose my Paul Veroner monoplane for the job. There's nothing like a monoplane when real work is to be done. Beaumont found that out in very early days. For one thing it doesn't mind damp, and the weather looks as if we should be in the clouds all the time. It's a bonny little model and answers my hand like a tender-mouthed horse. The engine is a ten-cylinder rotary Robur working up to one hundred and seventy-five. It has all the modern improvements— enclosed fuselage, high-curved landing skids, brakes, gyroscopic steadiers, and three speeds, worked by an alteration of the angle of the planes upon the Venetian blind principle. I took a shotgun with me and a dozen cartridges filled with buckshot. You should have seen the face of Perkins, my old mechanic, when I directed him to put them in. I was dressed like an Arctic explorer, with two jerseys under my overalls, thick socks inside my padded boots, a storm cap with flaps, and my talc goggles. It was stifling outside the hangars, but I was going for the summit of the Himalayas, and had to dress for the part. Perkins knew there was something on and implored me to take him with me. Perhaps I should if I were using the biplane, but a monoplane is a one-man show—if you want to get the last foot of life out of it. Of course I took an oxygen bag; the man who goes for the altitude record without one will either be frozen or smothered—or both.

"I had a good look at the planes, the rudder bar, and the elevating lever before I got in. Everything was in order so far as I could see. Then I switched on my engine and found that she was running sweetly. When they let her go, she rose almost at once upon the lowest speed. I circled my home field once or twice just to warm her up, and then with a wave to Perkins and the others, I flattened out my planes and put her on her highest. She skimmed like a swallow downwind for eight or ten miles until I turned her nose up a little and she began to climb in a great spiral for the cloudbank above me. It's all-important to rise slowly and adapt yourself to the pressure as you go.

"It was a close, warm day for an English September, and there was the hush and heaviness of impending rain. Now and then there came sudden puffs of wind from the southwest—one of them so gusty and unexpected that it caught me napping and turned me half-round for an instant. I remember the time when gusts and winds and air pockets used to be things of danger—before we learned to put an overmastering power into our engines. Just as I reached the cloudbanks, with the altimeter marking three thousand, down came the rain. My word, how it poured! It drummed upon my wings and lashed against my face, blurring my glasses so that I could hardly see. I got down onto a low speed, for it was painful to travel against it. As I got higher it became hail, and I had to turn tail to it. One of my cylinders was out of action—a dirty plug, I should imagine, but still I was rising steadily with plenty of power. After a bit the trouble passed, whatever it was, and I heard the full, deep-throated purr— the ten singing as one. That's where the beauty of our modern silencers comes in. We can at last control our engines by ear. How they squeal and squeak and sob when they are in trouble! All those cries for help were wasted in the old days, when every sound was swallowed up by the monstrous racket of the machine. If only the early aviators could come back to see the beauty and perfection of the mechanisms which have been bought at the cost of their lives!

"About nine thirty I was nearing the clouds. Down below me, all blurred and shadowed with rain, lay the vast expanse of Salisbury Plain. Half a dozen flying machines were doing hackwork at the thousand foot level, looking like little black swallows against the green background. I dare say they were wondering what I was doing up in cloud land. Suddenly a grey curtain drew across beneath me and the wet folds of vapors were swirling round my face. It was clammily cold and miserable. But I was above the hailstorm, and that was something gained. The cloud was as dark and thick as a London fog. In my anxiety to get clear, I cocked her nose up until the automatic alarm bell rang, and I actually began to slide backwards. My sopped and dripping wings had made me heavier than I thought, but presently I was in lighter cloud, and soon had cleared the first layer. There was a second—opal-colored and fleecy—at a great height above my head, a white, unbroken ceiling above, and a dark, unbroken floor below, with the monoplane laboring upwards upon a vast spiral between them. It is deadly lonely in these cloud-spaces. Once a great flight of some small waterbirds went past me, flying very fast to the westwards. The quick whir of their wings and their musical cry were cheery to my ear. I fancy that they were teal, but I am a wretched zoologist. Now that we humans have become birds, we must really learn to know our brethren by sight.

"The wind down beneath me whirled and swayed the broad cloud-plain. Once a great eddy formed in it, a whirlpool of vapor, and through it, as down a funnel, I caught sight of the distant world. A large white biplane was passing at a vast depth beneath me. I fancy it was the morning mail service betwixt Bristol and London. Then the drift swirled inwards again and the great solitude was unbroken.

"Just after ten I touched the lower edge of the upper cloud stratum. It consisted of fine diaphanous vapor drifting swiftly from the westwards. The wind had been steadily rising all this time and it was now blowing a sharp breeze—twenty-eight an hour by my gauge. Already it was very cold, though my altimeter only marked nine thousand. The engines were working beautifully, and we went droning steadily upwards. The cloud-bank was thicker than I had expected, but at last it thinned out into a golden mist before me, and then in an instant I had shot out from it, and there was an unclouded sky and a brilliant sun above my head—all blue and gold above, all shining silver below, one vast, glimmering plain as far as my eyes could reach. It was a quarter past ten o'clock, and the barograph needle pointed to twelve thousand eight hundred. Up I went and up, my ears concentrated upon the deep purring of my motor, my eyes busy always with the watch, the revolution indicator, the petrol level, and the oil pump. No wonder aviators are said to be a fearless race. With so many things to think of there is no time to trouble about oneself. About this time I noted how unreliable is the compass when above a certain height from earth. At fifteen thousand feet mine was pointing east and a point south. The sun and the wind gave me my true bearings.

"I had hoped to reach an eternal stillness in these high altitudes, but with every thousand feet of ascent the gale grew stronger. My machine groaned and trembled in every joint and rivet as she faced it, and swept away like a sheet of paper when I banked her on the turn, skimming downwind at a greater pace, perhaps, than ever mortal man has moved. Yet I had always to turn again and tack up in the wind's eye, for it was not merely a height record that I was after. By all my calculations it was above little Wiltshire that my air-jungle lay, and all my labor might be lost if I struck the outer layers at some farther point.

"When I reached the nineteen thousand foot level, which was about midday, the wind was so severe that I looked with some anxiety to the stays of my wings, expecting momentarily to see them snap or slacken. I even cast loose the parachute behind me, and fastened its hook into the ring of my leather belt, so as to be ready for the worst. Now was the time when a bit of scamped work by the mechanic is paid for by the life of the aeronaut. But she held together bravely. Every cord and strut was humming and vibrating like so many harpstrings, but it was glorious to see how, for all the beating and the buffeting, she was still the conqueror of Nature and the mistress of the sky. There is surely something divine in man himself that he should rise so superior to such unselfish, heroic devotion as this air conquest has shown. Talk of human degeneration! When has such a story as this been written in the annals of our race?

"These were the thoughts in my head as I climbed that monstrous, inclined plane with the wind sometimes beating in my face and sometimes whistling behind my ears, while the cloud-land beneath me fell away to such a distance that the folds and hummocks of silver had all smoothed out into one flat, shining plain. But suddenly I had a horrible and unprecedented experience. I have known before what it is to be in what our neighbors have called a *tourbillon*, but never on such a scale as this. That huge, sweeping river of wind of which I have spoken had, as it appears, whirlpools within it which were as monstrous as itself. Without a moment's warning I was dragged suddenly into the heart of one. I spun round for a minute or two with such velocity that I almost lost my senses, and then fell suddenly, left wing foremost, down the vacuum funnel in the center. I dropped like a stone, and lost nearly a thousand feet.

It was only my belt that kept me in my seat, and the shock and breathlessness left me hanging half-insensible over the side of the fuselage. But I am always capable of a supreme effort—it is my one great merit as an aviator. I was conscious that the descent was slower. The whirlpool was a cone rather than a funnel, and I had come to the apex. With a terrific wrench, throwing my weight all to one side, I leveled my planes and brought her head away from the wind. In an instant I had shot out of the eddies and was skimming down the sky. Then, shaken but victorious, I turned her nose up and began once more my steady grind on the upward spiral. I took a large sweep to avoid the danger spot of the whirlpool, and soon I was safely above it. Just after one o'clock I was twenty-one thousand feet above the sea level. To my great joy I had topped the gale, and with every hundred feet of ascent the air grew stiller. On the other hand, it was very cold, and I was conscious of that peculiar nausea which goes with rarefaction of the air. For the first time I unscrewed the mouth of my oxygen bag and took an occasional whiff of the glorious gas. I could feel it running like a cordial through my veins, and I was exhilarated almost to the point of drunkenness. I shouted and sang as I soared upwards into the cold, still outer world.

"It is very clear to me that the insensibility which came upon Glaisher, and in a lesser degree upon Coxwell, when, in 1862, they ascended in a balloon to the height of thirty thousand feet, was due to the extreme speed with which a perpendicular ascent is made. Doing it at an easy gradient and accustoming oneself to the lessened barometric pressure by slow degrees, there are no dreadful symptoms. At the same great height I found that even without my oxygen inhaler I could breathe without undue distress. It was bitterly cold, however, and my thermometer was at zero, Fahrenheit. At one thirty I was nearly seven miles above the surface of the earth, and still ascending steadily. I found, however, that the rarefied air was giving markedly less support to my planes, and that my angle of ascent had to be considerably lowered in consequence. It was already clear that even with my light weight and strong engine-power there was a point in front of me where I should be held. To make matters worse, one of my sparking-plugs was in trouble again and there was intermittent misfiring in the engine. My heart was heavy with the fear of failure.

"It was about that time that I had a most extraordinary experience. Something whizzed past me in a trail of smoke and exploded with a loud, hissing sound, sending forth a cloud of steam. For the instant I could not imagine what had happened. Then I remembered that the earth is forever being bombarded by meteor stones, and would be hardly inhabitable were they not in nearly every case turned to vapor in the outer layers of the atmosphere. Here is a new danger for the high altitude man, for two others passed me when I was nearing the forty thousand foot mark. I cannot doubt that at the edge of the earth's envelope the risk would be a very real one.

"My barograph needle marked forty-one thousand three hundred when I became aware that I could go no farther. Physically, the strain was not as yet greater than I could bear, but my machine had reached its limit. The attenuated air gave no firm support to the wings, and the least tilt developed into sideslip, while she seemed sluggish on her controls. Possibly, had the engine been at its best, another thousand feet might have been within our capacity, but it was still misfiring, and two out of the ten cylinders appeared to be out of action. If I had not already reached the zone for which I was searching, then I should never see it upon this journey. But was it not possible that I had attained it? Soaring in circles like a monstrous hawk upon the forty thousand foot level, I let the monoplane guide herself, and with my Mannheim glass I made a careful observation of my surroundings. The heavens were perfectly clear; there was no indication of those dangers which I had imagined.

"I have said that I was soaring in circles. It struck me suddenly that I would do well to take a wider sweep and open up a new air tract. If the hunter entered an earth-jungle, he would drive through it if he wished to find his game. My reasoning had led me to believe that the air-jungle which I had imagined lay somewhere over Wiltshire. This should be to the south and west of me. I took my bearings from the sun, for the compass was hopeless and no trace of earth was to be seen—nothing but the distant, silver cloud-plain. However, I got my direction as best I might and kept her head straight to the mark. I reckoned that my petrol supply would not last for more than another hour or so, but I could afford to use it to the last drop, since a single magnificent vol-plané could at any time take me to the earth.

"Suddenly I was aware of something new. The air in front of me had lost its crystal clearness. It was full of long, ragged wisps of something which I can only compare to very fine cigarette smoke. It hung about in wreaths and coils, turning and twisting slowly in the sunlight. As the monoplane shot through it, I was aware of a faint taste of oil upon my lips, and there was a greasy scum upon the woodwork of the machine. Some infinitely fine organic matter appeared to be suspended in the atmosphere. There was no life there. It was inchoate and diffuse, extending for many square acres and then fringing off into the void. No, it was not life. But might it not be the remains of life? Above all, might it not be the food of life, monstrous life, even as the humble grease of the ocean is the food for the mighty whale? The thought was in my mind when my eyes looked upwards and I saw the most wonderful vision that ever man has seen. Can I hope to convey it to you even as I saw it myself last Thursday?

"Conceive a jellyfish such as sails in our summer seas, bell-shaped and of enormous size—far larger, I should judge, than the dome of St. Paul's. It was of a light pink color veined with a delicate green, but the whole huge fabric so tenuous that it was but a fairy outline against the dark blue sky. It pulsated with a delicate and regular rhythm. From it there depended two long, drooping, green tentacles, which swayed slowly backwards and forwards. This gorgeous vision passed gently with noiseless dignity over my head, as light and fragile as a soap bubble, and drifted upon its stately way.

"I had half turned my monoplane, that I might look after this beautiful creature, when, in a moment, I found myself amidst a perfect fleet of them, of all sizes, but none so large as the first. Some were quite small, but the majority about as big as an average balloon, and with much the same curvature at the top. There was in them a delicacy of texture and coloring which reminded me of the finest Venetian glass. Pale shades of pink and green were the prevailing tints, but all had a lovely iridescence where the sun shimmered through their dainty forms. Some hundreds of them drifted past me, a wonderful fairy squadron of strange unknown argosies of the sky—creatures whose forms and substance were so attuned to these pure heights that one could not conceive anything so delicate within actual sight or sound of earth.

"But soon my attention was drawn to a new phenomenon—the serpents of the outer air. These were long, thin, fantastic coils of vapor-like material, which turned and twisted with great speed, flying round and round at such a pace that the eyes could hardly follow them. Some of these ghostlike creatures were twenty or thirty feet long, but it was difficult to tell their girth, for their outline was so hazy that it seemed to fade away into the air around them. These air-snakes were of a very light grey or smoke color, with some darker lines within, which gave the impression of a definite organism. One of them whisked past my very face, and I was conscious of a cold, clammy contact, but their composition was so unsubstantial that I could not connect them with any thought of physical danger, any more than the beautiful bell-like creatures which had preceded them. There was no more solidity in their frames than in the floating spume from a broken wave.

"But a more terrible experience was in store for me. Floating downwards from a great height there came a purplish patch of vapor, small as I saw it first, but rapidly enlarging as it approached me, until it appeared to be hundreds of square feet in size. Though fashioned of some transparent, jelly-like substance, it was nonetheless of much more definite outline and solid consistence than anything which I had seen before. There were more traces, too, of a physical organization, especially two vast, shadowy, circular plates upon either side, which may have been eyes, and a perfectly solid white projection between them which was as curved and cruel as the beak of a vulture.

"The whole aspect of this monster was formidable and threatening, and it kept changing its color from a very light mauve to a dark, angry purple so thick that it cast a shadow as it drifted between my monoplane and the sun. On the upper curve of its huge body there were three great projections which I can only describe as enormous bubbles, and I was convinced as I looked at them that they were charged with some extremely light gas which served to buoy up the misshapen and semi-solid mass in the rarefied air. The creature moved swiftly along, keeping pace easily with the monoplane, and for twenty miles or more it formed my horrible escort, hovering over me like a bird of prey which is waiting to pounce. Its method of progression—done so swiftly that it was not easy to follow—was to throw out a long, glutinous streamer in front of it, which in turn seemed to draw forward the rest of the writhing body. So elastic and gelatinous was it that never for two successive minutes was it the same shape, and yet each change made it more threatening and loathsome than the last.

"I knew that it meant mischief. Every purple flush of its hideous body told me so. The vague, goggling eyes which were turned always upon me were cold and merciless in their viscid hatred. I dipped the nose of my monoplane downwards to escape it. As I did so, as quick as a flash there shot out a long tentacle from this mass of floating blubber, and it fell as light and sinuous as a whiplash across the front of my machine. There was a loud hiss as it lay for a moment across the hot engine, and it whisked itself into the air again, while the huge, flat body drew itself together as if in sudden pain. I dipped to a vol-piqué, but again a tentacle fell over the monoplane and was shorn off by the propeller as easily as it might have cut through a smoke wreath. A long, gliding, sticky, serpentlike coil came from behind and caught me round the waist, dragging me out of the fuselage. I tore at it, my fingers sinking into the smooth, gluelike surface, and for an instant I disengaged myself, but only to be caught round the boot by another coil, which gave me a jerk that tilted me almost onto my back.

"As I fell over I blazed both barrels of my gun, though, indeed, it was like attacking an elephant with a pea-shooter to imagine that any human weapon could cripple that mighty bulk. And yet I aimed better than I knew, for, with a loud report, one of the great blisters upon the creature's back exploded with the puncture of the buck-shot. It was very clear that my conjecture was right, and that these vast, clear bladders were distended with some lifting gas, for in an instant the huge, cloudlike body turned sideways, writhing desperately to find its balance, while the white beak snapped and gaped in horrible fury. But already I had shot away on the steepest glide that I dared to attempt, my engine still full on, the flying propeller and the force of gravity shooting me downwards like an aerolite. Far behind me I saw a dull, purplish smudge growing swiftly smaller and merging into the blue sky behind it. I was safe out of the deadly jungle of the outer air.

"Once out of danger I throttled my engine, for nothing tears a machine to pieces quicker than running on full power from a height. It was a glorious, spiral vol-plané from nearly eight miles of altitude—first, to the level of the silver cloudbank, then to that of the stormcloud beneath it, and finally, in beating rain, to the surface of the earth. I saw the Bristol Channel beneath me as I broke from the clouds, but having still some petrol in my tank, I got twenty miles inland before I found myself stranded in a field half a mile from the village of Ashcombe. There I got three tins of petrol from a passing motorcar, and at ten minutes past six that evening I alighted gently in my own home meadow at Devizes, after such a journey as no mortal upon earth has ever yet taken and lived to tell the tale. I have seen the beauty and I have seen the horror of the heights—and greater beauty or greater horror than that is not within the ken of man.

"And now it is my plan to go once again before I give my results to the world. My reason for this is that I must surely have something to show by way of proof before I lay such a tale before my fellowmen. It is true that others will soon follow and will confirm what I have said, and yet I should wish to carry conviction from the first. Those lovely iridescent bubbles of the air should not be hard to capture. They drift slowly upon their way, and the swift monoplane could intercept their leisurely course. It is likely enough that they would dissolve in the heavier layers of the atmosphere, and that some small heap of amorphous jelly might be all that I should bring to earth with me. And yet something there would surely be by which I could substantiate my story. Yes, I will go, even if I run a risk by doing so. These purple horrors would not seem to be numerous. It is probable that I shall not see one. If I do, I shall dive at once. At the worst there is always the shotgun and my knowledge of . . ."

*   *   *

Here a page of the manuscript is unfortunately missing. On the next
page is written, in large, straggling writing:

"Forty-three thousand feet. I shall never see earth again. They are
beneath me, three of them. God help me; it is a dreadful death to
die!"

Such in its entirety is the Joyce-Armstrong Statement. Of the man
nothing has since been seen. Pieces of his shattered monoplane
have been picked up in the preserves of Mr. Budd-Lushington upon
the borders of Kent and Sussex, within a few miles of the spot where
the notebook was discovered. If the unfortunate aviator's theory is
correct that this air-jungle, as he called it, existed only over the
southwest of England, then it would seem that he had fled from it at
the full speed of his monoplane, but had been overtaken and devoured by these horrible creatures at some spot in the outer atmosphere above the place where the grim relics were found. The
picture of that monoplane skimming down the sky, with the nameless terrors flying as swiftly beneath it and cutting it off always from
the earth while they gradually closed in upon their victim, is one
upon which a man who valued his sanity would prefer not to dwell.
There are many, as I am aware, who still jeer at the facts which I
have here set down, but even they must admit that Joyce-
Armstrong has disappeared, and I would commend to them his own
words: "This notebook may explain what I am trying to do, and how
I lost my life in doing it. But no drivel about accidents or mysteries,
if *you* please."

Going Buggy

by J. P. McLaughlin

Alma was mopping the floor, running the sponge mop over the linoleum in a very leisurely fashion in tune with the music on the radio. She had no place to hurry to, no one to see, and her time was her own, so she enjoyed doing things at a more relaxed pace than she had been able to in her younger days. Being retired in Florida, at the Funky Flamingo Estates, was a welcome respite from years of keeping up with husbands, friends, and the usual round of socializing.

She was just thinking about how lucky she had been not to have kids when a big, shiny, brown-gold palmetto bug scuttled toward her. She drew in a gasp of surprise and was about to hit it with the sponge mop when it stood on its backmost legs, waved the others, and yelled, "Don't!"

"Huh?" she said, surprised, holding the mop in the air.

"Don't hit me, Alma. You've done enough damage already."

She froze as if she had been playing the children's game of Statue and glared at the palmetto bug.

"You look silly, Alma," it said. "Put the mop down, and let's talk. We never did have enough time to talk when we were married."

"Reggie?"

"I was wondering if you'd be able to recognize my voice. Yeah, it's me."

"What're you doing in that bug?"

"Isn't that what you asked when I bought that VW in '65?"

"Reggie, is that really you?"

"Who else would know about the VW bug in 1965, Alma? After all, woman . . ."

"Well, why are you here?"

"I've wanted to talk to you for a long time. I thought maybe you'd get the message when I broke that vase in the house on Long Island in '79. I hoped you'd go to a medium. I have to tell you a few things, and . . ."

"If Marty comes, he'll think I'm really off my rocker, talking to a bug, for Heaven's sake."

"Marty? Is he the latest?"

"If you've been following me around all this time, you should have seen me with Marty last night at the dog races."

"Alma, I only just got into this bug last night. If Marty's a new man in your life, I must have missed him."

"Reggie, you died eighteen years ago. Why aren't you in Heaven . . . or . . . the other place?"

"Not good enough, and not bad enough. I have to earn my way upstairs, in a manner of speaking."

"By becoming a glorified cockroach?"

"No. By having a good conversation with you, which I never really did while I was alive. I have to make up for it now."

Alma went to the table, pulled out a chair, and sat down, leaning the mop handle against the table. She stared at Reggie. Stared at the cockroach, a.k.a. palmetto bug, that claimed to be Reggie.

Reggie the bug approached her but stopped a few feet from the mop.

"Alma, I loved you so much."

"I know. You were stupid that way."

"To you, love was stupid. To me, it meant a lot. I had a responsibility to you, and I was so happy about that."

"So happy that *you* became the burden. All you ever wanted was to do things with me. And you wanted a baby. After I told you I never wanted any."

"I wanted six, Alma. I'd have been happy with at least one."

"Well, *I* wouldn't." She pouted.

"And you didn't want to go dancing when I asked you out, and you didn't want to do a lot of other nice things with me. But when you married Jake, you went dancing, and you had a little career. Why didn't you do that earlier?"

"I think you helped me find some direction in life, Reggie. It may sound odd, but when we got married, we were both still so young, and I just wanted to be myself for a little longer."

"Oh, I see. Then why did you marry me?"

"You were cute, and everyone was telling me to do something with my life, and I was tired of being a waitress at the diner, and you had good money."

"Oh. You see, Alma, that's the sort of thing I have to know about. It has something to do with getting wisdom."

"Are there other people in other palmetto bugs?"

"Maybe. Most of them go into animals for a while, so they can watch and learn. Some of the pushy ones take over other people's bodies. If the people are weak, they're easy to take over.

"Why did you kill me, Alma? That's one of the things I have to know."

"I was afraid you'd ask that. I don't know."

"You don't know! Alma, you took my life. I didn't even have a chance to make a commitment to life, and you took it away. When people go to gas chambers, they at least have a chance to speak with a minister, make their peace with God."

"Well, it was kind of spur-of-the-moment. What're you complaining about? At least you're not . . . down there."

"No thanks to you, Alma. Would you have cared if I was?"

"I probably wouldn't know. All along, I never questioned it, really."

"Alma, why did you kill me?"

"Hmmm. Wasn't that the day you came in and tracked up my floor after you had been fishing?"

"Yes."

"Well, that's why I did it."

"You killed me because I tracked up the floor? But the way you did it, with that poisonous tea, made with toadstools; that showed some premeditation. You had it planned, didn't you, Alma?"

"I think I considered it after the mess you and your friends made in the yard that time and I had to clean most of it up."

"But I cleaned everything up that time. I put all the beer cans in the garbage. What did you have to do?"

"Wash the picnic table, rake the lawn. You never did notice details, Reggie."

"Oh."

"That was why I didn't want kids. And you were as bad as an overgrown kid."

"Oh."

"Reggie, were you around when I was married to Jake?"

"Yes. I tried a few times to get your attention then, but you were too absorbed in life, finally. You were always talking about your paralegal career in that law office. And when Jake was around, the two of you fondled like you had just met. It was sickening."

"You mean you saw all that?"

"I tried not to see it, Alma. Heck, I'm no peeping Tom. Never have been. But there were times I couldn't avoid it, and it hurt."

"Gee, Reggie, this whole thing is weird. I mean, it's bad enough that I'm talking to a bug that claims to be my long-lost first husband, but to find out that you watched me and Jake . . ."

"It was nothing that sordid, Alma. Will you please drop the subject? After all, you had a right. How did Jake die?"

The sudden question startled her, coming as it did out of left field. She thought she might remember, if she wanted to.

"You don't want to remember that, do you?" Reggie asked.

"That's not it. It's just that I was in such a haze of shock . . ."

"Shock, my left eyeball," Reggie sounded querulous. "I remember you sitting on the bed and telling yourself, 'Forget the whole thing. Forget it ever happened. Forget Jake. He was a bad dream. Forget it.'" As he repeated the words, his voice changed, mimicking her higher pitch.

Alma began to cry. "I loved Jake. I didn't want to do it."

"Yeah, I know. I saw you drain the oil pan that night, after the car was all tuned up and ready for Jake to take it upstate for that big meeting. You didn't know the engine would seize up when it did and the eighteen-wheeler would topple over on the car. But you *did* want to cause trouble, didn't you?"

"I thought he had a little chippie on the side. That's what he called women, little chippies. I wanted him to get upset and lose control of the car and be stuck in the middle of nowhere."

"Well," said Reggie, sounding reasonable and forlorn. "I know that. I have to tell you, Alma, that this Marty guy is a nice guy, and if you're planning to do anything to him, lay off. Orders from Above."

Alma stopped crying, and stared at Reggie. "You mean . . ."

"I mean that you've pulled enough evil in your time, and if you don't change your ways, you'll be headed for that other place."

"It really exists?"

"It sure does. And I want you to have something better, even if you don't care. It's not fire, like you read about. The fire is figurative. It's the anguish at missing out on the good things. It eats you up and burns you away, for all eternity."

"I don't believe you. When we die, there's nothing."

"Hoo-boy. I should have known. People believe what they want to believe. Okay, Alma, that's really all I wanted to say. I do still love you, you know. Is it okay if I come back tomorrow, and we can talk some more?"

"I don't know, Reggie. I really don't like talking with you like this."

Reggie turned and started away.

Alma got up, walked over, and stepped on him.

"Track up my floor again, will you?" she said, and got a paper towel to wipe up the mess.

Old Flame

by Taylor McCafferty

After a funeral you're supposed to feel sad. And maybe a little scared, after coming face to face with the finality of death and all. I don't think, however, that you're supposed to feel angry, but that's what I feel, all right. Real angry. With nobody left to be mad at any more. Except maybe Pa.

I'm sitting out here on the front porch, and I can hear him real plain in the kitchen, sniffling. Everybody that came by to pay their respects has finally gone, and Pa's out there, rattling pots and pans, like maybe he's going to make us something to eat.

Now *that* would be a first. Pa, cooking. He's just making all that noise so I'll hear him and get up and fix something for us. In a minute he'll be yelling at me, "Ida Sue, ain't it about time for dinner?" How he can even think about eating is beyond me.

And all that pan rattling out there sure doesn't cover up his sniffling. I'm trying to keep calm, but that sniffling is a real irritating thing to listen to.

Because I know Pa's just crying for Jenelle. Not for anybody else. Not for me, not Chandler. Just Jenelle. I know Pa blames me for all this, too. I can see it in his eyes. And, of course, I can't forget what he screamed at me that day.

I know Pa won't ever admit the part he played in all this, either. After all, he did start it, didn't he? If he hadn't spoiled Jenelle so bad, giving her everything she ever wanted, maybe things would've been different. And if Pa hadn't ever told us how our mama really

393

died, maybe none of this would've happened. Part of being able to do a thing is believing you can do it, isn't it? And Papa helped me and Jenelle with the believing part. He helped us with that real good.

I was just thirteen the day Pa decided to break the news. Jenelle was fourteen; and if there was such a thing as a line between pretty and beautiful, Jenelle had crossed it that year. She made you want to gasp just looking at her.

I admit it, back then I couldn't help being jealous of her. Pa had been worshipping at her feet ever since she was a baby. And my mirror plainly told me she had me beat real bad in the looks department. Jenelle had long, wavy chestnut-colored hair, creamy-white skin, and big blue eyes with lashes so thick they looked false. At fourteen she had the kind of figure grown women envy.

I, on the other hand, had the kind of figure they call skinny, and the kind of hair they call dishwater blonde. It was real limp, too, like maybe some of that dishwater had been left in it.

It didn't help any, either, to know that your father plain and simple liked your sister best. Who was it that Pa put his arm around while he was telling us about Mama? Jenelle, of course. I was standing right next to him, too, but Pa reached over and pulled Jenelle close. "Now, Jenelle, Ida Sue," he said, "it's high time you two finally knew about what happened to your mama. And I want to be the one to tell you before you hear it from somebody else."

To this day I'm still not sure why Pa told us. Neither Jenelle nor I even remembered our mama. She'd died when I was still a baby. And it wasn't like we still lived in Pigeon Fork where it all happened. We'd moved from there to Bullitt Lick right after Mama died. And nobody here even knew about it. Or if they'd heard about it long ago, they never connected the story to us.

Still, Jenelle was starting junior high the next week. Maybe Pa was afraid she would look it all up in the high school library. I'd heard tell that the new library the high school had just built had years of back issues of a dozen Kentucky newspapers. So maybe Pa was worried. Because even though Pigeon Fork was a hundred miles away, Mama had made news statewide.

I can still remember the way Pa's voice dropped to a whisper when he told us. Like he was talking about something sacred. Or maybe something too frightening to talk about out loud.

"Your mama was sitting out on the back porch swing, holding her cat Muffin on her lap. I was in the kitchen, right on the other side of the screen door. So I could see her real plain out there, staring straight ahead, swinging back and forth. She was in a snit about something or another." Here Pa's eyes dropped for a second.

Even at thirteen I could guess what Mama might've been mad about. As far back as I could remember Pa had been something of a ladies' man; he was real goodlooking, dark and slim—and he must've dated every available woman around these parts. And he even dated some that weren't available. Both Jenelle and I had heard the gossip about Pa. In a town the size of Bullitt Lick, you couldn't keep something like that a secret. Jenelle and I exchanged a knowing look before Pa went on.

"She was just sitting, with that dang cat of hers. Then, all of a sudden, as sure as I'm sitting here, your mama just burned up."

Jenelle and I looked at him for a second without saying a word. Then I asked, my voice shaking a little, "What do you mean, burned up?"

"I mean, she just caught fire. That's all." Pa's eyes got this haunted look in them. "I—I tried to save her. I ran out there, thinking I'd get her to roll on the ground, like you're supposed to do. But you couldn't get near her. She was all blue flame." Pa's voice trailed off. "Just blue flame is all."

Jenelle's eyes were even bigger than usual now. She swallowed once, and then asked, "Was she sitting by a stove?" Now, you've got to understand here that while Jenelle may have been heavy on looks, she was a quart low on smarts. Pa was used to it by now, though, because all he did was take a deep breath before he answered her.

"I said your ma was out on the porch, Jenelle. There aren't too many stoves out on a porch." Pa's voice was slow and patient. He rubbed his hand over his eyes like he was trying to rub the memory away. "That was what was so weird. The fire looked like it was coming from *inside* her."

Jenelle's eyes seemed to fill her whole face. Me, I was trying real hard not to smile. Because I was thinking, you mean to tell me that all these years we've been told that our mama died in a fire, and now you expect us to believe that Mama *was* the fire? Right.

"What happened to the cat?" My voice must've sounded a little skeptical, because Pa gave me a sharp glance.

"Now look, little girl," he said, "I'm trying to warn you. The same thing happened to that cat as happened to your mama, and I don't want it happening again. Ever." Pa looked away then, scowling. When he spoke again, his voice was real low, almost as if he were talking to himself. "You know, that porch swing she was sitting on wasn't even singed. Or the floor around them. But your mama—" Pa actually shuddered. He got up then, real abrupt. "Look, I don't ever want to talk about it again. I felt like you two should know. That's all."

Then he went on into the living room, and started reading the paper. Like what he'd just told us about wasn't anything more interesting than what happened at the church social last week.

After Pa went inside, Jenelle wrinkled her pretty nose and said, "Well, that was a disgusting thing for him to tell us. Yuk."

Seeing my big strong father actually shudder had done a lot to convince me that Pa was telling us the truth. "I think he was trying to warn us," I said.

"About what? I think he was being mean, telling us a creepy thing like that." Jenelle was pouting by then, so I gave up trying to talk to her.

In fact, we didn't talk about it for a long time after that. I thought about it, though, wondering about poor Mama. Sometimes I even cried for her—for that woman I never got to know. But every time I'd start to bring it up with Jenelle, she'd cut me off with, "Look, that's disgusting, okay?" And she'd flounce out of the room.

The next year when I started junior high myself, I looked it all up in the library. Sure enough, Mama was written up in a lot of papers. All of them called it the same thing. Spontaneous human combustion. Like the way oily rags catch fire in a shed sometimes. Those newspapers said that there have been quite a few people over the years who've died like that. The papers said there's a lot in your body that could catch fire, like fats and oils, phosphorus, stuff like that.

After I read all those articles about Mama, it all seemed more real to me. More real, and more frightening. I started thinking about it a lot. Thinking about how they say your brain operates by making electrical connections. Like tiny sparks in your brain. I figured maybe what happened to Mama was like that. Maybe she got so upset that day that one of those brain sparks got out of control—and it caught her on fire.

I tried again to tell Jenelle about it, too. "We'd better be careful," I said, "because you can never tell. Maybe we're like Mama, and if we get too upset, it could happen to us, too."

Jenelle looked real pale for a minute. Then she shrugged and tossed her dark curls. "Look, our mama made an ash of herself a long time ago." She smiled at her little joke. "It's got nothing to do with us."

I tried to make her listen, but she wouldn't hear of it. Eventually I realized Jenelle probably had nothing to worry about anyway. Because everything she wanted she seemed to get. Looking at her perfect face and perfect figure, I decided it was real likely that Jenelle might live her whole life and never once get upset.

It was me that had to be careful.

So I worked on getting to be real easygoing. About everything. When I'd forget to do one of my chores—and Jenelle would tell Pa—I learned to just keep cool. It got to where I could stand there and have Pa yell at me right in front of Jenelle, and I wouldn't feel a thing. Even when Jenelle made up stuff that I did, and she'd stand there, with that little half-smile on her face, all the time Pa was smacking me. Nothing was worth dying over, so I got laid back. After a while there wasn't anything in the world that I cared about enough to get upset over.

Until I met Chandler Farris. Chandler had just transferred to our high school in my freshman year, and even though he was a year ahead of me, we were assigned to the same study hall.

I noticed him the first day he walked in. Chandler wasn't exactly the handsomest guy I'd ever seen, but he had the kind of face you don't get tired of looking at. Blue eyes, freckled nose, easy smile. A shock of sandy hair always falling in his eyes. I guess I was in love the minute I saw him, sitting across from me. When he asked me out, I thought I might actually faint from happiness.

When he asked me to go steady, I practically did faint. I guess those months I went steady with Chandler were the happiest I've ever known. Before or since. Suddenly, it didn't matter if the phone rang constantly for Jenelle, or if Pa practically ignored me, or anything else. I had Chandler, and that was all I needed.

I couldn't believe how lucky I was. One night driving home from the movies in Chandler's old Ford, he kept looking over at me and smiling. And looking over at me and smiling some more. Finally, I said, "What is it?"

That's when he told me. "You know what I really like about you?"

I shook my head no. It was the truth. I really had no idea.

"You're pretty and you don't know it."

I must've turned bright red. Chandler reached over and took my hand. For a minute we just grinned at each other.

"You're real smart, too." Now, I wasn't sure about that, either. Oh, I made good grades, all right. But if you never went out on dates—and before Chandler, I didn't—then you had a lot of time to study.

My grades didn't suffer any when I started dating Chandler, either. Because Chandler was a real serious student, too. He wanted to be a doctor, so he studied as much as I did. A lot of times we studied together. Jenelle used to laugh at us, calling us "the bookworms," like it was a dirty word. But that was before Chandler won that award in his junior year.

We'd been going together about a year when Chandler got selected something called a "President's Scholar." It's a big honor around here. It got Chandler's picture in the paper; it got him a full scholarship at any Kentucky college; and, let's face it, it got him Jenelle.

I'll never forget the expression on Jenelle's face while she read about Chandler in the Bullitt Lick *Gazette*. It was like watching a cat read about a mouse. I remember feeling real uneasy, watching her face.

Pa was impressed with Chandler, too. He took that paper right out of Jenelle's hands and said, "This here boy's going to be rich one day. You mark my words. Rich." He beamed at me the whole time he was talking. It was probably the first time he'd ever said an approving thing to me.

Jenelle looked like she'd been slapped. She didn't look any better when Pa went on, "Jenelle, you'd do good to find yourself a catch like Ida Sue has. Somebody who's going to have some money. Instead of all those football idiots you're always mooning over." Jenelle had just started going steady with yet another football idiot that week; she turned without a word and stomped out of the room.

Up to then Jenelle had made it a point not to be around when "The Drip"—that's what she called Chandler—came around. But after that little scene with Pa, she was suddenly hanging all over Chandler the minute he walked in the door.

The first time she did it, I got as mad as I could let myself get. "He's mine, Jenelle," I told her as soon as Chandler left.

Jenelle gave me a look that said, "Oh, yeah?" Her mouth said, "All's fair in love and war." And she gave me one of those little half-smiles of hers as she walked away.

I watched her, feeling a little sick. And Chandler. Poor Chandler. He never knew what hit him. Even today it seems as if one day he was mine, and the next day I walked into the living room and saw them. Jenelle and Chandler, wrapped in each other's arms, so close together they seemed to be one.

I'd seen it coming by then, of course. I couldn't help but notice the new dazed look Chandler was wearing lately. Or how all of a sudden Jenelle seemed to need Chandler's help with every subject she had. I also noticed how Jenelle's hand lingered on his when she handed him her schoolbook, or got him a Coke. How she was always leaning real close to him so he could smell all that perfume she wore.

I could see it happening, all right, but I didn't know how to stop it. How could somebody like me fight somebody like Jenelle? Chandler and I had been sleeping together for almost six months by then, but even in bed with me, Chandler seemed a little distracted.

It must've taken Jenelle a little time to take Chandler away from me, but it seemed like fifteen minutes. Max. After I walked in on them that night, I just stood there, not wanting to believe my eyes. For a second I couldn't breathe. My heart started pounding real funny, and my face got real hot. Jenelle and Chandler both started talking at once. Chandler was almost stammering. "Oh, Ida Sue, I am so sorry. Jenelle and I—we—"

I didn't wait around to hear the rest. I just turned and ran upstairs as fast as I could. There I took a long, long shower, standing under the cool water and crying and crying. Until finally I was all cried out. Finally, I'd washed that awful scene right out of my mind.

I never broke down again. After that, when Chandler started coming by to pick up Jenelle, I made sure I was out of sight. I still watched him, though, from behind the curtains in my room. Watched him going off with Jenelle, smiling into her eyes. I wanted to hate him, but I just couldn't. Hating Jenelle, however, was real easy.

When Chandler went away to Centreville College that next year, I didn't know which hurt the most—seeing him with Jenelle or not seeing him at all.

Before he left, Chandler and Jenelle got engaged. Jenelle showed me that diamond ring just like I'd never dated Chandler myself. Like he'd always been hers. It was as if she'd put the whole thing out of her mind. "I think Chandler and I were meant for each other," Jenelle told me. She actually told me that.

After Chandler left for college, Jenelle moped around the house for about two weeks. Pa started complaining weakly about her running up a phone bill calling Chandler long distance.

Then, of course, Jenelle couldn't sit at home. She started dating other guys.

"Jenelle, what are you doing? What about Chandler?" I asked her the first time she went flouncing out of the house with some guy she'd met at the restaurant where she'd started working.

Jenelle looked at me as cool as you please. "What about him?" she said.

I couldn't think of a thing to say back to her. I just stared at her, open-mouthed.

She shrugged, and smiled that little half-smile of hers. "Now don't get all uppity with me, Ida Sue. I still love Chandler just like always. He's going to give me everything I've ever wanted. But *he* wouldn't want me sitting around this house getting bored. There's no harm in me having a little fun."

I had to clench my hands together to keep from slapping her. I thought about telling Chandler, too. But I knew he wouldn't believe me, or else he'd hate me for trying to stir up trouble. So I kept still. And waited.

That was during my senior year in high school. To keep my cool, I buried myself in my studies. I ended up with straight A's and a full scholarship. To any college I wanted. That fall I decided to go to Centreville College, just like Chandler.

I guess in the back of my mind I knew what I was up to. That what finally happened I'd planned all along. But I told myself that I was going to Centreville just to be near Chandler, that was all. I realized he belonged to Jenelle now, but I just wanted to see him again. Nothing more. Just to see him.

I think I believed that. I know it never occurred to Jenelle I could be going to Centreville because of Chandler. For one thing, Jenelle could never think of me as competition. I'd filled out some, and I'd learned to wear makeup right; but Jenelle had me beat so long ago, I don't think she even saw me any more.

As a matter of fact, the day before I left, Jenelle actually gave me a hug and said, "Now you keep an eye on my man. Make sure he doesn't get away from me." Then she laughed like the idea was preposterous. This, even though she herself was dating other people.

I ended up in two of Chandler's classes, and it seemed as natural a thing in the world that Chandler and I would end up studying together. And even more natural that one night Chandler would lean over and kiss me just like he used to almost three years before.

He pulled back right away, and then just stared at me. "You know what's happened, don't you?" His eyes were so blue. "I've fallen in love with you all over again. I can see now it's you and me. It always has been."

My heart was pounding so hard I could hardly say what had to be said. "But, Chandler, what about Jenelle?"

His face reddened, and he said, "I realize now that was just an infatuation." He looked away and added, his voice real low, "I been hearing things about Jenelle for a long time now. You know how folks in Bullitt Lick love to spread bad news."

So he'd heard about Jenelle's running around, after all. I hadn't had to say a word. "I guess maybe I'm old fashioned," Chandler went on, "but I need a wife who'll be faithful." He reached over and took my hand. "I need you, Ida Sue. You and I—well, we've got so much in common. We belong together."

He ran his hands through his hair and added, "It's going to be hard telling Jenelle. But it's got to be done."

I started feeling real hot, just thinking about it, wondering how Jenelle would take it. But Chandler said, "Don't worry. She'll understand. You'll see. She'll realize you and I were meant for each other."

Jenelle was waiting for Chandler on the front porch when we went home for Christmas that year. When she lifted her hand to wave at him, I could see that diamond on her finger sparkling in the cold winter sun.

Jenelle's smile faded as soon as she saw me get out of the car, too. "Why, Ida Sue, I didn't know you were driving back with Chandler. I thought you might take the bus—" Her voice trailed off when she got a good look at our faces. I guess what we had to tell her was written all over them because Jenelle's face went chalky white. "What is going on?" Her voice went so loud and shrill that it brought Pa to the front door in back of her.

Chandler plunged right in, though. "I'm real sorry, Jenelle, but I've found out I love Ida Sue here. I always have." He went on, saying how he wouldn't hurt her for the world, but it was surely a lot kinder just to tell her outright than to lead her on.

I was watching Jenelle's face while Chandler talked. As pale as it was before, it went slowly deep, deep red.

"I know you'll wish us well," Chandler finished. I'll never forget what he looked like at that moment. So sweet, so earnest, so sure that this was the best way to handle everything.

Jenelle looked like she might faint. She swayed on her feet, and Chandler rushed forward to catch her. Jenelle started to speak, and for a second not a sound came out of her mouth. Then it was like a wail, the wail of an animal, wounded and hurting. "No-o-o-o." That was all she said. But she flung herself at Chandler, wrapped herself around him, as if she never meant to let go.

I knew right then what was happening. I'd seen her eyes, like something was smoldering in them. "Chandler!" I yelled. "Get away from her!"

Chandler turned to me, his face registering surprise; and it seemed suddenly as if everything was happening in slow motion. Chandler made a move as if to pull away, but it was already too late. He opened his mouth to scream, and then they were both engulfed by a blue flame. A blue flame that burned and burned and burned— but didn't seem to ignite anything else. Nothing else but my sister and the man I loved.

I stood there, watching those awful flames, and it felt like a part of me was dying, too. Even from where I stood, a good three feet away, the heat was so intense I had to step back. I realized dimly that Pa had rushed outside, screaming Jenelle's name. Over and over he screamed it until it was just a whimper.

Then Pa turned to me. I can't forget what he said. "WHAT HAVE YOU DONE?" I keep hearing Pa say that. Over and over.

It's hard to believe, sitting out here, that this is where Jenelle and Chandler both died. Out here on this very porch. The floorboards aren't even singed.

Pa is still whimpering out in the kitchen. Still sniffling. I heard Pa telling everybody at the funeral and all those reporters that showed up that what happened was a terrible accident. That Jenelle didn't mean to do what she did. And that she sure didn't mean to take Chandler with her. I know that's a lie.

If Pa had seen what I saw that day, he'd know it, too. In the midst of the flames, for just a moment I could still see Jenelle's face. She was looking straight at me. And smiling that little half-smile. Until the flames rose so high, so hot, you couldn't see anything. Only her and Chandler's shapes, looking as if they were whirling in the blaze. Jenelle took Chandler from me on purpose. The only way she could, any more.

It makes me so mad to think about it. But there's no one left to be mad at any more. Nobody left to vent this awful anger on. I'm sitting out here, trying to cool down, trying to put it all into perspective. But the whole thing makes me so horribly mad. And Pa's sniffling out there keeps making me madder. And madder. I feel like I could just explode.

There Are Fantasies in the Park

by Marion M. Markham

I hear police sirens. The sound gives me a funny feeling in my tummy. I know they are going to the park where it is dark and scary.

There are fantasies in the park. I have seen them sleeping in the trees. They look so funny. Sometimes they lie on their backs, and I can see the shaggy white fur on their tummies. Sometimes they lean their chins in the places where two branches meet, and I see how large their jaws are.

The fantasy I like best sleeps up close to the tree trunk. He curves his body around the trunk and puts his legs over the branches to keep from falling. I call him Tibby. I don't know his real name. He has a long shaggy mane, and when he sleeps with his mouth open, his tongue is bright red—like blood. I think he must have asthma because sometimes he makes funny noises when he breathes, the way Daddy does.

"See, there's one," I told my sister.

"One what?" she asked, though she never stopped walking.

"A fantasy." I pointed up into the big dead oak tree. "You can see it really plain 'cause there aren't any leaves in the way. Look, Donna. Please look, just this once."

She grabbed my elbow so hard it hurt.

"I haven't time for your baby games."

When she said that, the fantasy yawned. I saw the long sharp teeth, and I was glad Donna wasn't looking. She would be scared. Then the fantasy growled softly, so softly that even I could hardly hear it. I knew the growl wasn't meant for me, because Tibby was my friend.

At first I thought the fantasies were lions asleep in the trees. I told my kindergarten teacher about the lions in the park. She told me about a Cheshire Cat that faded away, but sometimes it left its grin behind. A man named Lewis something saw it and wrote a story about it. I think she said his name was Lewis Harold. But then she said it wasn't his real name anyway, just the name he put on the story. And she said the cat was a fantasy.

The lions in the park never fade while I'm watching. Maybe Tibby would, if he knew that's what fantasies are supposed to do. Or maybe the man who wrote the story only saw the grin, even though the rest of the cat was there. Sometimes I don't notice anything but Tibby's sharp teeth. They made me shiver until I knew that he was my friend.

He always watched my sister and me through large, half-open eyes. Once he winked. But I've never seen him grin.

My sister never saw Tibby at all. At first I thought she was saying that to get me mad. She liked to make me so mad that I cried—except when Daddy was around. Donna never made me cry if Daddy was around. When we were alone, though, she teased me or pinched me until I screamed. Donna was eight years old when I was born, and she was used to playing with her toys all alone and never having to share her candy. She didn't like to share with a little brother.

I stopped talking about the lions. She didn't see them, so she thought I was making them up anyway. I don't know why she couldn't see how pretty they were—all golden in the morning sun. But she didn't. So I didn't say anything more—unless she got too close to one of them.

Tibby and the other lions didn't like my sister much. I warned her when she got near a tree where one was sleeping. Then she teased me about seeing things that weren't there. That's why I stopped calling them lions. She didn't tease if I said she was getting too near one of my fantasies. Sometimes she even laughed. I didn't like to have her laugh at me and my friends.

If we went to the park real late, the lions were gone. I don't think they went very far. They must have had a hidey-hole. It couldn't have been far away, though, because they could see when Donna made me cry. Then I would hear them howl.

She said she didn't hear them. But she always said she didn't hear Daddy if he told her to take me with her when she was going somewhere. I knew she heard him, but she didn't want me around. Sometimes I'd cry when she left me home, and then Daddy would punish her. I liked that.

Since school started, I haven't seen the lions so much. My sister had to be on the corner very early for the yellow bus, so she couldn't take me to the park in the morning. I go to afternoon kindergarten, and after school, she picked me up and we rode home together on the bus. Sometimes we got off and took the shortcut home through the park. When red and orange leaves began falling from the trees, the lions didn't sleep in them any more. I guess they were in their hidey-hole.

Once when we got off the bus, I saw Tibby and his wife with their cub hiding in the bushes along the path. Or maybe it was just shadows I saw, because it was getting dark earlier and earlier and even I was a little scared to walk that way.

Today on the bus I told my sister what my teacher said about the fantasy that faded to a grin. Donna made fun of me and said I didn't understand what my teacher meant. She's the one who didn't understand. A fantasy is something one person can see that another can't. The Cheshire Cat was a fantasy because the man with the two first names could see only the grin most of the time, and no one else ever saw any of it at all.

Why can't anyone understand that just because they don't see things the same doesn't mean those things aren't real?

As we got off the bus to walk through the park she pinched my shoulder hard and said, "I suppose your fantasy lion is waiting to pounce on us right now."

"Not us," I said. "You."

After I heard the sirens, two policemen in blue uniforms with shiny buttons came to our house. I told them about the lions with the sharp teeth and how I warned my sister not to get too close to them. I said the lions didn't like her being so mean to me. The policemen didn't understand. They kept saying they didn't know who had slashed my sister, but they were going to keep on looking. I guess they've never seen fantasies either.

One of them called me a goofy kid. I hope Tibby heard him.

My mother cried a lot and didn't like me talking about the lions. She got awful upset and sent me to my room. She even gave me a push 'cause I didn't go fast enough. Sometimes she's just like my sister.

Now that my sister is dead, I probably won't get to the park very much. I'll miss Tibby. But maybe he isn't in the park any more. Maybe the sirens scared him, and he took his wife and cub and ran away.

Lately I've noticed that there are fantasies in our house. They're sort of like spiders except that they're white and fuzzy with big red eyes that look in every direction at once. They're awful small, and sometimes even I can hardly see them. But I'll bet if I think about them hard enough they'll grow big. As big as the lions in the park. And then my mother will have to be careful about being mean to me.

I bet fantasy spiders kill mean mothers.

The Ronnie

by K. D. Wentworth

Drawing in the rich, earthy, greenhouse smell, Sarah Hopsteader bent to examine the sleeping vegetable faces nestled among the glossy leaves."Well," she said to the green-uniformed VegeTot nurseryman, "I'm sure that these Eleanor Roosevelts are quite sweet-natured, just as you say, but I was hoping for something a little more . . ." she hesitated as she caught George's scowl out of the corner of her eye ". . . a little more attractive."

The man nodded. "Perhaps you'd like to see one of our Elvises or James Deans, or . . ." He thought for a moment. "I think we still have a few nice Ronnies left in the back."

Summer sunlight gleamed down through the translucent overhead panels, turning the floating dust motes to airborne flecks of gold as she followed him down the narrow, leafy aisles. Behind her, even without looking, she could feel George spreading his disapproval over her birthday like a noxious fog.

"Listen . . ." George caught at her sleeve. "When Allison sent you that wad of cash for your birthday, she didn't mean you should just throw it away. If you're so hot for a pet, I'll buy you a god-damned goldfish."

Her mouth trembled as she smoothed a humidity-dampened strand of graying hair back into place, knowing from the experience of ten long years that it wasn't smart to go against her husband. Still, several of her friends had bought VegeTots in the last few years, and the little creatures always seemed so dear when she visited, scampering about the house on their stumpy legs, peering up at her with round green faces that always looked like someone famous, and— she sighed—when would she ever have so much money of her own again?

Kneeling down, the nurseryman pulled the dark-spotted foliage back to expose a small, leaf-shrouded form. "This is our Ronnie line, very popular with the politically minded."

Bending over, Sarah saw the dark green vegetable child stir as the muted light struck its closed eyelids, moving one tiny fist as if in protest. "It really does look like him, doesn't it?" She thought for a moment. "Does it—"

"Give speeches?" The nurseryman smiled. "No, I'm afraid that all resemblance to their famous namesakes is purely superficial. Still . . ." Releasing the leaves, he stood up. "They're affectionate and loyal, and almost no trouble at all." He punched a few numbers into the com-link on his wrist. "I'm afraid this lot is so ripe that they'll have to be composted in a few days if they don't sell."

"Composted?" Her lips pressed together, then she brushed the broad leaves aside again, studying the firm little face with its eyebrow ridges and precious dimples. Something about the cast of the eyes even reminded her a little of Myron, her long-dead first husband and Allison's father.

The small mouth opened in what could almost have been a yawn, revealing tiny green vegetable teeth, then closed again. Her heart gave a great leap, and she stood up and brushed the black soil off her jeans. "I'll take this one."

"An excellent choice." Handing her a soft green blanket, he produced a short, sharp knife and, with a single decisive motion, sliced through the thick stem growing from the little creature's head. "This is a very vigorous strain, bred out of our heartiest zucchini stock. It's sure to give you months of pleasure."

Sarah accepted the squirming bundle and held it still while he dabbed yellow dust on the dripping stump on the back of its head.

"You'll need to apply this compound every day until the stalk dries and drops off." Folding the blanket over the dark green body, he pressed a packet into her hand. "Just be sure that it gets at least two hours of real sunlight every day, not just indoor light, and has a shallow pan of water available all the time."

A great tenderness surged through her with the feel of the tiny body through the blanket, but when she looked up, George was scowling down at the small green face. Her arms tightened protectively. It's my money, she thought, then walked back to the front counter to give the clerk her birthday money, hoping that George wouldn't make her pay in a different way for defying him.

"Three hundred dollars!" George glared at the glossy-green Ronnie, playing amidst his blocks on the floor. "And I don't care if it does slightly resemble some half-wit, long-dead president, it can't even talk." He wedged his arms across his pudgy chest. "For three hundred, you could have bought one hell of a mynah bird."

Leaning back in her easy chair, Sarah let his voice run over her until it was like so much rain, all movement and no meaning. At her feet, the Ronnie fiddled with his plastic building blocks, erecting tower after tower that had no chance of standing because he stacked them so crookedly.

He was such a dear, she thought; unlike dogs and cats, he didn't even need to be housebroken and asked for nothing but a patch of sun and a bowl of water to soak his root-feet in each day. In the three months that he had been with her, he had already reached his guaranteed height of two feet with no sign of his growth slowing, obviously a superior VegeTot in every way. Sometimes she even pretended to herself that he was like the real Ronnie had been as a child, and even if it weren't true, she finally understood how lonely she had been before. The house would feel unbearably empty without him now.

"Clever Ronnie," she said as he balanced a large yellow block on top of a smaller red one. Turning his pupilless green eyes to her, the Ronnie reached out to pat her leg with curly, vinelike fingers.

Then George's voice broke back into her musings. "—smells."

"What?" Startled, she looked at his sour expression.

"I said that stupid plant is beginning to smell." He ran a hand back through his thinning gray hair, then took another long pull on the frost-beaded bottle of beer. "I think it's time you sent it back to be composted."

The plastic blocks clattered to the floor. Reaching down, she gathered the Ronnie's cool green body into her arms. "It's all right," she whispered, pressing her cheek against the soft vine tendrils that covered his little head. "Go outside and play in the yard for a while."

He clung to her wrist with persistent ropy fingers, surprising her with the strength of his grip, but when she urged him, he let go and wavered toward the terrace door, balancing precariously on his short stumpy legs. She waited until he had pushed through the little dog door, then turned to George, her face stiff. "You don't have to say such things in front of him."

"*Him?* Don't be ridiculous. That thing is nothing more than a glorified squash." He tipped his head back and blinked at the ceiling. "It probably understands a little body language, maybe the tone of your voice, nothing else."

In the silence between them, the television droned on and on, some bit of nonsense about singing toilet bowls. She took a deep breath, feeling from the heat of her cheeks how flushed her face must be. "He understands every word. You have only to look at his poor little face to see that." Her hands clenched together in her lap. "Besides, he can't be rotting. He's guaranteed for a whole year."

"Well, I don't care." George turned back to the screen. "Just keep the stinking thing away from me."

"But you said that you would take care of him when Allison has the baby." She bit her lip, trying not to think of leaving her Ronnie alone with him. "You promised."

"Well, if I promised, then I guess I'll do it, won't I?" Draining the bottle of beer, he slammed it down so hard that she jumped and bit her lip. "I want another brew."

The autumn made dull, warped mirrors of the street as the taxi brought Sarah back through town from the airport. Her trip to

Allison's had been wonderful, of course, and the baby, little Colleen, had been so dear that it had been difficult for her to leave, but Ronnie had been on her mind the whole time.

When the taxi pulled up in front of her house, she stared out at the white-painted brick for a moment. Had she really been gone only a week? The house that she had shared with George Hopsteader for ten long years looked almost unfamiliar. Then she nodded to the cab driver and got out to dash through the chill, pelting rain to the covered front porch. She should have brought an umbrella, of course, but as George was so fond of pointing out, she never remembered things like that. Shivering, she unlocked the door and stepped aside so that the cab driver could deposit her single suitcase inside the threshold. "Thank you," she said, then handed him a handful of bills and waved the change away, knowing that George would be furious if he saw her tip like that.

Leaving the heavy suitcase in the hall, she looked around as she pulled off her dripping coat. "Ronnie?" It would have been best to take him with her, but Allison and her husband lived in a highrise apartment building where he wouldn't have been able to get the sunlight that he needed. Actually, she'd come home from the airport by herself just so that she could have some time alone with him. "Ronnie, where are you?" she called again, but there was no answering whisper of little root-feet hurrying to meet her. Well, maybe he was out on the terrace, she told herself, although he usually didn't stay outside much when it was raining.

Draping her coat over a kitchen chair, she peeked out through the sliding terrace doors into the small yard where the Ronnie loved to play when it was sunny, but there was no sign of him among the potted crape myrtles and azalea bushes. Strange . . . She walked back into the master bedroom and looked in the corner where his little wicker basket stood, so close to her side of the bed that she could dangle her hand down and stroke his head in the night. No Ronnie.

Her heart beat faster as she checked her sewing room, the den, the guest bedrooms, but there was no sign of Ronnie's glossy dark green body anywhere. Where could he be?

Coming back into the kitchen, she saw the puddle that her coat had dripped on the floor, so she took it outside for a quick shake, then went to hang it in the hall closet. When she opened the door, something stirred faintly in the far corner. Frightened, she dropped the coat and stumbled back, but then she heard it again, a weak scrabbly sound—and thought that she recognized it.

Falling to her knees, she reached back behind the snow boots, feeling more than seeing, touched something dry and scratchy, and pulled Ronnie's limp, wasted body into the light. His vine-hair was dried and frazzled, his eye closed, his skin a sallow, faded yellow-green. "Ronnie?" she whispered.

The vine-like fingers moved against hers slightly, then one of them cracked and fell to the floor.

Tears welled up in her eyes. How could this have happened? How long had the poor thing been shut up without sun and water? This was all her fault; she should never have left him.

A warm tear fell on Ronnie's emaciated body and his eyes opened slightly. Water, she told herself, first he must have some water, then she would call the nursery and see what else could be done. Handling the husk-light little yellow-green body carefully, she carried him into the kitchen in the crook of her arm. Filling the sink with cool water, she immersed him up to his chin.

Her fingers shook as she punched the number for VegeTots, Unlimited, and her voice broke as she told the secretary what she needed. After a moment, the green uniformed consultant came on screen, looking doubtful as she haltingly told him the story.

"I don't know, Mrs. Hopsteader." He shook his head. "When they're that far gone, it's usually kinder to bring them in for composting and just start over. Once those interior veins start cracking from lack of moisture, there's not really much that can be done."

Her fingers tightened on the kitchen counter as she stared back at his sympathetic young face. "Composting?" Horror rose up in her throat like a river in dark angry flood. "My Ronnie? You can't be serious. He's only four months old."

"They only last a full year if you take proper care of them." He looked grim. "And being without sun for that long, it could have permanent neural damage. You don't want it to suffer, do you?"

"N—" The answer stuck somewhere in her chest, fighting to remain unsaid.

"Well, let us know if we can be of any assistance."

She only nodded, afraid she would cry if she tried to say more, then punched the connection off. The Ronnie stirred in the sink, making tiny splashes with one of his little arms. Dabbing fiercely at the hot, ready tears that threatened to overwhelm her, she nodded down at his yellow-green face. "Don't worry," she whispered, "it's going to be all right."

As she stroked his poor withered vine-hair, her mind raced ahead, trying to think of what she would say to George when he came home. How could he believe that he could explain this?

Three hours later, she still didn't know what to say to him as she watched Ronnie through the plate glass window, propped up against a crape myrtle out on the rain-drenched terrace, soaking up what little light penetrated through the dull clouds.

She heard the front door open, then close, but she didn't move, indeed felt that she couldn't move if her life depended upon it.

"I thought you were going to call me when you got in." George's voice rumbled through the house like sullen thunder. "So, how are Allison and the brat anyway?"

She opened her mouth to answer, but the stupid, useless tears started as they always did at times like this when she wanted so desperately to be calm and reasonable, adult and secure. She took in a great wrenching breath. "The baby is fine, but . . ." She broke off then, her voice wavering, asked, "Why?"

"Why what?"

She heard the thump of his coat thrown over the counter, then the whish of the refrigerator door opening as he rummaged for the first of his daily six-pack, and finally the tortured creak of the easy chair as he plopped into it. She made herself turn around. "Why— Ronnie?"

"You mean that damn plant?" Twisting the cap off the bottle of beer, he shook the paper open and settled back to read it, one arm tucked behind his head and his black sock feet pointing toward the ceiling. "Haven't seen it for days."

"You said that you'd take care of him." The words almost choked her. "You promised."

"Can't very well water the little bastard if I can't find it." He turned the page.

"You locked him in the closet." Her throat closed up hard and tight. "You left him there for days without water or sun."

He met her eyes briefly over the top of the paper. "So that's where it got to." The paper came up again with a rustle. "I wondered."

"You did it on purpose!"

Then he was up out of the depths of the easy chair faster than any man as soft and lethargic as George Hopsteader had a right to be, his forearm catching her hard across the throat, crushing her back against the cold, smooth glass. "This is *my* house," he said into her face, his breath heavy with beer. "My house that *I* have gone out and worked like a slave for. The minute I'm ready to get rid of that damn squash, I'll put it down the garbage disposal one inch at a time."

He leaned harder against her windpipe until she could think of nothing but the brittleness of the rain-spattered glass beneath her, which could give way any second under their combined weights and send her flying out onto the terrace in a pile of gleaming shards, any of which could slice her throat almost as an afterthought. "George— please," she wheezed as her vision fuzzed and his voice faded to a distant roaring in her ears. "Let me—please—"

Abruptly, he released her, returning to his seat as though nothing had ever happened. "I'm hungry." His voice was gruff. "When's dinner?"

She caught herself against the window, trying to blink the grayness away, fighting to keep from falling to her knees. Outside, the chill autumn rain drummed against the window, streaming down it in rivulets, cascading over the Ronnie's head and outstretched arms as he pressed up against the glass, watching her with staring yellow-green eyes.

* * *

After she got her nerves under control, she slipped out the front door and quietly brought Ronnie in from the rain, sneaking him into the guest bathroom where she stood him in the tub and dried him off with a soft thick towel. Her hands trembled as she heard George clatter through the refrigerator after yet another beer.

How had it come to this, she wondered, lifting Ronnie out and setting him on the tiled floor. Little by little, she had gotten so used to George's casual cruelties and drinking that she sometimes forgot she'd once had another, more civilized life—before her soft-spoken first husband had died.

Taking Ronnie's withered little arm, she peered into the shadow-filled hall, but there was no sign of George. Picking up the Ronnie, she pressed his wasted body to her as she hurried into the master bedroom, treading as quietly as she could.

As soon as they entered the familiar room, the VegeTot wriggled out of her grasp and wobbled over to his basket, still unsteady from dehydration and lack of sunlight. "Oh, Ronnie." She sighed, then tucked him into the soft green blanket in which she'd first brought him home. His unblinking eyes followed her every move, speaking his misery as clearly as if he could talk. Tenderly, she touched the few remaining broken bits of vine-hair that still clung stubbornly to his head.

"When the hell are we gonna get some dinner around here?" George bellowed suddenly from the den.

Her stomach gave a sickening wrench. Dinner . . . dear God, she hadn't given it a thought since that heart-stopping moment when she'd found Ronnie shut up in the closet. "In—in a minute." Gathering the wicker basket into her arms, she hurried toward the door, intending to hide Ronnie in her sewing room until tomorrow.

Suddenly the doorway filled with George's bulk. "Here." He thrust something large and metallic at her. "I got tired of waiting, so I started dinner for you."

Numbly, she stared at the huge panful of steaming water dangling from his hand, sloshing over at the edges to soak into the rug in dark splotches at her feet. "I—don't understand."

"Well . . ." He leered crookedly at her, his face garish in the half-light from the hall. "We are having *squash* for dinner, aren't we?"

Then a belly laugh rolled out of him, filling the room until she thought she would scream.

She tried to avoid his eyes. "Please, George, if you'll just let me by, I'll get busy on dinner."

" 'Please, George,' " he mimicked her in a high falsetto. " 'Please, George!' " He lurched toward her and splashed her shoe with scalding water.

She bit her tongue to keep from crying out as the pain ate through her foot. *If he spilled that on Ronnie* . . . "George," she said, fighting to control her voice, "I'm sorry about dinner. Let me by."

"Hurry up, I'm hungry." Laughing again, he swung the pan toward her, slopping more boiling hot water over her legs. "Or would you rather fry the little bastard?"

How many times had the two of them done this? Lightheaded from the pain, she stared at his smirk; they had played this scene a thousand times in a thousand different ways, her pleading while he laughed in her face, hurting her in any way that amused him, then pretending the next day that none of it mattered.

"Stop it!" Her heart thumping so hard that she thought it would escape her chest, she put Ronnie's basket on the floor and hastily shoved it out of sight underneath the bed. "I'm not going to live like this any more."

"Is that so?" He wiped one handback across his face, then set the kettle on the floor and blinked unsteadily at her. "What are you going to do, move?" For some reason, the notion struck him as funny, and he began to snicker again.

She heard a rustling behind her as something husk-like moved. Her heart lurched. "Ronnie, no!"

"I keep telling you that the stupid thing doesn't understand a word you say." George shoved her out of the way and made a grab as the little green face peered out from under the bed.

Her face went ice cold. "Don't touch him!"

George paused, his face hidden in shadows. "Don't worry, darling, you're next." He giggled. "Here, Ronnie, here, you little bastard." He staggered forward, groping under the bed.

"No." She seized his arm. "Go sleep it off."

With an almost casual flick of his wrist, he threw her back against the heavy wooden dresser, cracking her head so hard that the room flickered around her—black—white—black—like a photographic negative. She tried to crawl after him, but her arms and legs seemed to be somewhere else, and it was all she could do to hold onto consciousness.

There was a sudden flurry over by the bed; then she heard George exclaim, "Gotcha!"

Blinking hard, Sarah thought she saw him raise something up in the air with one hand.

"Here's hoping that you make a better dinner than you did a president." He turned around on his knees, reaching for the pan of boiling water.

No, she tried to whisper, but her mouth was a million miles away and none of this could possibly be real.

George laughed again, then stopped abruptly. Hazily, she saw him stagger upright, then tear at his face, which seemed suddenly bulky.

Ronnie! She realized that her lips had moved, but had produced no sound. Why was it that George couldn't bear someone else to love her, even if it was only a poor VegeTot?

George collapsed to his knees, croaking while his hands clawed and beat at something that had fastened itself over his mouth and nose. Her vision kept losing focus as she summoned every remaining bit of strength to reach out a trembling hand and brush the stubble of Ronnie's broken vine-hair. Then the room and Ronnie and George all faded away into a soundless blackness.

"I don't think you should go back to that place." Allison's face was porcelain-pale as she folded the last nightgown and packed it into Sarah's suitcase. "I want you to move to Topeka and watch your new granddaughter grow up. There're some beautiful retirement condos only a few miles from our complex. You'd like that, wouldn't you?"

Opening the blind, Sarah looked down at the little park across the street from the hospital. Bright light still hurt her eyes, but it soothed her to watch the tiny figures of children at play, so happy and carefree . . . almost like Ronnie.

"I . . . really don't . . ." each word came slowly, as though imported from some faraway country ". . . don't know what I want." Her fingers sought the tender back of her head where the doctors had taken twenty stitches. "I still have trouble remembering what happened."

"And you ought to leave it that way." Taking her arm, Allison guided her back to the hospital bed.

Feeling a little dizzy, she lay back against the crisp white pillow. "You're sure . . ." she mumbled. "You're sure that he's . . . gone?"

"The funeral was two days ago." Strain lines reappeared around her daughter's eyes. "You remember that, don't you?"

"No, not . . . him." She turned her cheek to the freshly-laundered pillowcase and closed her eyes, trying hard to compose her thoughts. "No, I meant, you're sure that—Ronnie—*Ronnie* is really gone?"

Silence filtered through the room for a long moment. "Well, it was pretty broken up. The police took what was left away with the—body, but . . ." She hesitated. "When I went back to pack your clothes, I did find something."

Opening her eyes, Sarah watched her daughter put one hand in her pocket and then draw it out again. In the middle of her outstretched hand lay two slim golden ovoids. She blinked hard to make sure that her shaky vision wasn't betraying her again. No . . . she reached out and took them from the palm of Allison's hand, feeling the smoothness of . . . seeds . . . *squash* seeds.

Watching her closely, Allison sat down beside her and touched her face. "Mom, are you all right?"

Closing her fingers around the firm cool shapes, Sarah met her daughter's eyes. "Do you suppose that those condos have—gardens?"

The Canterville Ghost

by Oscar Wilde

When Mr. Hiram B. Otis, the American minister, bought Canterville Chase, everyone told him he was doing a very foolish thing, as there was no doubt at all that the place was haunted. Indeed, Lord Canterville himself, who was a man of the most punctilious honor, had felt it his duty to mention the fact to Mr. Otis, when they came to discuss terms.

"We have not cared to live in the place ourselves," said Lord Canterville, "since my grand-aunt, the Dowager Duchess of Bolton, was frightened into a fit, from which she never really recovered, by two skeleton hands being placed on her shoulders as she was dressing for dinner, and I feel bound to tell you, Mr. Otis, that the ghost has been seen by several living members of my family, as well as by the rector of the parish, the Reverend Augustus Dampier, who is a fellow of King's College, Cambridge. After the unfortunate accident to the duchess, none of our younger servants would stay with us, and Lady Canterville often got very little sleep at night, in consequence of the mysterious noises that came from the corridor and the library."

"My lord," answered the minister, "I will take the furniture and the ghost at a valuation. I come from a modern country, where we have everything that money can buy; and with all our spry young fellows painting the Old World red, and carrying off your best actresses and prima donnas, I reckon that if there were such a thing as a ghost in Europe, we'd have it at home in a very short time in one of our public museums, or on the road as a show."

"I fear that the ghost exists," said Lord Canterville, smiling, "though it may have resisted the overtures of your enterprising impresarios. It has been well known for three centuries, since 1584, in fact, and always makes its appearance before the death of any member of our family."

"Well, so does the family doctor for that matter, Lord Canterville. But there is no such thing, sir, as a ghost, and I guess the laws of nature are not going to be suspended for the British aristocracy."

"You are certainly very natural in America," answered Lord Canterville, who did not quite understand Mr. Otis's last observation, "and if you don't mind a ghost in the house, it is all right. Only you must remember I warned you."

A few weeks after this, the purchase was completed, and at the close of the season the minister and his family went down to Canterville Chase. Mrs. Otis, who, as Miss Lucretia R. Tappan, of West 53rd Street, had been a celebrated New York belle, was now a very handsome middle-aged woman, with fine eyes, and a superb profile. Many American ladies on leaving their native land adopt an appearance of chronic ill health, under the impression that it is a form of European refinement, but Mrs. Otis had never fallen into this error. She had a magnificent constitution, and a really wonderful amount of animal spirits. Indeed, in many respects, she was quite English, and was an excellent example of the fact that we have really everything in common with America nowadays, except, of course, language. Her eldest son, christened Washington by his parents in a moment of patriotism, which he never ceased to regret, was a fairhaired, rather goodlooking young man, who had qualified himself for American diplomacy by leading the German at the Newport Casino for three successive seasons, and even in London was well known as an excellent dancer. Gardenias and the peerage were his only weaknesses. Otherwise he was extremely sensible. Miss Virginia E. Otis was a little girl of fifteen, lithe, and lovely as a fawn, and with a fine freedom in her large blue eyes. She was a wonderful amazon, and had once raced old Lord Bilton on her pony twice round the park, winning by a length and a half, just in front of Achilles' statue, to the huge delight of the young Duke of Cheshire, who proposed to her on the spot, and was sent back to Eton that very night by his guardians, in floods of tears. After Virginia came the twins, who were usually called The Stars and Stripes, as they were always getting swished. They were delightful boys, and with the exception of the worthy minister the only true republicans of the family.

As Canterville Chase is seven miles from Ascot, the nearest railway station, Mr. Otis had telegraphed for a waggonette to meet them, and they started on their drive in high spirits. It was a lovely July evening, and the air was delicate with the scent of the pine-woods. Now and then they heard a wood pigeon brooding over its own sweet voice, or saw, deep in the rustling fern, the burnished breast of the pheasant. Little squirrels peered at them from the beech trees as they went by, and the rabbits scudded away through the brushwood and over the mossy knolls, with their tails in the air. As they entered the avenue of Canterville Chase, however, the sky became suddenly overcast with clouds, a curious stillness seemed to hold the atmosphere, a great flight of rooks passed silently over their heads, and, before they reached the house, some big drops of rain had fallen.

Standing on the steps to receive them was an old woman, neatly dressed in black silk, with a white cap and apron. This was Mrs. Umney, the housekeeper, whom Mrs. Otis, at Lady Canterville's earnest request, had consented to keep on in her former position. She made them each a low curtsey as they alighted, and said in a quaint, old-fashioned manner, "I bid you welcome to Canterville Chase." Following her, they passed through the fine Tudor hall into the library, a long, low room, panelled in black oak, at the end of which was a large stained-glass window. Here they found tea laid out for them, and, after taking off their wraps, they sat down and began to look round, while Mrs. Umney waited on them.

Suddenly Mrs. Otis caught sight of a dull red stain on the floor just by the fireplace and, quite unconscious of what it really signified, said to Mrs. Umney, "I am afraid something has been spilt there."

"Yes, madam," replied the old housekeeper in a low voice, "blood has been spilt on that spot."

"How horrid," cried Mrs. Otis, "I don't at all care for bloodstains in a sitting room. It must be removed at once."

The old woman smiled, and answered in the same low, mysterious voice, "It is the blood of Lady Eleanore de Canterville, who was murdered on that very spot by her own husband, Sir Simon de Canterville, in 1575. Sir Simon survived her nine years, and disappeared suddenly under very mysterious circumstances. His body has never been discovered, but his guilty spirit still haunts the Chase. The bloodstain has been much admired by tourists and others, and cannot be removed."

"That is all nonsense," cried Washington Otis; "Pinkerton's Champion Stain Remover and Paragon Detergent will clean it up in no time," and before the terrified housekeeper could interfere he had fallen upon his knees, and was rapidly scouring the floor with a small stick of what looked like a black cosmetic. In a few moments no trace of the bloodstain could be seen.

"I knew Pinkerton would do it," he exclaimed triumphantly, as he looked round at his admiring family; but no sooner had he said these words than a terrible flash of lightning lit up the somber room, and a fearful peal of thunder made them all start to their feet, and Mrs. Umney fainted.

"What a monstrous climate!" said the American minister calmly, as he lit a long cheroot. "I guess the old country is so overpopulated that they have not enough decent weather for everybody. I have always been of opinion that emigration is the only thing for England."

"My dear Hiram," cried Mrs. Otis, "what can we do with a woman who faints?"

"Charge it to her like breakages," answered the minister; "she won't faint after that"; and in a few moments Mrs. Umney certainly came to. There was no doubt, however, that she was extremely upset, and she sternly warned Mr. Otis to beware of some trouble coming to the house.

"I have seen things with my own eyes, sir," she said, "that would make any Christian's hair stand on end, and many and many a night I have not closed my eyes in sleep for the awful things that are done here." Mr. Otis, however, and his wife warmly assured the honest soul that they were not afraid of ghosts, and, after invoking the blessings of Providence on her new master and mistress, and making arrangements for an increase of salary, the old housekeeper tottered off to her own room.

2

The storm raged fiercely all that night, but nothing of particular note occurred. The next morning, however, when they came down to breakfast, they found the terrible stain of blood once again on the floor. "I don't think it can be the fault of the Paragon Detergent," said Washington, "for I have tried it with everything. It must be the ghost." He accordingly rubbed out the stain a second time, but the second morning it appeared again. The third morning also it was there, though the library had been locked up at night by Mr. Otis himself, and the key carried upstairs. The whole family were now quite interested; Mr. Otis began to suspect that he had been too dogmatic in his denial of the existence of ghosts, Mrs. Otis expressed her intention of joining the Psychical Society, and Washington prepared a long letter to Messrs. Myers and Podmore on the subject of the Permanence of Sanguineous Stains when connected with crime. That night all doubts about the objective existence of phantasmata were removed forever.

The day had been warm and sunny; and, in the cool of the evening, the whole family went out for a drive. They did not return home till nine o'clock, when they had a light supper. The conversation in no way turned upon ghosts, so there were not even those primary conditions of receptive expectation which so often precede the presentation of psychical phenomena. The subjects discussed, as I have since learned from Mr. Otis, were merely such as form the ordinary conversation of cultured Americans of the better class, such as the immense superiority of Miss Fanny Davenport over Sarah Bernhardt as an actress; the difficulty of obtaining green corn, buckwheat cakes, and hominy, even in the best English houses; the importance of Boston in the development of the world soul; the advantages of the baggage check system in railway travelling; and the sweetness of the New York accent as compared to the London drawl. No mention at all was made of the supernatural, nor was Sir Simon de Canterville alluded to in any way. At eleven o'clock the family retired, and by half past all the lights were out. Some time after, Mr. Otis was awakened by a curious noise in the corridor, outside his room. It sounded like the clank of metal, and seemed to be coming nearer every moment. He got up at once, struck a match, and looked at the time. It was exactly one o'clock. He was quite calm, and felt his pulse, which was not at all feverish. The strange noise still continued, and with it he heard distinctly the sound of footsteps. He put on his slippers, took a small oblong vial out of his dressing case, and opened the door. Right in front of him he saw, in the wan moonlight, an old man of terrible aspect. His eyes were as red as burning coals; long grey hair fell over his shoulders in matted coils; his garments, which were of antique cut, were soiled and ragged, and from his wrists and ankles hung heavy manacles and rusty gyves.

"My dear sir," said Mr. Otis, "I really must insist on your oiling those chains, and have brought you for that purpose a small bottle of the Tammany Rising Sun Lubricator. It is said to be completely efficacious upon one application, and there are several testimonials to that effect on the wrapper from some of our most eminent native divines. I shall leave it here for you by the bedroom candles, and will be happy to supply you with more should you require it." With these words the United States minister laid the bottle down on a marble table, and, closing his door, retired to rest.

For a moment the Canterville ghost stood quite motionless in natural indignation; then, dashing the bottle violently upon the polished floor, he fled down the corridor, uttering hollow groans, and emitting a ghastly green light. Just, however, as he reached the top of the great oak staircase, a door was flung open, two little white-robed figures appeared, and a large pillow whizzed past his head! There was evidently no time to be lost, so, hastily adopting the Fourth Dimension of Space as a means of escape, he vanished through the wainscoting, and the house became quite quiet.

On reaching a small secret chamber in the left wing, he leaned up against a moonbeam to recover his breath, and began to try and realize his position. Never, in a brilliant and uninterrupted career of

three hundred years, had he been so grossly insulted. He thought of
the dowager duchess, whom he had frightened into a fit as she stood
before the glass in her lace and diamonds; of the four housemaids,
who had gone off into hysterics when he merely grinned at them
through the curtains of one of the spare bedrooms; of the rector of
the parish, whose candle he had blown out as he was coming late
one night from the library, and who had been under the care of Sir
William Gull ever since, a perfect martyr to nervous disorders; and
of old Madame de Tremouillac, who, having wakened up one morning early and seen a skeleton seated in an armchair by the fire
reading her diary, had been confined to her bed for six weeks with
an attack of brain fever, and, on her recovery, had become recon-
ciled to the Church, and had broken off her connection with that
notorious skeptic Monsieur de Voltaire. He remembered the terrible night when the wicked Lord Canterville was found choking in
his dressing room, with the knave of diamonds halfway down his
throat, and confessed, just before he died, that he had cheated
Charles James Fox out of fifty thousand pounds at Crockford's by
means of that very card, and swore that the ghost had made him
swallow it. All his great achievements came back to him again, from
the butler who had shot himself in the pantry because he had seen a
green hand tapping at the window pane, to the beautiful Lady
Stutfield, who was always obliged to wear a black velvet band round
her throat to hide the mark of five fingers burnt upon her white skin,
and who drowned herself at last in the carp pond at the end of the
King's Walk. With the enthusiastic egotism of the true artist he went
over his most celebrated performances, and smiled bitterly to himself as he recalled to mind his last appearance as "Red Ruben, or the
Strangled Babe," his *début* as "Gaunt Gideon, the Bloodsucker of
Bexley Moor," and the *furore* he had excited one lovely June evening by merely playing ninepins with his own bones upon the lawn-
tennis ground. And after all this, some wretched modern Americans
were to come and offer him the Rising Sun Lubricator, and throw
pillows at his head! It was quite unbearable. Besides, no ghosts in
history had ever been treated in this manner. Accordingly, he determined to have vengeance, and remained till daylight in an attitude
of deep thought.

3

The next morning when the Otis family met at breakfast, they discussed the ghost at some length. The United States minister was naturally a little annoyed to find that his present had not been accepted. "I have no wish," he said, "to do the ghost any personal injury, and I must say that, considering the length of time he has been in the house, I don't think it is at all polite to throw pillows at him"—a very just remark, at which, I am sorry to say, the twins burst into shouts of laughter. "Upon the other hand," he continued, "if he really declines to use the Rising Sun Lubricator, we shall have to take his chains from him. It would be quite impossible to sleep, with such a noise going on outside the bedrooms."

For the rest of the week, however, they were undisturbed, the only thing that excited any attention being the continual renewal of the bloodstain on the library floor. This certainly was very strange, as the door was always locked at night by Mr. Otis, and the windows kept closely barred. The chameleon-like color, also, of the stain excited a good deal of comment. Some mornings it was a dull (almost Indian) red, then it would be vermilion, then a rich purple, and once when they came down for family prayers, according to the simple rites of the Free American Reformed Episcopalian Church, they found it a bright emerald green. These kaleidoscopic changes naturally amused the party very much, and bets on the subject were freely made every evening. The only person who did not enter into the joke was little Virginia, who, for some unexplained reason, was always a good deal distressed at the sight of the bloodstain, and very nearly cried the morning it was emerald green.

The second appearance of the ghost was on Sunday night. Shortly after they had gone to bed they were suddenly alarmed by a fearful crash in the hall. Rushing downstairs, they found that a large suit of old armor had become detached from its stand, and had fallen on the stone floor, while, seated in a high-backed chair, was the Canterville ghost, rubbing his knees with an expression of acute agony on his face. The twins, having brought their peashooters with them, at once discharged two pellets on him, with that accuracy of aim which can only be attained by long and careful practice on a writing master, while the United States minister covered him with his revolver, and called upon him, in accordance with Californian etiquette, to hold up his hands! The ghost started up with a wild shriek of rage, and swept through them like a mist, extinguishing Washington Otis's candle as he passed, and so leaving them all in total darkness. On reaching the top of the staircase he recovered himself, and determined to give his celebrated peal of demoniac laughter. This he had on more than one occasion found extremely useful. It was said to have turned Lord Raker's wig grey in a single night, and had certainly made three of Lady Canterville's French governesses give warning before their month was up. He accordingly laughed his most horrible laugh, till the old vaulted roof rang and rang again, but hardly had the fearful echo died away when a door opened, and Mrs. Otis came out in a light blue dressing gown. "I am afraid you are far from well," she said, "and have brought you a bottle of Dr. Dobell's tincture. If it is indigestion, you will find it a most excellent remedy." The ghost glared at her in fury, and began at once to make preparations for turning himself into a large black dog, an accomplishment for which he was justly renowned, and to which the family doctor always attributed the permanent idiocy of Lord Canterville's uncle, the Honorable Thomas Horton. The sound of approaching footsteps, however, made him hesitate in his fell purpose, so he contented himself with becoming faintly phosphorescent, and vanished with a deep churchyard groan, just as the twins had come up to him.

On reaching his room he entirely broke down, and became a prey to the most violent agitation. The vulgarity of the twins, and the gross materialism of Mrs. Otis, were naturally extremely annoying, but what really distressed him most was that he had been unable to wear the suit of mail. He had hoped that even modern Americans would be thrilled by the sight of a Spectre in Armor, if for no more sensible reason, at least out of respect for their national poet Longfellow, over whose graceful and attractive poetry he himself had whiled away many a weary hour when the Cantervilles were up in town. Besides, it was his own suit. He had worn it with success at the Kenilworth tournament, and had been highly complimented on it by no less a person than the Virgin Queen herself. Yet when he had put it on, he had been completely overpowered by the weight of the huge breastplate and steel casque, and had fallen heavily on the stone pavement, barking both his knees severely, and bruising the knuckles of his right hand.

For some days after this he was extremely ill, and hardly stirred out of his room at all, except to keep the bloodstain in proper repair. However, by taking great care of himself, he recovered, and resolved to make a third attempt to frighten the United States minister and his family. He selected Friday, the seventeenth of August, for his appearance, and spent most of that day in looking over his wardrobe, ultimately deciding in favor of a large slouched hat with a red feather, a winding sheet frilled at the wrists and neck, and a rusty dagger. Towards evening a violent storm of rain came on, and the wind was so high that all the windows and doors in the old house shook and rattled. In fact, it was just such weather as he loved. His plan of action was this. He was to make his way quietly to Washington Otis's room, gibber at him from the foot of the bed, and stab himself three times in the throat to the sound of slow music. He bore Washington a special grudge, being quite aware that it was he who was in the habit of removing the famous Canterville bloodstain, by means of Pinkerton's Paragon Detergent. Having reduced the reckless and foolhardy youth to a condition of abject terror, he was then to proceed to the room occupied by the United States minister and his wife, and there to place a clammy hand on Mrs. Otis's forehead, while he hissed into her trembling husband's ear the awful secrets of the charnel house. With regard to little Virginia, he had not quite made up his mind. She had never insulted him in any way, and was pretty and gentle. A few hollow groans from the wardrobe, he thought, would be more than sufficient, or, if that failed to wake her, he might grabble at the counterpane with palsy-twitching fingers. As for the twins, he was quite determined to teach them a lesson. The first thing to be done was, of course, to sit upon their chests, so as to produce the stifling sensation of nightmare. Then, as their beds were quite close to each other, to stand between them in the form of a green, icy-cold corpse, till they became paralyzed with fear, and finally, to throw off the winding sheet, and crawl around the room, with white bleached bones and

one rolling eyeball, in the character of "Dumb Daniel, or the Sui-
cide's Skeleton," a *rôle* in which he had on more than one occasion
produced a great effect, and which he considered quite equal to his
famous part of "Martin the Maniac, or the Masked Mystery."

At half past ten he heard the family going to bed. For some time
he was disturbed by wild shrieks of laughter from the twins, who,
with the lighthearted gaiety of schoolboys, were evidently amusing
themselves before they retired to rest, but at a quarter past eleven
all was still, and, as midnight sounded, he sallied forth. The owl
beat against the window panes, the raven croaked from the old yew
tree, and the wind wandered moaning around the house like a lost
soul; but the Otis family slept unconscious of their doom, and high
above the rain and storm he could hear the steady snoring of the
minister for the United States. He stepped stealthily out of the
wainscoting, with an evil smile on his cruel, wrinkled mouth, and
the moon hid her face in a cloud as he stole past the great oriel
window, where his own arms and those of his murdered wife were
blazoned in azure and gold. On and on he glided, like an evil
shadow, the very darkness seeming to loathe him as he passed.
Once he thought he heard something call, and stopped; but it was
only the baying of a dog from the Red Farm, and he went on,
muttering strange sixteenth century curses, and ever and anon
brandishing the rusty dagger in the midnight air. Finally he reached
the corner of the passage that led to luckless Washington's room. For
a moment he paused there, the wind blowing his long grey locks
about his head, and twisting into grotesque and fantastic folds the
nameless horror of the dead man's shroud. Then the clock struck the
quarter, and he felt the time was come. He chuckled to himself, and
turned the corner; but no sooner had he done so, than, with a
piteous wail of terror, he fell back, and hid his blanched face in his
long, bony hands. Right in front of him was standing a horrible
spectre, motionless as a carven image, and monstrous as a madman's
dream! Its head was bald and burnished; its face round, and fat, and
white; and hideous laughter seemed to have writhed its features
into an eternal grin. From the eyes streamed rays of scarlet light,
the mouth was a wide well of fire, and a hideous garment, like to his
own, swathed with its silent snows the Titan form. On its breast was

a placard with strange writing in antique characters, some scroll of shame it seemed, some record of wild sins, some awful calendar of crime, and, with its right hand, it bore aloft a falchion of gleaming steel.

Never having seen a ghost before, he naturally was terribly frightened, and, after a second hasty glance at the awful phantom, he fled back to his room, tripping up in his long winding sheet as he sped down the corridor, and finally dropping the rusty dagger into the minister's jack-boots, where it was found in the morning by the butler. Once in the privacy of his own apartment, he flung himself down on a small pallet bed, and hid his face under the clothes. After a time, however, the brave old Canterville spirit asserted itself, and he determined to go and speak to the other ghost as soon as it was daylight. Accordingly, just as the dawn was touching the hills with silver, he returned towards the spot where he had first laid eyes on the grisly phantom, feeling that, after all, two ghosts were better than one, and that, by the aid of his new friend, he might safely grapple with the twins. On reaching the spot, however, a terrible sight met his gaze. Something had evidently happened to the spectre, for the light had entirely faded from its hollow eyes, the gleaming falchion had fallen from its hand, and it was leaning up against the wall in a strained and uncomfortable attitude. He rushed forward and seized it in his arms, when, to his horror, the head slipped off and rolled on the floor, the body assumed a recumbent posture, and he found himself clasping a white dimity bedcurtain, with a sweeping brush, a kitchen cleaver, and a hollow turnip lying at his feet! Unable to understand this curious transformation, he clutched the placard with feverish haste, and there, in the grey morning light, he read these fearful words:

> **ÐE OTIS GHOSTE**
> De Onlie True and Originale Spook.
> Beware of De Imitations.
> All others are Counterfeite.

The whole thing flashed across him. He had been tricked, foiled, and outwitted! The old Canterville look came into his eyes; he ground his toothless gums together; and, raising his withered hands high above his head, swore, according to the picturesque phraseology of the antique school, that when Chanticleer had sounded twice his merry horn, deeds of blood would be wrought, and Murder walk abroad with silent feet.

Hardly had he finished this awful oath when, from the red tiled roof of a distant homestead, a cock crew. He laughed a long, low, bitter laugh, and waited. Hour after hour he waited, but the cock, for some strange reason, did not crow again. Finally, at half past seven, the arrival of the housemaids made him give up his fearful vigil, and he stalked back to his room, thinking of his vain hope and baffled purpose. There he consulted several books of ancient chivalry, of which he was exceedingly fond, and found that, on every occasion on which his oath had been used, Chanticleer had always crowed a second time. "Perdition seize the naughty fowl," he muttered, "I have seen the day when, with my stout spear, I would have run him through the gorge, and made him crow for me an 'twere in death!" He then retired to a comfortable lead coffin, and stayed there till evening.

4

The next day the ghost was very weak and tired. The terrible excitement of the last four weeks was beginning to have its effect. His nerves were completely shattered, and he started at the slightest noise. For five days he kept his room, and at last made up his mind to give up the point of the bloodstain on the library floor. If the Otis family did not want it, they clearly did not deserve it. They were evidently people on a low, material plane of existence, and quite incapable of appreciating the symbolic value of sensuous phenomena. The question of phantasmic apparitions, and the development of astral bodies, was of course quite a different matter, and really not under his control. It was his solemn duty to appear in the corridor once a week, and to gibber from the large oriel window on the first and third Wednesday in every month, and he did not see how he could honorably escape from his obligations. It is quite true that his life had been very evil, but, upon the other hand, he was most conscientious in all things connected with the supernatural. For the next three Saturdays, accordingly, he traversed the corridor as usual between midnight and three o'clock, taking every possible precaution against being either heard or seen. He removed his boots, trod as lightly as possible on the old worm-eaten boards, wore a large black velvet cloak, and was careful to use the Rising Sun Lubricator for oiling his chains. I am bound to acknowledge that it was with a good deal of difficulty that he brought himself to adopt this last mode of protection. However, one night, while the family were at dinner, he slipped into Mr. Otis's bedroom and carried off the bottle. He felt a little humiliated at first, but afterwards was sensible enough to see that there was a great deal to be said for the invention, and, to a certain degree, it served his purpose. Still, in spite of everything, he was not left unmolested. Strings were continually being stretched across the corridor, over which he tripped in the dark, and on one occasion, while dressed for the part of "Black Isaac, or the Huntsman of Hogley Woods," he met with a severe fall, through treading on a butter-slide, which the twins had constructed from the entrance of the Tapestry Chamber to the top of the oak staircase. This last insult so enraged him that he resolved to assert his dignity, and determined to visit the insolent young Etonians the next night in his celebrated character of "Reckless Rupert, or the Headless Earl."

He had not appeared in this disguise for more than seventy years; in fact, not since he had so frightened pretty Lady Barbara Modish by means of it that she suddenly broke off her engagement with the present Lord Canterville's grandfather, and ran away to Gretna Green with handsome Jack Castleton, declaring that nothing in the world would induce her to marry into a family that allowed such a horrible phantom to walk up and down the terrace at twilight. Poor Jack was afterwards shot in a duel by Lord Canterville on Wandsworth Common, and Lady Barbara died of a broken heart at Tunbridge Wells before the year was out, so, in every way, it had been a great success. It was, however, an extremely difficult "make-up," if I may use such a theatrical expression in connection with one of the greatest mysteries of the supernatural, or, to employ a more scientific term, the high-natural world, and it took him fully three hours to make his preparations. At last everything was ready, and he was very pleased with his appearance. The big leather riding boots that went with the dress were just a little too large for him, and he could only find one of the two horse-pistols, but, on the whole, he was quite satisfied, and at a quarter past one he glided out of the wainscoting and crept down the corridor. On reaching the room occupied by the twins, which I should mention was called the Blue Bed Chamber, on account of the color of its hangings, he found the door ajar. Wishing to make an effective entrance, he flung it wide open, when a heavy jug of water fell right down on him, wetting him to the skin, and just missing his left shoulder by a couple of inches. At the same moment he heard stifled shrieks of laughter proceeding from the four-post bed. The shock to his nervous system was so great that he fled back to his room as hard as he could go, and the next day he was laid up with a severe cold. The only thing that at all consoled him in the whole affair was the fact that he had not brought his head with him, for, had he done so, the consequences might have been very serious.

He now gave up all hope of ever frightening this rude American family, and contented himself, as a rule, with creeping about the passages in list slippers, with a thick red muffler round his throat for fear of drafts, and a small arquebus, in case he should be attacked by the twins. The final blow he received occurred on the nineteenth of September. He had gone downstairs to the great entrance hall, feeling sure that there, at any rate, he would be quite unmolested, and was amusing himself by making satirical remarks on the large Saroni photographs of the United States minister and his wife, which had now taken the place of the Canterville family pictures. He was simply but neatly clad in a long shroud, spotted with churchyard mold, had tied up his jaw with a strip of yellow linen, and carried a small lantern and a sexton's spade. In fact, he was dressed for the character of "Jonas the Graveless, or the Corpse-Snatcher of Chertsey Barn," one of his most remarkable impersonations, and one which the Cantervilles had every reason to remember, as it was the real origin of their quarrel with their neighbor,

Lord Rufford. It was about a quarter past two o'clock in the morning, and, as far as he could ascertain, no one was stirring. As he was strolling towards the library, however, to see if there were any traces left of the bloodstain, suddenly there leaped out on him from a dark corner two figures, who waved their arms wildly above their heads, and shrieked out "BOO!" in his ear.

Seized with a panic, which, under the circumstances, was only natural, he rushed for the staircase, but found Washington Otis waiting for him there with the big garden syringe; and being thus hemmed in by his enemies on every side, and driven almost to bay, he vanished into the great iron stove, which, fortunately for him, was not lit, and had to make his way home through the flues and chimneys, arriving at his own room in a terrible state of dirt, disorder, and despair.

After this he was not seen again on any nocturnal expedition. The twins lay in wait for him on several occasions, and strewed the passages with nutshells every night to the great annoyance of their parents and the servants, but it was of no avail. It was quite evident that his feelings were so wounded that he would not appear. Mr. Otis, consequently, resumed his great work on the history of the Democratic Party, on which he had been engaged for some years; Mrs. Otis organized a wonderful clambake, which amazed the whole county; the boys took to lacrosse, euchre, poker, and other American national games; and Virginia rode about the lanes on her pony, accompanied by the young Duke of Cheshire, who had come to spend the last week of his holidays at Canterville Chase. It was generally assumed that the ghost had gone away, and, in fact, Mr. Otis wrote a letter to that effect to Lord Canterville, who, in reply, expressed his great pleasure at the news, and sent his best congratulations to the minister's worthy wife.

The Otises, however, were deceived, for the ghost was still in the house, and though now almost an invalid, was by no means ready to let matters rest, particularly as he heard that among the guests was the young Duke of Cheshire, whose grand-uncle, Lord Francis Stilton, had once bet a hundred guineas with Colonel Carbury that he would play dice with the Canterville ghost, and was found that next morning lying on the floor of the card room in such a helpless paralytic state that though he lived on to a great age, he was never able to say anything again but "Double Sixes." The story was well known at the time, though, of course, out of respect to the feelings of the two noble families, every attempt was made to hush it up; and a full account of all the circumstances connected with it will be found in the third volume of Lord Tattle's *Recollections of the Prince Regent and His Friends*. The ghost, then, was naturally very anxious to show that he had not lost his influence over the Stiltons, with whom, indeed, he was distantly connected, his own first cousin having been married *en secondes noces* to the Sieur de Bulkeley, from whom, as everyone knows, the dukes of Cheshire are lineally descended. Accordingly, he made arrangements for appearing to Virginia's little lover in his celebrated impersonation of "The Vampire Monk, or, the Bloodless Benedictine," a performance so horrible that when old Lady Startup saw it, which she did on one fatal New Year's Eve, in the year 1764, she went off into the most piercing shrieks, which culminated in violent apoplexy, and died in three days, after disinheriting the Cantervilles, who were her nearest relations, and leaving all her money to her London apothecary. At the last moment, however, his terror of the twins prevented his leaving his room, and the little duke slept in peace under the great feathered canopy in the Royal Bedchamber, and dreamed of Virginia.

5

A few days after this, Virginia and her curly-haired cavalier went out riding on Brockley meadows, where she tore her habit so badly in getting through a hedge, that, on her return home, she made up her mind to go up by the back staircase so as not to be seen. As she was running past the Tapestry Chamber, the door of which happened to be open, she fancied she saw someone inside, and thinking it was her mother's maid, who sometimes used to bring her work there, looked in to ask her to mend her habit. To her immense surprise, however, it was the Canterville ghost himself! He was sitting by the window, watching the ruined gold of the yellow trees fly through the air, and the red leaves dancing madly down the long avenue. His head was leaning on his hand, and his whole attitude was one of extreme depression. Indeed, so forlorn, and so much out of repair did he look, that little Virginia, whose first idea had been to run away and lock herself in her room, was filled with pity, and determined to try and comfort him. So light was her footfall, and so deep his melancholy, that he was not aware of her presence till she spoke to him.

"I am sorry for you," she said, "but my brothers are going back to Eton tomorrow, and then, if you behave yourself, no one will annoy you."

"It is absurd asking me to behave myself," he answered, looking round in astonishment at the pretty little girl who had ventured to address him, "quite absurd. I must rattle my chains, and groan through keyholes, and walk about at night, if that is what you mean. It is my only reason for existing."

"It is no reason at all for existing, and you know you have been very wicked. Mrs. Umney told us, the first day we arrived here, that you had killed your wife."

"Well, I quite admit it," said the ghost petulantly, "but it was a purely family matter, and concerned no one else."

"It is very wrong to kill anyone," said Virginia, who at times had a sweet Puritan gravity, caught from some old New England ancestor.

"Oh, I hate the cheap severity of abstract ethics! My wife was very plain, never had my ruffs properly starched, and knew nothing about cookery. Why, there was a buck I had shot in Hogley Woods, a magnificent pricket, and do you know how she had it sent up to table? However, it is no matter now, for it is all over, and I don't think it was very nice of her brothers to starve me to death, though I did kill her."

"Starve you to death? Oh, Mr. Ghost, I mean Sir Simon, are you hungry? I have a sandwich in my case. Would you like it?"

"No, thank you, I never eat anything now; but it is very kind of you, all the same, and you are much nicer than the rest of your horrid, rude, vulgar, dishonest family."

"Stop!" cried Virginia, stamping her foot, "it is you who are rude, and horrid, and vulgar; and as for dishonesty, you know you stole the paints out of my box to try and furbish up that ridiculous bloodstain in the library. First you took all my reds, including the vermilion, and I couldn't do any more sunsets, then you took the emerald green and the chrome yellow, and finally I had nothing left but indigo and Chinese white, and could only do moonlight scenes, which are always depressing to look at, and not at all easy to paint. I never told on you, though I was very much annoyed, and it was most ridiculous, the whole thing; for whoever heard of emerald green blood?"

"Well, really," said the ghost, rather meekly, "what was I to do? It is a very difficult thing to get real blood nowadays, and, as your brother began it all with his Paragon Detergent, I certainly saw no reason why I should not have your paints. As for color, that is always a matter of taste: the Cantervilles have blue blood, for instance, the very bluest in England; but I know you Americans don't care for things of this kind."

"You know nothing about it, and the best thing you can do is to emigrate and improve your mind. My father will be only too happy to give you a free passage, and though there is a heavy duty on spirits of every kind, there will be no difficulty about the Custom House, as the officers are all Democrats. Once in New York, you are sure to be a great success. I know lots of people there who would give a hundred thousand dollars to have a grandfather, and much more than that to have a family ghost."

"I don't think I should like America."

"I suppose because we have no ruins and no curiosities," said Virginia satirically.

"No ruins! no curiosities!" answered the ghost; "you have your navy and your manners."

"Good evening; I will go and ask papa to get the twins an extra week's holiday."

"Please don't go, Miss Virginia," he cried; "I am so lonely and so unhappy, and I really don't know what to do. I want to go to sleep and I cannot."

"That's quite absurd. You have merely to go to bed and blow out the candle. It is very difficult sometimes to keep awake, especially at church, but there is no difficulty at all about sleeping. Why, even babies know how to do that, and they are not very clever."

"I have not slept for three hundred years," he said sadly, and Virginia's beautiful blue eyes opened in wonder; "for three hundred years I have not slept, and I am so tired."

Virginia grew quite grave, and her little lips trembled like rose-leaves. She came towards him and, kneeling down at his side, looked up into his old withered face.

"Poor, poor ghost," she murmured; "have you no place where you can sleep?"

"Far away beyond the pine woods," he answered, in a low dreamy voice, "there is a little garden. There the grass grows long and deep, there are the great white stars of the hemlock flower, there the nightingale sings all night long. All night long he sings, and the cold, crystal moon looks down, and the yew tree spreads out its giant arms over the sleepers."

Virginia's eyes grew dim with tears, and she hid her face in her hands.

"You mean the Garden of Death," she whispered.

"Yes, Death. Death must be so beautiful. To lie in the soft brown earth, with the grasses waving above one's head, and listen to silence. To have no yesterday, and no tomorrow. To forget time, to forgive life, to be at peace. You can help me. You can open for me the portals of Death's house, for Love is always with you, and Love is stronger than Death is."

Virginia trembled, a cold shudder ran through her, and for a few moments there was silence. She felt as if she was in a terrible dream.

Then the ghost spoke again, and his voice sounded like the sighing of the wind.

"Have you ever read the old prophecy on the library window?"

"Oh, often," cried the little girl, looking up; "I know it quite well. It is painted in curious black letters, and it is difficult to read. There are only six lines:

When a golden girl can win
Prayer from out the lips of sin,
When the barren almond bears,
And a little child gives away its tears,
Then shall all the house be still
And peace come to Canterville.

But I don't know what they mean."

"They mean," he said sadly, "that you must weep for me for my sins, because I have no tears, and pray for me for my soul, because I have no faith, and then, if you have always been sweet, and good, and gentle, the Angel of Death will have mercy on me. You will see fearful shapes in darkness, and wicked voices will whisper in your ear, but they will not harm you, for against the purity of a little child the powers of Hell cannot prevail."

Virginia made no answer, and the ghost wrung his hands in wild despair as he looked down at her bowed golden head. Suddenly she stood up, very pale, and with a strange light in her eyes. "I am not afraid," she said firmly, "and I will ask the Angel to have mercy on you."

He rose from his seat with a faint cry of joy, and taking her hand bent over it with old-fashioned grace and kissed it. His fingers were as cold as ice, and his lips burned like fire, but Virginia did not falter as he led her across the dusky room. On the faded green tapestry were broidered little huntsmen. They blew their tasselled horns and with their tiny hands waved to her to go back. "Go back! little Virginia," they cried, "go back!" but the ghost clutched her hand more tightly, and she shut her eyes against them. Horrible animals with lizard tails, and goggle eyes, blinked at her from the carven chimneypiece, and murmured "Beware! little Virginia, beware! we may never see you again," but the ghost glided on more swiftly, and Virginia did not listen. When they reached the end of the room he stopped, and muttered some words she could not understand. She opened her eyes, and saw the wall slowly fading away like a mist, and a great black cavern in front of her. A bitter cold wind swept round them, and she felt something pulling at her dress. "Quick,

quick," cried the ghost, "or it will be too late," and, in a moment, the wainscoting had closed behind them, and the Tapestry Chamber was empty.

6

About ten minutes later, the bell rang for tea, and, as Virginia did not come down, Mrs. Otis sent up one of the footmen to tell her. After a little time he returned and said that he could not find Miss Virginia anywhere. As she was in the habit of going out to the garden every evening to get flowers for the dinner table, Mrs. Otis was not at all alarmed at first, but when six o'clock struck, and Virginia did not appear, she became really agitated, and sent the boys out to look for her, while she herself and Mr. Otis searched every room in the house. At half past six the boys came back and said that they could find no trace of their sister anywhere. They were all now in the greatest state of excitement, and did not know what to do, when Mr. Otis suddenly remembered that, some few days before, he had given a band of gypsies permission to camp in the park. He accordingly at once set off for Blackfell Hollow, where he knew they were, accompanied by his eldest son and two of the farm servants. The little Duke of Cheshire, who was perfectly frantic with anxiety, begged hard to be allowed to go too, but Mr. Otis would not allow him, as he was afraid there might be a scuffle. On arriving at the spot, however, he found that the gypsies had gone, and it was evident that their departure had been rather sudden, as the fire was still burning, and some plates were lying on the grass. Having sent off Washington and the two men to scour the district, he ran home, and despatched telegrams to all the police inspectors in the county, telling them to look out for a little girl who had been kidnapped by tramps or gypsies. He then ordered his horse to be brought round, and, after insisting on his wife and the three boys sitting down to dinner, rode off down the Ascot Road with a groom. He had hardly, however, gone a couple of miles when he heard somebody galloping after him, and, looking round, saw the little duke coming up on his pony, with his face very flushed and no hat. "I'm awfully sorry, Mr. Otis," gasped out the boy, "but I can't eat any dinner as long as Virginia is lost. Please, don't be angry with me; if you had let us be engaged last year, there would never have been all this trouble. You won't send me back, will you? I can't go! I won't go!"

The minister could not help smiling at the handsome young scapegrace, and was a good deal touched at his devotion to Virginia, so leaning down from his horse, he patted him kindly on the shoulders, and said, "Well, Cecil, if you won't go back I suppose you must come with me, but I must get you a hat at Ascot."

"Oh, bother my hat! I want Virginia!" cried the little duke, laughing, and they galloped on to the railway station. There Mr. Otis inquired of the station master if anyone answering the description of Virginia had been seen on the platform, but could get no news of her. The station master, however, wired up and down the line, and assured him that a strict watch would be kept for her, and, after having bought a hat for the little duke from a linen draper, who was just putting up his shutters, Mr. Otis rode off to Bexley, a village about four miles away, which he was told was a well-known haunt of the gypsies, as there was a large common next to it. Here they roused up the rural policeman, but could get no information from him, and, after riding all over the common, they turned their horses' heads homewards, and reached the Chase about eleven o'clock, dead tired and almost heartbroken. They found Washington and the twins waiting for them at the gatehouse with lanterns, as the avenue was very dark. Not the slightest trace of Virginia had been discovered. The gypsies had been caught on Broxley meadows, but she was not with them, and they had explained their sudden departure by saying that they had mistaken the date of Chorton Fair, and had gone off in a hurry for fear they might be late. Indeed, they had been quite distressed at hearing of Virginia's disappearance, as they were very grateful to Mr. Otis for having allowed them to camp in his park, and four of their number had stayed behind to help in the search. The carp pond had been dragged, and the whole Chase thoroughly gone over, but without any result. It was evident that, for that night at any rate, Virginia was lost to them; and it was in a state of the deepest depression that Mr. Otis and the boys walked up to the house, the groom following behind with the two horses and the pony. In the hall they found a group of frightened servants, and lying on a sofa in the library was poor Mrs. Otis, almost out of her mind with terror and anxiety, and having her forehead bathed with eau-de-cologne by the old house-keeper. Mr. Otis at once insisted on her having something to eat, and ordered up supper for the whole party. It was a melancholy meal, as hardly anyone spoke, and even the twins were awestruck and sub-dued, as they were very fond of their sister. When they had finished, Mr. Otis, in spite of the entreaties of the little duke, ordered them all to bed, saying that nothing more could be done that night, and that he would telegraph in the morning to Scotland Yard for some detec-tives to be sent down immediately. Just as they were passing out of the dining room, midnight began to boom from the clock tower, and when the last stroke sounded they heard a crash and a sudden shrill cry; a dreadful peal of thunder shook the house, a strain of unearthly music floated through the air, a panel at the top of the staircase flew back with a loud noise, and out on the landing, looking very pale and white, with a little casket in her hand, stepped Virginia. In a moment they had all rushed up to her. Mrs. Otis clasped her passionately in her arms, the duke smothered her with violent kisses, and the twins executed a wild war dance round the group.

"Good heavens! child, where have you been?" said Mr. Otis, rather angrily, thinking that she had been playing some foolish trick on them. "Cecil and I have been riding all over the country looking for you, and your mother has been frightened to death. You must never play these practical jokes any more."

"Except on the ghost! except on the ghost!" shrieked the twins, as they capered about.

"My own darling, thank God you are found; you must never leave my side again," murmured Mrs. Otis, as she kissed the trembling child, and smoothed the tangled gold of her hair.

"Papa," said Virginia quietly, "I have been with the ghost. He is dead, and you must come and see him. He had been very wicked, but he was really sorry for all that he had done, and he gave me this box of beautiful jewels before he died."

The whole family gazed at her in mute amazement, but she was quite grave and serious; and, turning round, she led them through the opening in the wainscoting down a narrow secret corridor, Wash-

ington following with a lighted candle, which he had caught up from
the table. Finally, they came to a great oak door, studded with rusty
nails. When Virginia touched it, it swung back on its heavy hinges,
and they found themselves in a little low room, with a vaulted ceiling, and one tiny grated window. Embedded in the wall was a huge
iron ring, and chained to it was a gaunt skeleton, that was stretched
out at full length on the stone floor, and seemed to be trying to grasp
with its long fleshless fingers an old-fashioned trencher and ewer,
that were placed just out of its reach. The jug had evidently been
once filled with water, as it was covered inside with green mold.
There was nothing on the trencher but a pile of dust. Virginia knelt
down beside the skeleton, and, folding her little hands together,
began to pray silently, while the rest of the party looked on in wonder
at the terrible tragedy whose secret was now disclosed to them.

"Hallo?" suddenly exclaimed one of the twins, who had been
looking out of the window to try and discover in what wing of the
house the room was situated. "Hallo! the old withered almond tree
has blossomed. I can see the flowers quite plainly in the moonlight."

"God has forgiven him," said Virginia gravely, as she rose to her
feet, and a beautiful light seemed to illumine her face.

"What an angel you are!" cried the young duke, and he put his
arm around her neck and kissed her.

7

Four days after these curious incidents a funeral started from Canterville Chase at about eleven o'clock at night. The hearse was
drawn by eight black horses, each of which carried on its head a
great tuft of nodding ostrich plumes, and the leaden coffin was
covered by a rich purple pall, on which was embroidered in gold the
Canterville coat of arms. By the side of the hearse and the coaches
walked the servants with lighted torches, and the whole procession
was wonderfully impressive. Lord Canterville was the chief
mourner, having come up specially from Wales to attend the funeral, and sat in the first carriage along with little Virginia. Then
came the United States minister and his wife, then Washington and
the three boys, and in the last carriage was Mrs. Umney. It was

generally felt that, as she had been frightened by the ghost for more than fifty years of her life, she had a right to see the last of him. A deep grave had been dug in the corner of the churchyard, just under the old yew tree, and the service was read in the most impressive manner by the Reverend Augustus Dampier. When the ceremony was over, the servants, according to an old custom observed in the Canterville family, extinguished their torches, and, as the coffin was being lowered into the grave, Virginia stepped forward and laid on it a large cross made of white and pink blossoms. As she did so, the moon came out from behind a cloud, and flooded with its silent silver the little churchyard, and from a distant copse a nightingale began to sing. She thought of the ghost's description of the Garden of Death, her eyes became dim with tears, and she hardly spoke a word during the drive home.

The next morning, before Lord Canterville went up to town, Mr. Otis had an interview with him on the subject of the jewels the ghost had given to Virginia. They were perfectly magnificent, especially a certain ruby necklace with old Venetian setting, which was really a superb specimen of sixteenth century work, and their value was so great that Mr. Otis felt considerable scruples about allowing his daughter to accept them.

"My lord," he said, "I know that in this country mortmain is held to apply to trinkets as well as to land, and it is quite clear to me that these jewels are, or should be, heirlooms in your family. I must beg you, accordingly, to take them to London with you, and to regard them simply as a portion of your property which has been restored to you under certain strange conditions. As for my daughter, she is merely a child, and has as yet, I am glad to say, but little interest in such appurtenances of idle luxury. I am also informed by Mrs. Otis, who, I may say, is no mean authority upon art—having had the privilege of spending several winters in Boston when she was a girl—that these gems are of great monetary worth, and if offered for sale would fetch a tall price. Under these circumstances, Lord Canterville, I feel sure that you will recognize how impossible it would be for me to allow them to remain in the possession of any member of my family; and, indeed, all such vain gauds and toys, however suitable or necessary to the dignity of the British aristocracy, would be completely out of place among those who have been brought up on the severe, and I believe immortal, principles of republican simplicity. Perhaps I should mention that Virginia is very anxious that you should allow her to retain the box as a memento of your unfortunate but misguided ancestor. As it is extremely old, and consequently a good deal out of repair, you may perhaps think fit to comply with her request. For my own part, I confess I am a good deal surprised to find a child of mine expressing sympathy with medievalism in any form, and can only account for it by the fact that Virginia was born in one of your London suburbs shortly after Mrs. Otis had returned from a trip to Athens."

Lord Canterville listened very gravely to the worthy minister's speech, pulling his grey mustache now and then to hide an involuntary smile, and when Mr. Otis had ended, he shook him cordially by the hand, and said, "My dear sir, your charming little daughter rendered my unlucky ancestor, Sir Simon, a very important service, and I and my family are much indebted to her for her marvelous courage and pluck. The jewels are clearly hers, and, egad, I believe that if I were heartless enough to take them from her, the wicked old fellow would be out of his grave in a fortnight, leading me the devil of a life. As for their being heirlooms, nothing is an heirloom that is not so mentioned in a will or legal document, and the existence of these jewels has been quite unknown. I assure you I have no more claim on them than your butler, and when Miss Virginia grows up I daresay she will be pleased to have pretty things to wear. Besides, you forget, Mr. Otis, that you took the furniture and the ghost at a valuation, and anything that belonged to the ghost passed at once into your possession, as, whatever activity Sir Simon may have shown in the corridor at night, in point of law he was really dead, and you acquired his property by purchase."

Mr. Otis was a good deal distressed at Lord Canterville's refusal, and begged him to reconsider his decision, but the good-natured peer was quite firm, and finally induced the minister to allow his daughter to retain the present the ghost had given her, and when, in the spring of 1890, the young Duchess of Cheshire was presented at the Queen's first drawing room on the occasion of her marriage, her jewels were the universal theme of admiration. For Virginia received the coronet, which is the reward of all good little American girls, and was married to her boy-lover as soon as he came of age. They were both so charming, and they loved each other so much, that everyone was delighted at the match, except the old Marchioness of Dumbleton, who had tried to catch the duke for one of her seven unmarried daughters, and had given no less than three expensive dinner parties for that purpose, and, strange to say, Mr. Otis himself. Mr. Otis was extremely fond of the young duke personally, but, theoretically, he objected to titles, and, to use his own words, "was not without apprehension lest, amid the enervating influences of a pleasure-loving aristocracy, the true principles of republican simplicity should be forgotten." His objections, however, were completely overruled, and I believe that when he walked up the aisle of St. George's, Hanover Square, with his daughter leaning on his arm, there was not a prouder man in the whole length and breadth of England.

The duke and duchess, after the honeymoon was over, went down to Canterville Chase, and on the day after their arrival they walked over in the afternoon to the lonely churchyard by the pinewoods. There had been a great deal of difficulty at first about the inscription on Sir Simon's tombstone, but finally it had been decided to engrave on it simply the initials of the old gentleman's name, and the verse from the library window. The duchess had brought with her some lovely roses, which she strewed upon the grave, and after they had stood by it for some time they strolled into the ruined chancel of the old abbey. There the duchess sat down on a fallen pillar, while her husband lay at her feet smoking a cigarette and looking up at her beautiful eyes. Suddenly he threw his cigarette away, took hold of her hand, and said to her, "Virginia, a wife should have no secrets from her husband."

"Dear Cecil! I have no secrets from you."

"Yes, you have," he answered, smiling, "you have never told me what happened to you when you were locked up with the ghost."

"I have never told anyone, Cecil," said Virginia gravely.

"I know that, but you might tell me."

"Please don't ask me, Cecil. I cannot tell you. Poor Sir Simon! I owe him a great deal. Yes, don't laugh, Cecil, I really do. He made me see what Life is, and what Death signifies, and why Love is stronger than both."

The duke rose and kissed his wife lovingly.

"You can have your secret as long as I have your heart," he murmured.

"You have always had that, Cecil."

"And you will tell our children some day, won't you?"

Virginia blushed.

The Last Crime Story

by Robert Loy

*When a man undertakes to create something, he establishes a
new heaven, as it were, and from it the work that he desires
to create flows into him. For such is the immensity of man
that he is greater than heaven and earth.*
PHILIPPUS AUREOLUS PARACELSUS

The moral of this story is that IT IS VERY IMPORTANT TO BE-
LIEVE IN SOMETHING, AND VITAL TO KNOW JUST EX-
ACTLY WHAT IT IS YOU BELIEVE IN.

I'm placing the moral at the beginning of this tale rather than at its
more customary encampment in the rearmost sector because it has
come to my attention that some of you people out there select which
stories you're going to read in this magazine by skimming through
the first three paragraphs and then either continuing on if that
paltry prose sample strikes your fancy or skipping over to the next,
hopefully-more-instantly-compelling story if it does not. (This puts
a tremendous burden on the author, who must sacrifice his vision of
the intrinsic artistic structure of his piece just so he or she can grab
potential readers by the vitals in the first two hundred fifty words or
so, but I won't go into that here except to say I sincerely hope you
people out there appreciate all this trouble we put ourselves
through for you.) The point is, I want everybody—even the finicky

and the slovenly readers among your number—to hear at least the moral of this story. It's that important. (That, of course, is also why I violated some more rules and wrote the moral all in capital letters— "all caps," as we in the business say.)

Okay, here we go: Norman Novellis had a heart attack on Friday. It perhaps might not have been a fatal one had he not lost control of his Buick Skylark and crashed into a telephone pole. As it was, he was killed instantly.

(How's that? Compelling enough? I tried to work a little sex into this scene of violence and death, but it just couldn't be done. Sorry. I'll try to throw in some gratuitously a little later—I know how you guys love that stuff.)

I'm getting ahead of myself, I realize. You don't even know who Norman Novellis was, do you? But, you see, I still have not shaken those three-paragraph phantoms. I'm still playing by their rules, still trying to hook readers by the third paragraph. That, of course, is why I broke the rules of good writing once again and made my second paragraph so run-on and unwieldy, just so I could get the violence and death in by this reader-enforced deadline. The moral will be a lot more meaningful to these people if they can get it in context, with all the illustrations and symbols that I have racked my brain here in my lonely ill-lit study to come up with, and intend to use to support this thesis of mine (see the first paragraph if you've forgotten the thesis). I ask the indulgence of the more diligent readers out there, those of you who read each story from beginning to end before deciding if the work a stranger poured his heart out on to entertain and enlighten you with is worth your time. Bless you, all shall be revealed.

Perhaps I can best explain who Norman Novellis was by explaining what he wasn't. He was not a believer—in anything. (That he knew of.) He did not believe in Jesus, Buddha, Krishna, Mohammed, Bhagawan Shree Rajneesh, Reverend Moon, or Shirley MacLaine. He did not believe in capitalism, communism, socialism, or any of the other isms man inflicts upon himself. He did not believe in philosophy, theology, Scientology, evolution, creationism, the big bang, abortion, or right-to-life. He had never even believed in Santa Claus, the Easter bunny, the tooth fairy, or the boogeyman.

He called himself a nihilist, but he was really just a cynic. There's a difference. Nihilists believe in nothing, but Norman Novellis did not believe in anything—again, anything that he knew of; actually, as we shall see, it is impossible not to believe in something, but we're getting ahead of ourselves again.

As an example of the difference between nihilism and cynicism: If a competent physician told a nihilist that his lifestyle was killing him and he'd better change his eating and exercise habits or get ready for a massive heart attack, the nihilist would probably pull that dusty old exercise bicycle out of the attic and start pumping it for all he was worth. No doubt he would also immediately cut down on—if not cut out entirely—red meat, butter, sour cream, and all that good stuff. DIET, THAT'S THE MAIN KEY TO PREVENTING HEART DISEASE. (We're having a special on morals today—buy one, get one free.)

But Norman Novellis was such a cynic he did not even believe in oat bran, the erstwhile manna of our era.

And when Norman Novellis's physician told him he was cruising for a coronary, he laughed in her face.

"Don't hand me that stuff," he told his physician. "All that cholesterol jazz is just an AMA conspiracy to deprive people of whatever *joie de vivre* they might possibly be able to wring out of their sordid little existences. It's the same thing you guys have always done. Whether it's leeches or radiation 'therapy,' you guys are always the spoilsports of life."

"All I'm saying, Mr. Novellis, is that your arteries are clogged with cholesterol. You need to make a few changes in the way you've been eating. Specifically I want you to cut down on saturated fat and alcohol and try to get more soluble fiber into your diet. Also, I want you to try to exercise a little, three times a week or so. Otherwise your life may very well be shortened. Considerably."

"Hey, if I don't have long to live, then I damn sure don't want to spend what time I have eating sellable fabric or whatever it is —the doctorese term for horse chow—and jumping and jogging around with no destination. Why should I deny myself the few simple, basic pleasures of life, doc, when I might step outside your office here and get run over by a bus, or be stabbed to death in my sleep tonight by Lebanese terrorists? Sell it to some other gullible fool."

Here the physician lost some of her temper—not all of it, but some.

"Well, you'll be singing a different song before long is all I can say. When that pain in your chest comes, and it feels like a big muscle has just ripped right in two, you'll be thinking, 'God, I wish I hadn't been so hard-headed. I wish I'd done something to prevent this while there was still time.'"

But this physician, although she was absolutely right about the congested condition of Norman Novellis's capillaries, was not a seeress.

When the pain in Norman Novellis's chest struck him and he knew, though he hadn't felt one before and wasn't expecting it now, that it was a heart attack, knew that it was going to kill him, his last earthly thoughts were not on the texture of his skull. Nor was his mind filled with regret over sins of omission.

What he actually thought was, "Damn. Why did this have to happen on the way *home* from work—on a Friday! Right before a bowling weekend. I guess this means no pizza and beer with the guys tonight."

And it was truer than he knew.

For Norman Novellis had ingested his last anchovy, consumed his last Coors, avoided his last aerobic workout.

As I said before (though I didn't really want to, I prefer to have these little tales of mine emulate life as much as possible and give you folks these events in chronological order), this was not a massive coronary, but Norman Novellis lost control of his Buick Skylark and smacked into a telephone pole, and that was the end of his earthly existence.

But it is just the beginning of this story.

(Actually, it's more like an allegory, but let's just call it a story. Keep things as simple as possible. Matters are going to get complicated enough on their own very shortly.)

* * *

As you probably expected, Norman Novellis did not believe in an afterlife. So just opening his eyes again at all after he knew he was dead (and believe me, you know when you're dead, you always do. Regardless of what you may have read or heard, nobody is unaware of what is happening, nobody thinks they're dreaming or anything. They know.), was a tremendous shock.

Opening them to see a man with a burlap face and painted-on eyes and mouth and to hear the man ask him if he was all right was so astonishing he passed out again.

Understandably, he was still a little weak from his recent traumatic experience. And perhaps this is as good a time as any to point out that had Norman Novellis been a fundamentalist Christian he would right now be opening his eyes to robe-clad, harp-playing, halo-topped, hymn-singing cloud hoppers. Had he been a Hindu, he would be reviewing his life and preparing for his next incarnation. Had he been a Viking (unlikely in this day and age, I realize, but bear with me. I'm trying to prove a point here), he would wake up with a sword in one hand, a horn of mead in the other, and a slew of monsters and giants to slay in Valhalla, the happy hunting ground of the Norsemen. If he was L. Frank Baum or Dorothy Gale, he'd be exactly where he was now. (Intriguing, huh?) Had he been a true nihilist—pay attention, this is where it starts to get tricky, because nihilists believe in nothing, but nothing is the only thing that really *doesn't* exist. Nihilists believe that after they die they're just dead and that's it. Unfortunately, that's not possible, so nihilists go off to a dark, quiet corner of the universe where they can lie around with their eyes closed and think they're dead. They're not really dead, of course. They could get up and walk around if they wanted to, play a little handball, take in a movie or a show, even get out and try to hunt up a happier hereafter, but they don't believe they can so the effect is much the same as if they actually couldn't.

(If you're not sure you caught all that, you need to back up and reread it. The rest of us will wait here for you. It's important that you not get behind or you're going to be completely lost when we start building on what we've already learned.)

The main point (so far) is this: What you believe is going to happen to you after you die (as well as what happens to you while you live, but that's another allegory) is pretty much what does happen to you. If you honestly believe that after you die you will wind up screaming and crying in brimstone-scented flames while a cloven-footed beast with horns and a sharp tail prods you with a pitchfork, this is precisely what will happen. You will not be disappointed.

But Norman Novellis was not a Christian or a Buddhist or a Muslim or a Viking or a nihilist, so he couldn't go to any of the more popular promised lands. Where did he go? What happens to you if you don't believe anything is going to happen to you?

When Norman Novellis came to, the burlap man was still there.

"I would ask you if you were all right," said the burlap-faced man, "but it seems that question makes you faint. So, how about: 'Hello, friend. How are you today?' Do you like that question any better?"

And he smiled.

But how can he smile? Norman Novellis wondered. His face is painted on.

"I said, 'Hello, friend. How are you today?' "

Norman Novellis sat up and looked at this man. He was dressed in rags and had straw sticking out of his chest, gloves, boots, and neck.

Oh, my god, thought Norman Novellis, this guy's a scarecrow. I've lost my mind.

"Where am I?" Norman Novellis asked the straw man. (You've noticed, no doubt, that he is completely ignoring the scarecrow's question. Cynics are often rude like that.) "And why aren't I dead?"

"Hmmm," said the Scarecrow as he scratched his head (which being filled with straw probably itched quite a bit). "That's a toughie—not your first question, that's simple; you're in the Emerald City of Oz, more specifically in Princess Ozma's rose garden. But as to why you're not dead, I must say that even with my magnificent mind I can't figure that one—"

"Wait a minute. Where did you say I am?"

"You're in Ozma's rose garden."

"In Oz?"

"Well, of course, where else would Ozma's rose garden be but in Oz? I mean, think about it for a minute. Why would Ozma plant her—"

The Scarecrow kept on talking, but Norman Novellis wasn't listening. He put his right hand on his chest and felt his heartbeat clear and strong. Clearer and stronger than it had been since he was a teenager.

He stood up. Everything—the trees, the grass, the sky, the roses—was greener or bluer or redder, as the case may be, and sharper somehow than he had ever seen trees and grass and sky and roses look since he was a child. And the air was so fresh—fresher than he had ever felt in his life. You could actually taste the air, and it tasted great.

You might think that Norman Novellis is taking all this incredibly calmly. You might even be starting to doubt my abilities as a belletrist (a fancy word for writer; I love fancy words) and think that Norman Novellis's reactions are unrealistic, unbelievable. Maybe you think that if you all of a sudden landed in a place you had always assumed was nothing more than a fairytale land, you'd exhibit a bit more hysteria than Norman Novellis is demonstrating. But the truth is you don't know. I mean, after all, you've never been dead, so how you're going to react to it when it happens is a mystery, isn't it?

(And really, there is one thing you have to give cynics, and that is that they adjust to changes—even rapid future-shock-like changes—remarkably well, much better than optimists. Norman Novellis figured if he was in Oz, then he was in Oz. He could worry about the whys and wherefores later, now he had something more important on his mind.)

"Tell me something," Norman Novellis said to the Scarecrow, "what do people eat here in Oz?"

"Eat? Why, whatever they want, as much as they want, whenever they want."

"Anything they want?"

"Sure. Hot dogs, cupcakes, pizza, double fudge chocolate brownies with whipped cream. Anything."

"No oat bran?"

"Sure, you want oat bran, you can have oat bran."

"I don't want it."

The Scarecrow wasn't used to people inquiring about foodstuffs they *didn't* want to eat. He had to think for a minute before he answered. (Contrary to what MGM led you to believe, the wizard actually did give the Scarecrow a brain, and a very brilliant brain it is, too.)

"Well, if you don't want it, don't eat it. You don't have to eat anything you don't want to eat. And me, I don't have to eat anything at all. I'm made out of straw, not meat, so I don't have to eat—or sleep, for that matter. Nick Chopper and Jack Pumpkinhead are the same way—well, they're not made out of straw, but they don't have to sleep is what I meant. We have some of our best conversations late at night, early in the morning when everyone else is asleep, and we don't have to interrupt our talk to fill our mouths with popcorn or potato chips or—"

"I suppose you guys talk about philosophy and religion and politics and all that kind of stuff."

(Norman Novellis hated philosophical and religious discussions. "A waste of perfectly good oxygen," he called them.)

"No," said the Scarecrow, "mostly we talk about different adventures and fun times we've had, and places we haven't been and things we haven't done but would like to see and do someday."

Only now did it really start to sink in on Norman Novellis that he wasn't in Kansas any more (so to speak). It started to sink in and it felt wonderful. Somehow Norman Novellis had landed in Paradise, a much cooler paradise than the boring heaven his mother and father and other born-again do-gooders had tried to get him interested in during his earth life. He closed his eyes and let the sensation of living permanently in Paradise pervade his spirit.

"So what do you do?" he asked the Scarecrow, several minutes later.

"Oh, I do lots of things," the Scarecrow said. "I think about lots of different things. I dance—generally, if I'm not thinking, I'm dancing." And here the Scarecrow stood up and did a few loose-jointed charleston steps to demonstrate his terpsichorean (yes, fancy word) talents. "And I read a little, write a little—"

"No, I mean, what do you do for a living? What is your job?"

"Oh, I don't have a job. No one in Oz has a job—unless of course he really wants one."

Now Norman Novellis threw back his head and laughed. He had

hated his job even more than he hated philosophical discussions. He didn't know how he got here to Oz, and he didn't really care. He only knew it was the most peaceful, the most perfect place he had ever seen—or even dreamed about (Not that that's saying much. Cynics' dreams tend to be depressingly prosaic.), and he wanted nothing more than to live here forever.

"This Oz sounds like quite a place."

"Oh, it's great. There's no crime, no disease, no pollution, people never get any older. We have Christmas every month, and it only rains at night here and then only so the children will have mud puddles to play in. You're going to love it here."

"You mean I can stay?"

"Oh, well, I guess so." The Scarecrow appeared momentarily puzzled. "I mean, that's not really up to me. Princess Ozma will have to decide about that."

"Who is this prin—"

But just then a horse pulled up—only it wasn't a horse like Norman Novellis was used to; it wasn't a meat horse, as the Scarecrow would say. It was a wooden sawhorse, but it galloped just like a real horse and it carried a coach all by itself, just as a real horse might do if it were incredibly stronger than the average horse. The only thing the sawhorse did that other horses don't do is talk.

"Princess Ozma sent for you, friend stranger," said the knotholed nag. "Hop in."

But Norman Novellis did not immediately hop.

"How did this Ozma person know I was here? Was she expecting me?" he asked the lumbering beast. ("Lumbering," get it? A wooden horse—lumbering. Usually we authors ruthlessly redline all extraneous literary frivolities such as puns. Particularly puns. We don't do it because we want to, but because every editor in the world believes that you guys, the readers, find anything that does not directly advance the plot confusing. Personally, I think you're all a lot more intelligent than that, but try telling that—or anything else, for that matter—to an editor. Anyway, you people have no idea how much this hurts us. All authors love puns more than we love our own children, and just to uproot them from a manuscript and—

well, I'm leaving that one in. It adds nothing to the story, but I'm leaving it in. As an experiment. I want to see if Western literature implodes as a result.)

"No," answered the sawhorse, "but she has a magic mirror in which she can see everything that happens in Oz as it happens. And she saw you land here in her rose garden."

"Oh, okay. I see," he answered absently.

Norman Novellis answered absently not because he was thinking, as a more logical, linear-deductive man might be at this moment, What? A magic mirror? Nothing doing, that is scientifically impossible. No, Norman Novellis was thinking, Gee, a magic mirror. Maybe sometimes when this Ozma person isn't looking I can borrow it and check out what's going on the University of Oz girls' locker room.

(See what I mean about cynics adjusting rapidly?)

He hopped in the carriage. So did the Scarecrow.

"I'll point out some of the sights to you on the way," the cornfield custodian said to Norman Novellis.

And what wondrous sights there were, too. Rolling meadows, brooks that actually babbled, beautiful women everywhere, rainbows with real pots of gold at the end, plants and animals and colors that Norman Novellis had never seen and had no adjectives with which to describe them to himself. All he could do was sit back breathless and try to absorb all this wonder and beauty.

Truly, this is heaven, thought Norman Novellis.

And here he shed a tear of joy. (I know, I know, cynics don't shed tears of joy. But Oz can do strange things to a man. Besides, I'm telling this story, and if I say he shed a tear of joy, he shed a tear of joy.)

The only unpleasant thing at all he witnessed on their journey was a small blue man stepping out of an alley, conking another small blue man on the head with an umbrella, and lifting his wallet. Norman Novellis started to point this out to the Scarecrow, who had not seen it, and ask him how it jibed with his assertion that there was no crime in Oz. (Cynics love to catch other people's misstatements and rub their noses, even painted-on noses, in them.)

But Norman Novellis was already feeling less cynical by the minute, and he figured why spoil the magic?

Unfortunately, Ozma was called away on an emergency (there was a bank robbery in the Gilliken country north of the Emerald City) before she could meet with Norman Novellis, and he was taken directly to his new home, a cottage in the Munchkin country, which is east of the Emerald City.

Unlike what the 1939 MGM motion picture classic *The Wizard of Oz* (which Norman, like most cynics, despised) had led him to believe, the Munchkins were not abnormally small, certainly not midgets. They were about the size of the average Japanese. And that suited Norman Novellis just fine because he was a little on the short side himself.

In fact, nearly everything about his new neighborhood suited Norman Novellis just fine. There were only a couple of things wrong with Munchkinland, and they were so trivial that they did not at all detract from Ozheaven (as Norman Novellis now mentally referred to his new home). One was that the Munchkins all wore blue—all day, every day. It was the only color of clothing—the only color of fabric—available in stores. (Now that is just a loose end. I'm not going to explain why the Munchkins all wear blue, nor does their inclination toward indigo have anything to do with what happens from here on in. As an author, you're not supposed to do that. In fiction, as we've discussed before, if it doesn't advance the plot, out it goes. Again, because editors don't think you're smart enough to handle it. Insulting, is it not? You ought to get down on your knees every night and thank Whoever, or whoever, it is you think deserves the credit or blame for your reality, that you've got us authors in the trenches, fighting—at a ridiculously low, few-pennies-per-word wage rate, I might add—every day for your right to quality literature. There are supposed to be no loose ends, no meaningless events—which is why fiction is not, and will never be, realistic. Real life—real life on earth anyway—is mostly loose ends.)

And every once in a while there was a pocket-picking or an aggravated assault or a trademark infringement to break up the joyful monotony of good news. One night Norman Novellis returned home from a party to find that his cottage had been broken into and entered—robbed.

But this did not upset Norman Novellis a great deal, partly because he had consumed a great deal of Munchkin wine at the party, but mostly because it's easy to replace your possessions in a country that doesn't use money and where everything you need is free for the asking.

Besides, there wasn't nearly as much crime here as there was back in Texas. (Oh, did I not mention that Norman Novellis was from the Lone Star State—Fort Worth, to be specific? Well, it doesn't matter, he could be from anywhere. In fact, it's probably better if you don't think of him as having come from anywhere more specific than earth. After all, Norman Novellis is a symbol, remember.)

But the Scarecrow had said there was *no* crime. What can he have been thinking of, Norman Novellis wondered.

Norman Novellis settled into his new lifestyle with no problem whatsoever. Mornings he read the newspaper—the *Munchkin Monitor*—from cover to cover, a luxury he never had time for back on earth. Afternoons were spent exploring the other areas of his new homeland, the Winkie country to the west of the Emerald City, the aforementioned Gilliken country, and the delightfully balmy (though all of Oz is quite temperate) southern land of the Quadlings.

Evenings were when Norman Novellis socialized with his friends—and he had lots of them. It's impossible not to make friends in Oz. Everyone there is so open, so giving—so friendly.

Ironically, Norman Novellis's best friend in Oz was probably Nick Chopper, the Tin Woodman. (I know his name was not given in the movie, but take my word for it, it's Nick Chopper.) I say ironic because Nick Chopper has to be the least cynical guy in all the vast realms of creation. I mean, here's a guy who travels many miles, tangles with flying monkeys, humbug wizards, wicked witches just to get a heart. If Norman Novellis had been born without a heart, he would not have gone to that much trouble. He would have just gotten used to it. (I know, I know, if he had been born without a heart, he wouldn't do anything, he'd be stillborn—on earth. But we left earth several paragraphs ago. Keep up—we're taking the cosmic view here and it's going to get even more cosmic before we're finished.)

Norman Novellis used to have long talks with his friend Nick Chopper. Nick had a theory about how it was that Norman Novellis ended up in Oz. Everybody knew (that is, everybody in Oz knew) that you go where you believe you're going to go. Nick further postulated that people like Norman Novellis who didn't believe they were going anywhere ("The only place people can't go is nowhere," Nick reasoned. "Even if you take off without a map or a compass you're still going to wind up *somewhere*. It might not be where you want to go, but it won't be nowhere."), just sort of take pot luck and end up in some random place.

"Maybe whatever gods or goddesses are in charge of that sort of thing just close their eyes and more or less toss you out somewhere, off into creation," Nick told Norman Novellis.

I guess I can go ahead and tell you here that Nick's theory is essentially correct. Although the beings—actually, a computer now—in charge of assigning nonbelievers to their final rewards don't close their eyes and toss anybody. It's more of a turn-taking type of process. But Nick was right in that it's pretty much a crapshoot where you're going to end up if you don't know what it is you believe in. Every supposedly fictitious realm (I say supposedly fictitious because there is truly no such thing as a fictitious realm. Every place from heaven to Mayberry to Never-never land is real if somebody believes in it, even if it's only the man or woman who invented it. Therefore, every place anyone has ever thought about is real, also every person, every animal, every thing, but I don't want to overload your minds with too much too fast), anyway, every supposedly fictitious realm takes turns offering sanctuary to these orphans of faith like Norman Novellis. It just happened to be Oz's turn when Norman Novellis ran into that telephone pole back in paragraph three.

Nick's theory chilled Norman Novellis to the bone (and he didn't even know it was true).

Why, just think, he thought. I might have ended up in Wonderland and have to worry about getting my head chopped off—or been sent to Lake Wobegon and be bored to death—or, geez! Dante's inferno. (And Norman Novellis was right to be chilled. The mind of man has created many heavens and many earths, but not many—well, why mince words? None of them is as nice as Oz.)

Norman Novellis told Nick about his former home, about earth and its peoples and its customs. Nick, of course, tried, as all Ozmopolitans try at all times, to be polite and positive, but he couldn't help but remark that earth sounded pretty hellish.

Norman Novellis had to agree.

And then one day Norman Novellis was summoned before Princess Ozma (full title *Her Royal Highness, the Eminent Empress, Princess Ozma the First and Only of Oz, Beloved and Benevolent Ruler of all the Myriad Mysterious Places and Peoples East of the Deadly Desert and West of the Shifting Sands*). The Cowardly Lion escorted him, and when they reached the palace, a structure so much more magnificent than anything on earth I'm not going to insult it by even trying to describe it (Hey, why don't you do it? I shouldn't have to take you by the hand and point out everything for you. It's time you readers started standing on your own two feet and helping out a little in this creative process. Oh, all right, since you're used to being babied, I'll help you out a little. Just imagine the most breathtaking, incredible castle you've ever dreamed, something that makes the Taj Mahal look like an outhouse, a fortress where everything from the foundation to the finial is made of precious jewels and metals. Then multiply it by ten.), he was grabbed by guards and tied up with some kind of rope made out of green light. Some kind of escape-proof, very tight rope made out of green light.

"Hey, what's going on here? What's the meaning of this?"

A tall, imposing, but breathtakingly beautiful woman stepped out from the shadows. No doubt you're curious as to what she looks like, but again I don't feel qualified to do the descriptions here (And no, I'm not copping out. I heard you there in the back row, and believe me, if you'd ever laid eyes on this lady you'd be at a loss for modifiers too, wise guy.) so I'm going to let somebody who has actually seen her describe her to you:

"No one knows her age, but all can see how beautiful and stately she is. Her hair is like red gold and finer than the finest silken strands. Her eyes are as blue as the sky. Her cheeks are the envy of peach-blows and her mouth is as enticing as a rosebud. She wears no jewelry, for her beauty would shame them."

(No, I'm not sure what a peach-blow is either, but I think you get the idea.)

(And by the way, I am quoting from L. Frank Baum, who invented this heaven when he wrote *The Wizard of Oz*, as well as thirteen other books on this wonderful country. If you thought there was only one, you probably spend more time watching television than you do reading, and you ought to be ashamed of yourself.)

I probably should say right here that this is *not* Princess Ozma. This is Glinda, the *Good Witch and Official Sorceress of the Kingdom of Oz*. Princess Ozma could not see Norman Novellis (except in her magic mirror) and Norman Novellis could not see her at all. (Which was really Norman Novellis's loss, since if you think Glinda is a knockout . . .) The reason is that all Norman Novellis knew of Oz was from the movie, and Ozma was not in the movie. (Actually she was in it briefly, but you wouldn't have recognized her. It was during a period in her life when she'd been turned into a boy. Yes, life does sometimes get complicated in Oz.) Norman Novellis could not see Ozma because he did not believe in Ozma. (Of course, he did not, prior to his death, believe in the Scarecrow, Nick Chopper, the Cowardly Lion, or Glinda either. But he did believe they were characters in the story.)

"The meaning of this, Norman Novellis, is that you must leave Oz." Her voice was lilting and beautiful (One of the few things the movie did get right was Glinda's voice. She sounds exactly like Billie Burke.), but the words turned Norman Novellis's blood to slush. "And you must leave Oz now."

"But I don't want to leave Oz. I like it here," said Norman Novellis.

"I realize that," said Glinda, raising her magic wand gracefully but distinctly menacingly, "and if there was any way to arrange things so that you could stay I would do that for you, but there is not. You must go."

"But where are you going to send me?" Norman Novellis asked, trying to keep down the hysteria in his voice. He was not adjusting well now.

"Your destination is a mystery to me. People in Oz do not die, but I am sending you to one of the countless hereafters they might end up in if they did die. More than that, I cannot say. This inter-reality magic thing is still in its infancy."

"But you can't do that. You can't just kick me out of here for no reason."

Glinda put the wand down on a nearby table. She didn't let go of it, but she set it down.

"It's not without reason, Mr. Novellis. You have brought crime to Oz. The crime must stop. The crime will not stop as long as you are here. Therefore you must go."

"Wait a minute! How do you figure I'm responsible for the crime?"

"Prior to your arrival there was no crime. Now there is."

"Well, all right, so it started when I got here. It's a coincidence. It's got to be a coincidence. I'm not a crook. I haven't stolen anything since that bottle of Dad's Wild Turkey when I was in the eleventh grade. Surely you're not going to deport me for that. So how—"

"I have given you the benefit of the doubt for quite a long time, Mr. Novellis, but I'm afraid there is no longer any doubt for you to benefit from. I've done some research on this phenomenon, and while there is not time for me to explain all to you in any detail, I can simplify it by saying that you come from one of the few realms where there is such a thing as crime, and when you came to Oz you brought this criminality with you as ideological baggage. In some realms this would not be a problem, but here in Oz I am afraid it is intolerable. In other words, Mr. Novellis, you are not being deported because you are a criminal. You're being deported because you believe in crime."

"Not me, sister. I don't—I mean, I didn't—believe in crime. I don't believe in anything." Which was even more untrue now than it was when he was on earth. The truth is, Norman Novellis had recently come to believe in a whole lot of things—chief among them that Oz was where he wanted to spend eternity—but he had not examined his belief system in some time (see paragraph one, if you think that's a good idea) and he was denying belief in anything out of long-ingrained habit.

Glinda let go of the wand and put the palms of her hands lightly together. Norman Novellis breathed for the first time since being summoned there.

"Let me ask you one question, Mr. Novellis," said the Good Witch and Official Sorceress of the Kingdom of Oz. "Do you believe it is possible to get away with murder?"

Norman Novellis squirmed in his green-light ropes and said, "Literally or figuratively?"

(He was stalling while he tried to figure out what it was Glinda wanted to hear.)

"Either way," answered Glinda.

Well, thought Norman Novellis, she didn't ask me if I thought murder was okay. She asked me if I thought it was possible to get away with it, and everybody knows you can—even though it's wrong. So, trying his best not to sound cynical, Norman Novellis said:

"Sure, people do it every day."

"Then you believe in crime. Some of your beliefs have leaked out" (This is another complicated concept, but you've noticed how Norman Novellis has gotten less cynical just by being around Oz people. Well, the process works in reverse too.), "and now there is crime in Oz. You must go, Norman Novellis."

(Actually, Norman Novellis had brought a whole bunch of other nasty things to Oz with him as ideological baggage—things like disease, death, religion, hemorrhoids, tabloid television, old age, greed, lust, the concept of condom humor, and other various and assorted aberrations that we here on earth accept as normal but were previously unknown in Oz. But I'm mentioning only crime here because crime is probably the worst thing he brought, and because this is a mystery magazine; it concerns itself primarily with crime. Therefore I have to play up the crime aspect of this story, and downplay other aspects, such as characterization. This, by the way, is called slanting, and it's just another of those things that we inkstained wretches do for you guys that you probably do not appreciate even slightly.)

Glinda picked up the wand.

"No, wait!" Norman Novellis screamed. "Wait! Didn't Oz have witches that kidnapped and tried to kill Dorothy and who sent their flying monkeys out to tear up the Scarecrow? Yes, I know you did, Nick told me about it. There, that's assault, attempted murder, kidnapping, God knows what all else. All before I got here."

Norman Novellis let out a soft "Whew!" He actually thought he was off the hook now. But Glinda pooh-poohed his argument with an airy wave of her hand.

"The witches did what they did because they wanted power," Glinda explained, "so their actions, Mr. Novellis, were essentially political. And politics, while it resembles crime in many regards, is not precisely the same thing."

Glinda never lost her patience, but she was anxious to get this over with. Every minute Norman Novellis stayed in Oz the concept of criminality became more deeply embedded in the minds of her fellow Ozmopolitans.

She raised the wand.

"But look," Norman Novellis continued to protest, "if you send me off somewhere, God only knows where, you could be sending me to hell or someplace worse. Isn't that a crime? Doesn't that make you a criminal?"

"Oz has always had strict immigration policies. After all, we're not a democracy. We're a utopia."

"Then send me back to Texas," pleaded Norman Novellis, "don't zap me with that thing that you don't know what it's going to do to me. Send me back to Texas. Please, please!"

"I can't do that, Mr. Novellis."

"Yes, you can," Nick Chopper had told Norman Novellis about Ozma's magic belt which could send people anywhere she wanted them to go, and Norman Novellis was still under the impression that this was Ozma he was talking to.

"Perhaps I did not phrase that well, Mr. Novellis," said Glinda. "I could indeed *send* you back to Texas. But you cannot *go* back to Texas."

"But why not?"

"Because nobody in Texas *believes* that you can come back.

"Now, goodbye, Mr. Novellis." Glinda intoned some magic words, waved the magic wand, and Norman Novellis screamed and vanished.

Well, no, he didn't really vanish. Norman Novellis went *somewhere*—to some other hereafter. I don't know which one, and I wouldn't tell you if I did. But as we've already ascertained, none of them is as pleasant as Oz.

(No, hang on a minute here, that doesn't sound nearly forceful enough. I don't think it brings home the horror of not knowing what you believe in in as graphic and unforgettable a manner as I had in mind when I sat down to write this thing. I damn sure don't want to let you guys slip off the hook right when we're getting to the end, so let me back up and try it again.)

Well, no he didn't really vanish. Norman Novellis was sent to a planet where people with two eyes were considered freakish aberrations and were tortured unmercifully, unspeakably, thirty-nine hours a day, sixty-six days a week. A planet that had no concept of death, so there was no chance of escaping to another hereafter.

(Yeah, that's much better.)

And that was the end of Norman Novellis—as far as we're concerned. We leave him in a place that makes hell look like Disneyland. And remember, Norman Novellis is there not because he didn't believe in anything, but because HE DID NOT KNOW WHAT IT WAS HE BELIEVED IN UNTIL IT WAS TOO LATE.

(See? I told you it was dangerous.)